MW01420453

To Kalai, my sister, my master, my muse;
for all the nights we stayed up too late, laughed too
loudly, and together created Two Sides of the Coin,
I am, and always shall be, your devoted slave.

Two Sides of the Coin

Knight of the Rising Star

Malia Davidson

authorHOUSE

AuthorHouse™
1663 Liberty Drive
Bloomington, IN 47403
www.authorhouse.com
Phone: 1 (800) 839-8640

© 2016 Malia Davidson. All rights reserved.

No part of this book may be reproduced, stored in a retrieval system, or transmitted by any means without the written permission of the author.

Published by AuthorHouse   04/27/2016

ISBN: 978-1-5049-8261-0 (sc)
ISBN: 978-1-5049-8260-3 (e)

Library of Congress Control Number: 2016903309

Print information available on the last page.

Any people depicted in stock imagery provided by Thinkstock are models, and such images are being used for illustrative purposes only.
Certain stock imagery © Thinkstock.

This book is printed on acid-free paper.

Because of the dynamic nature of the Internet, any web addresses or links contained in this book may have changed since publication and may no longer be valid. The views expressed in this work are solely those of the author and do not necessarily reflect the views of the publisher, and the publisher hereby disclaims any responsibility for them.

PROLOGUE

On a bustling street of a certain town, there was a certain shop. And in that certain shop was a certain man who, rumors tell, was responsible for a few certain crimes. Over the shop hung a sign that would have you believe the owner was an honest man. The shop was connected snugly to another house which, as the locals knew, had been haunted for years. Dusty, black curtains hid the shop's interior. Still, on one dreary, grey afternoon, a crowd of girls and boys gathered about the doorway like guests invited to a party.

Doink, doke, dingy! The cowbell over the door jangled as the door swung open. An old man with scruffy white hair beamed at the children from the doorway. "Eh, now what are you hooligans doing 'round Honest Erwin's? Come to see Matilda?"

They shook their heads, laughing. "No, Honest! We wanna story!"

He winked. "A story, is it? Who said I tell fables on Friday?"

However, the children were used to their friend's mischief and bounced into his cozy shop. The man peeked up and down the street and locked the door behind him. When he smiled at the children, laughter lines crinkled around his sea-blue eyes. Seating themselves cross-legged on the bear skin rug, the children gazed up at him with expectant grins.

Honest sank onto his favorite stool and immediately assumed his narrating voice. "Oh, I've a story the likes you've never heard before! Now hold onto yer hats, boys, and yer skirts, girls, 'cause if we start this new tale, we may never come out of it alive. It's called..." he held up his hands, pausing for effect, "Knight of the Rising Star!"

"Oooooooh," they chorused.

"Ahem!" He cleared his throat and the children hushed each other. Then the storyteller learned forward, a smile on his craggy face. "Once upon a tragedy," he began, "there was a man who had a very dangerous idea. Why was it dangerous? I can't tell you that yet. After all, that's why we take the journey of a story, eh? Just give me your ears and a little blind faith, and perhaps we'll figure the rest out as we go along…"

CHAPTER 1

Of Bosses and Boats

Knock, Knock! Mr. Morri, a tiny, bespectacled man, looked up from his papers and chirped, "Come in, come in!" The digital clock at his elbow flashed 9:34. As always, a steady chorus of rumbles, honks, and the humming of car motors sang in the streets below. It was the song of business and opportunity, the theme of Sanfran Cisco.

Two men in suits entered the room carrying briefcases. Morri's eyes twinkled. In their black and grey suits, they resembled penguins. He motioned for them to sit, and they shuffled to their seats. The black penguin had wavy, dirty-blonde hair and hazel eyes. Thin and pale, with a long, narrow face, the penguin didn't seem to get much sun wherever he lived. With an air of condescending composure, he sat down with perfect posture. Morri wondered where the man's snuff box was, for he seemed the type who would take it out and dab his nose serenely.

The other penguin, the one with the grey suit, was taller than his companion and slightly chubby. He had military cut brown hair and dark eyes to match. Unlike his companion, who looked completely at home, he fidgeted in his seat. Nervous as a dog at the vet, he tapped his foot in cut time tempo on the carpet and kept adjusting his tie as if it was too tight.

Having labeled the penguins, Morri went back to gazing at his paperwork. The men waited for him to speak, but he had his nose buried in a sea of papers. The clock buzzed, and Morri gave it a distracted poke. As the black penguin checked his watch for the third time, the grey penguin craned to see the paper which their employer examined with such concentration.

"Morri's Medical: We Save lives!" It proclaimed in an obnoxious font. The little man folded his hands and leaned back in his chair, cackling with triumph. "You've done it again, Morri, you ol' rascal!" he crowed.

The black penguin cleared his throat. "Excuse me, Mr. Morri. If you have a moment, I believe we had a meeting scheduled for 9:30."

Morri ran his hand through his messy, grey hair, appearing like he was trying to look dignified now. He jabbed a finger at the men. "Ah, yes, I remember. You're the new 'uns workin' for my company." He puffed out his chest and shouted, "Morri's Magazines: always the best!"

Old Mr. Morri went on to ramble about his other companies: Morri's Furniture, Morri's Estates, Morri's Transport, Morri's Magazines, and now the newest, Morri's Medical, each with a rather off-putting motto. Chatting all the while, Morri spun around to dig though a mountain of folders, supposedly for their employment records.

The grey penguin leaned over and whispered to his coworker, "How Mr. Morri came to own most of the companies in Sanfran Cisco, I'll never understand."

"It may have something to do with the fact that his sister married Frank Harder," whispered the other.

"Harder? That sounds familiar."

"It should. He's Sanfran Cisco's current mayor who is going on third time in office."

Morri had his feet up on the desk, and he waved a hand at the reporters. "You boys are quite lucky to be here in my office at such a monumental time in our city's history. Watch out, world! Here comes Mr. Morri with his medical: We save lives!"

"Of course, sir," they answered. Their faces were the picture of polite perplexity.

Their employer twirled in his chair and then turned to size them up. "I've heard of you. Morri's Magazines' rising stars, they say." He pointed at the black penguin. "I know you! The one and only Steve Johnson! You're practically a celebrity, aren't you?"

The black penguin gave a modest shrug. "Well, I don't know—"

"You wrote that article about our new brand of toilets from Morri's Furniture!" He paused for dramatic effect and declared, "Break a leg!"

The grey penguin made a suspicious sound and covered his mouth. Flushing, the black penguin murmured, "Among many others, sir."

"Yes, yes, and one of your best, young man. I kid you not, I read that thing over and over again. T'was the best of the year!" There was an awkward silence as Mr. Morri rocked back in his chair, musing on that article so dear to his heart. He glanced at the dark-haired man and stopped rocking. "And… what have you written?"

This time it was the other reporter who hid a smile. Straightening in his chair, the grey penguin seemed to forget his nervousness. "I wrote that article on the kidnapped children who ended up in a haunted mansion," he protested. "I also investigated the mystery of the disappearing trains, but it was not published."

Morri nodded. "Well, guess all your stories about disappearing stuff just made them disappear right out of my head!" He laughed at his own joke, and the reporters humored him with smiles. Finally, Morri clasped his hands on the desk and adopted a more businesslike attitude. "So, what can I do for you boys?"

"My name's Shawn Rossow," the grey penguin began.

"And yes, I'm Steve Johnson, writer of a few award-winning articles."

Shawn shot him an exasperated look. "Me and Steve have been traveling from town to town for a while, working on new stories for Morri's Magazines every week. But we were thinking the other day…" He paused as they had planned to let Steve work his magic.

Steve stood up and paced to the open window, gazing out across the tops of the buildings. On the horizon, the ocean was as blue as a sapphire. Steve gestured towards it. "Why limit ourselves to Sanfran Cisco, where the writing business is an endless competition between newspapers? Why not explore the sea where it is not charted by fathoms and acres and discover something new that would capture our readers' imagination?"

Shawn was impressed by his partner's speech. Morri looked impressed too. Shawn leaned forward in his chair, allowing himself a smile. "If you could lend us a boat from Morri's Transport—"

"All in one piece!"

"—yes. We could even leave today, if you hook us up with a ride."

"Well, I'd be delighted!" said Mr. Morri, smiling at the reporters. "Such adventurous spirits. Kinda reminds me of myself. I'd love to go exploring myself someday, but Morri's Medical is calling my name! So where exactly do you wish to go?"

"The Bermuda Triangle," said Steve.

Morri spun his chair around so fast that the pencil fell from behind his ear. He cleared his throat. "Well, you sure know how to pick interesting places, don't you? I've heard that area can be pretty deadly."

With a nod, Shawn recited, "On December 5, 1945, a bomb-squad of U.S. Navy Avenger planes called Flight 19 disappeared on a training mission. The triangular area where the losses took place became known as the Bermuda Triangle and was suspected to have paranormal or supernatural forces. Several other disappearances have been reported in or near the Triangle." He added under his breath, "According to Wikipedia."

Steve chuckled. "I've been trying to convince Mr. Rossow of the true facts about the Bermuda Triangle, but he's pretty set in his ways." Shawn scowled as Steve explained in a matter-of-fact tone, "It has been observed by researchers that the number of ships and aircraft that disappeared in the area is no larger than the disappearances in other places. A number of large tropical storms often blow over the Bermuda Triangle. Those writers who thought up all the supernatural nonsense did not mention the storms, probably because there is nothing mysterious about them. Many of the disappearances have been exaggerated or did not even happen. This so-called legend of the Bermuda Triangle is really just a mystery made up by sensational writers." Mr. Johnson leaned back against his chair in satisfaction. The other reporter looked as frazzled as a wet rooster.

I'm sure you'll forgive Mr. Morri for bursting out laughing at this point. He slapped his knee. "Me oh my! Such a show, gentleman. I

Two Sides of the Coin

understand everything now. You," he pointed to Shawn, "want to prove that there is something fishy in the Triangle. But you, Mr. Johnson, want to prove that there is absolutely nothing fishy. Ho ho ho! What dramatic contrast! This is exactly what the readers of Morri's Magazine (always the best!) want to hear."

The reporters exchanged puzzled yet excited looks.

"Uh-huh, oh yes, that will do…" Their employer scribbled something on the back of an important looking paper. "I'll arrange to have a boat ready for you in Florida. Hope you boys know how to get to Miami. And I'll tell Mrs. Andrews to give you some money for airplane tickets. Heh, heh! I wish I could see her face when I intercom her. I suppose you'll be needing a pilot for your boat too?"

"Actually, Shawn here has a boating license," said Steve.

Shawn nodded. "As long as it has some parts I can recognize, no problem!"

Morri clapped his hands. "Great, great! Now you've got me so excited, I'll give you boys a deal. If you, Mr. Johnson, can prove that there's nothing weird going on, then I'll start a new cruise with Morri's Transport through the infamous Bermuda Triangle. You'll get a good share in the profits."

"I'm always glad to do business with you," Steve leaned back in his chair, already dreaming of the house he would buy on the rich side of Sanfran Cisco.

"But," Morri turned to Shawn, "if *you* can prove that something bizarre is going on in the so-called Devil's Triangle, I'll *double* your paycheck."

Shawn blinked. "Th-thank you, sir!" he managed to say.

"Now remember our motto, boys: 'Morri's Transport: All in one piece!' So you'd better keep it that way, and yourselves too."

"Yes, sir!" exclaimed Shawn.

"We will be back within a month. Thank you very much," said Steve.

The reporters rose with murmured farewells and scurried from the room. "Have fun!" shouted Morri, even as the door slammed shut behind Shawn. The two reporters made a dignified dash down the hallway of the office building, took an elevator to the main floor, collected cash from a glaring Mrs. Andrews, and slipped through the revolving door.

The reporters were greeted by the usual clamor and honking of Sanfran Cisco's main street traffic. The towering buildings grimly watched over all the activities below them. People hurried down the sidewalks, cell phones in ears, checking their wrist watches. Ladies in high heels and men in suits stepped from taxis into shops. The streets were a parade of organized chaos. Sleek limos, monstrous buses, ear-splitting motorcycles, road construction trucks, police, pizza delivery, and a thousand other cars filled the city with a unified motor-engine hum. It was a chilly spring afternoon. The sky was mostly overcast, but if anyone cared to notice, the sun peeked through windows of a blue. The breeze smelled of gasoline, McDonald's, and mud.

Steve and Shawn faced each other outside *Morri's HQ*, grinning at each other in excitement. "I can't believe it," said Shawn. "We're really going!"

Steve reached out his hand, and they shook on it. "Get your suitcases," he instructed. "I'll call a taxi and pick you up. We're going to leave on the one o'clock plane."

"See you then."

The reporters turned their own ways. Steve waved down a taxi and rode back to the quiet neighborhood where he lived. Steve Johnson's house was a lot like the man: neat, narrow, and solemn. There was a place for everything, and everything was in its place… the perks of hiring a maid to clean while he was away. He checked the fridge and was satisfied that nothing was left to spoil. Walking into his spotless room, he found his suitcase packed and ready. Steve took a moment to go over all his gear to make sure he was not leaving anything behind.

The house seemed quieter than usual. As Steve rechecked his wallet, he let his eyes wander around the bedroom. For the first time, he was struck by how bare it was once the equipment and other necessities were packed away. There were no keepsakes on the writing desk, no novels on the shelves, no pictures of loved ones by his bed. The reporter frowned. *I was planning on making my place a little homier, but I suppose it will have to wait until I return.* Standing, he took his suitcase, his camera bag, and the writing gear to the door. He called the cheapest cab on the list to meet him. Without a second thought, he left his house to brood on in silence.

Meanwhile, Shawn raced as fast as his worn dress shoes would allow. Without waiting for the cross sign to flash on, he took off across the street. A car turning right screeched to a stop. The car honked and the driver shouted exactly what he thought about Shawn. The reporter waved. "Sorry! Good day to you!" Nothing could flatten his good mood.

Shawn flew down the sidewalk, passing huge skyscrapers of various shapes and sizes. He skirted the iron fence which enclosed Sanfran Cisco's factories and passed through a busy suburb. Here the city workers were easily distinguished from the factory workers by their clothes, faces, and demeanor. Shawn slowed to a walk. In these places, it was better not to appear chased. At last, he turned into an alleyway that led him to a flight of stairs: his apartment.

Shawn found his room number 676 and unlocked it after a moment's hesitation. Stepping into the darkness, he flicked on the lamp-light. Three of the five light-bulbs overhead had gone out, and the remaining two did not cast the room in a favorable light. In his excitement over his trip to L.A. with Steve, Shawn had literally emptied his drawers to pack. Hardly a square inch of the floor was visible, except for a stained spot where he had accidently knocked over his coffee mug.

A greasy pizza box decorated the table, accompanied by a host of bills. One new envelope in particular caught the reporter's eye. The grey envelope was stamped with the official symbol of the renting homes: two boxes stacked on top of one another with a red fireplace spouting curly smoke. He had to hop-scotch through the maze of clothes and trash to reach the table. As if he were handling an explosive, Shawn opened the envelope and unfolded the letter.

```
Mr. Rossow:

It has come to our attention that again you
have failed to pay your rent when it is due.
We are giving you a week to pack your things
```

```
and move. Perhaps you will take paying rent
more seriously in the future.

Our deepest apologies,

The Sanfran Cisco Home and Board Co.
```

Shawn glanced over the high titles and official-looking print with a sinking feeling in his stomach. "Hmm, I guess a week's not too bad," he consoled himself. Then he saw the date on the inside address: March 12, 2014... five days ago. Shawn crumbled the letter. "Deepest apologies, indeed!"

He took a step towards the trash can, then thought better of it and tucked the wad of paper in his suit pocket. "Well, Shawn," he said, "it doesn't matter yet, but just wait 'till you get back." Sighing, he rubbed his neck and beheld the destruction. There was nothing else to do; he bent down and began to sort through the mess. *This is what I get for thinking up this wild idea,* he thought as he threw a pile of clothes into his hamper. *And for being single.*

Although Shawn had pursued several relationships over the past two years in Sanfran Cisco, they all ended as swiftly as they began. Somehow, he had never found a girl who fit his personality type. But Shawn would rather think about the month-old dirty dishes in the tiny sink than his life-long singleness. Over a short period of time, his apartment room had fallen into miserable disarray. Shawn grumbled, "As if a reporter's life in the big city isn't enough. I mean, I have to compete with all the veteran reporters in Sanfran Cisco, somehow get where I'm supposed to go without a car, dodge gangs at night and my touchy landlord during the day. But no! I have to catch the fever of ocean exploration. Not just any exploration trip though. Nope, I get myself hooked on going to the Bermuda Triangle, also called the Devil's Triangle."

Shawn examined his watch which had mysteriously stopped ticking yesterday. Shrugging, he tossed it into the overflowing garbage. "Still, I can't believe Steve actually listened this time. He's usually a snob about my ideas. If that's not a good omen, I don't know what is."

Half an hour later, there came a muted yet insistent sound from outside: the blaring of a car horn. Shawn jumped and whirled upon the kitchen clock. It took him a moment to calculate the real time by subtracting an hour. The reporter gasped, "Shoot, it's almost 12 o'clock! I haven't even changed yet!" Rushing around his apartment, he grabbed his half-made suitcase and stuffed clothes frantically. "Oh boy. Oh boy. Steve's going to kill me!"

Into his suitcase went all of Shawn's valuables: his only suit, his savings box, his books, movies, video games, and the three magazines with his published articles. The next time he came back, the place was sure to be cleaned out. Dragging the suitcase along, with his notebook under one arm and the camera dangling from his neck, Shawn the reporter paused at the doorway and looked for the last time at the apartment room, stripped clean of everything he cared about. "Good riddance," he muttered and slammed the door behind him.

Shawn had an ordeal lugging his suitcase down the steps, but the impatient growl of the taxi urged him on. The taxi man leaned out the window. "Youz Mr. Rawzo? I thought I'd grow a beard waitin' for youz."

"Sorry!" Shawn shoved his suitcase into the trunk next to Steve's. He barely had time to slip into the car, buckle his seat belt, and give Steve an apologetic shrug before the car jerked backward. Tires screeched on the pavement as the man did a 90-degree back up, knocked over a trash can, and butted right into traffic. Shawn and Steve held tight to their bags as the taxi man put the pedal to the metal and laid on the horn. The rest of the very short ride to the airport you can image yourself, as I'm afraid the rest is too frightful for either of the two men to relate.

An hour later, Steve and Shawn relaxed in their seats. The hum of the airplane's engine soothed their nerves. "Welcome to Coastal Airlines," the pilot said over the speakers. "Our scheduled arrival time in Miami is 4:30. Please keep your seat-belts buckled until the indicator goes off. Thank you for joining us today."

9

As the airplane raced down the runway and lifted above the clouds, both men found themselves jotting down random details in their notebooks. They looked at each other and laughed. "You're a reporter alright," said Steve in his patronizing way.

"Not one like you," murmured Shawn. He took Tolkien's *Fellowship of the Ring*, his favorite book, out of his travel bag and opened to the first page.

Steve blinked, unsure whether to take that as a complement or insult. "You know, I find it hard to believe we're only a month apart in age."

"Yep."

Frowning, Steve reclined in his seat for a long, well-deserved nap. Three hours and seven chapters later, the plane dipped below the clouds to land. Shawn closed the book and rubbed his eyes. Of course, many of the passages he knew so well he could quote them. Upon landing, Steve called another taxi to take them to their hotel. As they drove along the road with palm trees on either side, Shawn gazed at the Atlantic. It seemed to beckon to him, saying, "Tomorrow your real journey begins!"

* * *

The solitude was complete on those tropical seas. Only the wind and a lone albatross held a conversation. These were wild oceans: untamed, unmarked!

But one day, the silence was broken by the roar of an engine.

Faster and faster, a boat from the west skimmed over the water. One man crouched on deck, watching their progress, and another sat in the pilot's cabin, gunning the engine. As the boat sped on into uncharted waters, the swirling white trail of their boat vanished.

"Shawn, Shawn! Come quick!" Steve yelled. Shawn pulled the key from the boat and the engine died with a sputter.

He joined Steve up on deck. "What's the matter? It could take me another fifteen minutes to figure out how to start this old piece of..."

Shawn trailed off. Steve clutched the rail of the boat so hard his knuckles turned white.

"Look at that smudge up ahead. It's an island! I could've sworn it was not on our maps."

Shawn glanced down at the map in Steve's hand. Sure enough, Cocoa Isle was a day's journey away. Beyond Cocoa Isle were acres and acres of empty water. "It must be pretty big for us to see it from this distance!" Shawn exclaimed. "So why hasn't anyone seen it before? You have to admit that's pretty weird."

Steve shrugged. "New islands are discovered all the time. It just so happens that this one may bear our names when we introduce it to the world."

"No kidding?" Shawn laughed. "That would be something." He reached into his briefcase and pulled out a sleek, black camera, his most precious possession. Cradling it for a moment, Shawn brought it to his eye and snapped the picture. "So," he said at last, "here's our mystery. Time to find out just how devilish this triangle is. May the best man win."

Always the practical one, Steve gestured to the island. "Let's get closer, shall we?"

CHAPTER 2

The Island of Despair

It didn't take fifteen minutes to start the boat again. Actually, it took half an hour. Steve yelled, "We're being pulled into some kind of current! We're going to lose our island!"

Shawn felt ready to pull out his hair. "All in one piece, huh?" he roared. "We'll see about that when we get back!" He twisted the key viciously and gritted his teeth. The engine squealed in protest at this rude awakening and began muttering at him. Shawn whooped. "We're back in business! Next stop, Reporter Island!" Following Steve's finger, Shawn turned the wheel and fought back against the current.

It seemed to take forever and a day to get closer. Shawn had never experienced a current quite as contrary as this one. For every two acres forward, the boat was pushed one acre back. He longed to flip out his notebook and record the strange fact, but only Steve had that luxury. Instead of writing, though, Steve kept his gaze fixed on their destination, as if afraid to lose it if he blinked. Little by little, the misty blob gradually became lines on the horizon.

Steve shouted, "There are two islands!"

The pilot smiled at this and fought the current harder, which revolted with equal zeal. When Shawn thought he couldn't keep battling anymore, it was suddenly over. Pulling the lever back, Shawn stopped the motor. The boat floated in place. Shawn snatched his notebook and wrote down his observations of the strange phenomena before leaving the cabin.

Wind ruffled the wave into white crests and blew into Shawn's face. He closed his eyes and breathed deep of the fresh, briny aroma. "Well, well. Two islands, two of us, huh?" Steve didn't reply; he was as still as an ice sculpture. Shawn gripped the rail as the boat rocked and glanced at his fellow reporter. "Steve?"

Steve was paler than usual. He cleared his throat and pointed. "Is it normal for islands to look like that?"

Shawn looked at the islands, rubbed his eyes, and looked again. It was as if they had discovered the place where day met night. Though it was a clear day where their speedboat floated, a huge thundercloud clung to the island on the left. Somehow the wind that whipped their clothes and chilled their faces failed to move the black cloud. Its shadow hung over the entire island. Out on the open sea, it looked especially dark and forbidding. A single mountain pierced the sky on the farthest edge of the island. It seemed to cast an aura of evil towards them.

However, as soon as Shawn turned his face towards the other island, a warm puff of air blew past him, smelling of roses and honey. The island was as green as could be, so green it hurt Shawn's eyes to look at it for long. A pure shaft of light shone down on it from the skies, making it shimmer like a mirage. It also had a large mountain which rose in sloping, emerald curves. As soon as his eyes fell on that picture of perfection, Shawn felt drawn to it as if by an invisible force. "Let's name that one Rossow Island," he said.

"No way," Steve protested, jabbing a finger at the dark island. "You think I would give my name to that – that creepy excuse for an island? I discovered them, so I should choose which one I want to name."

Shawn scowled. "I suppose you *also* want me to explore that creepy excuse for an island?"

"You're more adventurous than I am."

"Well, you're in better shape than I am!"

"Maybe you should get in better shape."

"I will! As soon as I can stop living from pay check to pay check…" Shawn glared at Steve. "And don't look so surprised. You know I'm dirt poor. If I could introduce the next Jamaica, I would finally have a chance to get back on my feet!"

Though Steve didn't say anything for a minute, his pitying expression seemed to say, "If only you were an award-winning writer like me, you'd have a chance."

It wouldn't work on him this time. Shawn crossed his arms. "It was *my* idea to come here, so I should be the one to write about it."

"Actually, it was *your* idea to look for supernatural phenomenon," Steve pointed out. "It's my job to find the next destination for Morri's cruises. Look, we're both getting what we asked for. You get a mysterious island, and I get the next Jamaica.""

Steve shook his head. "Do you really think people are going to be so happy with your Jamaica when they see that black one just across the street? It could be a volcano, for all we know."

"Which is precisely why you should go check it out."

Shawn's scowl deepened. *Oh, I get it. Just send Mr. Expendable to explore an island with a volcano ready to explode like Pompeii. Sounds perfect.*

"We came here for an interesting story," Steve reminded him. "Something that would blow all the other reporters out of the water, and that place," he pointed to the dark island, "is one of the greatest stories I've ever seen. Maybe there is something supernatural about it. Or maybe that dark cloud caused your planes to disappear. You might even discover a crew of stranded people! Who knows? You could be a hero."

There was a reason Steve was known as a successful advertiser, but Shawn wasn't fooled. He had been fooled far too many times for that. "You might be right," he conceded. Stealing a longing glance at the green island, he was struck by an idea. "Let's flip a coin to decide who goes where. It's much fairer that way." So saying, he searched his pockets and grimaced. "Got any spare change?"

Shawn was usually loaded with coins. However, he had given them all away recently to a *Pennies for Hope* organization which bought food and clothing for certain third-world countries. Steve rarely kept change, but he checked his wallet anyway. It was astonishing. Even between the two of them, they had no coins. The reporters resorted to checking the ratty cushions of the driver's seat. Results: a dime, a quarter, and three rusty pennies.

"What a load of junk," muttered Steve.

"Morri's Transport," croaked Shawn, perfectly imitating Morri's squeaky voice. "All in one piece!" The two men forgot their argument for a moment and laughed.

Shawn held up the quarter. "Whoever gets their side will explore the next Jamaica. I'm heads!"

"Tails!" urged Steve.

The dime flicked up in the air...

... and landed with a *sploosh* in the sea.

The men glanced over the rail. Shawn chuckled. "I guess we're both out of luck."

At Steve's glare, Shawn shrugged and picked up a penny. "Tales for me this time." With a snap of his fingers, the penny flashed up and back down. Shawn caught it in his fist. "And just for kicks," he slapped it on the back of his hand and held it out for both to see.

It was heads.

Steve smirked and lounged back in the deck chair as if he was already soaking in the sunshine on the emerald island. "Look, can't we just forget about this and go together?" Shawn begged. "It makes more sense to stick together, and we can just spend a little time on both—"

"Don't try to cheat your way out of the deal. Haven't you heard the saying, 'divide and conquer'?" said Steve.

Shawn glanced at the dark island, muttering, "Haven't you heard the saying, 'united we stand, divided we fall'?"

Still the victor refused to relinquish his triumph. "You'll get your chance later. It's only two days, and you've got more than enough beef jerky to last you that long. Explore a bit. Do some camping. Have one of those adventures you're so fond of reading about." When Steve saw that Shawn's argument was quenched, he opened a bottle of green tea from the cooler to celebrate.

Scowling, Shawn ducked into the driver's seat. He cracked his knuckles and twirled the wheel. "Next stop: the island of eternal happiness!"

It seemed to take only a few moments to reach the sandy shore of Steve's island, as if the waves themselves rushed towards that destination. Shawn pulled the boat up so close that he could see the surf breaking on the golden sand. The engine's roar lowered to a growl as Shawn inched the boat forward, looking for some sign of people. There was not a dock or house to be seen. The shore, twinkling as if strewn with diamonds, stretched for miles with a thick forest beyond it. Shawn laughed to himself to think of Steve Johnson hiking though the wild like Robinson Crusoe.

After fifteen minutes, there was still no good landing in sight. Shawn asked Steve at least three times if he wouldn't mind taking off his boots, rolling ups his pants, and wading to the shore. Steve only gave him a look that said, "Are you crazy? Award-winning reporters do not *wade*."

"Well, that's just great," grumbled Shawn. "Too proud to get his fancy pants wet, is he? I'm about ready to chuck him overboard myself if something doesn't show up soon. Please, oh please give me something to dock him—"

"Hey, Shawn! This spot is perfect!" Steve waved his arms and pointed. Branching off from the shore about five yards away, a large, flat, marble stone lay in wait for them. The waves lapped at its smooth sides.

Shawn pulled back on the lever and stared for almost a full minute. "That can't be right," he muttered. "I didn't see anything like that for miles…" Confusion made him cautious, but Steve kept waving for him to continue. Still staring, he eased the boat forward. Soon it had pulled up next to the makeshift dock. Shawn left the engine running and climbed out on deck, squinting at the sudden light. *Huh. Maybe the sun's glare kept me from seeing it,* he mused.

Gathering his bags, Steve straightened up and shook Shawn's hand. "I really appreciate you driving us here."

Two Sides of the Coin

"Don't mention it," Shawn grumbled.

Steve patted his shoulder. "Don't look so sad! This expedition will be over before you know it, and then you can have your relaxing vacation."

Shrugging, Shawn toyed with the remaining quarter; glaring in the sunlight, it burned a circle in his vision. Steve vaulted over the rail and stepped onto the rock. His face lit up with wonder, or maybe it was simply reflecting the brilliance of the light on the marble rock.

Shawn forced a smile and handed him his suitcase and tent-bag. Returning to the driver's seat, he pointed the ship's prow to the dark island. Steve waved until the boat faded from sight, but Shawn did not look back at the place he had left. Instead, he focused on the approaching apparition before him. The dark island, as he had come to think of it.

Shawn held the wheel steady with his knee and flipped out his notebook. He wrote as fast as he could:

- *On the afternoon of March 20, I and my fellow reporter Steve discovered two islands no more than two miles apart.*
- *They are both very large; from the sea I cannot calculate their width and length.*
- *At approximately 3:05, I have passed under the shadow of what looks like a huge nimbostratus cloud, low in the sky and dark gray varying to black. May perhaps be smoke coming from volcano?*

Shawn glanced up and shivered at the motionless clouds. *If that's a real volcano, I'll never forgive Steve. That is, if I'm still alive to not forgive him.*

The boat also seemed unwilling to head towards the coming land. Several times it turned left and right, forcing Shawn to put away the notebook so he could grapple with the wheel. "You're stubborn," he growled. "But I can be stubborn too!" The sound of creaks and hollow groans answered his words. "Come on, baby," he encouraged. "Almost there!"

Just like before, the fight ended all of a sudden, leaving a loose feeling on the wheel. Instead, the currents seemed to be dragging the boat towards the dark island. Shawn glanced at the water and shook his head. "Weird."

After the fairy tale glow of Steve's island, this one appeared even more shadowy. A blanket of fog shrouded the shore from sight. Chills went through Shawn the moment they entered the whiteness. "Cut it out, Shawn," the reporter muttered. "It's just like sailing through a cloud... a sad cloud, that is."

Still, he pulled the motor to a standstill and allowed the waves to draw them in. Shawn flipped on the lights, but the visibility became even worse. He turned them off again, allowing the shadowy outlines of objects to guide him. Waves pounded against the toothy cliff as far as he could see. The land grew closer, but Shawn's hopes of a smooth landing faded farther away. He navigated the boat along the shore at a good distance from them to avoid shoals of submerged rocks. The crashing of waves against the shore drowned out all other sounds. Clammy mist floated through the windows of the cabin, and goose bumps prickled his skin.

Could the whole shoreline be like this? Shawn wondered. He let the boat drift a bit while he considered what to do. *Ha, maybe I should beg for a landing place like I did at the last island. That seemed to work.* Shawn cracked a smile and drove a bit closer. "Please, I need to park my boat somewhere," he whined. "Just give me a little sandy shore, and I'll—Oomph!"

The boat bucked as it struck something underwater. Since Shawn's seat belt – like most accessories in this boat – was broken, he was almost thrown into the windshield. He seized the wheel and veered away from the shore.

"That's it!" he yelled. "I'm out of here. I don't care if I saw a dock with freshly painted wood and blinking lights. Steve can come here himself if he's so interested in it."

However, as Shawn turned the wheel, something dark seemed to materialize out of the mist. It looked like a giant crocodile lounging halfway on land, halfway in the water. "What the..." Shawn muttered.

He leaned forward and eased the boat closer. Pulling up next to it, the reporter stared once more.

It was a dock! An ancient, rotting, broken-down thing, but a dock nonetheless, which meant people lived there... or had.

Shawn gazed at the unfriendly land. Questions whirled through his mind. *Who would want to live here? Unless... unless they're stranded here! Maybe Steve was right. Maybe this is my opportunity for the story of the year!*

Yes, his idea to turn back was stale now. The boat crept towards the dock. Shawn jerked the keys out and listened to the engine shut down. "That's that. No turning back," he said. Glancing at the gas meter, he reminded himself to fill it up next time.

"Just two days," Shawn repeated and threw open the door. As he stepped out, the boards creaked. It wasn't the cold that made him shiver now. "Think light thoughts," he murmured. He peered through the fog and could barely make out a warm glow from the other island. "Yeah. Light," he sighed. "I bet Steve has a surplus of that."

Soon Shawn stood on the dock holding his suitcase. He slung the tent-bag, stuffed with food, across his back, and let his precious camera dangle around his neck. The surf rolled underneath his feet and bashed the rocks like a battering ram. Tiny droplets blew into Shawn's face, and the salty taste awakened his thirst.

I'll open a Coke when I get to shore, Shawn promised himself. He took a baby step. Then another. The water-logged wood squeaked with each step. Despite the cold, sweat broke out on Shawn's forehead. When a high-pitched squeal of tortured wood rent the air, Shawn halted, heart pounding. "Oh no. I'm gonna die."

Nothing happened. Shawn gulped for air and fixed his gaze on the shore. From what he could see, the land was no more welcoming than the shoreline. Gritty sand lined the shore as if the powerful current had battered the rocks to bits. A stone's throw away, the land rose in craggy walls which seemed to frown at him. Shawn bit his lip. *As long as it's firm ground, I don't care. I'm about halfway... like ten more steps.* He took a shaky step. *One... two.* Shawn had to stretch out his foot to avoid a broken board. *Three. Four. Five—*

SNAP! The board under his foot caved, and the new hole swallowed up his left leg. Shawn fell, screaming, and caught himself on the dock. Icy water enveloped his leg up to the hip. Shawn tried to stand up, but his sock caught on the jagged wood board. The bridge shuddered. Fabric ripped as Shawn jerked his foot out and made a wild dash to the shoreline.

Shawn felt like kissing the sand as he stumbled — clothes, bags, and arms going every which way — off the treacherous dock. Instead, he slumped to the ground and stared down at his bare foot.

"Oh, boy. What have I gotten myself into?"

* * *

A large fly, flashing iridescent purple and green, buzzed through the open window to land on a long, cedar table. It rested its wings for a moment, all the while alert for danger. Still, even the sensitive creature could never have guessed that in the darkness something lurked. Facing each other from opposite sides of the table, two motionless figures sat silent and watching.

The fly fidgeted. Some sixth sense quivered with danger, and it started to open its wings to fly away.

Faster than a striking serpent, the person on the right pinned it down with white, slender fingers. The fly buzzed its wings hopelessly as the lady stared down at it with cruel, black eyes. And then a murmuring sound broke the silence. Though the fly couldn't understand the words, it lay still as though mesmerized by the soft voice.

"So I've caught you now, my grotesque, little friend. And you wonder what I shall do. By all the laws of nature, you are a dirty pest, even a threat to our health. You show up here from an unknown land, stupidly unaware of the diseases you may carry. Should I kill you in cold blood because you landed on my property? No... I do not think even you deserve that punishment for scarcely any fault of your own."

She picked up the motionless insect and cupped it in her hands. "For such a lowly creature, you have given me an idea. Thus, I'll spare your life." The darkness fell away, and the fly found itself standing on her open palm: free! It lay frozen in shock for a moment. Then it scratched its tiny head, scurried in a circle, and flew out the window.

Also unnoticed by the fly, the person on the left watched this monologue without a word. When the sound of the insect's wings faded away, the man chuckled. "Somehow, my dear, I feel you weren't talking about an insect."

She sighed and sat back, the shadows once again falling over her face. "Hardly. But I did not speak deceptively when I said it has given me a new look on this dilemma."

"Do tell, my vixen."

The lady picked up a thick scroll and held it out. "This new report I've read and reread, trying to make sense of it. Four days ago, a man sailed into Cobra in a strangely-shaped vessel around the third hour. He carried large bags, and his clothes were unlike any of the island. They say that he made his way to the nearest town and asked probing questions, scribbled notes in his book, and made flashes everywhere with a magic box that he carried around his neck. The town guards wished to lock him in a cell, but he departed before they could lay hands on him. Our spies report that he was last seen headed in this direction, following a path through the Stag Forest."

The man contemplated her words, though he'd heard them all before.

"Never before has anything like this stranger appeared. He's disturbing the silence, searching out secrets, practically *begging* to be killed. And the worst of it? Nobody on the Island of Despair can tell me where he came from, which makes me suspect he could not possibly have come from... that *other place*." Lifting her hand toward the window, she pointed at a distant speck of light over the turbulent sea.

The man drew deeper into his cloak and refused to look. The lady took a dagger from her cloak and inspected its edge. "He's a true outsider, without a place on either island. Who knows how much damage an outsider could cause? Perhaps it would be best to forget all about him and let the stags deal with him as they deal with all intruders... by making them disappear." Her mouth curved upward as if the notion held a sweet taste.

"Yet," the man prompted her.

She sheathed the dagger and leaned forward, meeting the man's gaze. "Yet he could also be innocent— a lost, clueless stranger. Like the insect, he may be unaware of how dangerous he is. In that case, it would be no fault of his own that got him thrown into prison, or worse."

"You're thinking of taking him under your wing, aren't you?"

"I am resolved not to lift a finger for the deranged creature. His blood is not my concern. All the same, he appears to be so senseless that it would be murder to do nothing."

"Have you considered asking Gilen to go after him?" the man asked.

The lady pondered this. "Yes, I'm sure Gilen would find him an interesting diversion. It could keep both of them out of trouble. Where is he?"

The man smirked and stroked his beard. "He left after supper to go hunting."

"Without permission? Again?" she snapped.

He lifted his hands in protest. "Don't look at me, dear. He's your son for the week."

Smiling, the man stood and offered his arm to his wife. She allowed him to lead her to the window. From there they could see the path that led to a dense forest, the forest of the stags.

"You're right," said the lady. "And I am proud of *my* son." She laughed deep in her throat. Thunder rumbled in the distance. Her husband placed an arm around her waist and laughed with her, higher and more sinister. This time lighting split the sky and the ocean in two, filling the world with a piercing light before the darkness once again closed in.

Change was coming, one need only to feel it in every raindrop, every breath of wind. Together, they waited in expectation.

* * *

Shawn trudged down a gravel road overshadowed by trees. Back and forth, the trail squiggled around the ancient giants. If Steve could have seen Shawn now, he would have been astonished at the difference.

Shawn's business coat was wet, dirty, and wrinkled. His tie was gone, and the once white shirt underneath was torn and muddied. He looked disinterested in the world around him — which is never a good frame of mind for a reporter — and downright miserable. All he noticed was that it was cold and dark, and he longed for food and a warm bed.

Only weak trickles of light could make it through the ceiling of leaves and branches, casting an air of gloom over the forest. Shawn leaned against a tree and took out his notebook. The reporter looked up and down the path as if to make sure no enemy was approaching. He flipped through the pages and reread what he'd learned in the past week, which was undoubtedly the longest week of his life.

March 20

I can hardly believe what I'm seeing! The people that inhabit this rocky, barren land seem to be locked in time near the medieval ages. Their houses are built almost like little cabins, but the village itself seems more like an old western town. I scoff at myself now, but I believed then that the village was simply a historic institute, making its living off visitors who came to the see the type of life-style medieval people lived.

Out on the main street, I saw men and women coaxing travelers to buy from their stalls. They had fresh vegetables, eggs, milk, meat, yarn, fabric, clothes, pots and pans, jewelry, shoes, hot cakes, sundials! The whole place stunk, actually, and there were flies everywhere. Not your typical idea of a medieval market.

The first thing I did after I'd walked through the town was to look for someplace to get information. Heaven knows I needed some! I saw a wooden sign decorated with a bottle of wine surrounded by smiling faces and noted the location of the bar for later.

I asked some of the people lounging about where I could find a visitor's building, but all they did was stare at me like I was an alien. At the time, I was very impressed by their acting. I suppose if it were really a village from the past, I would look as funny to them in my suit as they look to me in their old-fashioned clothes.

Speaking of clothes, the townsmen wear tunics of rich, dark colors with snakeskin belts. As for pants, most people here wear short, woolen stockings that go about to their knee, but never white stockings, oddly enough. Oh, and there are capes everywhere. Not super hero capes, mind you, but black, weather-beaten capes that always include a hood. Almost everyone has a cape, even the women.

I also observed that the bigger the boots, the greater the status here. As you can imagine, this makes life difficult for me, as I'm missing my left boot. Already I've had several people knocking me aside or refusing to speak to me. They wouldn't even accept my money.

The women here enjoy scandalous dresses, it seems. Most of them are tight-fitting, long-sleeved dresses that almost trail behind them. Some women wore leggings like the men, but nobody called them a witch, like they would in medieval times. I wonder at this strange place. Everything that I see is both familiar and different.

Finally, I asked a teen selling tomatoes if there was someplace to get information. She looked me up and down and said, "I daresssay you need ssssome of it. Are you going to buy any tomatoesss?" Her face was sly.

After a moment, I understood that she wouldn't tell me anything until I bought a tomato. It reminded of that time I had to buy some information about a crime scene from a street-wise boy, and I smiled. I gave her two dollars, wondering if she would lick it to see if it was real.

She examined the money and then handed it back with a scornful, "You're not from around here, are you?"

I shook my head. "Nope, I don't even live on this island. I sailed here from Sanfran Cisco."

Her eyes got really big. I asked again if there was a place to find information. She pointed at a large building across the street. "You can exchange your foreign money for shekelsssss in there."

Then she turned her back on me to hiss at a grubby boy who was about to bite into a tomato as if it were an apple. I hurried across the street while trying not to get jostled by the crowd. The building loomed above me, intimidating as a haunted house. I plucked up my courage and entered the dark room.

Once I got in, I felt very silly for being frightened. All I found was an old man snoring in his chair by a desk. I rapped on the table, and he opened one eye. "Yezzz?" He asked in a slurred voice.

I wondered if he were drunk or just sleepy. "Hello, my name's Shawn Rossow, and I'm a reporter from Sanfran Cisco. I'd like to know a few things about this town. Who are all these people? Am I in a history institute or something? Why does everybody pronounce their 's'? Where can I find the nearest gas station? Are any hotels nearby? And do you know anything about the disappearing planes in this area?"

The old man blinked several times. Then he yawned, pushed his cap over his eyes, and made a snoring sound. I grew even more frustrated. "Don't fall asleep! I came here for information, not lazy, old men!"

A wide smile grew under the brim of his hat. In a clear voice, he told me without opening his eyes, "If you wish to exchange foreign money for shekelsssss, I'll help you there out of courtesssy. But as for what you really want—information—you can jussst turn around and walk right back out that door for being sssso rude to the mayor of thissss town."

...That awkward moment when all you can think is, "Words! Come back!" I apologized and begged him to forgive me. Sitting up and pushing his hat back, I saw now that he was not quite as old as I'd first thought.

I started to apologize again, but he interrupted, "Now, what wassss your firsssst question?"

"Who are you people?"

"Cobrasss," he said, as if that should be enough explanation.

Next I asked, "Is this place some sort of history establishment?"

"Eh?"

"Well, your whole village is acting like it's in the medieval ages," I counted the odd things I had seen on my fingers. "There are candles instead of light bulbs, the women wear dresses instead of pants (well, most of them), there are horses instead of cars, and pumps instead of indoor plumbing. Plus, everybody acts different too. I'm amazed at how realistic your village is. If I didn't come from a modern place myself, I would've though the whole world lives like this!" I stopped to catch my breath.

The mayor looked at me like I was crazy. "You're ssssspeaking nonsssenssse."

"Ha!" I said. "All right, ssssir. You're doing a great job staying in character. Last question: do you know anything about the disappearing planes?"

"Eh... plainssss?" the man scratched his head. "You mean sssssinking ssssand? It'ssss quite treacherousssss, but we mark them off mossst of the time."

"I give up," I growled. "Seriously, would you just point me in the direction of the nearest hotel and bathrooms?"

"Bath-room?" the man seemed confused by the word. After a moment, I saw that he was truly perplexed and experienced a moment of panic at the thought of having to explain what a bathroom was.

"Er, you know... the men's room, toilets, restrooms, outhouse, er..."

"A privy?" the mayor guessed, and I nodded, relieved. He jerked his thumb at a back door. "You can use one out back. As for hotelsss, try The Ssssleepy Sssssnake Inn. Jussst go down Ssssouth Street until you ssssee the building. They have tolerable lodgingsss for only five shekelssss a night. And," he added with a grin, "their beer izzz the besssst in the region."

I was growing very impatient with the man, but I decided to play his game. So I gave him twenty dollars for twenty shekels, thin, silver coins engraved with twisting cobras and unintelligible words. The mayor put on a pair of crooked spectacles to examine my dollars, and he practically danced with glee. "Ssssso unique! I've never sssseen thisss kind of money in my life!"

I couldn't help smiling. "You should try out at Hollywood. They can use good actors like you." Ignoring his baffled expression, I went "out back" and used the privy, a stinky, primitive thing.

As I left, the mayor waved with one of my dollars. "Good luck!"

I guess he wasn't such a bad source, just ill-informed. I figured there must be someone else higher up in control of the town.

I strolled down South Street for awhile, seeing all sorts of amazing things: cattle, sheep, and chickens roaming free, men on horseback, but the people most of all never ceased to amaze me. Once I saw a noisy ring in the street with a huge crowd of men shouting at a snake fight. I was appalled at the writhing, hissing creatures and moved on. It seems these people have a strange attachment to snakes. Even the hoods of their capes resemble a cobra's hood.

At last, I found the wooden sign that said, "The Sleepy Snake." On the sign was a passable picture of a cobra curled up around a goblet of wine and loaf of bread. While I observed the sign, a man came out from the building. He wore a short sword at his side and a bow and quiver full of arrows on his back. Who wouldn't stare at something like that?

Catching my stare, he hissed. "What are you looking at, sssssssir?" When you see the word "hissed", you think that I mean he simply said it with a hissing attitude. But no, this man actually hissed at me like an angry snake.

"Relax, stares are not going to kill you," I said.

He glared and put his hand on the hilt of his dirk. "But thissss might. You'd be wisssse to watch your back."

When he had stalked away, I realized that both my backpack and twenty shekels were nowhere to be found! That meant no food, no tent, and no clothes. I was furious, wondering how on earth a thief had taken them without my noticing. I consider myself lucky that I still have my notebook and camera! But without my supplies, what more can I do? I guess I'll have to rely on Steve.

I've decided to get back to the ship early, for it seems these people grow more hostile with every passing hour. I can't think of what I'm doing wrong, but I somehow manage to offend everyone I talk to. I'm so confused. Anyways, this crazy place is more than enough of a good story—everybody likes to hear about loonies.

March 21

The worst possible thing has happened. My boat is gone! I followed that gravel path back to the sea, and then followed the shore until I found the dock, yet there was no boat! I know it was the right dock. There was a broken board with half of my sock pinned to it. What am I going to do?!

March 22

This is a terrible, cruel land. Yesterday, a toothless old woman had "pity" on me and dragged me to a soup kitchen where I was forced to sit with a number of other smelly vagrants. The soup was actually quite good, mostly broth with a few potatoes. It was the spiciness I enjoyed most. I quickly drained my first bowl and lined up for a second.

When I returned, one of the men, whose coat seemed to be a bug hotel, grinned at me. "Ah, I ssssee you're a native. You mussst be if you can drink thissss broth without a wink."

"Why is that?" I asked.

"Don't you know?" the bug-coat man looked very amused. "Hey, boysssss, this ssstranger has never heard of our sssoup before! He's already had one serving."

To this, they grinned and commented, "Ooh, I hope you didn't get an extra dose."

"Heheh, I shouldn't wonder if he'll be dead by morning."

"Well, he was the one being adventurousss."

By this time, my stomach began to tense up from sheer nervousness. "Dose of what?" I managed a pathetic grin. "It's just soup."

The man serving the soup burst out laughing. "Not just sssoup, boy: venomousssss soup!"

"Poisoned!" shouted the men gleefully.

My buggy friend added, "Don't look so pale, sssssir. It won't kill you... probably. It's only the poison of a Sssand Ssserpent. It'll only kill you if you're not immune to it, like most of ussssss are. None of usssss even show ssssymptoms of it."

"S-symptoms? What kind?"

"Oh, the most common: rashes, swelling, inability to breathe, shock, paralysisss, and death."

No, I did not die. That night I did suffer unpleasant symptoms, but on the whole the experience was pretty anticlimactic considering the scare they gave me.

This morning, I resolved to research this strange tradition of theirs. Quite by luck, I found my way back to the mayor's building. The mayor was awake this time and looked rather happy to see me. I found out many interesting facts from him.

- All people born in the land of Cobra already have a slight immunity to poison.
- They put the venom of snakes in almost all their drinks and soups. When I asked why, he looked at me as if I was stupid. "Because it tastesss good!"
- They are known for their quick-working poisons. The mayor also mentioned their "ssssuperb" darts.

Note: I have the oddest feeling someone's watching me.

The words here are illiterate in some places and covered with dirt smudges.

(Scribble, scribble) — being chased! They look like soldiers with (scribble, scribble) I'm hiding in a barrel but I- (mud splotch) —help!

* * *

March 24? 25?

I need to get out of here! I'm starting to lose track of time... a side effect of spending the night in a stinky barrel. I've heard the men talking about other regions, though they never tell me a thing when I ask for a map or at least point me to the nearest road out of Cobra. Maybe all the people on this island are jerks, but I'll never know until I meet them, I guess. I found a little path branching off from the main one.

Without much hope, I'm going to follow it. I'll walk through the night and rest in the morning.

Shawn picked up where he had left off.

March 25... or 26.

Things to remember:

- *Do not, if you value your life, walk at night. It was a nightmare.*
- *These people like to do the opposite thing you ask them. Be careful.*
- *Watch out for cows. Especially the fat ones.*

I have entered a very large forest with a narrow path that zigzags through the trees. It's so dark I know it's time for dinner, but then I remember that I have no food whatsoever, nor any hope of finding some tonight.

How I long to take a nap in the sunshine and wake up to the smell of barbecued ribs and

"Aaaah!!!" One moment Shawn was writing and imagining. The next, as he shifted his weight onto his other foot, he was upside down. The ground bobbed up and down as the limb tested his weight. A tough rope encircled his ankle. Shawn kicked and struggled like a hooked fish.

"No! No, no, no!" he screamed. "Why me?" He proceeded to moan for another five minutes. After the brief monologue of his loathsome life, Shawn felt ready to escape.

Grunting, he pulled himself up and grabbed hold of his foot. *What now?* he wondered, staring at the thick rope. After attempting to pick at it with his fingers, and then his teeth, he concluded that it was impossible to gnaw through. Maybe if he could grab onto the tree, he could somehow pull himself up on the branch and untie the rope around his foot. After all, upside down he was only a foot or two from the ground.

Letting himself down, Shawn began to rock his body towards the trunk of the tree. However, every time he reached out to grab it, he only swung back clutching a piece of bark. While Shawn rocked, he considered calling for help. But even if somebody heard him, would they help him? Most likely they would just laugh and walk away or do something worse to him. Shawn's foot began to sting, and his fingers were full of splinters. All the blood had rushed to his head, making his mind as thick as pudding… or maybe that was his stomach thinking.

Finally he gave up. He began to wish that he had eaten more soup, poisoned or not. Hunger gnawed at his belly, and his mouth felt desert dry. Shawn wondered if he'd ever be able to tell this story to Steve. Half asleep with weariness, he began to chuckle. "Hey, Steve, guess what I found out today? The world looks much different hanging upside down from the limb of a tree. Seriously, you should try it sometime."

Chapter 3

The Island of Joy

Steve watched the speedboat zoom away and felt a pang of guilt in his stomach. As soon as he turned away, however, he forgot to feel guilty. On an aromatic breeze, a beautiful song met his ears. It filled Steve with a rare emotion akin to curiosity but so much grander. It filled him with wonder. Though the reporter couldn't identify the words of the melody, he imagined that the singer was calling someone… calling to him? Steve crept towards the trees, his ear cocked to hear the distant song. As he drew closer to the forest, the music became clearer. Steve halted at the edge of the beach and peered into the forest. To his astonishment, it was no darker underneath the trees than it was where he was standing on the warm sand.

Steve spoke to himself, something he had never done in Sanfran Cisco. "I guess I should find out whoever's singing in the woods."

"You've got that right, young man," said a man's voice. It was so clear that the speaker could've spoken right in his ear.

Steve whirled around, but all he saw was the sparkling, golden sand around him and the frothing white waves washing against the beach. "Who said that?" he asked.

A different voice, this one female, said in a scolding tone. "Don't bother, my friend. You know that it won't do any good talking to the crazy humans from the land of shadow. They are simply too far gone to help... not at all like the people we know."

Steve kept looking around; still there was not a soul in sight.

"He doesn't look like one of *them*, does he?" a new voice commented.

Steve stepped into the forest to look among the trees, wondering if someone was playing a prank. He even looked up into the branches and called, "Anyone up there? Show yourself!"

As soon as he said that, the branches of the trees began to wave, making the leaves clatter together. With a cry, Steve jerked backwards so fast that he landed on his bottom in the sand. The leaves clattered even louder, yet there was hardly a breeze blowing. *This can't be happening,* Steve thought.

"Look, now you've scared the poor stranger," said the woman's voice. "Perhaps he's *not* one of them. Look! Not even a weapon."

"I think he's a nice man," a child's voice chimed in. "We should be friends."

"Ah, you never said a truer word."

"Hear, hear!"

"More power to the lovely maple!"

Steve raised his voice, "Excuse me..."

A host of voices answered together: "Oh, it's quite alright, sir. Quite!"

"You're very much excused."

"Please grace us with your excused reply."

"We are all ears. Or mushrooms, you might say."

"Hey!" shouted Steve. The voices quieted at once. "Could one of you come out and talk to me face to face?"

"Face to bark, you must mean."

A tree to his left rattled. "Oh, dear, oh dear! Stop talking for goodness sake before you end up giving the stranger a signed confession."

Steve took a step back. "Are you talking trees?!"

No more voices were heard, but the reporter did not dare get closer. Now that the voices had stopped, he could once again hear the beautiful song somewhere beyond the forest. The trees waved their branches as if dancing to the tune. *It's the wind,* Steve told himself. *But how could*

I have thought up the voices? I hope I'm not becoming like that Shawn Rossow.

Worried, Steve felt his forehead. Then his expression cleared, and he began to laugh in relief. "Microphones!" he exclaimed. "Embedded in the trees somewhere, probably to scare away intruders. What a clever invention." He felt very clever himself for figuring it out. "Of course, that means that there must be people already here, unless it's just a recording. As soon as I find that singer, I'm sure everything will be cleared up." With a nod, Steve entered the dancing forest.

But as soon as he was gone: "Goodness gracious, do you think the poor boy might get lost?"

"A likely problem, indeed. Perhaps you could call little Nifty and have him show the man to the village."

A universal groan went through the trees. "If that squirrel was not as cute as he was a pest, I'd give him a nice switching!"

"No, no, please, we don't want scare away our new visitor before he's even gotten settled in."

"My limbs are still sore from him hanging and bouncing on them. Ugh!"

The first one spoke again, "Why don't we just let him follow the song until he finds Melody?"

"By Rainbow's Summit, now that's an idea!"

"Heeheehee, there's nothing like a song to start a romance."

"Wait! What if he really is one of *them*? He might be after a captive!" spoke the second voice. "And since Melody has no True Love, she will be lost!"

There were horrified gasps all around, and they agreed to send Nifty. A towering oak bent its graying leaves and sighed. "My, my, us trees bear all the weight of our fair island, don't we?"

"For the greater good of the people," an old birch replied.

Steve walked through the woods as if in a trance. Yet he never bumped into a tree, stumbled into bushes, or hit his head on an overhanging limb. The bushes scurried out of his way, and the trees lifted their thick arms away from his head and feet. If Steve had been his usual self, he might have noticed the sly winks and giggles passed by the enchanted creatures of the wood. Whispers followed him, *"The stranger is following Melody's song."* The magical air of the island had started to do its work on Steve.

If Shawn could have seen him now, he would have noticed that Steve's usual bored expression was dreamy, and the worried lines between his eyes had started to fade. His step grew bouncier, and he threw his arms as he strolled. Why, he even felt like whistling!

Recognizing the ridiculousness of the thought, Steve remembered why he was there; he was on a mission. The realization stopped him in his tracks. What was he doing, following a song blindly through an unknown forest? He hadn't even taken one note since he reached the forest's edge.

These worries were almost lost amid a multitude of happy thoughts. Thoughts like singing, skipping, climbing a mountain, going on picnics. He tried to push these thoughts away, but it was like digging a hole in the sand. There was always more to replace the thoughts that he shut down. Steve slapped his forehead as a hard as he could. The pain subdued the nonsensical emotions. "Thank goodness," he muttered.

Steve set his briefcase down and took out his notebook. Checking for sap, he sat down against a huge pine. It took only one look around to set the pencil dancing across the paper.

- *There is something very strange about this forest. As far as my eyes can reach, there are trees everywhere. Yet there are no rotting logs or dead plants anywhere. In fact, there are no signs of anything dead. It seems more like a garden than a wild forest.*
- *Besides the unidentified voice from far away, there's a very strange sort of music that fills the forest to its brim.*

- *I find my mind wandering to sunlit pastures and cool waterfalls. Could it be something in the air that is clouding my thoughts?*
- *After sniffing the air, I found that besides the usual forest scent, there is an intoxicating perfume that hangs about the place. It's so sweet, it gives one a dizzy, faint feeling.*

"What does 'intoxicating' mean?"

Steve glanced up from his writing to see a plump, red squirrel hanging on a limb mere inches from his shoulder. It's curious, beady eyes stared right at the page. The squirrel twirled his tail, opened its mouth, and the cheery voice came again, "Oh, I know what 'faint' means, that's what the girls do when something frightens them. Either that or their T.L. has just proposed."

Note that if Steve had been sitting on a street back in Sanfran Cisco and this same animal had spoken to him, he would have done only two things: run and go to the doctor saying he was having hallucinations. But like I said before, the very air of that that island had been working on him from the moment he stepped onto the rock. This was a new Steve; a Steve that responded to animals, for example, which is exactly what he did. "A t-talking squirrel? How in the world…?"

The squirrel narrowed his eyes and said, "Oh, yes, it was a challenge. But I am Nifty, the Wizard of Words, the king of—"

Suddenly the limb dropped, sending Nifty tumbling harmlessly to the ground. A voice cried, "Come off it, Nifty. Everybody but that human with the dirty hair knows that all animals can speak the human language."

"The *animals* can *talk*?"

Nifty scrambled up onto Steve's leg. "Yep, and all the trees too, though they are more the sort of thing that like to talk for years about stuff like T.L. and weddings and who just fell for who." His little snout curled in a disgusted face.

"Impossible!" gasped Steve.

"Impa-what? Never heard that one before. You're just chock-full of fancy words, aren't you?"

Steve leaned back against the tree. "What's going on? This can't all be a hallucination."

"Ha-loo-sin-a-tion? What's that?"

"What's happening to me? Have I stumbled into Narnia? Shall I see a unicorn next?" Steve began to hyperventilate. Immediately, the tree brushed Niftee off Steve's knee and began to fan him gently. Steve closed his eyes and took deep breaths. *Just breathe. It's okay. Smell that beautiful air!* With every breath, he felt his panic ebb away. When the dizzy feeling faded, he opened his eyes. The squirrel peeked at him from behind a tree. "You sounded like my friend Wheezy the hound. Was that a hallucination?"

"No, no," Steve managed to say. "My asthma. I've… I've just never heard things other than people talk."

With one bounce, Niftee landed back on his knee. "It's the way it is here, that's all," he stated. "I've heard stories of other places where animals couldn't talk. Seems like such an inconvenience. I mean, what would you do if you wanted someone to scratch behind your ear?" He cocked his head.

Almost mechanically, Steve reached out and scratched Nifty's ear. The squirrel sighed with delight. Despite himself, Steve began to smile while he stroked the downy fur of the squirrel. *I guess talking animals aren't that absurd, are they? Parrots and crows can talk, and no one is surprised. I just wonder how I'm going to explain that my source was a talking squirrel named Nifty.*

Nifty spoke again, "You're definitely more interesting to converse with than most people. All they want to talk about is their T.L."

"What do those initials stand for?"

The tree behind Steve waved its branches. "Don't you know? It is truly the wonderfullest thing of all."

"I don't think wonderfullest is a word," interjected Nifty.

"True Love!" the tree burst out. "Our island was built upon it!"

Steve retrieved the notebook, rescued his pencil from a crowd of curious animals, and stood for nearly fifteen minutes, writing everything down. Nifty, looking over his shoulder the whole time, made comments like, "Heheh, you didn't spell mischievous right."

When Steve looked up, he almost glowed with excitement. "Nifty, I think I'm beginning to understand about this island. It's the picture of paradise. Thus, all the inhabitants are good, aren't you?"

A tree to his left shook its pine branches, which Steve now recognized as laughter, and said in its odd, hollow voice, "Of course we're all good! Though a few creatures I know cut it pretty close." Nifty sniffed.

Steve pocketed his notebook and snatched up his bags. "Quick, Nifty, show me where the other people are!"

Nifty leaped to a branch and bobbed up and down, his tail batting the air. "Juuuust one thing!"

"Yeah?"

For the first time, the squirrel got a solemn look on his face. He put his right paw over his heart and recited, "You must promise by Rainbow Summit that you are not one of *them*."

"One of whom?"

"The evil humans that inhabit the Island of *Despair*," he pronounced the word *despair* in a fierce way.

Immediately, there were gasps and whispers around them. "Don't say such things, you naughty squirrel! That word is a pain to my heartwood."

Steve shook his head. "I don't understand."

"You will," declared Nifty. "But first you have to promise!"

"I promise by Rainbow Summit that I'm not one of the people from the Island of—mmmph!" Steve found his mouth muffled by a handful of leaves. He pushed the branch away and muttered an apology.

The creatures graciously forgave him. Nifty giggled. "Well, since we've decided that you're not one of *them*... Follow your ear, or maybe your heart. Whichever works better." And with that, the squirrel scampered up the tree. Half a second later, he slid back down. "By the way, what's your name?"

The reporter opened his mouth, closed it again, and had to think for a few seconds. "My name is, umm... Steve! That's right. Imagine forgetting your own name!" He trailed off when he saw that no one was listening anymore except the trees, but they could hardly help that. Just then he heard the sweet call of the song drifting towards him.

Now, the old Steve would probably have gathered his dignity and marched towards the voice. But this new Steve felt his heart give a colossal leap, and he forgot everything else. With a yell, he abandoned his bags and bolted through the trees, shouting, "I'm coming! I'm coming!"

Nifty smirked. "Yep, he's following his heart. Good thing Melody's not spoken for, eh?"

* * *

The forest began to thin up ahead, but Steve barely noticed. He ran with an energy that knew no bounds. When the forest ended, Steve found himself standing at the edge of a field of colors. Flower of every color you can imagine covered the ground. The air was heavy with the aroma, and Steve's mind was assailed with the colors which bounced out at him like paint off a canvas.

That's when he saw the lady, lying in a bed of yellow and red flower bushes. Thick, golden locks of hair fell about her shoulders like a waterfall. She wore a white dress with lace sleeves as gossamer as a spider's web and twice as pretty. In her hand, she held a flower and sniffed it in pure bliss.

Even from where Steve stood, paralyzed, he could see that her eyes were bright green like emeralds. Her face was a sculptor's masterpiece. Long bangs fell over one side of her face as she tilted her head toward the sky and burst into song. The lady's voice soared higher and higher, but never fell out of tune.

"Oh, beautiful flowers, how dost thou grow?
Through joy and love and happiness; this I truly know!
Your beauty is unexplainable, the words I cannot speak
Your purity is unmatchable, humble and meek.

The smell of Freedoms flourishing by Heaven's Treasure

Two Sides of the Coin

*The caress of Sweet Friendship and the Love Giver
Close to Lovely Lake, the Violet Kisses grow
The Spring Dew, the Sky Petal, oh, I love them so!*

*In the silver moonlight, Angel's Touch shall appear
While Honey Drop is always there to cheer
But of Joywish, what can compare?
It's like every flower dancing in the air.*

*Oh, beautiful flowers, how dost thou grow?
Through joy and love and happiness; this I truly know!"*

The lady began to sing the chorus again. A burst of energy pulsed through Steve, spurring his feet into a run. The words of the song poured from his mouth. In a strong, clear voice he sang, "Your beauty is unexplainable. The words I cannot speak! Your purity is unmatchable, humble and meek."

He stopped a foot from her, gazing down at her sweet, heart-shaped face. The girl's green eyes met his hazel ones, and a smile parted her pink lips. Steve felt a hundred emotions tear at his heart. The vivid colors, the overwhelming aroma, the girl's perfect voice, and the sound of his own voice singing.

Perhaps that was really what surprised him the most. *I just sang to her, didn't I?* Steve thought. *And she liked it!* The man who never cried found his eyes brimming with tears. His heart somersaulted like a trapeze artist. Never had he felt such keen joy. It struck his heart like a mortal blow. *I could die of happiness,* he thought with a booming laugh. *And I wouldn't mind!*

As if in slow motion, the ground rushed to meet him. Steve didn't feel any alarm. The soft grass tickled his nose before all his senses faded into warm oblivion.

CHAPTER 4

The Queen's Son

"Hahah! This is great! Ooh, now I'll try it in Sylindra's voice. Heeheehee! *Ahem*. Ah, my poor pet, Rossow... My spies tell me that you have been too happy lately. Well, I've come to tell you that we need the money, and we need it today. *Don't* tell me you spent it all trying to buy yourself some measly bread. You have until the clock strikes midnight to gather your petty belongings and be gone."

Shawn found himself coming awake to the sound of harsh laughter. "Mwahahaha! Perhaps someday you will find that paying us money is a requirement, you pathetic rat! Or else, *we will burn your house to ground! MWAHAHAHA!*"

A huge thunder clap rattled the forest. A dark figure shook his fist inches from Shawn's face and screamed like a maniac. Shawn cried out in terror.

Something inside him snapped. With one swift motion, he punched the man square in the face. *Smack!*

Immediately, the tension in the forest ceased. The whole place lightened as the sun peeked from behind the clouds, as if to see the show better. The man lay on his stomach, apparently stunned into silence. Shawn stared at his stinging fist for a full five seconds. "Shoot!" he said. "Now I'm in trouble." He craned his neck to see the man, whose back had begun to shake. "Are... are you okay, sir?"

Two Sides of the Coin

The man rolled over on his side, gasped for breath, and laughed out loud. He sounded like a normal human now; that is, one dying of laughter. Whatever was tickling him was totally lost on Shawn. The trees rattled in the chill wind, as if they too were chuckling at the reporter's series of unfortunate events.

Shawn shook his head. *I'm never going to understand these people.* "Hey, a little help would be appreciated up here!" he yelled down. When the man took no notice, Shawn peeled off a section of the bark and chucked it at him. "Stop laughing!"

Faster than Shawn's eye could follow, the man leapt up, unsheathed his sword, and severed the rope with one stroke. Shawn crashed to the ground in a pile of legs, arms, and leaves. "OUCH. Thanks for the warning," he muttered.

The reporter felt a jab in his side and heard a merry, "You're welcome!" Sitting up, he got his first good look at the strange man. Like Shawn, he appeared to be in his early twenties. With wind-tossed, dark hair and a bristly chin, he was in need of a haircut. A few long bangs fell into his gleaming, amber eyes. Sharp and narrow, his face would have looked sly if not for the good-natured expression. Whenever he smiled, as he was doing now, lines appeared around his eyes and mouth. He held himself with a confidence that Shawn had hardly ever seen, and certainly never felt.

The man wore baggy, black trousers that sported several pockets as well as several holes. His dark brown tunic went almost to his knees, and a thick leather belt showed off his trim waist. Like Shawn's shoes, the man's boots were muddy. Unlike Shawn's, his looked perfectly suited to the outdoors. A long, black cape was fastened at his shoulder with a silver brooch. The only other item he wore that looked worth anything was a silver ring on his left hand. The ring was engraved with a fox's face with tiny rubies for eyes.

Shawn sat up, rubbing blood back into his aching limbs. The man sheathed his sword and seated himself beside the reporter. "Are you a storyteller?" he asked. After all the screaming, Shawn was surprised to hear a normal, friendly voice.

"No, I'm a reporter," he said. "I only write stories about real things. You know, the news. After I give my story to my boss, he sends it out for the people to read."

The man raised an eyebrow. "I know what news is."

"Yeah, but the difference between my news and yours is that you probably get your news from spies," growled Shawn. As the blood sank back into his limbs, it brought a needling sensation.

The man rubbed his chin. "Hmm, got me there." He murmured to himself, "So you *are* a spy."

"I'm not a spy," Shawn protested, but the man took no notice.

He grinned and held up a torn, dirty paper. "In your news, I discovered a vast store of amusement behind the tedious script."

Shawn snatched the paper from his fingers, his gaze darting over it. "Dear Mr. Rossow," the wrinkled letter began. "It has come to our attention that you have again failed…" The reporter glanced from the letter to the stranger and wondered how on earth he had taken a boring thing like rent and thought of burning down houses.

"I didn't write this," he stated. "It's a letter from the apartment owner saying that I forgot to pay my rent."

"Ha!" crowed the man. "I knew it had something to do with money."

Shawn ran his fingers through his matted, brown hair. It felt like there was a layer of dirt caked on his scalp. The reporter turned again to his strange rescuer. "Why were you screaming at me when I woke up?"

The man's smile faded. "Oh. *Well*. I didn't plan for you to wake up the moment my story came to its climax." He rubbed a spot on his cheek that was already turning black and blue. "I was going into a perfectly brilliant imitation of Sylindra, and—"

"Who's Sylindra?"

The man narrowed his eyes and gave a knowing smile. "Oh, you'll find out sooner or later."

"How do you know?" asked Shawn.

"Last I heard she was looking for you," he commented as if Sylindra were an old friend of his. "You know, you're quite lucky I showed up when I did. You would be in real trouble if she had found you first. Now that I'm here, you have no need to worry."

"What do you mean, 'now that I'm here'?"

The man rubbed his neck. "Well, she can't kill her own brother, can she?"

Mortified, Shawn shook his head. "I'm so confused."

"Poor fellow," said the stranger. "I suppose you cannot know what a curiosity you are. My sister Sylindra and other inquisitive people have been searching for the trouble-maker of Cobra. But don't worry. I won't let the vixen take my game."

Shawn sighed. *What a pity. First friendly person I've met, and he's nuts, just like the rest of this island.*

"Would you like me to cut off the rest of the rope?" the stranger asked, gesturing to the loop encircled around Shawn's ankle. At Shawn's nod, the man produced a dagger hidden somewhere in his tunic and seemed to cut the rope as easily as a string.

Shawn stood up and gave the rope a kick. "Who would put up such a dangerous trap by the side of the road where anyone could step into it by accident?"

"That was me," the man stated. He untied the trap and began to coil it up. "I suppose I should be upset by your ruining my bear trap—I mean, you have to make a living somehow—but I'm not in the slightest. Regardless of black eyes, you gave me the best laugh I've had in months." He tousled Shawn's hair. "You are *not* from around here, are you? Other people would never get caught in a simple, old bear trap. Even if they did, they'd cut themselves loose easily with their dagger. Decent folk would leave a shekel to pay for the damage."

"What dagger?" Shawn spread his arms with a scowl. "And what about the damage done to *me*, ever think about that?"

"That's your loss, and a reminder to be more careful next time."

"I didn't even know that people were putting up traps around here!"

The man chuckled. "You know, the purpose of traps *is* to catch creatures by surprise. I never expected to catch something this big though."

Is that a fat joke? Shawn wondered. Everything in his body hurt, his stomach gurgled in agony, and yet this guy wanted to lecture him about paying for a broken trap! He crossed his arms. "Who are you, anyways?"

The man whirled around, flapped his cape to the side, and bowed. "Call me Len."

"Is that your real name?" Shawn asked.

Len looked puzzled at the reporter's question. "What does it matter?" Without waiting for an answer, he turned on his heel and swept over to a tree where a bulging sack hung. Retrieving this, he got to work. In a matter of minutes, Len had a fire going and a tin coffeepot hung expertly over the licking flames. After offering Shawn an extra cape from his pack, he set about carving two cooking sticks.

Shawn found himself cooking beef over the fire, all the while bolting down bread and cheese and chugging water from a canteen. Soon Len took over cooking both sides of meat after Shawn's meat dropped once or twice into the fire. Instead, Shawn sipped the tongue-scalding, bitter coffee with relish.

For the first time on that island, Shawn felt good. His belly was warm with the hot coffee. He scorched his clothes sitting so close to the fire, but he didn't even mind. And when Len handed him a steaming, luscious side of a meat, he even forgot about silverware. Flapping his burning fingers in the air, he tore off chunks of meat with his teeth like a wolf.

Besides asking for his name and how he liked his meat, Len said nothing the rest of the night. Shawn was glad for the silence. After dinner, Len cleaned up the leftovers and arranged a bed with his cape and a pile of leaves. For a bear-trapper, he was sure civilized. When Len returned to stoke up the fire, Shawn said, "Thank you for dinner. But why are you helping me?"

Len looked up. "You're my catch of the day, aren't you? I thought I should have you for dinner. No charge."

The reporter laughed at that. "Maybe I should get caught in bear traps more often!"

"I wouldn't," he warned. "The stags are pretty inhospitable to trespassers."

"Stags?"

"This *is* the Stag Forest," Len said, as if stating the obvious.

"There were no signs," Shawn defended himself. "Is this forest some kind of no-man's land, where anybody can hunt for deer?"

"You really don't know anything, do you?" Len marveled, not unkindly. "In every region, the people are called by the names of that animal. For example, the men of the Stag Forest are called bucks; the women are does, and the children fawns."

"Why?"

"It's been a tradition of the island since its beginning." Len's eyes shone in the firelight. "It's odd, having to explain to you what children know."

Shawn bristled. "Hey, I just got here a couple days ago, and you expect me to know everything? You're the only person who's told me anything useful since I got here."

Len lowered his gaze into the flames and stroked his whiskers. "You're not a very good spy, you know."

"*I'm not a spy!*"

"Tell that to the stags. They were ready to use you as target practice until I caught you. Then you became my rightful property and thus, off limits."

Shawn's skin prickled. "How do you know that? Did you talk with them?"

Len shrugged. "No need. I know they're watching even if you can't see them, and they don't like strangers."

The reporter glanced over his shoulder. Somewhere, hiding in the shadows of the trees, were dangerous people who didn't like him any more than the aptly named cobras. Shawn shivered. "Can you... will you show me the way out?"

"Fear not," Len said. "You will not fall by a Stag arrow or a Cobra dart while I'm around."

"But why?" Shawn repeated. "Why are you helping me?"

"You're different, Rossow. Different is dangerous. I like danger." Len nodded as if t. Shawn rubbed his face, worn out from all the strangeness. "Get some sleep," Len gestured to the bed he had made in the leaves.

Shawn considered the offer in silence. *If he was out to kidnap or kill me, he could've done that while I was tied up, hungry, and numb. Well, it's not like I've got anywhere else to go.* "Thank you," he finally said. Trudging around the fire, he dropped face first onto the cape. It felt like lying on a cloud. In another minute, he was fast asleep under the watchful gaze of his strange, new friend Len.

* * *

"*Rossow, wake up!*" came a voice from far away.

"Okay, coming..." Shawn muttered. That taxi driver was really impatient, but there was no way he could leave yet. He wandered around his apartment, searching for something important. Something he knew he had forgotten. It was painful to walk on all the trash littering the floor. Just then, something cold and wet touched his face, and Shawn remembered that he needed to fix his sink.

Hoisting himself under the sink, he began to fix the pipe, but it kept dripping on him. As he used a wrench to tighten the screw, it fell off. A fountain of icy water doused him in the face.

The reporter gasped and sat bolt-upright. He blinked. Everything had gone dark, as if someone had flipped off the lights. Water dripped from his hair down his shirt, making Shawn shiver. "I must have turned that screw the wrong—mmmph!" Somebody clapped a hand over Shawn's mouth. He tried to pull the hand off to scream for help, but his attacker was too strong.

"It's only me," whispered a familiar voice. Shawn squinted in the dark and was barely able to make out Len's face. The memory of the dark island hit Shawn like a sledgehammer. Len brought a finger to his lips, and Shawn nodded in comprehension. "You sleep like a dead man," Len whispered, letting him go. "Which you soon shall be if you can't learn otherwise. Gather your things *quietly*."

Frowning, Shawn rubbed his face dry with the cape he had been sleeping on. *What a lovely way to wake up. There better be an explanation for this.* He pulled on the cape, hung the camera around his neck, and clutched his notebook like a lifeline. Meanwhile, Len scattered all the evidence that they had been there. The fire had already been put out and covered with dirt so that Shawn could scarcely tell where it had been last

Two Sides of the Coin

night. Suddenly, the sound of distant voices wafted through the forest. Shawn whirled towards the sound. "Are those stags?" he whispered.

The man drew his hood over his face. "Stags don't make noise in the forest. Those are soldiers of Cobra."

Shawn shivered and drew deeper into the cloak, welcoming the darkness. "What are they doing here? I thought—"

"You thought you were safe," snapped Len. "Well, I was mistaken as well. I didn't think they would be fool enough to come after you here. Now it's too late to run."

Shawn gestured at the dark forest. "So we're just going to wait here and twiddle our thumbs until they find us?"

"I said it's too late to *run*," said Len. "I didn't say we're going to wait here. I'll get us out, but you have to promise not to scream or do something stupid. Understand?"

Shawn opened his mouth to say that no, he didn't understand, and he doubted that he ever would. This denial was interrupted by a twang and a sharp hiss. Len ducked as an arrow bit into the tree next to him, showering him with woodchips. A shout rang through the forest, "Sssssurrender and give yoursssselves up. You are sssssssurrounded!"

"Quick, wrap your arms around my back!" Len yelled.

"What? Why?"

"Shut up and do it!"

Mystified, Shawn obeyed. As he hugged Len's back, he glanced into the forest. Dark figures raced towards them from all sides. Their cobra-hoods flapped out, and Shawn felt like a mouse ambushed by a brood of vipers. He stared, too terrified to scream, while another row of cobras loaded arrows onto their bows.

When he looked back at Len, he *did* scream. Huge, bat-liked wings had appeared from Len's back. They were black with a leathery appearance, each larger than a man. As the wings unfurled, they blocked out the moonlight, and the veins in them were black against the lighter skin. Len's back muscles bunched as he flapped his wings. Again and again, faster and faster, the great wings beat at the air. With a yell, Len launched himself upwards and left the ground with the reporter hanging on for dear life. Arrows pierced the tree trunks in the clearing they had just left.

It was like being pulled by a string. Up and up they went, gaining speed and height. The search party milled about below them. "That accurssssed foxsssss!" they hissed with rage.

"You sssssordid serpentssssss!" Len jeered back.

Shawn kept his eyes fixed on the ground, his last grasp onto reality. "Prepare to fire!" yelled the commander. Archers loaded their arrows and aimed for Len as if he were an escaping partridge. The order was never given.

Shadows seemed to materialize out of the forest, and the shouts of the soldiers turned to screams. One by one, the cobras vanished from sight, their screams cut off abruptly. Shawn gasped, goose bumps prickling on his skin. "Never cross a stag, Rossow," said Len. "We're lucky they chose our side."

Shawn was too numb with shock to feel grateful. He squeezed his eyes shut, thinking to himself, *It's just a dream. Just a crazy nightmare. My alarm clock will be going off any minute now.* He hoped that thinking it would make it come true. Still, the sound of wing-beats did not cease.

Len coughed. "Stop squeezing so hard before you crush my ribs, Tubby!"

Shawn barely loosened his grip. "I'm not tubby," he said between gritted teeth.

"Really? Have you ever tried to fly carrying twice your own weight? I thought we weren't going to make it for a second. I dare say you're the heaviest thing I've had to fly with yet."

Fly? thought Shawn. *We can't be flying. That's impossible. Gravity pulls too hard on our weight for us to fight against it. Humans are not built for flying.*

The reporter cracked an eye open. Darkness surrounded them, and the rolling clouds looked close enough to step onto. Len's hood had slipped off, leaving his long hair to blow about in the wind. They glided about a mile from the ground, and the gusts of air chilled Shawn to the bone. Yes, it was impossible, but somehow Len *could* fly.

Shawn kept stealing glances beneath them to see the forest shimmering like a huge, green lake. Up ahead in the distance was the massive, bulky shape of the mountain the cobras called Mordoom. To his left were great stretches of forest followed by brighter patches that Shawn guessed were fields. To his right was the ocean, black and motionless, except for one white, egg-shaped reflection. It took Shawn a moment to realize it was the moon.

Suddenly, Shawn saw something beyond the reflection of the moon that made his jaw drop. On this island, the water near the shore was as dark as could be. But the closer it got to that other island across the channel, the lighter the water became until it was practically daylight blue.

The island itself *shone*. Not a creepy sort of glow, but so radiant compared to this dark island that Shawn found himself squinting. It was like the island's light had ceased to grow darker after sunset.

Once again, Shawn felt a definite pull inside himself towards that beautiful place. However, the longing seemed fainter than before, which surprised and perturbed the reporter. Surely after seeing how unfriendly this dark island was, he would want to go to that other place even more? Eventually, Shawn tore his gaze from the bright island. It took a while for his eyes to adjust once again to the gloom.

"When are we going to land?" he asked.

"As soon as possible, believe me," Len grunted.

Shawn got an idea. Picking up his camera, he aimed it at the forest below and clicked the button. The flash blinded him and lit up the whole woods.

Len glanced upwards at the clouds. "Funny, it doesn't smell like a storm."

"Storm?"

"Didn't you see the lightning? It was close, but no thunder. How odd," Len murmured.

Shawn glanced down at his camera. How to explain? He decided to save that for later. "I'm sure it's nothing to worry about." Grinning, he turned the camera off. *Ha, I wonder what the guys back home will think when I tell them I didn't take the pic from a helicopter but on the back of a bat-creature!*

About fifteen minutes later, Len shouted back. "We've made it out of the Stag Region. Unless I'm wrong—and I'm usually not—the stags will have no further reason to come after you."

"Ah, this from the guy who thought the cobras wouldn't follow us into the forest?" said Shawn.

Len frowned, tossed his head, and said in a devil-may-care voice, "Whatever. By the way, you might want to hang on." The bat-like wings angled downward, and Shawn had no time to catch his breath before the aerial rollercoaster plummeted. All he could do was hold tight to Len while his insides tied themselves in knots.

Tears sprung to Shawn's eyes as the wind blew up against them, knocking the men back and forth like toys. "Leeeeeeeen!" Shawn screamed. The man in question cackled with glee, folding his wings in close like a bird of prey. Nearly five feet from collision with the ground and certain death, Len opened his wings. He flapped hard once, twice. The two hovered in the air for a second and dropped to the ground.

As soon as Shawn felt the ground beneath his feet, he threw himself facedown upon it with a cry, "Oh sweet, sweet earth! I'll never leave you again!" A moment later, he was back on his feet, glaring from the ground to the new grass stains on his suit. Len smirked and strode down the path while Shawn followed. "Where are we going?" he asked.

"Thonfirm," Len replied. "The capital of the Fox region and my home. It's still a fair distance, so we can discuss everything on the way."

Shawn nodded. *So, my rescuer is a fox, is he? It wasn't just an insult the cobras threw at him.* Now that the danger was over, Shawn began to feel curious again about the island. The reporter checked his belongings and was relieved to find that nothing had gotten lost during the take off or the landing. He examined his camera three times before hanging it back in place. *Finally, it's my turn to ask the questions.* He pulled out the worn notebook, poised a rather dull pencil, and turned to Len.

Len began to talk without urging. "So, Rossow, if that's your real name..."

"Shawn Rossow," he corrected.

"Where should I begin, I wonder? You show up on our island with no knowledge of anything. It's almost as if you bashed your head, lost your memory, and now have to learn everything anew." He gave a shudder of delight. "Perfect!"

"Perfect?" *I might describe this situation as many things, but not perfect,* Shawn thought.

"Well, let me start with a few introductions." Len gestured around him. "This, our beautiful home, is called the Island of Despair."

Len waited for a reply but only heard a rather annoying: *Squeak, squeak. ...scribble, scribble. Squeak, squeak!*

He did his best to ignore Shawn's pencil, continuing, "There is so much for you to learn, I hardly know where to begin. All our customs will be completely new to you. Well, you have probably noticed by now that all our people are like the island itself. Sinister. Shadowy. How we love it! Don't get me wrong now. We're not evil. Or at least, not all of us are. Take me for example. I like to think of myself as a rather reckless, handsome, and mysterious fellow, correct?"

Squeak, squeak, squeak.

"But my dear Rossow, you must understand: we are bad, simply nasty. It's lovely. Oh yes. We plot, sneak, spy, kidnap people, investigate dark secrets, chase each other around, throw sharp objects, feud, and then simply add an evil laugh—we love to have fun. On the other hand, even villains have goals in life far bigger than making others miserable. We keep the wheels of life turning, so to speak. Oh, Tubby, we are the *balance,* if you would understand such things." He cackled and jabbed Shawn in the belly, who glared at him.

"Of course, to understand us, you must understand..." Len glanced around and lowered his voice, "... *them.* The other island that lies only a few miles from ours is known as," putting a hand over his mouth, he uttered, "*the Island of Joy.*" The grass under his feet almost seemed to wither at the very name.

"The people that inhabit the island are obsessed with light. Even the people themselves never have dark hair or eyes. Black and other wholesome colors are nowhere to be found. They are all vegetarians, and they never chop down trees. There are *no* predators there, for the animals and people live in peace, of all things!"

"The people so happy, it's rather sickening. They enjoy things like," he shuddered, "singing songs about sunshine, love, and *flowers!* The girls are as fragile as flowers themselves. The men think themselves heroes, carrying blunt swords around. Obviously, they're just for looks. They barely know how to use them really, let alone protect themselves and their maidens against, heheh... *enemies.*"

"And that, O Scribbler, is where we come in. You see, over there they have a certain tradition. Unless the man can rescue his beloved nuisance, the girl he wishes to marry, and prove that he truly," and here he gagged, "*truly* loves her, they cannot be joined in *holy* matrimony. But in that place of halos and harps, what is he supposed to rescue the squeaky squealers from?"

Shawn paused mid-sentence. "Squeaky squealers?"

Len rolled his eyes. "Oh, forgive me. The damsel in distress. Except there would no distress if they were left alone. But give them a phantom in the night, a shadow in the trees, or a ghost on the wind?" He drew his cape over his face and murmured in a deep voice, "At last, danger has come."

"You mean *you* pose as the danger?"

Len perked up. "Yes, Rossow! We, the protectors of life, are here to help. Tell me, if no one ever married over there, but went about in the wooing stage for the rest of their lives, what then?" Len waved his arms about for emphasis.

Scribble, scribble...

"It's quite clear that life would soon vanish on that island. Understood?"

"Yeah, I get it," said the reporter. "You terrorize innocent people, supposedly in the name of life, and have a fun time doing it."

"Haven't you been listening? It's for their own good! What more do you want, man? Of course, there is a high level of sadistic and malicious enjoyment, I will not deny that."

A sudden idea hit Shawn. He gestured to the Island of Joy, "But my companion Steve went to the other island. What about him?"

Len rubbed his bristly chin. "Well, I cannot think of a single instance in our history where someone from our island turned good and left. Neither has anyone on the other island converted to darkness and come here. It will be interesting to see what happens to your friend, what's-his-name."

"His name's Steve, and what do mean, interesting? There's no way Steve Johnson will become a nature-loving goody-two-shoes."

"Don't underestimate their power," Len muttered.

This time it was Shawn who rolled his eyes. He looked over his notes and thought up new questions to ask. Madman or not, Len was a good source of information. Already, he had a name for both islands and actually knew something about the people. That is, unless Len really was crazy.

The two travelers passed by an old pond with a solid floor of green algae. The reeds and cattails stood tall in the water, their tops fluffy as duck down. *Conk-la-reeeeeee!* A red-winged blackbird rocked back and forth on a sturdy brown cattail. His handsome red and yellow wing shone bright in contrast to the shiny black of his feathers.

Len paused to admire the bird, and Shawn was glad for a rest. Folding his hands behind his back, Len smiled, "Very human-like, birds. This one just said 'I am the most handsome bird on the island, and this parcel of land is all mine.' Well, you're welcome to it, sir." He whistled in perfect imitation of the blackbird, *Conk-la-reeeeeee!*

Shawn stared. The bird jumped to a closer reed and made a clucking sound. As if they were having a conversation, Len clucked back at the bird a few times before inclining his head in farewell and strolling on. Shawn raised his camera and snapped a picture of the bird. It flew away scolding, and he had to jog to catch up with Len.

For about half an hour, they walked side by side down the road. Both were accompanied by their own thoughts. Shawn spoke first, "Len, now that you've told me about the other place, I'd like to know more about this island."

Len grinned. "Oh yes… the Island of Despair. What a lovely country! It has such a comforting darkness about her which some say comes from Mt. Mordoom. Others have their own superstitious ideas, but we all love it. I'm sure you'll grow to love it as well."

The darkness? Fat chance, thought the reporter.

"Our island is divided into eight regions. Each region is independent of the others, and is ruled by its own set of laws and royal mucky-mucks." Reaching into his pocket, Len pulled out a rolled-up map and handed it to Shawn.

The reporter drank it in as if it was water, and he was dying of thirst. The whole island was laid out before him. At the top of the thick page, *Island of Despair* was written in scarlet, flowing letters. The land was sketched in excellent detail: the forests, mountains lakes, and stretches of open land. The cities and villages were placed expertly with their names close beside them. Shawn could see whether a village was walled or open, small or large. Some had castles, others had moats and gates. Thin lines marked roads, thicker lines marked rivers, and the thickest lines marked the boundaries that separated the regions.

Every region had its own unique shape. Some such as Lion were long and thin. Others like Fox were short but fat. The Stag region was all forest and right below it were the stony desert dunes of Cobra. The Sea Dragon, Cobra, Hawk, Crow, and Lion regions were beside the sea. The Stallion region sat below Mt. Mordoom, and the Fox region was surrounded by all of these.

Len peered over his shoulder. "You have already witnessed the Cobra Region, aye? And Stag has also given you a rather pleasant greeting." He beckoned to the lands around him. "Now get a look at your first *civilized* region. We are quite proud of our land, us Foxes."

Shawn glanced up from the map. Rolling hills, forests, and plains of tall grass waved in the breeze for miles in each direction. The crisp air smelled of dirt and wet grass. A choir of birds sang all around them. Though clouds blocked the sun's light, the day had grown warm.

Two Sides of the Coin

The Fox region was indeed a welcome change from the sand and rocks of the harsh Cobra region, and the looming darkness of the Stag Forest. Still, Shawn shrugged and took out his notebook again. "It doesn't look civilized," he replied without thinking. Len gripped his sword hilt for a moment, and then reluctantly let it go.

The reporter straightened his coat collar and poised his pencil. "Does everybody on this island carry weapons?"

Len's teeth flashed in a smile. "Just the smart ones."

"Are you a knight?"

"That depends on who you ask."

"Do you enjoy hurting animals?"

"Only the annoying ones."

"Where did you get your wings?"

"It's a long story."

"Has anyone ever tried to kill you?"

"Aye," was Len's glib response. "Approximately sixteen times."

Shawn froze and glanced towards the other man. "Have *you* ever killed anyone?"

Len counted on his fingers and murmured, "We-ell, my hand may have slipped once or twice." Shawn stopped in his tracks, and Len looked back at him. "What's wrong?"

The reporter tucked away the notebook. "I have just realized something," he said. "You are all completely mad." And with that, he spun around and raced down the road the way they had come as fast as his legs could carry him. A pencil dove down to the muddy path from Shawn's ear. His bag, camera, and suit flapped about him so he could hardly hear anything—even the sound of Len's pursuit. Soon he grew quite out of breath.

Risking a glance over his shoulder, Shawn saw to his surprise that Len had not followed him. He had remained where Shawn had left him as if rooted to the spot. Len looked after him, seemingly lost in thought about this odd behavior. Shawn turned away and nearly twisted his ankle as he lurched off the road. Stumbling, he scampered into a grove of tangled grape vines, back into Stag Forest.

57

Len watched until Shawn disappeared from view. Then a big smile spread across his sharp features. He folded his arms. "Heh. This guy is going to be more fun than I thought."

A gust of wind blew down the plain, whipping his cape out with an audible *whoosh,* and his long hair blew back and forth. The sound of the wind whistled in his ears, rising to a keening howl. Lightning lit up the sky, and thunder accompanied the man's evil laugh.

"Yes, this is only the beginning, Rossow."

CHAPTER 5

Love at First Sight

Lost in song, Melody hardly noticed when a second voice joined in with hers. Then a gypsy wind blew right in her face, and as she opened her eyes, she saw him. Melody gasped, and the flower dropped from her hand. A strange man had appeared from nowhere, garbed in black. He kept singing as he walked closer, and his face was radiant. "Your purity is unmatchable," he sang. "Humble and meek."

Melody gazed up at the strange man, and he gazed back. His beautiful hazel eyes didn't leave her. She felt a blush rise in her cheeks, but it wasn't an unpleasant sensation. She couldn't stop a smile from spreading across her face. The man laughed as if he'd never laughed before.

Of all the laughter I've ever heard, surely this is the most joyful! thought the maiden. She felt like a flower perking up after a gentle rain.

The fantasy ended abruptly as the man collapsed into a bush of flowers and moved no more.

"Oh my goodness!" Melody cried. Her dress rustled as she stood and rushed towards the man. Then she stopped, uncertainty clouding her face. The man's hair wasn't dark, but it wasn't light either. His face was pale and drawn, with dark circles under his eyes. Worst of all, he wore black clothing. *I don't recognize him,* she thought. *Could he be one of… of them?*

He looked so helpless, lying limp as a doll with his head encircled by the tiny flowers known as Sweet Friendships. Although Melody knew she should be frightened of the stranger, all she felt was compassion. Slowly, she reached out a delicate, ivory hand to touch his cheek. His skin was cold.

"Hi, Melody!" Nifty bounced towards her in big squirrely leaps. "Isn't the mysterious stranger interesting?"

Nifty is so adorable when he uses big words, Melody thought. The squirrel perched on the man's chest and chattered, "What did you do to him? I've never seen a man faint like you girls." Nifty bounced a couple times on the man's chest. "Wake up! Wake up!"

Melody shooed him off. "Stop, Nifty! You might be hurting him."

Nifty made a face. "No more than you did, begging your pardon, ma'am!"

"Oh dear, I didn't mean to. Who is he?" she asked.

"I dunno. But he promised by Rainbow's Summit that he's not one of *them*."

"He will be alright, won't he?" she asked, her pretty face crumpled in anxiety.

The squirrel twitched his ear. "I should think so. At least, he sounded pretty happy right before he fainted."

Melody nodded. Taking another look at him, her heart leapt with joy. With a laugh, she clapped her hands together. "I just had a wonderful thought! What if he has come to be my True Love?"

At the last two words, the flowers all brightened, the trees let out a sigh of delight, and Nifty's eyes widened. "Wow! You think?"

Melody twirled in a circle. "Here I was singing by myself, dreaming of the man who might someday sing with me. And then O! he appeared like an angel from heaven and began to sing."

"Well, I saw him right before he found you, so I guess he couldn't be an angel," commented the squirrel. "Anyways, the trees told me that they saw him get out of a weird, white boat from the ocean. I don't think he has true goodness in him yet. Maybe that's why he fainted."

"Poor man!" said Melody. "We must rescue him from his darkness. I'm sure Steadfast would give him a home in the village. Maybe in time

Two Sides of the Coin

he will learn our joyful ways and... and choose to be one of us." She beamed with hope.

Nifty leapt almost a foot into the air. "That's the spirit! Well, what are you waiting for? Do you choose to rescue this unconscious, shadowy fellow from his prison of darkness?"

Melody smiled. "I do." Gracefully, she knelt by the stranger's side, laid a hand on his chest, and leaned over him. Her golden locks fell to one side, allowing the world a perfect view of the young man and woman's First Kiss.

As her lips met his, a beam of golden light fell down on them from the sky, and a rush of song burst out all around them. A sudden wind set the flowers bowing and dancing and blew Melody's hair around her face. It ruffled Steve's hair, and his cheeks flushed with color. His chest rose as he breathed it in. He opened his eyes.

A slim, feminine figure bent over Steve, smiling. A halo of light rested on her golden hair. He reached out a hand towards her face. "Are you an *angel?*" It is doubtful that Steve had ever used the word before, and it sounded strange even to his own ears.

The girl merely laughed, her perfect teeth framed by pink lips. Steve's heart pounded against his chest like a trapped bird. She took his larger hand in her small ones and said, "My name is Melody."

The light on them began to dim, and Steve looked around at the pink and white flowers which surrounded them on all sides. He had never bothered to imagine heaven, but if he had, the name might've appeared in his mind as he sat there in the light with the girl beside him. She cried with delight, "Another bud opened!" and leaned over to sniff the flower's perfume.

Steve sat up and felt his forehead. *What happened? I feel like I've been knocked out by a drug. I guess that would explain the talking animals and this odd, ecstatic feeling.*

Nifty hopped in his lap. "You alright?"

"Uhh, yeah. Never been better," he said.

"Good! I brought some friends for you to meet," he gestured to a crowd of animals standing at a respectful distance: rabbits, squirrels, mice, hedgehogs, and a lone lizard.

One chubby, brown squirrel pushed through and was the first to greet Steve. "Nak's the name, matchmakin's the game," he drawled. "In this case, you've most likely already booked one. What a shame, plotting is half the fun." The animals tittered.

"Umm… thanks?" Steve mumbled. The reporter's eyes widened as each creature scampered up to him and shook his hand, all the while chattering:

"Spiffen' good show, an' all that, sah! Here's to you!"

"Did you see that, children? That's True Love, sure enough. Oh my, you did splendidly."

"I dare say you didn't do much but lie there…"

"Jackie, don't be rude. Say you're sorry. Though lie there may be all the poor chap did, he played his part perfectly."

"Sorry… you did a great job lying there, poor chap."

"Mazal Tov!"

"Aye, you're a real trump."

"Aw'll be telling dis to my grandhogs for years!"

Steve was baffled. "Nifty," he whispered out of the corner of his mouth, "What are they talking about?"

Nifty gave a small grunt but didn't reply, so Steve repeated the question. The red squirrel shrugged and pointed at Melody. "Ask her in a few weeks. You'll understand by then."

Greetings over, the animals scurried past Steve, their downy fur tickling his legs. They danced around Melody, squeaking, "Sing us a song, Miz Melody! Pleeeeeaaase?"

Melody clasped her hands and beamed at the fuzzy creatures. "Oh, alright." The animals hopped into a circle and gazed up at her. She took a deep breath and began the song. Her voice reached all the high notes without effort. The song didn't seem to have any set rhythm, but the rabbits still thumped their feet to the tune.

"Come my friends, come play with me;
For everyone loves a happy dance, O sing so cheerfully!

O the handsome Sun salutes the Lady Moon,

Two Sides of the Coin

*She takes his hand and around they spin,
On a starlit stage, they dance to a heavenly tune!*

*Come my friends, come play with me;
For everyone loves a happy dance, O sing so cheerfully!"*

The song changed to an octave lower. It slowed gradually, building in drama and emotion.

*"Strangers meet to dance for the first time,
The lady sings to him, he answer so faithfully,
They look to each other, their eyes shine!*

For a moment, Melody's eyes met Steve's. Then she burst back into the chorus with more energy, and all the animals, trees, even Steve sang along,

*"Come my friends, come play with me;
For everyone loves a happy dance, O sing so cheerfully!"*

The animals collapsed in a big dog pile, laughing so hard that the lizard, who for this whole time had listened to Melody's song with delight, now flicked his blue tongue at them and scuttled to a safer location, which of course made them laugh even harder. The laughter was contagious. Steve chuckled simply for the absurdity of it all.

When the giggles began to subside, Melody rose and walked past the reporter, beckoning him with a finger. He followed as though pulled by an invisible string. She led him to a large, clear river that flowed at a gentle pace. They sat side by side at the water's edge, and the ground was warm and sandy. "I love Sparkle River!" she exclaimed. Lifting one pink slipper off her foot, she dipped her foot in the bluer-than-real water.

Steve looked all around him. The vivid colors made it seem like he'd stepped into a storybook. A mixture of sounds rose together like a choir: the birds in the trees sang soprano, the river gurgled a tenor part, the fat, fuzzy bumblebees buzzed bass, and the trees hummed alto. Steve felt his old life and its worries fading away, lost in the light of this haven. *Wonderfullest?* thought Steve. *Hmm, I'm would never have thought that was a real word until I came here.*

Shaking his head, he readied his notebook and pencil. *You can do this, Steve. You are Steve Johnson the reporter. Remember, only a few days, and Shawn's coming to pick you up.* He assumed his reporter voice, "So, Melody, how many people live on this island?"

"Oh, I could never guess. The Joyful Village has grown even bigger this year, and I couldn't be happier. They're like my family."

"The whole village? That's pretty incredible. I mean, there's got to be fights every now and then."

"Of course not!" she replied and pointed towards the other island. "We leave that sort of thing to *them*."

Steve followed her finger. "I've heard *them* mentioned twice now, the people who live on the other island. What's so bad about them?"

The girl was silent for a minute, her brow furrowed in thought. Even thinking about the other people made her shiver, and Steve wished he hadn't asked. Finally, she burst out, "They're terrible people! They're always grim and horrid, and they never sing songs—I don't why— I think they might have forgotten what it feels like to be happy. What's worse, they kidnap our girls and carry them off to their dark island."

Steve's pencil flew across the page. "That's awful! Isn't there anything you can do to stop it?"

Her face brightened. "Oh, yes! Good will always triumph over evil. Our courageous men follow them across the ocean and over the lands to save their dear True Love. When the hero completes the daring rescue, he proves to the maiden's family the depths of his love for her. The two can be married!"

The reporter gave a low whistle. *Villains, fair maidens, and heroes… just like a fairy tale.* He couldn't help asking, "Is there something inhuman about these villains?"

"Yes," she lowered her voice to a whisper. "They have wings."

"Wings! Can they really fly with them?"

"Yes, they are like bats. Big, mean bats."

"Have you ever seen one?"

Melody nodded. "I was out walking by the waterfall when this horrible creature stepped out of nowhere. His face was ugly and bruised. He was limping as if his leg hurt. He asked in a mocking voice, 'Where's

Two Sides of the Coin

your True Love, my small one?' I told him that I had none, and I was *not* his small one!"

"What did he do then?"

Meldoy shuddered. "I was lucky. The villain gave me a nasty look, flipped a cruel-looking dagger, and pulled out his wings. He flew right over my head, up the waterfall, and then I saw him no more."

"Amazing!" Steve exclaimed. "Back where I come from, we've never mastered the art of flying."

"Why would anyone want to fly in the sky? That's for birds and butterflies, silly!" she teased.

Melody and Steve talked and talked. At first, Steve asked questions and jotted down tiny notes. By the end of the conversation, however, he listened more and wrote less. Every word the pretty maiden spoke seemed to flow like poetry from her lips. Steve was mesmerized by the twinkle in her eyes and the shine of her golden hair. Soon only Melody spoke, while Steve absorbed the rays of light from the sun shining thousands of miles away, and from the young woman, sitting right beside him.

Hours or perhaps only minutes later, Steve asked her how she'd gotten such a beautiful name. She smiled. "The name has been in my family for years. My grandmother's name was Melody too. I don't remember much about her." The girl looked down at her hands. For the first time since she stopped talking about the other island, she didn't wear a carefree, happy smile. It made Steve's heart ache.

"Did she pass away when you were little?" he asked. "I'm so sorry."

"No, I think it was a few months ago—or was it a year?—but please don't be sorry. We had a lovely memorial for her, up on the top of the mountain. She was one of the oldest ladies on the island, one hundred and forty-seven years old!" Melody exclaimed.

Steve wrote down the number in awe. "That's incredible. Back where I come from, people hardly live past ninety."

"How dreadful!" cried Melody. "What a good thing you came to this island. We stay young for many years because of the air here. Can't you feel it already making you younger?"

Steve inhaled the perfumed air. He could feel his blood quicken, his senses sharpen, and his lungs tingle. He rubbed his chin. "How is this possible?"

Melody trailed a finger in the water. "It has always been so. This is how life is supposed to be, dear. But how is it possible, I wonder, for the people outside to pass away so fast?"

Somehow the question completely caught Steve off guard. He tried to focus on the past, but the details had become fuzzy. It was as if his mind was trying to forget all of his life up to the point of the landing. Even that had begun to fade. It seemed like months ago when he had haggled with Shawn about which island to land on. Of course, some details he could recall as if from a dream: towering building, cement roads, honking cars and buses. Nothing like this wonderful world he had stumbled across: a world of talking creatures, joy, and *Melody*.

"I think," Steve murmured, "that sadness shortens life. If that's true, then perhaps it's the joy here which sustains you all."

Melody gasped, covered her mouth with both hands, and gazed at the stranger with shining eyes. "You do understand," she whispered. "I've never heard anyone speak it so truly."

It sounds strange, thought Steve. *But isn't this whole island strange? Or was that other place I came from strange, and this really is how life's supposed to be?*

"You're not like any person I've ever met, but I know you'll fit in soon, sir, umm, sir…" Melody suddenly laughed. "Why, I don't even know your name! Please, what do they call one such as you?"

One such as you. The words pounded through his brain.

"I—I don't know," the reporter stammered, and it was true.

He had even forgotten his *name*.

Just as this revelation dawned on him, and before he could fully comprehend it, the whole area around them exploded with shouts, cheers, and whistles.

"There they are!"

"Three cheers for our newest islander! Hurrah, hurrah!"

"Look at the man, isn't he magnificent?"

Hundreds of people poured from the trees, all talking at the same time. Not one of them was garbed in dark colors; they all wore light, colorful clothes. Their golden hair was breathtaking in its *lightness*. The crowd almost overwhelmed the poor newcomer, whose back was pounded it seemed by every man, woman, and creature on the island.

To the reporter, every person appeared identical unless he scrutinized their faces. They all wore bright smiles, had shining, gold hair, and talked in a funny, gallant accent. There is no easy way to describe the way the people of joy spoke. Try talking in your most ridiculously dramatic, high voice with a hint of a Middle English accent, and you may come close to their language. Thus, amid much pandemonium, the "one, big family" from Melody's village welcomed the stranger.

A giant, broad-shouldered man approached the stranger last of all, "Friend, we have brought some clothes for you to change into, as your present black garb is not befitting of this lovely land of light."

"Oh," he said. "I'm sorry. I didn't realize."

"Of course not!" the giant gave a great, belly laugh which seemed to shake the ground. "Don't apologize! We're all here to help, and I most of all. That is the duty of the leader of the Joyful Village. My name is Steadfast." The giant shook Steve's hand with a gentle but firm grip.

"Good to meet you," said the stranger. When he tried to introduce himself, he was tongue-tied. *How do you explain forgetting your own name?* But the giant didn't seem to notice. He handed over the outfit and showed him to a secluded place where he could change. The stranger put on the green, woolen tunic, light brown pants, moccasin-like boots, and a belt woven of some tough material.

When he strode back towards the group of men, they nodded in satisfaction. The stranger no longer looked strange except for his hair, which seemed dull in comparison to theirs.

Steadfast raised his voice. "Now that our new friend has changed, let's get to the business of destroying his old garments." He pointed toward the west. "We shall wash them in Lovely Lake! Come hither."

Carrying the black suit with a puzzled expression on his face, the reporter was led through another forest to the shore of an immense, sparkling lake. The man gawked at the water. No matter how deep it got, he could see all the way to the bottom. Silver fish meandered close to the golden sand, light flashing off their scales. *I've never seen anything more beautiful. Well, except...* he blushed at his own thoughts.

Steadfast beckoned to the water and called, "O stranger, do you wish to wash away the horrid life you once lived in that land of shadow and enter into the glorious light?"

"I think so."

Steadfast learned in closer. "Do you *know* so?" The stranger could hardly remember the "land of shadow," and he certainly didn't want to leave Melody. He nodded his head, and Steadfast continued, "If you truly want to enter into our land, then throw that vile cloth into the lake and let it be purified!"

The men cheered and applauded his speech. The reporter looked puzzled. "Purified? But I always keep my suits clean."

"Ah, but how clean can it be when it's black, the color of night?"

"Uhhh..."

"Come, come! You have said you want to join us. Now prove that you want to be as we are: full of light! For without light, all would be darkness."

It made sense while Steadfast spoke. The reporter glanced at his best suit and shrugged. Before he could reconsider, he threw it into the water.

Like a bathtub being drained, the water gave a slurping noise and the suit disappeared. The whole area of the water began to shake and churn. Waves battled each other, clashing together and throwing spray into the air like a giant washing machine. Sometimes they saw a glimpse of the suit, whipping about frantically. Every man leaned in as close as he dared.

Finally, the pool ceased shaking. In a blink, the water was once again as smooth as glass. Something white rose to the surface, and the men cheered. A benevolent wave washed the cloth, brighter than snow, straight into the waiting hands of the reporter. He stood up and showed it to them with his mouth hanging open.

The black suit had transformed into a white cape. As he held it up, it seemed to light up their faces with pure brilliance. Without hesitation, the reporter threw it over his shoulders and buckled it with the golden clasp at his shoulder. It was hardly wet at all. The men cheered again, clapped him on the shoulder, and exclaimed how gallant he looked with it on. They assured him that he would win the heart of Melody.

"Why do I want to win her heart?"

Everyone stopped talking at once and glanced at each other, baffled at this ridiculous question. "You mean, you don't want to?" asked Steadfast.

"Well, I guess I do. It's only… I've just met her and…" He held up his hands. "I don't know how to win a girl's heart."

The men were stunned to silence. Steadfast turned to them with his arms crossed. "We must be patient with our new friend. He doesn't know our customs yet." Catching the droop of the stranger's shoulders, he exclaimed, "Don't look so worried, my good fellow! It's simple. To begin your loving relationship with Melody, you must first rescue her!"

"I thought that was when I wanted to marry her."

"No, no, no, you misunderstand me. If you wish to be her True Love, you first must rescue her from her *loneliness*."

"Oh, I see. I'm supposed to ask her to be my girlfriend!"

"… girlfriend?"

"Excuse me, my True Love."

"Precisely!" said Steadfast, delighted by his new student.

Another villager spoke up, "Ah, but you forget. It seems the damsel has rescued the man this time!"

The men chuckled, and the reporter himself had to smile at them. They were like boys, ever eager for a laugh, yet without a speck of meanness in them.

As if on cue, the laughter quieted, and all grew serious again. "Friend," Steadfast said, "here on this island you will find love, courage, and joy. Never again shall you chase shadows. Therefore, you should also forget that past life you once lived."

A sudden thought struck him, and he spoke it out loud, "What about Shawn?"

The men blinked at one another and echoed "Who?" like a parliament of owls.

"I arrived here with another guy, I mean, fellow. I think his name was Shawn. I came here, and he left for... for *that other place*," the man pointed towards the dark island.

Steadfast bowed his head and looked sincerely sorrowful. "My son, if your friend has gone to that terrible land, one of two things will happen."

"What?"

"They will kill him, or he will join them."

There was a long pause.

"Now who wants to see what the ladies are cooking up?"

* * *

Feeling fuller than he could ever remember, the stranger strayed from the joyful feasting table for a moment by himself next to the river. Since he always thought better when he wrote, he took out his notebook and put his jumbled thoughts into words.

Truly, I don't know what to think. Everything I once felt or wanted has faded. I can barely remember how I got here. I don't even know my name anymore! And yet... I'm happy. Maybe this is really how life is supposed to be, like Melody said. Ah, Melody, my dearest! Even if I tried to leave this blessed island, I would probably pine to death for her lovely voice. When I think of her, I know I shall never wander again.

The only thing that holds me back is the thought of that other fellow, Shawn, (it is a wonder I can still remember his name!) Perhaps someday when the goodness of this island has worked its magic on me, I will find my way to that island and search for him. If he is alive, there may still be a chance to save him and bring him to the light.

My dear, faithful notebook, you have served me well over the years. However, I shall not need you any longer. Your final resting place is where I stand. When I have finished this last entry, I will bury this book and my past. No longer will you haunt me as I turn my face to the light and begin my new life. Farewell.

CHAPTER 6

Esssssscape!

It was raining again. Not pouring-down-cats-and-dogs raining, but a steady patter of freezing droplets. The dusty streets of the cobra village had turned to mud, while puddles lay here and there waiting for some unfortunate traveler to step in. The town slept in silence, except for the occasional laughter from within a house or the sneeze of a sentry on the wall.

Decorating the main square of the town was a gallows, which was never used, and stocks, which were seldom used. However, when the opportunity came for some vagrant to be put into the stocks.... well, the people of the little town had their fun.

"Look on the bright side, Shawn—"

"What bright side?" he grumbled.

"Now that the rain's started, people aren't coming out to throw trash at you anymore!"

Shawn put his hands up as far as they could go in the hand-holes, "Oh, *thank you*, Mr. Optimist! Anything else to cheer me up?"

"Well, if you stretched your head as far as you could to your *right*, you may be able to scratch that itch on your nose."

"Don't try it, Shawn! With the way your luck's going, you'll still be an inch away from that wonderful, comforting scratch on your irritated nose."

Two Sides of the Coin

"Like you would know anything about that, Pessimist!"

"Admit it, Opti, from the moment we landed on this stink-hole of an island, you've had to work harder than ever. I, on the other hand, have been negatively thriving!"

"Hey, I think the rain is starting to slow down."

"Trying to change the subject, eh? And in reality, it's getting harder and colder by the minute."

"All you do is make Shawn feel worse! You're just a bully."

"What are you talking about? I'm an honest fellow."

"Well, if the shoe fits!"

"Nope, you got a size too small. Either that or your shoes are shrinking in all this confounded rain."

"*Stop it*!" yelled Shawn, "I don't need both of you toying with my emotions so just clear off!"

Clear off! Clear off! Nothing but the echoing of his shout answered him. "I'm going crazy," the reporter whimpered. He tried to sit on his feet to ease the pain in his back, but found that his neck was too short. Because of adjusting his position, droplets from the gallow's beam fell not on his head but down his shirt. Shawn was too exhausted to move again. His suit was already soaked and clung to his skin.

How did I get in this mess? Shawn wondered. *I didn't do anything wrong, yet those cobras were so riled up they left their village to catch me. I guess since I ran away from that crazy killer, I was no longer his "rightful property," and thus, easy bait for the stags.*

Thinking of Len, Shawn remembered the campfire, the coffee, and the steak in his hands, dripping with juice. His stomach gurgled in agony. Going hungry hadn't been the worst of his troubles though. He had spent a whole day in the stocks, enduring the jests and junk thrown at him from all passer-bys. Rotten egg was still encrusted in his hair where one boy broke it over his head with great ceremony.

"Oh, food, food; wherefore art thou food?" moaned Shawn. He recalled the time he had interviewed a director after watching a performance of the Shakespeare play, *Romeo and Juliet*. Needless to say, the lines of the play perfectly aligned with what he felt.

"Alack, there lies more peril in starvation than twenty of their swords!" Shawn soliloquized. "What's in a cheeseburger? That which we call a pizza by any other name would taste as delicious. O wilt thou leave me so unsatisfied?"

"Always thinking with your stomach, eh, Tubby?" came a voice from beside him. Leaning against the stocks, grinning ear to ear, was Len himself.

"Len!" Shawn cried. "It's so good to see you, I—" he stopped talking, thinking of the last time he had left the strange man. Half-indignant and half-relieved, Shawn exclaimed, "Wait, I ran away from you! Why are you following me?"

"You amuse me, Rossow," Len stated.

"It's Shawn."

"That too."

Seething with frustration, Shawn shut his mouth. *I will not be a diversion for this madman.*

Len was not at all discouraged. He perched on top of the stocks and began carving a piece of wood with his knife. "This is a happy reunion, aye? You would never guess the trouble it's taken me to get here. The guard was much more vigilant than usual. Not the bribing sort, you know." While Len chatted away, Shawn forgot about being stubborn and listened with interest to Len's story. Since he had nothing better to do, Shawn answered Len's questions about how he'd come to end up in this mess, how long he'd been there, and if the villagers had been nice.

"Nice!" he snorted. "They were the opposite of nice! I haven't met anyone nice since I got here."

Len tsked and flicked a wood shaving over his head. "That's why you shouldn't get put in the stocks."

"I don't even *know* what I did! Those stags gagged me, tied me up, blindfolded me, and left me like a stuffed chicken on the doorstep of the cobra city… along with all the other soldiers. You would think it was *my* fault, the way they carried on, hissing and kicking me! Without a trial or anything, they dragged me back into the city. They forced me to kneel with my hands and my head still. I nearly jumped out of my skin when they closed the stocks over my head. I called for help, but no one would listen."

"They only put people who are being a public nuisance in the stocks," said Len. "It's common sense that helps you around it, if you have any in that brain of yours. My guess is that they didn't like you asking so many questions. People around here like their secrets. You'd be better off not asking questions at all."

"Well... sorry. I didn't think they'd be so sensitive."

Len chuckled to himself. "Ignorant too! By Mordoom's Peak, I love this fool."

The rain still pattered on the puddle-strewn streets, and it grew even darker as the night deepened. Shops closed while the inns opened wide, beckoning travelers to find shelter. Those who were not already tucked inside their homes hurried through the streets with their hoods down.

"You see, Tubby," Len explained, "after evening falls, few people want to get caught outside when the lights turn off and meet those who come *out*."

"Why?"

"Because if you met someone in the street stalking through the shadows, chances are one in fifty it's going to be an innocent, lost traveler like yourself."

"Oh."

"Night time is the best time for those who wish to be unseen," Len drew a deep breath and let it out, creating a cloud of steam. "I *love* it."

"So these dangerous people are nocturnal?"

"Somewhat. You might compare them to wolves."

"That makes sense," Shawn murmured.

The last light of the day faded out. Shawn was sure that a strange, new feeling was in the air. It was the prickly feeling of being watched, and it was impossible to see anything behind him.

Something scrabbled about in the darkness from the nearby alleyway. Two grubby faces peeked out from behind a horse trough and sneered at Shawn. Ducking down, they rummaged through the garbage until they had a rotting apple and an onion, respectively. Shawn cowered against the wood. "Hey, Len?"

"Hmm?" Len squinted at his wood figurine and didn't seem to notice the men.

The two scoundrels crept closer. Shawn spoke quickly, "I saw your sword when you cut me down from the bear trap and if you still have it could you, er, do your stuff?"

Len pocketed his figurine, unsheathed the sword, and roared, "Whenever you go into a battle, you must be merciless!"

The two men stopped in their tracks, their mouths in danger of catching flies.

Len chopped left and right until the sword whistled. "Hold the sword with both hands for extra penetration into your target. Swing right, then left! Mwahahah! Your enemy may try to escape, *but you mustn't let them get away!*"

A few articles of trash fell to the ground, and the sound of shoes slapping on the cobblestone gave away the men's frantic retreat. Shawn burst out laughing, but Len's face was stern. "What are you chortling about, you guttersnipe? Here I am trying to give you a basic lesson in vegetable chopping, and you can't keep at least one little titter inside?"

By the time he was done, Shawn gasped for breath, and even Len allowed a slight chuckle at his own genius.

At that moment, footsteps gave away the approach of another person. *How on earth could those rats return so soon?* Shawn wondered. But as the figure strayed into the light of a nearby inn, his long spear was silhouetted against the light. This was no tramp. Catching sight of Len, the man broke into a run. "What do you think you're doing, converssssing with our prisssoner?" he hissed.

Aww, shucks, thought Shawn. *Someone does care about me.*

The soldier was dressed in light armor that clinked as he ran. Besides the spear, he carried a short sword at his side. His scarlet tunic was embroidered with the sign of a black, rearing cobra. His shaggy hair was dark brown, but his short, spiked beard was dyed red. A wide hood with red and black circles flared with every step.

The man pointed his spear at Len. "Get off!"

Len hopped down. Despite the cobra's armor and weapons, he cut the more intimidating picture, standing at least half a head taller than the other man. Fingering his sword, Len glared down his nose at the man. Apparently, this was yet another of his character changes. "Are you the soldier in charge of this prisoner?"

"Aye, one of 'em."

"In that case, I am sure you will be pleased to know that you are released from your duty guarding this wretched creature. I am here to remove him." While Len spoke, he made dramatic sweeping gestures with his hands. It would've looked ridiculous on anyone else.

The guard stroked his beard and eyed Len. "By what authority? And what do you want with him, anywayssss?"

Without a word, Len clenched his left hand in a fist and held it up to the Cobra's face. The silver ring with the fox emblem seemed to glow in the moonlight. The man gasped. His expression changed from suspicion to fear, and he dropped onto his belly in the cobra's bow. "Ssssire! Forgive me, I had no idea."

Len inspected his nails. "My, my, such a change of heart! If you must know, I need a man for sword practice. But if you have a problem with that… would you care to take his place?"

The cobra trembled like a leaf in a gale. Shawn actually began to feel bad for him, but Len's wink assured him. The cobra, however, was still on his belly in the mud. Fumbling in his pockets, he threw it down at Len's feet. "Please, take thisss key, and go," he whimpered. "But be warned: when morning comessss, I will have to tell the captain where the prisssoner hasss gone, and you'd better be out of our region by then!"

Len flipped the key in the air and caught it. "Put your fears to rest, pitiable worm. I'll be out of your hair faster than you can say, 'O Masster, Massster! A wicked foxsssss has sssssstolen our chicken *again!*'" With that, he unlocked the stocks and strode into the nearest alley. "Come, Rossow."

"Wha- wait! Len, wait up!" Shawn leaped up and banged his head on the gallows beam. Rubbing his head, he dashed after the disappearing figure.

* * *

"Len, how much longer?" Shawn groaned. "We've been bouncing up and down on this ruthless horse since last night! Can't we stop for lunch?"

"You're worse than a cub," Len snapped. "At least they know when to speak up and when to shut up!"

Shawn sighed and watched the trees go by. *Once upon a time, I wanted to be a cowboy and learn to ride. Now I am learning to ride and it's killing my butt.*

As if he could read Shawn's thoughts, Len chuckled. "Lackaday, you're going to be so sore tomorrow."

"I'm sore *now*. Can't we stop?"

This time Len didn't even dignify him with an answer. Shawn grumbled to himself. After two days of riding, he wanted nothing more than to lie down and never feel a saddle again. When he had asked where the horse had come from, Len told him it was a gift, but Shawn had his doubts.

A horse neighed in the distance, and Len's horse whinnied in response. A second later they left the shadow of the trees and found themselves standing on top of a hill. Shawn strained to see over Len's shoulder.

A great meadow spread below them like a fuzzy, green blanket. A bright blue stripe meandered down the midst of this blanket until it vanished underneath a arched stone bridge. The cobblestone road was nearly invisible for the people, animals, and carts covering it.

Shawn followed the path of the road and grinned. *That's no Cobra village. That's what I call civilization!* Built into the side of the cliff, the city was designed with tiered levels, the largest at the bottom of the cliff and the smallest at the peak. The buildings were made from red stone with round, glass windows. Chimneys spouted curls of white smoke and graceful steeples rose above the smaller buildings. Without a wall to hide behind, the city seemed to welcome in the weary travelers with open arms. In sharp contrast to the suspicious Cobra village, the city had an aura of bold freedom about it. However, when Shawn lifted his eyes to the top of the cliff, he forgot all about the city in his excitement. He pointed. "Look, Len! A castle! I mean, it's a real castle!"

It was a castle straight for medieval lore. The walls were built on the very edge of the cliff, defying gravity. Though tall, they did nothing to hide the magnificent architecture of the keep, which rose above the land like an oak in a valley. Its towers and pinnacles seemed to cut into the sky, sending their shadows far behind them. Crowning the peaks of each tower were scarlet flags decorated with the sign of the silver fox.

Len rolled his eyes. "Your powers of observation are real impressive."

Shawn couldn't stop staring. "It's…" he wanted to say, "It's just like Gondor from Middle Earth!" Instead, he finished, "It's just how I imagined a castle should be."

Len reached out a gloved hand to pat the horse's neck. He smiled at the city spread out below him. "Thonfirm, the pride of foxes. Her architecture is superb, her houses strong, and Castle Fox is her father. It may not be as artistic as Teken'Eils, the Sea Dragon's capital, or as rich as the Crow's capital city Ravenlocke. But I assure you, it is a far better place to live than either."

I can't wait to hear what Steve says when I show him these pictures! Shawn thought as he raised the camera and snapped a perfect photo.

Len winced and glared at the box. "You seem to have a secret weapon. Light."

"Sorry."

Muttering something about witchcraft, Len urged the horse down the hill. The horse, eager to be back at his comfortable stable, sped like a toboggan down the grassy hill. The giddy, falling sensation made Shawn forget about his soreness. All too soon, they reached the bottom. People on the road glanced towards them, and a few raised their hands in salute.

Shawn noticed many immediate differences between foxes and cobras. Unlike the cobras, who favored fancy boots with curly toes, many of the people walked barefoot. Most went with their hoods down as well. They dressed in sleek yet simple clothes in contrast to the more extravagant, trailing cobra robes. The men wore clothes that resembled Len's, and most women wore knee-length dresses with leggings.

Their skin was paler than the cobras, as if they spent more time in the shadows. While the cobras had long noses, sharp chins, and narrow faces, most foxes and vixens had rounder faces and pronounced cheek bones. Shawn noticed with relief that nobody held their S's. Compared to the cobras' hissing, the foxes' sharp speech was a welcome change.

The noise of clattering horse hooves, trumping feet, and scraping wagon wheels deafened Shawn. Beside them two oxen pulled a cart overflowing with bales of hay, and several barefoot children ran behind it. Over all this noise, an even greater clanging resounded from an odd-looking wagon. The wagon was pulled by a teensy donkey that followed its master at what seemed like a snail's pace. On the wagon was placed a box-like structure made of old boards from which a multitude of pots and pans clattered against each other. Shawn wondered if the poor donkey had become deaf pulling that contraption.

After a few minutes, the river of people began to break up where a small crowd congregated in the grass just off the road. In the middle of the circle stood a dwarf of a man with dark red hair, a curly beard, and a fiddle. He played a tune so lively that Shawn wanted to dance a jig. In fact, several men and women began to dance. They joined hands and move one direction and then the other, shouting along with the music, clapping, and kicking up their heels. Even the man with the fiddle managed to do a jig in the center of the circle.

"What's with the random dance party? Is this like a flash mob or something?" Shawn asked.

"A mob, Tubby? On the contrary, many of these people have been traveling for days. You can't blame them for being happy to come home safe to our beloved city."

By the looks of the people, they had certainly seen hard times. Families traveled all around Shawn: fathers, mothers, teenagers, children, and babies. They all looked worn out and dirty, yet the whole crowd hummed with excitement.

"Thonfirm, at last!" someone called out. The party of impromptu dancers ended their song with a loud cheer. Len pulled up his horse to let a girl in a ragged dress pass by. As he glanced about at the people, he sighed and shook his head.

Is he upset that so many people are emigrating to Thonfirm? Shawn wondered. But no, Len scowled not at the people but down at the strap behind the horse's ears. What went on in that man's head, Shawn could not begin to guess.

Soon Len was back to normal, grinning at the city of foxes as if he hadn't a care in the world. He called over his shoulder, "I live on the tallest level, so we still have some riding ahead of us. I wonder if we can make it by tea time. Lunch is usually not a grand affair, but everyone shows up for tea and cake around this time of day... except for that one time when Mother made Sylindra bake some cakes as part of her training. Heh, heh, that time everybody found an excuse not to show up."

"Is she that bad at cooking?"

"No, that wasn't the concern. Knowing Sylindra and my dear mother, they feared poison."

"Poison?!"

"You know, Tubby, you have this odd habit of repeating my words back to me in a question. Is that one of those things you reporters do?"

An hour or so later, Len and Shawn entered Thonfirm. It was perhaps three times the size of Cobra village, and the streets were clogged with people. Len seemed to know the village well; he navigated through it as a pilot navigates rocky waters. As they finally started to break free of the newly-arrived crowd, a pair of screaming boys raced in front of Len's horse. "Look out!" Shawn cried, grabbing hold of Len's tunic.

Len pulled up just in time, and the boys scurried into a doorway. He shouted after them, "Take care not to get run over next time, lads!"

They poked their heads out and laughed. "Get run over?" said one. "Ha! I am the greatest horse dodger in Thonfirm!"

At that moment, a woman with graying black hair appeared in the doorway. The boy's smiles vanished. The mother opened her mouth to scold but froze at the sight of Len. "My liege!" she exclaimed and fell to her knees with her palms up. Shawn guessed this must be the Fox equivalent of the Cobra's bow, and he liked it much better. "Please, forgive my foolish cubs."

"Did she just say 'my liege'?" Shawn muttered.

Len ignored Shawn's question. "No harm done, good lady." He reached into his tunic and tossed a few items to the boys. One caught a little hand puppet, shaped like a comical, ragged crow and the others snatched the fox puppet.

"Thank you, sir!" each one cried and darted away down the road. The woman gave a helpless shrug, and Len chuckled.

"Good day to you, madam!" he slapped the reins to continue their journey again.

Shawn watched the woman until she disappeared from view. *Why did that woman address Len like royalty?*

The deeper they rode into Thonfirm, the more crowded the streets grew. Soon they were forced to dismount and lead the horse up the paved road. Shawn tried see past the giant of a man in front of him but his view was continually blocked. The noise of voices was overwhelming. Once, he started to follow a different horseman, like a child grabbing onto another woman's skirts instead of his mother's. Len pulled him back just in time. Shawn clutched the horse's bridal like an anchor.

Finally, a large bulk of the crowd moved away down a street perpendicular to theirs, allowing Shawn to look around. The path most of the people had followed led to a market-place. The brightly colored stalls competed for attention along with the merchants. Some sang clever ditties about their products, and others complemented shoppers. One particularly earnest peddler ran right up to Shawn and thrust a live turkey in his face. "See his fine feathers? See his healthy crown? You won't find any other poultry as delicious, sir!"

The turkey squawked and pounded Shawn with its giant wings. The reporter cried out and fell back into Len. As soon as the peddler saw Len, he wedged the turkey under his arm and showered apologies on Len. He laughed it off and dragged Shawn away. The man ran into the market shouting something excitedly, but it was lost in the great hubbub. People began to turn and point at Len, mouths gaping.

"How's that for subtlety, aye?" Len scowled. "Up on the horse quick, Tubby." He mounted the horse in one smooth motion and pulled Shawn into the saddle behind him. They galloped away from the confusion in the market, but Shawn felt he couldn't escape his own confusion.

Up, up, always up. Shawn clung to Len's waist to keep from slipping off the horse's rump. The road was well-kept but steep. They passed several wagons and travelers, who always moved to the side at the sight of their horse. Shawn wondered if all knights were so respected in the Fox region. Perhaps Len was an honored war-veteran, he figured. Or maybe he was a colonel or lieutenant in the king's army. *I guess I'll find out soon enough.*

The sun dipped in and out of the clouds. Whenever it shone, Shawn perked up. When it vanished behind distant thunderclouds, he shivered. The further they traveled up, the fewer people there were and the more elegant the houses became. Statues and fountains decorated the streets, and the fortification of the road gates became steadily more powerful. Still, Len did not stop the long climb. Shawn's stomach grumbled.

They climbed until the entire city was spread out below them. At last, Len turned off the main road to the right where it became level ground. A shadow fell over Shawn. Looking up, he gasped. The great castle that he and Len had viewed from afar towered over them, more intimidating than ever. He gaped at the sheer size of the walls—tall as ancient oaks, thick as a cottage, and long enough to hold five market places. U-shaped towers fortified each edge, and a large gate lay between two of these.

Shawn tapped Len's back. "What are we doing here? You don't live in the castle, do you?"

Len snorted. "Why else would we come here?"

"Well, no offense, but I thought you'd be living in some cottage beside the castle, you know, like in the barracks or something."

"I see." He sounded amused.

"But if you live in the castle, wouldn't that make you some a general or like royalty?"

At that moment, the horse halted at the closed iron gate, and two guards poked their heads up from behind the battlements. "Who comes to King's Rubin's castle?"

"State yer names an' yer business!"

Shawn's mind whirled. *What* are *we doing here?*

Len threw back his hood and shouted, "You rotters—Roanick, Simor! You couldn't recognize an honest friend of yours if he flew up and knocked you flat."

The men guffawed. The one called Simor, tall and lanky with a black moustache and beard, called back. "Ah, sar, as for you knockin' us flat, I can believe, maybe. But some'ow 'honest' does not registair in my mind when I pitchure you, Prince Gilen!"

He had an odd accent which confused Shawn for a moment. That moment passed all too quickly as Shawn comprehended what the guard had said. *PRINCE?!*

Shawn felt the revelation like a kick in his stomach. "Len," he managed to say.

Clanging, the gate began to rise, and the horse shied away. Len steadied him with one hand and hung onto Shawn with the other, who was in danger of falling out of the saddle. When the gate was halfway up, Len galloped straight for the low bars. Both men ducked. Len came out laughing, while Shawn moaned.

The man wasn't just crazy; he was a prince. Shawn suddenly wanted to punch him again. But what would the soldiers do if they learned he'd attacked their prince? Probably chop off his hand or something.

Pushing aside the glum thoughts, Shawn examined the marvelous castle. The keep was a square structure so tall it seemed to pierce the clouds. The foundation was made of giant-sized grey stones, each one about as long as a car and tall as a door. Higher up, the stones shrunk until they were brick-sized. Small windows were placed near the ground, stained-glass windows on the second story, and balconies on the tallest level. At every corner of the keep stood round towers with narrow, diamond-shaped windows. These would allow archers to shoot out without being endangered. To complete the picturesque castle, a bell tower crowned the castle top.

Two Sides of the Coin

At the front of the castle stood a stout, wooden double-door taller than two men. Strengthened by metal bars and an arch of stones, the doors looked ready to hold off an army. Leading up to the entrance were three wide, marble steps. Over this grand door, about mid-way to the top of the castle, was a huge, circular stained-glass window. A white fox paced in the center with its head turned to the front. Surrounding the brilliant white fox was an array of black and red shards. Its intelligent, green eyes seemed to follow Shawn. He could not stop gazing at it, even though he had to crane his neck and squint because of the sun's glare.

Two guards stood before the door with spears in hand. Unlike the cobras, the foxes' armor was far lighter. Neither of the guards wore a helmet, but both wore a gleaming, silver breastplate embellished with the Fox symbol. Underneath the breastplate, they wore a scarlet tunic and belt. They also had gauntlets, shoulder armor, and boots.

"Welcome back, Prince Gilen!" one of them called, bringing Shawn back from his daydream. The reporter, who had begun to forget his sad state, was reminded once again: Len was a prince, and he was what? A reporter from Sanfran Cisco, living barely above the poverty state.

Len stopped to chat with the soldiers about the possibility of venison for dinner before leading the horse away from the gate. They went down from the paved pathway onto a dirt road where people dressed in commoner's clothes surrounded them. Len— Gilen dismounted to lead the horse through the tangle. That is, until a servant recognized him.

With a cry, "Make way for the prince!" the road cleared as if by magic. The road led them away from the gatehouse and through a cluster of buildings. Wooden signs hanging before the doors announced the Royal Bakery, the Royal Blacksmith, and other such establishments.

Many people bowed to the prince, while others called a warm, "Welcome home, sir!" Soon Shawn and Len came out of the cluster of buildings to a stable swarming with horses, messengers, and stable boys. One such boy appeared out of the woodwork and took the prince's horse.

Handing the reins to him with instructions and jokes, Len strode onward without a single word of explanation. Seething, Shawn followed a step behind him. They passed the path leading to the gardens and climbed the marble stairs up to the doorway that stood underneath the awesome stained-glass window. Len paused in front of the imposing doors, leaned his ear against the wood, and flashed a grin at Shawn. "Aye, it's tea time."

The thought of walking through those doors (to interrupt a royal meal, no less) made Shawn gulp. "I guess we can slip in from a side door, right?"

Len winked. "Where is the fun in that?" He pulled the hood over his face and threw open the doors, and along with them throwing out Shawn's hopes of a subtle entry. The doors emitted a deafening *boom*. Len strode into the hall accompanied by a gale that seemed to shove Shawn inside. The reporter looked behind him and gasped. Black and menacing, a huge thundercloud had descended on the castle.

"What's happening?" shouted Shawn, but his voice was drowned out by a crash of thunder. *Another weather change? It seems to be at Len's beck and call! But that's impossible. Of course, that's what I thought about flying...*

Then all reasonable thought fled his mind as the doors slammed shut of their own accord, and he stood like a drowned rat before the king's table.

The people leapt to their feet. With the spine-tingling sound of metal on metal, they pulled swords free from their scabbards. The knights, dressed in striking red, black, and silver, brandished a dazzling array of weapons. A veiled lady in a trailing, black dress held a dagger in each hand. The man at the head of the table brandished a bow nearly as tall as himself with an arrow already on the string.

The tall archer's crimson robe distinguished him from the other men. Two leather straps crossed at his chest to form an X over a chain-mail suit. But it was his eyes, fierce and authoritative, which made Shawn's heart squeeze into his one remaining sock. He wanted to apologize for intruding and walk backwards bowing until he was a mile away. In his fear, it didn't even strike him as odd that the people carried weapons at the dining table, in their own castle, with a wall outside, and guards surrounding them.

Len held up a hand and walked straight for the table, ignoring the weapons trained on him. Glancing back, he beckoned to Shawn. *Are you crazy?* Shawn mouthed. Len waved harder. The reporter scampered to his side, and they walked slowly (oh so slowly!) past every chair to the head of the table. The great man still held the bow, though his grip had relaxed a little. Len stopped a pace away from the arrow, which was trained between his eyes. The tension was so great that Shawn could almost taste it. *Come on, Le- Gilen! Take off that stupid hood before you get us both killed!*

Finally, Len reached out his hand. "Hello, Father. I've come home with the biggest game of the season."

The man he addressed had the same sharp, chiseled features as Len. His keen eyes were amber-brown, and his black hair was streaked with grey. On it rested a silver crown with twisting patterns so intertwined Shawn could not see where they began or ended. The king's face was grim and lordly. He had thick eyebrows, and a prominent chin with a neat, red beard. Shawn knew, from the way he handled the bow, that this king was as much a warrior as Len.

When Len spoke, the king's face changed from wariness to amusement. He shook Len's hand and, chuckling, snatched off his hood. An audible sigh—of relief or exasperation—blew down the table. They sheathed their weapons but remained standing. Catching a few sharp glances, Shawn quickly pulled back his hood. Len bowed deeply to the veiled lady.

In turn, she dipped her head. "Congratulations on your catch, son." Shawn couldn't help shivering at the lady's voice. It was as delicate and deadly as a knife's edge.

Len pulled Shawn forward. "Meet my father and mother, King Rubin and Queen Alexi. And this is Shawn Tubby Rossow the Reporter Spy."

"Not a spy," Shawn muttered.

"Quite a title," said the king, examining Shawn with narrowed eyes. The reporter pretended to be very interested in the carving on the table so he wouldn't have to meet that piercing gaze. Although Shawn couldn't see the queen's eyes, he could almost feel her gaze fixed on him as if she could look into his soul.

Len whispered out of the corner of his mouth, "Bow."

Bowing. Of course. Why didn't I think of that? As if he were stepping on thin ice, Shawn shuffled forward and bobbed a quick bow. "Hello—I mean, greetings, your majesties!" He retreated to Len's side, half-wishing he could scurry under the table and not come out until everyone was gone.

King Rubin burst out laughing. His laughter was as a sudden as a thunderclap and merry as a spring rain. Everybody turned at the sound. "Where did you find this creature, Len?" he asked. "He bows just like those rotten crows!"

The hostile silence of the soldiers turned to laughter. At the king's gesture, they seated themselves and conversation resumed. Though the joke was made at his expense, Shawn let out his breath and grinned in sheer relief. Elegant music swelled from a small orchestra on the balcony high above. Finely dressed servants appeared as if from nowhere bearing trays of fish, bowls of fruit, toasted bread with a honey coating, and a whole pheasant, feathers and all. The reporter watched the procession with awe. *This is a snack? Dude, that's awesome.*

The queen and king had a whispered conference. Whatever they said, Shawn felt it could not be good news for him, for it finished with the king murmuring, "Whatever pleases you, my dear…" He strode over and patted Len's shoulder. "It's good to have you home again. You know how your mother worries." Len gave a knowing smile.

"As for this stranger you have brought to our door," the king's voice hardened, and Shawn felt a tingle of dread creep up his spine. King Rubin spread his hands and grinned like a wolf at a lamb. "Welcome, Shawn Rossow."

CHAPTER 7

Castle Life

In the weeks that followed Shawn's untimely arrival at the king's castle, he learned many useful and important pieces of information. All these he recorded in his notebook, now a precious lifeline in that dark, dangerous place.

Day 1. at Castle Fox

This morning I awoke with a determination to learn these people's many common-sense rules, as Gilen calls them. Basically, it's all those rules that are obvious for them, such as:

- *Never stare at people's faces. This I learned with the grouchy knight in the Cobra village.*
- *Never ask questions... yeah, I can't exactly follow that one.*
- *Never underestimate anyone. What I took for some insane hobo actually turned out to be the prince of Fox!*
- *To quote Gilen, "Always do something unexpected." ... I'm not sure whether I should follow this rule.*

These people aren't only crazy and weird, they're dangerous. When I mentioned this to the prince, he gave me a humble look. "Oh Rossow, you flatter us. We're actually somewhat average, when it comes to villains." I'd hate to see what their bad villains are like!

Day 2.

This morning, I was woken by a pail of icy rainwater in my face. Gilen warns me he'll do this every morning until I stop sleeping so deeply. Easy for him to say. I couldn't sneak up on him if he were dead!

Len presented me with some new clothes, and I'm loving them. Today I'm wearing a pair of leather boots with fur lining, black trousers (thank goodness they don't wear tights), a rich red tunic over the trousers, and a belt around my waist to hold them all together. Standing before a mirror, I was pleased to see that their clothing did not look like those cheap, Renaissance Fair outfits. These clothes are the real deal. The prince came in a little later to comment how "killing" I looked without those rags I had been wearing. I guess I'll take that as a complement.

I followed him through the castle back to the hall where we first arrived. I was unsure where to sit until Len nodded to the chair on his left. Relieved, I sat down. Others were arriving, but so far no food had yet been brought in. Len exchanged a polite greeting with one of the generals and spent the rest of the time chatting with some other palace people about the goings on in the castle. I could hardly understand a word of it. At last, a messenger arrived to tell us that the queen and king were taking their breakfast elsewhere.

Though I did not hear any signal given, it was like a bell rang to release the thundering herd. Servants poured from the kitchen, bearing trays of tempting morsels. It was more food than you can imagine! For the main dish they had fresh-baked black bread (try saying that five times fast!) slices of cheese, boiled eggs, a whole pig still on fire, and fruit. I could go on and on describing the food, the silver plates and goblets, and everything else, but it would take up five pages at least. It was everything one could imagine for a royal meal, and much more.

For drinks, we had fresh milk and wine to start (yes, there were different courses for drinks, too!) When Gilen offered me a goblet of wine, I said, "I don't drink." That's mostly true. In reality, I'm what the regulars call a "foul-weather friend." Meaning when papers sell and the sun shines, I stay away from that sort of thing. But when the papers don't sell, you might see me hanging around the bars.

Len gave me a strange look, so I explained that I didn't handle alcohol well. He waved my objection aside. "You would have to drink a lot of this to lose your wits," he replied. "And unless you want to drink milk the rest of your stay here, I think you might reconsider."

Then I remembered that people in medieval ages hardly drank water at all because it was so hard to purify. Instead, they drank diluted wine and beer. Just to be sure, I asked Len, "Don't you have clean water to drink?"

"Oh sure, Tubby," he said, "if you live right by a spring, mountain river, or have a good well. But seeing as Castle Fox only has one well, we make do with what we have. Unless you wish to try out the pond-water..." He gave a wicked grin.

I became accustomed to their drinks pretty quickly. Imagine my joy when I caught a familiar, aromatic smell coming from a servant's pot: coffee! "Len, where on earth does the Island of Despair get coffee?" I asked him.

He took a big gulp from his mug, slammed it down, and stated, "Stallion when we can bully them into it, and Lion when the king's in a good mood. The only time I've tasted Cobra coffee was after a raid." He wrinkled his nose in disgust. "Nastiest stuff you ever quaffed. No wonder they're ill-tempered with such bitter coffee! Now that stuff could make you lose your wits."

From there Len dove into another story. "The first time I had coffee, I was twelve. I took a liking to it and drank three cups. I started running up the walls, jumping off the tower into the pond, and swinging from the chandeliers." He laughed. "Aye, and the only reason I stopped is when Sylindra, who was nine, tackled me, tied me up, gagged me, and stuffed me in a closet. Such a loving little sister, isn't she?"

Speaking of which, I haven't met his sister yet. Apparently, she left the castle right after Len and still hasn't returned. To be honest, I'll be happy if our paths don't cross for awhile.

Later that day, as we took a tour in the palace gardens, I called the prince "Gilen". Even as I said it, Len filled his hands with thick, oozing mud and tackled me. After he painted my face with a generous portion, I was able to get him back with an equal handful of it. Thus, our two-hour mud war began. It certainly acquainted me with the gardens on both sides of the castle. Perhaps I will describe them later on.

About two hours later, shivering in the pond by the castle as we scrubbed ourselves clean, Len warned me. "Next time you call me that, I'll give you another scrumptious mud pie, no matter where we are!"

"Ha! Not if I bury your boots first," I retorted.

"Where did you bury those confounded boots?" he growled.

"Not a clue!"

Len blinked at me. "Shawn, I would congratulate you on your first villain-like deed, but, too bad for you, I was the victim. Not for long though..."

Just because Len's a prince doesn't mean he's not a terrific mud-slinger, or bear-hunter, or play-actor. Or a great friend... That is, when he's not beating the tar out of me. He was sure that I was lying about the boots and vows that he won't let me leave this island until I tell. The worst part is, I think he's serious! What have I started?

At this point, there is sticky, blue-black goo stuck to the page.

It wasn't me! I didn't do it! I tried to tell those stupid cooks it was Len who took the blackberry pie, but somehow, the remains of the pie and the pie dish magically showed up under my bed. What, someone at the door?
AAAAHHHH! I HAVE BEEN FRAMED! LEEEEEEEN!!!!!!!!!!

Day 4.

Note: Avoid the kitchen at all costs.
It's interesting to watch the servants skulking to and fro in the castle. There seems to be an unlimited number of them, ranging in age, shape, position, and character.

However, as I watch them about their daily duties, their core expression is the same: polite condescendence. Whenever I say something they deem stupid (which is most of the time) they get this mischievous glint in their eyes. It's as if they're thinking, "Heh, heh, just wait 'till the girls in the kitchen hear this moron's gobbledygook." Yes, that's a word, my reader.

Sometimes I hear the kitchen ringing with laughter. I'm not saying the joyful "tee hee hee," or more polite "ha ha ha," or the jolly "ho ho ho." No, it is more the laugh of malicious glee at other's misfortunes. Hence, the "heh heh heh," "Mwee hee hee," or "Mmm hmm hmm..."

This is simply a theory, you see, and I'm sure it sounds a bit foggy to you. What I mean to say is that on this island people don't laugh for happiness, unless they hear someone they despise has just died. Hahaha!

Day 5.

So there I was, feasting with Len and some of his castle buddies, and they all went off on a tangent about the Mushroom Wars. Yes, mushrooms. You had to be there to believe it. But they were talking on about it so earnestly, all about famous battles and knights that I was almost convinced it was an actual occurrence. Of course, when I asked what the Mushroom Wars were, they exchanged winks and tried to outdo each other coming up with the most outrageous stories. I resolved that I would somehow find out by myself and surprise them next time.

Where else can you go to find history besides the library? I was delighted to hear that Castle Fox had a large one. This way, I could find out all I need to know about the Island without having to ask anyone. I think they have a policy of never answering a straight-up question, or at least, never with a straight-up answer. This I discovered more and more as I searched for the library. I was beginning to think that it didn't even exist after several hours of searching and the blank stares of the servants.

At last, I noticed an old fellow with spectacles walking slowly down the hallway, holding a big book in front of his face. I let him go ahead and followed at a discreet distance. The fellow didn't look up even once. He must know the castle like the back of his hand! He went up one passage, down another, took a left, and went down that passage until he came to a door.

I waited until I heard the door close behind him before I ventured in myself. Sure enough, I had reached the library! Stepping inside, I was assailed by the smell of books and dust.

Two Sides of the Coin

It was an amazing, primeval library. The walls were lined with books and statues, and there were also large bookcases in the middle of the room such as you might find in a modern library. That's where I would draw the comparison, however.

Light shone down from tall windows on both sides of the room, illuminating legions of dust motes and casting shadows on the towers of books piled at random intervals in the room. Among these wandered the old man, the librarian himself, who was collecting an arsenal of hefty volumes. On the other side of the room, several men laughed at the top of their lungs as one of them shouted out course jokes from a book. I decided to remember one for when I saw Steve next.

I approached the librarian to ask him where to find books of wars and battles (I was not about to made a fool of myself asking about the so-called Mushroom Wars.) He peeked at me from behind the book and stated, "Back wall, left corner. Now begone!"

As I went to the back wall, I couldn't help overhearing more of the jokes and hurried past, blushing. The whole back row was filled with books about wars and battles. Some were illustrated; others were hardly legible, for all were handwritten. One book I found was almost as wide as my waist!

I would take one down, flip to the first page, and put it back reluctantly. There were titles such as The un-Civil War of Serpents, The Age of Chaos, The Battle of Mordoom's Peak, A Duel of Kings, and Battle of the Black Rose.

After about an hour, I found, to my astonishment, a book titled The Mushroom Wars, by E. Shmitt. I plopped down in the corner and began to read the scrawled handwriting, but the other men made so much noise I could hardly concentrate.

I wanted to yell back, "Don't you know this is a library? Go laugh in the stables!" Instead, I removed myself to the farthest corner away from them, and at last had some measure of peace and quiet. The scrawling print was almost impossible to understand. Just as I was getting into the story, I perceived as if from afar a strange sensation from my foot. It was almost like a vibration, except more like something was gnawing on my boot. Which, in fact, was exactly what it was.

I glanced up, and in that moment I screamed so loud I'm sure a thousand librarians around the world heard it and shouted, "Silence!"

Several men came running with swords in hand, and the librarian was in the lead asking, "What is it? A fire? An invasion? Discovered a blood relationship to royalty? Spit it out, man!"

I cried, "There was a rat eating my boot!" and pointed to the evidence—a little chunk taken out of my left boot. They all stared at me and then the men, of course, busted out laughing.

The librarian gave a world-weary sigh. "Well, that's why you don't sit in profound and absorbed silence. Don't you know your volume must exceed polite standards in libraries to frighten away the vermin that make their abode there?"

I was almost positive the old man was off his rocker. But it did make sense in a totally insane kind of way. Well, you can be sure I didn't hang around there long, for fear the rat would invite his relatives to come dine.

With The Mushroom Wars under my arm, I made for the door, but the way was blocked by none other than the queen! She glared at me as if I had done a hateful crime and did not move out of the doorway. The librarian rambled over and asked if she would like to find that book she wanted.

"No," she replied coldly. "I will come back another time."

"I was just leaving—" I began, but she was already gone.

Yeah, I learned a lot in an hour. One, where to find the library. Two, always be loud in the library. Three, there was such a thing as the Mushroom Wars. And four, the queen haunts the library as well, so go at your own risk!

Day 6.

Have you ever gotten the feeling you were being watched? Today I got that feeling as I strolled down the hallway to my room. I looked around, but nothing seemed amiss. Then I remembered how in the movies, when the hero was fighting the villain, they would get separated. In those tense moments, the hero keeps looking back and forth, and only the audience can see that the villain is actually perched right above the hero, ready to pounce. How irritating...

So I glanced up, just to be sure there wasn't some ninja or bat-creature peering down at me. It turns out, there was something watching me from the ceiling. It was a chiseled, three-dimensional likeness of a fox's head, the snout extending towards me with bared teeth. A brief investigation showed that this fox-face was the only one I could find on the ceiling. It's odd that there was only one.

Day 8.

I found another of the Watchers! This time, I was peacefully munching a russet apple out on the balcony when I turned to my left and saw another fox on the rail's edge. This one showed the whole fox with its head turned to me, eyes glaring. Oh, shall I have no peace?

Day 14.

Over the course of this week, I've spotted three other Watchers, all shaped different but always with the same burning eyes that eventually give away their presence. It might sound strange that I'm bothered by little, stone carvings, but at this point my life is past strange. I feel like the foxes are just waiting for me to make a mistake.

Day 15.

I almost died today. And no, this had nothing to do with the queen, just her husband's treacherous throne. Well, I should probably start at the beginning. Today the king and queen were called away into Thonfirm for some business. What business it was I don't know, and there's no way I'm asking!

Before the incident, I was viewing the portrait gallery of all the previous kings and queens of Fox who had dwelt in this castle. Some scowled at me while others gave me a cold stare. One king wore a ghost of a smile, as if he were thinking of a joke. Not a nice joke, mind you. King Rubin's father was the last picture. At first I thought it was Len. Although his hair was grey, and his face scarred, he looked just like the prince, smirk and all.

That's when Len found me. I asked him, "How come your parents' portraits aren't up here?"

Len shrugged. "It used to be a tradition not to put up pictures of the royalty until they were dead. Now, you might say it's a superstition."

"What?" I snorted. "You think if you hang up your picture here you'll die?"

He gave me a solemn look. "I wouldn't dare. Would you?"

My gaze strayed to the last queen of Fox, and I shivered. "Nope!"

"Good. Now that's settled, come with me!" so saying, Len grabbed my arm and dragged me through the castle. He wouldn't tell me where we were going. In a minute or two, the double-doors of the throne room were right ahead.

I pulled back. "W-we're going to see the king and queen?"

"Don't worry, they're gone," Len said with a smile. "Come on!"

I had to admit, I was curious to see the place without the commanding (and terrifying) presence of Len's parents. He burst through the doors, but I hung back until I could see the empty thrones.

It was a marvelous room. The roof, which appeared to be made of marble, was high, high above us. From the center of the room hung a huge chandelier, like the ones in the Dining Room. Supporting the roof were six marble pillars, three on each side. In between the chandeliers hung tapestries with pictures that made me want to stare for hours.

The room rectangular shaped, and at the far end were the two thrones on a raised platform. A scarlet carpet led up to them. The thrones themselves were beautiful but not extravagant. Tall, silver, and ancient, the king's chair was inlaid with vine patterns and a large ruby in the center. The hand rests were two foxes, one on the right and one on the left. I knew as soon as I saw them that these silver creatures must rule the Watchers. The queen's chair was not any smaller and just as lovely. The two thrones complemented each other.

To the left of the thrones was a little open space with a table, some chairs, and a wine-bottle. There was also a balcony a little further back. On the right of the thrones was another table with a chess set.

I wandered about in awe, forgetting my fears. Then Len called me over to the thrones. "How would you like to sit on one?" he asked.

I thought he was kidding. "Surely there's some superstition about that!"

"None that I can think of," he said. "Go ahead, try it out!"

"Seriously? I don't think I should."

"What's to be afraid of? I do it all the time," Len boasted.

"Your father won't mind?"

"My father isn't here."

Oh, why did I give in? I should've trusted my instincts. But deep down, I was curious what it felt like to sit on a throne. Len kept reassuring me it was safe. Finally, I walked up the steps, placed my hands on the Watchers' heads, and sat down gingerly.

No thunder rocked the palace, and no lightning bolt struck me dead. I settled back with a sigh. The throne was hard and cool, yet it warmed at once to my touch. I can't explain the feeling of sitting up there on that throne. It was as if the whole world was underneath me. Len bowed elaborately with his cape spread out, and I chuckled.

Something flashed in the corner of my eye. To the right of the throne lay a golden scepter. The temptation overcame me, and I reached down to pick it up. Oddly, it was stuck to the ground, and I gave it a sharp jerk.

Len cried out, "No!" and, with one great leap, snatched me out of the chair and threw us both to the ground. Something whistled through the air. It passed so close to my head that I felt a waft of air and struck the throne with a resounding clang!

Dazed, I sat up. "What the..." I trailed off when I saw what was quivering just under the headrest of the throne: a gigantic, two-sided battle-axe! I touched my throat and wished I could faint.

Len tugged the axe from the throne and whistled. "Oh, you're in trouble if Father discovers this scratch on his throne."

I somehow found my voice. "A scratch?"

"This throne's been here since King Jaxton I."

"I almost died!"

"Yes, and I'm sure you'll think twice now before you go pulling levers. You certainly have a knack for setting off traps, Rossow." With that, he threw back his head and laughed.

This was too much. I ran out of the room, yelling, "I'm through with this place!" It's times like these when I wish I was back in Sanfran Cisco again, where at least you don't have to worry about losing your head.

I am not stranded, not anymore with the help of the prince. I mean, he's my friend, right? Maybe he can give me money to buy a boat, and I'll get out of here, maybe at the end of this week. Poor Steve must be wondering where I am by now. There's still so much I want to know, but it's simply too dangerous!

Day 16.

Before I go, I am taking a tour of the castle, carefully interviewing several servants, and otherwise doing my reporter's duty. Today I explored outside. It took me all day just to get an overview of the place!

I had a great time running along the castle walls until two soldiers seized me and threatened to throw me over the side. I quickly explained that I was the prince's special guest. After that, they left me alone for the most part.

Anyways, the walls—Oh, the walls! I've always wanted to journey along the Great Wall of China. Though this wall was not even a tenth of the size and length, it was exhilarating to stroll along the top. I could view miles of forest stretching behind Castle Fox and the city of Thonfirm spread out below. It was fun.

The castle walls run in a unique half-rectangle, encircling the huge fortress on all sides but one, which is the side that has no windows, doors, or gardens. Along the other two sides of the castle are gardens and hedges, a genuine maze.

The corners of where the wall meets the castle are shadowy and chilling; all there was to see there was a tumble-down shack and a stone bench. The front, however, is much livelier.

Servants, messengers, and all sorts of carriers and merchants are constantly flowing in and out of the gates. On the side where the wall meets the castle is the tiny pond where Len and I washed.

Another common-sense rule to add is, "Never ask guards how strong their walls are." They'll either exaggerate or think you're some sort of spy. I'm starting to get used to the title.

Oh, did I mention that there is a sort of village living right inside the walls? Of course, there must be some way for the castle to sustain itself in case of a siege. As I walked through the village, I saw a blacksmith, a butcher, a bakery, even a bone store for the royalty's hunting dogs! The people that run these places are friendly enough, though I did get some suspicious looks from the old ones. They must think it strange that the prince has let a stranger like me into his confidence.

That concludes my research outside. I shall begin the tour inside tomorrow. The bell is ringing out for dinner now.

Day 17.

I began my tour at the main entrance, which is really the Dining Hall. This is where Len and I first showed up. Pillars of stone are placed along the wall supporting the ceiling. There are six of these on each side. Several chandeliers hang overhead to cast light across the auditorium. Remembering Len's story about coffee, I chuckled, and the walls echoed it back. Presently, there is only one long table set on a higher level than the rest of the gleaming, marble floor.

Off to the left and right sides of the room are snack bars. I suppose this is where the appetizers and such are found. The whole room is decorated richly with rare trinkets from around the island. Windows are furnished with scarlet drapes, but furniture is scarce except for the high-backed chairs around the feasting table.

At the back of the Dining Hall are two large doors placed symmetrically on both sides of the room. I tried the handles, but they were both locked. To be honest I was relieved. The doors are made of a dark red wood, and beautifully carved with strange signs and patterns. Something I've learned is that the most beautiful things here can also be the most dangerous.

Two large pathways branch off from both sides of the hall. The left path led to a variety of rooms, mostly empty. At the end of the hallway, I found a theater-like room. There are rows and rows of seats all the way down to the candle-lit stage. An aura of evil hung about the place, so I soon retreated to the Dining Hall.

To the right is another hallway that goes through the whole castle, twisting and turning. The first door I came to went right to the kitchens; trust me, I don't want to go there again! A couple feet farther, there are stairs that lead to the Guest Chambers. I wandered through several servant passages and closets before I recognized the winding stairs that brought me to the Royal Chambers. Despite its name, this is also where they house important guests.

At the top of the stairs, there is yet another hallway. Just to the left is a door with an ugly mask hanging on it. Yeah, that's Len's room. My room is connected to his by a door, almost like a suite. In fact, the rooms in the Royal Chambers are almost like a hotel, but much more confusing. What I would give for the rooms back home with those wonderful numbers that keep you from getting lost!

Across from the Royal Chambers are the Lady's Quarters. Most of the maid-servants stay here. Oddly enough, so does Len's sister. How did I discover this? Well, I didn't ask, that's for sure! That could get me killed. I was walking down the aisle of the Lady's Quarters and trying not to feel self conscious as maid-servants cast curious or hostile looks at me.

Just as I passed a particularly scary-looking door, I heard the matron, a sharp woman who rules the maid-servants with an iron hand, venting her spleen on this poor servant girl. I've never seen a woman so upset. I strode past without looking, but slowed my pace to hear the conversation. It went something like this:

Matron: Even a new servant girl like you should have the brains to know we never touch royalty.

Servant: But I didn't—

Matron Ah, but you did touch the property of royalty! What were you thinking, caressing the princess's door with your miserable, dirty paws?

Servant: It won't happen again.

Matron: It better not, or I might go to the princess herself and mention I saw a nosy girl hanging about her room. She doesn't take kindly to that sort of thing, you know. And she can't abide eavesdroppers.

To which she advanced on me brandishing a feather-duster, and I had to run for my life. I managed to find my way back once the matron had left to get a better look at the doors. They were at the end of the hall, fastened to the wall with silver clasps. Carved into the door was a picture of a blood-red rose with a black thorn curling around it. I could understand the servant's temptation to stroke the mysterious, beautiful door. There was a tiny knocker underneath the carving, but who'd want to knock on that door?

Well, that's it for now. Soon I will begin my exploration of all those miscellaneous tunnels and passages. You might think that I would have enough information to fill a hundred newspapers already, but who knows? America simply gobbles up information these days.

Two Sides of the Coin

Day 18.

I woke up to find Len toying with my camera. "Stop!" I yelled and snatched it away just as he was about to stick his dagger through the lens.

Len jabbed a finger at it. "What sort of devilry have you been hiding? How long did you think you could keep it secret? And why does it make an awful flash every time you press that circle down?"

"My camera is not a mystical device!" I protested. "It's a very delicate and expensive instrument that all the best reporters have." This was not necessarily true, but he didn't need to know that.

Anyways, it took forever for me to convince Len my camera wasn't, er, witchcraft. But eventually, I made him understand that at the place I came from, we can make things happen by science. He was baffled when I explained to him that a camera painted whatever scene you flashed it at. I took my photography book from my briefcase to show him.

Len's face was priceless! He kept turning the pages and staring with his face close to the picture like a kid. I showed him the pictures I had taken of the Island of Despair, the Cobra village, the Stag Forest, and Castle Fox. I thought he was going to burst with excitement!

After asking more questions than I could possibly answer, he begged me to take more pictures of him posing with weapons. Of course, I obliged. He was alarmed when the film appeared black, but waited in silence with the picture in his hands for nearly half an hour before it cleared.

Then he whooped at the top of his lungs and ran for more props. I took a picture of him with his bow at ready, and one of him whirling two swords. He also took pictures of me trying to pose, but he couldn't help correcting me on everything.

As I finished posing in a warrior's stance with a dagger in each hand, I was going to give them back to Len when he told me to keep them. He suggested I find someplace to hide the knives. I accepted the simpler of the two and tied the sheath onto my belt. The weight was unfamiliar, but somehow comforting. Len waved away my thanks. "Be patient until we get you a real sword, Rossow!" he said. Can you believe that?

After the impromptu photo shoot, we both sat exhausted but satisfied against the wall. He wanted to know more about "the science of the other world." I felt a little scared telling him about guns and bombs, but I did mention them. Electricity, I explained, was harnessing the power of nature to make heat, cool our homes, or cook food. I avoided the topic of cars altogether.

In the end, Len told me that the science of my land was indeed superior to theirs. "But," he said with a wry smile, "if the Island of Despair did have machine guns and Adam bombs, I doubt we'd survive long…" I tend to agree.

I don't know what to do. If I go back and tell the world about the Islands, these people's way of life would be forever changed. Even though I don't know much about them, I know that they like their freedom. What if cops, reporters, and tourists suddenly appeared? What on earth would become of them? It scares me to think of it. Perhaps when I go back to get Steve I'll say nothing about it, except that it would be a terrible place for tourists, which is true enough.

The next few paragraphs are damp, muddy, and almost illegible.

I hate to record this painful scene, but it is my duty in case anyone wants to learn what became of Shawn the Reporter. It all started when I headed up a mysterious passage I discovered behind a dark veil. At the top of the winding staircase were thick double doors, beautifully crafted, though marred by a gargoyle leering over it with a grimacing smirk.

This should have been warning enough, but how was I to know? I tried the door handle and found it unlocked. The only light came through a stain-glass window. The red glass threw a bloody look over the room and various pieces of furniture: a chest, a long, wooden table, two tall black chairs with red cushions, and several swords on the stone walls.

A completely evil setting... I turned to escape through the door to find a figure standing there like some nightmare come true. The red light shone on her face, and to my horror, it was the queen!

Now ever since I saw the queen of the foxes, I've been terrified of her. A most rational fear, in this case. I still shudder when I see that look on her face when she found me in her room. I thought she was going to flip out one of her daggers and kill me there and then, never mind I was a guest.

However, I was lucky. She swept out of the room, with a furious roar, "Guards!" Within a minute, the soldiers marched in, their armored capes clinking. I let them tie my hands and lead me out of the room. I had to bite my tongue to keep from thanking them for saving my life.

As the guards hauled me downstairs, I heard Lieutenant Simor and the queen talking. I wondered what punishment she had in store for me: the gallows, the guillotine, the stocks—no, anything but the stocks!

When the lieutenant came down, he smirked at me. "I shore hope Prince Gilen finds ye soon, ye poor knave," he said in his thick accent. The soldiers exchanged knowing grins.

So here I am. It seems the foxes have a different way of punishing trouble-makers than the cobras. Leading out of the city is convenient ditch by the side of the road for rainwater and... sewage. The victim is unceremoniously dumped in and *then chained to a pole like a dog. Yes, reader... that's where I am now. Can you guess what the weather's like? Rain. They must have a terrible atmosphere.*

* * *

Thud, thud, thud. Slam! Len banged the door shut and leaned on it, arms crossed. Shawn squirmed under his unreadable expression. Self-consciously, he reached up to wipe his face. *Don't be silly Shawn, there couldn't be a speck of dirt on you after those sinister, old women scrubbed and beat you like a piece of laundry at the pool.* He tried to meet Len's eyes but couldn't.

"This isn't working," said Len. There was no anger in his voice, just a tinge of scorn.

Shawn slumped on Len's bed and groaned, "I *know.*"

"I thought you had already learned your lesson at Cobra."

"What lesson?"

Len rolled his eyes. "Don't snoop!"

"Oh yeah. Guess I forgot."

"How could you be such a fool? You should know by now that you can tell a lot about a room by its entrance. Suppose you saw an ax hanging above the door. What should you do?"

"Don't snoop."

"Correct. What if you saw a picture of a man being swallowed by a lion?"

"Len-"

"I've seen them before! What do you do?"

"Don't snoop." Shawn sighed.

"You seem to be getting the idea. A gargoyle is just as much a hint as a knife hanging by a thread above your eye when you wake up in the morning! And what is that hint?"

The reporter gulped. "Don't snoop or you'll get killed?"

Gilen nodded in satisfaction. "Correct again, Tubby."

"I'm sorry. I didn't know."

Two Sides of the Coin

"That is exactly the problem. You don't know," Len murmured with a thoughtful look, as if it had just occurred to him. Len paced to the window and back. He scowled at Shawn. "You should know enough to steer clear of the queen. *Nobody* crosses my mother, not even the king!"

"Not even Sylindra?" Shawn couldn't help asking.

Len winced. "Well, she was always was the one who got away unpunished whenever the two of us got into trouble. Her deceptive nature doesn't fool Mother... it pleases her."

"Does the queen know I'm here now?" asked Shawn.

"She will," Len replied. He turned on his heel and ran his finger along the groove of his favorite sword. Shawn stared out the window. The sky was still grey, weeping tiny raindrops that settled to the ground like mist. As far as he could see were trees, trees, and more trees. *A great deal of this island must still be wild, with no people for miles,* he thought.

Len was deep in thought. The silence grew until Shawn could not stand it any longer. "What are we going to do?" he burst out.

The prince lifted the sword from the wall and inspected its edge. Satisfied, he sheathed it and pulled the scabbard over his back. "Run away."

Shawn jumped to his feet. "Run away?!"

Len turned with an endearing smile. "There you go again, Tubby, repeating my words like a deranged crow. My parents aren't too stern about me and Sylindra wandering, as long as we don't make trouble." He paused and confessed, "Technically, I am not allowed to stay away for more than three days, but I do it all the time."

The reporter toyed with a loose string on his tunic. "So why can't we just stay away for a few days and come back?"

Len raised an eyebrow. "First, that's not nearly enough time to teach you everything you need to survive on this island. You can't learn anything here, twiddling your thumbs and partaking of castle life. You will have to learn as we go along. After all, I can only save you so many times. We must get away from people for a good stretch of time."

As he spoke, Len moved around his room, packing up. Shawn got up to help but was shoved back onto his seat. He sulked there until Len had finished. From his own wardrobe, the prince packed two outfits suitable for traveling, one change of clothes for them both. Blankets weren't needed; they had their capes. He packed nothing that wasn't necessary. All in all, he acted with such calmness and efficiency that Shawn got the impression he'd done this all before. Somehow, the thought wasn't reassuring.

"Second," Len continued his discourse, "you can't stay here with my mother in such a deadly mood." He held up the bag, weighing it critically. Satisfied, he hoisted the bag over his shoulder, held a finger to his mouth, and motioned for Shawn to stay seated. He finished in a whisper, "And third, running away is so much more fun! Look," he pulled the hood over his head, "there's a clasp on the hood right below your chin that will keep it from slipping off. You'll find it to be quite useful for sword fights and escapes."

Then he eased open the door and left, sliding it shut behind him. The reporter noticed how the hinges on the old door looked as good as new.

What a scoundrel, Shawn thought. *He's kept the hinges oiled so they won't squeak.* Shawn fiddled with the clasp on his hood until it clicked together. Shaking his head, he was pleased to find that the hood stayed in place. He thought to himself, *Wow, they really—*

His thoughts were interrupted by footsteps outside and hushed voices, "Are you sure he isn't in here? If we were to walk in with both present…"

"*Relax.* The prince is busy with own schemes. The kitchen, it looked like. Come on, it'll be easier than taking a maiden from the Island of Joy."

"Indeed. All it takes is one arrow."

The speaker stepped up to the door and turned the handle.

CHAPTER 8

The Runaways

Shawn was galvanized into action as he saw the handle turning slowly. Without thinking, he dove to the floor and scurried under Len's bed like a frightened cockroach. *I bet it's much easier for them,* thought Shawn with a grimace. *They're naturally flat.*

The door cracked open. Shawn held his breath as one of the intruders growled, "Where is the man? She said he would be here!"

"Stop worrying, Mora. We'll find him."

"Ever the optimist, eh, Karis? I'll search this other room."

Shawn could not believe what his ears were telling him. Now that the two people were closer, he could distinguish the sound of their low voices. It was unmistakable; the intruders were two *women*.

He still remembered something Len had told him, "Beware of women, Shawn. Some people might say that a lady is more dangerous than a knight with his battle-axe." Now two women padded about the room, looking for him. Little, ol' him.

One moved into Shawn's room while the other checked Len's wardrobe. Shawn could see her shiny, black boots stalking the room with absolute silence. After a moment, the lady strode to the window, cupped her hands to her mouth, and mimicked a howl so realistic that Shawn mused to himself, *Geez, I hope they don't have werewolves here...*

"Gotcha!" the lady seized his boot. Shawn yelped and kicked his legs. Mora charged into the room to help while Shawn clutched the bed frame for dear life. Both women tugged on his leg until his fingers were pried from the frame, and out he popped like a worm caught by robins.

The women glared at him with contempt. The tall one, called Karis, had a noble yet fierce face. Her nose was large, and her cheekbones very pronounced. Her black hair was tied up into a thick, braided bun. She wore all black and carried a crossbow as well as a thin sword. She reminded Shawn of an evil elf.

Mora was shorter but no less frightening. Cat-like eyes, a sharp chin, and a fair complexion showed under her hood. A few bangs of carrot-red hair had escaped from her headband. Garbed all in black, her large belt stood out. The leather belt was embroidered with all sorts of imaginary creatures: griffins, dragons, minotaurs, phoenixes, and a fox with nine tails. Hanging from her belt was a chain-whip with an iron ball at the end. If you have never been hit with an iron ball going thirty or more miles per hour, you could hardly imagine how painful it can be. Never try it at home or anywhere else, for that matter.

Shawn started to ask, "What do you want?" but the words died in his throat.

One of Len's rules was, "Don't ask questions that you know aren't going to be answered." Oh, how Shawn would love to see him right now!

The tall woman gestured with her crossbow. "Up against the wall, mortal."

"Mortal?"

"Now!"

Shawn rose to his feet and walked as if in a trance to the wall with the hanging masks. Some of the masks seemed to mirror his feelings: terror, sadness, frustration. Others appeared to laugh at his plight. *So this is the end*, he thought. *I never imagined it would be like this. Why did luck have to be on Steve's side when we flipped that stupid coin?*

He heard the ladies whisper to one another, and the shuffling of the crossbow in their dangerous hands. Then, somewhere to his right, he heard a most unexpected sound.

"*Quack, wak, wak... quack! Quack, wak...*" It was, in fact, a duck... a duck with a cold, at least. Shawn risked a glance over his shoulder just as a corner of black cloth slipped above the window sill. Len's cape! He was here to rescue him!

Why is he making a duck noise, then? thought Shawn.

"Well, Mora, would you do the honors?" Karis spoke. Apparently, they saw no threat in ducks.

"I would not soil my hands on the like of him," Mora replied.

"Fine," Karis drew her sword, the sound sending chills down Shawn's spine.

"*Quack, quack, quack!*" went the "duck" more insistently.

What's that supposed to mean? Quacking... duck? Duck?! Even as it hit him, Shawn sucked in his breath and *ducked!*

The hilt of the sword swished over his head. Time seemed to slow down for a moment, allowing Shawn a thundering revelation. *They're not trying to kill me! She was using the hilt, not the blade! They were going to knock me out and kidnap me.*

A desperate energy filled him, and he spun to face the women. Karis, taken by surprise at his sudden duck, lost her balance and stumbled. Shawn raced for the door. Mora brandished her chain whip, and Karis put an arrow to the crossbow. "Stop or I'll shoot!" she threatened. But Shawn was already running, running for freedom, running for the door.

Click, click. The reporter had never heard a worse sound in his life. The door was locked. He shook the handle frantically.

If the dark-haired woman had released the arrow, as she very nearly did, poor Shawn's story would have ended there and then. Just as she squeezed the trigger, Mora's chain wrapped itself around the crossbow. Fragments of wood flew from the impact. "What are you doing?" snarled Karis, dropping the remains of the crossbow.

"Saving both our necks from Sylindra's wrath," Mora retorted. "She would kill us if anything happened to—"

"Mora..." she hissed.

But the damage was done. Shawn's stomach twisted in panic. *Len's sister is still after me!* Like a wild animal whose escapes had all been blocked, he faced his attackers. Drawing the dagger from his belt, he was strangely invigorated at how heavy it felt in his hands.

Shawn held up the blade and roared, *"Get out of the way I don't know how to use this!"* He sprinted towards them. Snarling, Mora snaked her chain at his legs. With adrenaline pumping through every vein, Shawn leaped over it as if it were nothing but a jump rope. As he landed, he rolled over his shoulder. Karis was right in front of him when he came up. Both froze with their daggers at ready, staring at each other.

A hundred thoughts sped through Shawn's mind in that split second. *What would Len do? Probably something unexpected. What would Steve do? Ask for an interview? What would Shawn the Reporter do? ... Give himself up?*

Shawn clenched the dagger tighter. Never in his wildest dreams had he imagined this; an adventure had come to him like something out of *The Lord of the Rings*. There was no way he would give that up.

Bellowing a war-cry, Shawn lunged towards Karis. Though taken by surprise again, the woman moved like lightning to block the strike with her next move already in mind. Instead of slashing, the reporter kicked the knife from her hand.

Shawn raced for the window, his only escape. Mora's chain whipped after him, but again, luck was with him. It snapped inches from his legs. Sheathing the dagger, Shawn reached the window. "LEN, YOU CRAZY BAT CREATURE YOU BETTER CATCH ME!" he screamed and dove headfirst out the window.

It was a lovely feeling of weightlessness that greeted the reporter out in the open air. That feeling went away all too soon as gravity kicked in. "Aaaaaaaaaaaah—Oomph!" As Shawn plummeted towards the rose garden and certain death, something seized him by the middle. All the air whooshed out of his lungs like a balloon. Huge wings beat the air on either side of him, and for a moment, Darth imagined they were his.

Then Len grunted in his ear, "Hang on. Tubby, we're going down!"

Indeed they were, despite Len's valiant efforts. Shawn's weight, coupled with ruthless inertia, dragged them downwards far too quickly. Panting, Len angled his wings, and they swooped just over a rosebush straight towards a haystack. Shawn didn't have the breath to scream a second time. Hay flakes flew in all directions at the collision. Floundering out of the haystack, Shawn gagged for air. Len emerged beside him, drew a breath, and laughed his head off.

Typical. When Shawn got his breath back, he snapped, "That woman almost brained me while you were perched on the window making duck noises! Why didn't you help me?" As he spoke, he pushed free from the haystack and sneezed three times.

Brushing hay off himself, Len still wore his customary smirk. "Where's the fun in that?" He spun on his heel to survey the territory. A veritable maze of hedges stood between them and the castle community. Judging by the haystack, the stable wasn't far. Just as the women bent over the window to search for Shawn's body, Len dragged him by the scruff into the maze.

"No time to gripe, Tubby," he whispered. "Those bounty hunters won't give up that easily."

"But, Len, they work for—"

"Shut up and run!"

Shawn tried to concentrate on running, but he couldn't stop thinking about what the bounty hunter had said. Sylindra was still determined to catch him. But why?

He had always dreamed of living an adventure-packed life. When he followed the reporter's trade, he hunted for great stories—not necessarily the most factual. Yet nobody seemed to appreciate this mythical aspect much. Steve himself had recommended he give up his strange fixation with fiction. Reluctantly, Shawn began to write what others expected: politics, scandals, gossip about Hollywood stars, the latest fashion, hunting and fishing in the National Parks, sports, etc. His dreams of adventure faded, drained away by the world's cynicism.

On the other hand, in Sanfran Cisco he'd never been chased by soldiers, strung up by his foot in a tree, or nearly kidnapped by women bounty hunters. Sanfran Cisco was tame in comparison to this medieval world.

If Len hasn't shaken off those women by now, my name's Luke Skywalker, thought Shawn. Len led him through the thorny hedges, dashing through one passage after another until Shawn was totally disoriented. Surely they weren't lost?

Just as he got the nerve to ask, they turned the corner and were free at last. Best of all, they were right behind the stables. The heavy aroma of hay, horses, and leather tickled Shawn's nose. A single door stood waiting for them

Len strode to the door and knocked a code: two hard knocks repeated three times. Shawn kept watch behind them. A minute later, the door creaked open an inch, and a freckled-faced boy with tangled, red hair peered at them. It was the stable boy who'd taken Len's horse.

The boy grinned and opened the door. "Hullo, your majesty! Need my help again?" He was dressed in the regular attire of a stable hand: a cape that fell to his waist, a long-sleeved scarlet tunic underneath a leather vest, trousers with pockets, tall boots, and a belt with the emblem of the fox on the silver buckle.

Len boxed his ear gently, smiling. "Still as cheeky as ever, you devilish kit! Go get two light horses with enough food to last them a week or so. After that, I'm going to need a little sabotage done on the gate."

The boy's face lit up. "*Sabotage?*"

"Oh yes, my friend. I want you to make sure the gate gets open and stays open until we get out." The red-head nodded and disappeared without a sound. Len commented, "Sometimes having a fortified castle is such a bother."

The red-head sprinted down the dim aisle, dodging other workers. Some of his friends waved, but he was too busy to greet them. He ran to the far left wall of the stables and saddled Len's finest stallion and another fresh horse. In the stables, the horses were classed as either light or heavy. Light horses were bred for the ability to run long distances, live off the land, and travel for days on end. Heavy horses, in comparison, were much larger, stronger, and faster. However, they tired much faster, as long-distance rides used their weight against them. Also, they required a regular diet to keep them in perfect condition. They were preferred for jousting, hunting, and skirmishes.

This corner of the stables was different from the others. Visibly, everything appeared normal. The wall was made of wood, resembling the rest of the stable. But with a hard push, the panel went back into the wall and slid to the side. Wide enough to let horses through, the door opened to a shadowy corner behind the stable. The door wasn't common knowledge. When the stable was built by the earliest king of Foxes, he purposely added it to the stables. He knew that once in awhile *someone* would need to use it to run away, and so they have.

When the stable boy finished saddling the horses, he checked that no one was around. He guarded the secret of the door jealously. Murmuring to the horses, he led them out one at a time and left the reigns in Len's hands. The prince patted his shoulder, pulled a coin out from behind his ear, and placed it in his hand.

The stable boy carefully pocketed the coin, pulled the door closed, and wiped his hands. Now only one duty was left.

Sabotage!

* * *

It was a typical day in the throne room of Castle Fox. The lady of the castle sat on her throne above the world, brooding in silence. The king was seated a table to the right of the thrones. On the table rested a marvelous chess set: the pawns, knights, rooks, and castles on one side shaped to resemble the men of Fox. Their clothes Fox style as well as their flags, armor, and weapons. The king and queen pieces were statuettes of the old king and queen of Fox, his grandparents.

The enemy on the opposite side was presently an army of Sea Dragons, each chess piece just as detailed. Their deep blue clothes contrasted the brilliant red of the foxes. This was the king's favorite game to sharpen his mind or simply for fun. The Fox army's left hand was now blocked on all sides by approaching pawns, their thin, black cutlasses in hand. Both queens stared at each other with malice from across the battlefield. A Fox knight seated on his tall war horse watched the castle, which dared not attack the line of pawns. The rooks, too, stood in tactful locations on the battlefield.

The king leaned back and gazed at the ceiling for inspiration. "Alexi, would you sacrifice a castle to perhaps break through the enemy's line? It just might work."

"Of course it won't work. Since you are the mastermind behind both armies, you'll see at once what the castle is trying to do and immediately bring your queen around to keep your wall firm."

"I almost wish you would simply state yes or no—for I know you care nothing about the game—yet you insist on presenting an even more confusing scenario," he complained.

"That's not what you married me for, Rubin."

He folded his arms with a wry smile. "True. It's too bad you dislike chess, my vixen. You'd be splendid at it."

They lapsed into silence, both boarded on their own train of thought. After a minute, the queen revealed her mind. "I confess, I'm still wondering what to do with that *thing* Len dragged home."

"I thought you already dealt with him."

"We both know that we can't keep him chained in the ditch forever. He's already wanted in Cobra. It won't be long until other regions hear of him as well. You know how fast word spreads."

"If another region did capture him, wouldn't that solve our problem? Throw the honey and the hornet's nest into the neighbor's yard." The king moved a piece and rose, stretching his arms as he slipped into the opposite seat.

"It's not the man I'm worried about." The queen gestured to the door. "Could it have escaped you that the moment he is taken, Len would go after them? Or have you forgotten how he went back to rescue him while he was in the stocks?"

The king hid a smile. "How could I forget with all those subtly aggressive messages from that Cobra town complaining about their 'sssstolen prissssoner'?"

The queen glanced at him in disdain. "You ask me for solutions, yet you offer none."

At that, the king tore his eyes away from the chess-board. "Forgive me. Perhaps, we should retrieve him from the ditch and lock him up until we can figure out what to do next."

The queen pondered this and gave a slow nod. "A year or so in the dungeon should dampen his fame."

"Whatever pleases you, dear." That usually meant the end of their conversation.

However, the silence was soon broken by a loud knock on the door and a shrill voice. "Your majesties! Sir Fink wishes an audience with you!"

The queen and king winced at the man's voice. "Who is *that?*" hissed the queen, glowering at the door.

The king moved a chess piece and went to sit beside her. "He's the new doorman. The other one resigned after that incident with the—"

"Don't remind me," she snapped. "Come in, Fink!"

The king and queen stood in unison as the door creaked open, and the man shuffled in. Fink was a short, thin man with a fez perched on his nearly bald head. Tufts of scruffy, white hair peeked around the hat's edges, looking remarkably like cobwebs.

In one arm, he carried a large, dusty tome which he held close to his heart. The book was bound in black leather, and its gold title read, *The Ancient History of Darkness and Light.* The cover depicted a man dressed in scarlet crossing blades with a man cloaked in blue.

The queen was quite attached in her own way to the old librarian. Fink had lived in the castle longer than she had been there. He usually went about with a preoccupied look on his face which some took for stupidity. However, he was much more intelligent than anyone thought. For the most part, Fink kept to himself in his own corner of the castle with books as his only companions.

Fink removed his fez and dipped his head to the royalty. "Majesties, you know that no one pays much attention to a deaf, little man with his nose buried in dusty pages. Indeed, many people to this day may still believe I am naught but a statue of some long-dead personage. But nay, I watched two hooded figures so rudely disturb our solace, yet they noticed me not."

"Where and when did you see them?" asked the king.

"Not but a few minutes ago, your majesty. Mine eyes watched these strangers creeping O so silently down our very castle hallways. They proceeded to a servant door where they made their departure."

The king and queen pondered the librarian's words.

It was the king who spoke first, "Alexi, do you know of these strangers?"

The queen curled her lip. "My spies do not sneak around in our own castle. Fink, did they have any clothes to give away their region?"

"They wore all black, my lady. I'm afraid I could not tell what their region was by their clothes, though one of them had a belt decorated with mythical creatures. It looked very old and the embroidery was nothing short of breathtaking—oh, pardon me. I digress," he apologized.

"Are you sure it wasn't a servant or guest?" asked the king.

"Your highness," said Fink with a stern look, "I know an intruder when I see one."

That was enough for them. Together they swept to the balcony that overlooked the courtyard and gate. The king put his fingers in his mouth and blew a piercing whistle. A guard appeared on the wall to hear the command, *"Shut the gate at once!"*

The guard disappeared into the gate house, and the queen departed to rally the palace guards. Meanwhile, the king questioned Fink to see if he could obtain any more clues. When his eyes strayed to the gate, he was taken aback to see that it had not been closed. He watched from the balcony for several minutes, but the gate remained suspended. What had happened?

"*Slimy*, flea-bitten, scrawny, wicked scum! The gutters ain't worthy of the likes of ya', doorknob licker. Gnome, rat, son of a frog-eating troll! I dare you to come out of the hole you're cowerin' in. I'll mop the floor with your filthy face!"

The stable boy covered his mouth with both hands, shaking with mirth. He was perched in the rafters right above the gate wheel, so he had an excellent view of the sabotage results. The guard heaved against

Two Sides of the Coin

the wheel while screaming the most blood-curling insults. He seemed to know an endless amount of them. As much as he cursed and strained against the wheel, however, it turned at a snail's rate.

Another guard poked his head in. "Gilbert! What's the problem? I know you're a rookie at gate duties, but any dunce knows how to throw the lever to release the gate."

Gilbert pointed to the lever which hung near the ground. "Someone put Fool's Glue in the axel. You know, that sticky, black stuff that'll dry hard as rock in a couple hours? And I bet I know just the rodent who did the unspeakable deed."

The other guard looked worried. "No time for that. The queen is on the warpath, and the king wants the gate down *now*. Come on: one, two, PUSH!" The two men bent their backs and strained against the wheel. It was like trying to move an obstinate animal.

"I'm gonna kill that kid," Gilbert muttered.

"Less talk and more push. We'll deal with the nuisance later, or the *queen* will."

The stable boy climbed higher into the rafters. Without a doubt, the guard's description of a rodent fit the nimble boy. Crawling out of a child-sized window onto the roof, the red-head slid down the rope he'd stashed there for such a time as this. He landed outside the walls, retrieved the rope, and walked off, whistling. With his duty done, he would hang out with the village boys for the rest of the day, and no one would be the wiser. The gate would stay open long enough. That is, if they were fast enough.

"Keep up, Shawn!" Len yelled behind his shoulder. That was quite a feat, considering that he simultaneously led two galloping horses down a narrow passage. But the prince of Fox was a true horseman, weaving his way through the clustered buildings in the courtyard square. He held the reins in one hand and placed his other on the horse's neck. The great stallion and Len were like one creature.

Right behind them, Shawn hung onto his horse's neck with all his might, but he still felt his grip slipping. When he had first climbed into the saddle and put his feet in the stirrups, he had said, "Len, there's something I have to tell you."

Len had told him it could wait until they were out of the castle. Now Shawn screamed inwardly. *Gah! It can't wait, you reckless villain! I don't know how to ride!*

"Duck!"

Not again... Shawn ducked his head just in time to miss a hanging sign for the blacksmith. His left boot came loose from the saddle, and he was almost bounced off the side. Panicked, he grabbed hold of the reins and hauled himself up, clueless how he was hurting the horse's mouth. It snorted and jerked the reins free from Shawn's hands. All the reporter could do was squeeze tighter with his legs.

Such an act can only be pitied. There's nothing worse for a horse than a rider who doesn't know what he's doing. Or for the rider. Sensing Shawn's panic, the horse put back its ears and bolted. "Whoah, horsie! Slow dowwwwwn!" Shawn cried.

They pulled ahead of Len, who shouted, "Don't lose your head, Tubby. Hang on!" Len urged his horse into a gallop to keep up with Shawn's horse. They thundered down the street, scattering people and animals. Just when Shawn felt he could hold on no longer to the horse's steaming neck, they broke out of the houses and the gate reared up at the far end of the courtyard.

Immediately, Len could see that the sabotage had worked. The heavy, iron gate teetered and groaned but stayed up. Inside the gatehouse, guards heaved at the wheel while others scrambled to scrape off the dreaded Fool's Glue. With all this going on, he and Shawn could make it through the gate!

"Len, this crazy horse is finally slowing down," said Shawn. "Don't leave me behind!"

Len tossed his hair out of his eyes. "Don't worry, just get past the gate." Soon Len's horse pulled ahead and Shawn's slowed to a trot.

Don't worry, don't worry, get to the gate. Shawn patted his horse's neck. "Look, it's no farther than half a parking lot. Keep going, horsie."

Two Sides of the Coin

There is a proverb in the Fox Region told to children at bedtime which illustrates Len and Shawn's predicament. Full from a night of hunting, a fox returned to his den at daybreak. It turns out he was being followed by a huge brown bear. The bear had searched everywhere for a den without any luck, but he was pleased to see that the fox's cave was just the right size. So he stopped before the entrance and growled at the fox to leave.

"You'll have to go through my fangs and claws before you steal my home!" the fox snarled.

The bear only smirked. "No matter. I am vastly stronger than you, and there's no denying it, you trickster."

"My cubs will return to avenge me and drive you out," the fox warned.

The bear laughed in scorn. "They will be a mere snack for me, foolish fox. I will have this den even if I have to fight ten of your cubs!"

At last, the fox sighed and shook his head as if in despair. "I see you really mean to take my home. Well, if that's the way it has to be, would you be a lamb and break the news to my poor wife? You wouldn't believe the way she acts when something upsets her—" and the fox went on to describe it.

At this point in the legend, the storyteller would show how the arrogant bear suddenly began to shiver and tremble. His eyes widened, and he whimpered like a puppy. Right in the middle of the fox's terrible descriptions, the bear shook his grizzly head. "Foxes and their tricks I can deal with, but never vixens!" He turned tail and trudged off, grumbling, "You can't cross a vixen."

Meanwhile, the fox laughed to himself and returned to his den to rest in solitude. "Maybe someday I really will get a vixen. Until then, I'll bide my seasons in perfect safety."

If this was one of Aesop's fables, it would probably end with the moral, *"Even the most powerful forces can be defeated by cleverness."*

But the moral that most storytellers would always communicate to their listeners is, *"Beware of vixens!"*

Sure enough, even as Len escaped, the queen appeared from the barracks with fire in her eyes. Behind her marched a score of guards, ready to cut off the strangers. She was truly "on the warpath." Shawn, who was still in the courtyard, saw them at the same time they saw him. The queen's scorching gaze scrutinized him, and Shawn was glad for the cover of his hood. The soldiers broke into a run to cut him off. They were, as Shawn would describe it, only a parking lot's length away. And the gate—it was almost halfway down!

"Giddy-up!" Shawn shouted and slapped the reigns. The horse moved lazily into a canter.

The queen instructed her soldiers, "Be careful, this man could be treacherous. Frighten the horse away from the gate and surround the horseman with arrows. He will have no time for tricks."

In desperation, Shawn squeezed his knees into the horse's sides. At once, the horse moved into a gallop. Oh, the stamina of those great beasts! They flew towards the gate, scarcely touching the ground. Finally, Shawn was the master of his horse.

"Yeeeaaaah!" he whooped as they passed within feet of the queen and soldiers. In vain did the men shout and wave their arms. They were like lemmings trying to scare a wolf. The horse flew by with the stranger in tow. In that brief, glorious victory, Shawn had never felt more alive with his cape fluttering and his hair blown from his face. He left confusion and chaos behind in the soldier's ranks.

Groaning, the gate slid down another foot. "Close the gate!" the guards screamed.

The five men heaving at the wheel pushed with all their might. Shawn examined the gate and saw that the horse could barely make it, but not him! *No, I'm not giving up yet,* he vowed. He gave the horse an encouraging pat to keep it on track. With less than three yards to go, Shawn suddenly leaned from the saddle until his body was nearly parallel to the ground. How close it looked, rushing away right below him! He gritted his teeth and held tight to the reins.

Either the horse knew exactly what Shawn wanted or it was slightly out of control. In any case, it did not turn away from the gate when its reins jerked to the left. Out they shot past the low gate, away from the thick walls, away from the group of angry soldiers, away from castle life. The gate shrieked and broke free of the glue's clutches. *Shhhhhink!*

Two Sides of the Coin

Thud! Its sharp pikes bit into the ground. The soldiers assembled around the gate, mad as hornets. Shawn's horse pranced at the commotion, but at Shawn's touch of the reins, it calmed and turned to the right. They cantered away with the shouts of the soldiers in their ears.

"Open the gate! Open the gate!"

Gilbert's sweaty face peeked out from the gatehouse window. "Make up your minds, you lumpy toads!"

The queen watched the preceding without a word. A moment later, she sensed the king standing next to her. "It seems the stranger was not trying to stall," she mused aloud. "Why then, had his attempts to move the horse been so pathetic? Was he merely attempting a more glorious escape? Only a man could be so ridiculous."

The king wrapped his arms around her from behind. "You are right, my love. We should check the village and make a careful search of the castle to see if we can find the strangers' identities. The worst they could be are assassins, but obviously they failed at that task. Sylindra is gone, Gilen's in the kitchen for an early lunch, and we are both very much alive." He leaned forward to kiss her cheek.

The queen allowed a thin smile. "Unless the assassins were after that poor creature called Tubby."

The king raised an eyebrow. "Maybe so," he chuckled. "Maybe so."

Shawn was relieved to see Len waving from the forest edge. As he approached, Len called, "What took so long?"

"I don't know how to ride, you fox!" he snapped.

To Shawn's dismay, Len burst into helpless laughter. "OH! *That* would explain the bolting horse, yes? And you slipping out of the saddle like a doll, and your close shave at the gate!"

Shawn shook his fist at the prince. "I'll make you will pay for this!" He waited for a burst of thunder, but none offered its assistance. Len gave him an odd look, and Shawn lowered his hand. "Ah well. I thought the thunder might work for me just this once."

The prince cocked his head sympathetically. "Poor Tubby. You don't have the touch yet. In time, perhaps."

Shawn shrugged. "Come on, let's scram."
"Beat it," agreed Len.
"Hit the road."
"Get lost."
"Burn some tires."
Len cocked his head. "Burn what?"

CHAPTER 9

Sylindra

Shawn and Len rode in silence as the forest closed in around them. Shawn tried not to wonder what would happen when the queen and king figured out who had sabotaged their gate and escaped with a score of soldiers on their tail. Bumping up and down in the saddle, he struggled to put down some facts on paper. At last, he admitted defeat and stowed the notebook in his saddlebag. With a heavy sigh, he murmured, "Len?"

The prince turned in the saddle and flicked his hair out of his eyes. "What's wrong? Is someone after us?"

"No, that's not it. Look, I don't belong here, do I? I thought I was only going to stay until I learned more about the island, and then I'd get home. Yet here I am running from men with swords and arrows, and doing all sorts of crazy stuff. I need to get back!"

"Why?"

Len's question wasn't a challenge. It wasn't taunting or even protesting. He was curious, and his curiosity unnerved Shawn. *He's got a point,* Shawn thought. *It's not like I've got a home or a car or even a pet dog to go back to.*

His least adventurous side protested. *What about running water, fast food, and friendly, normal people! What about light-bulbs, cars, and the police, for goodness sake?*

Honestly, Shawn, you sound like you care more about things than people. Just remember that back "home" you're alone. Shawn winced at the thought.

It was true that he had a few relatives. However, their relationship with his family was much like the hobbit Bilbo Baggins in *The Lord of the Rings* with his relatives, the Sackville-Bagginses. They were worse than fair-weather friends. If Shawn had ever succeeded in his reporter's career, which he never did, they would've been knocking each other over to become friends with him. But in the hard times, not one of them sent him so much as an I-hope-you-do-better card.

"Len, what should I do?" he pleaded.

Narrowing his eyes, Len whispered, "Join us, Rossow." And with that, he gave his horse a slap which sent it galloping down the path and disappeared from view. Shawn spurred his horse onwards; now that he was alone, the ancient forest felt hostile. As if drawn to his fear, clouds obscured the sun. A chill wind sprung up, biting his face and hands. The trees whizzed by him, their trunks dark and scarred. He tried to catch a glimpse of Len, but even the echoing of the horse's hooves had faded away.

Shawn pulled the horse to a stop. The forest seemed so empty. "Len?" he called. He could see the pale outline of his steed's neck and head, but after that it was like looking down a hole in the ground, from which anything might come out. The sound of thundering hoof-beats broke the eerie silence. Len's horse charged headlong into view. Len, riding like a madman, galloped straight towards Shawn. The horse thundered down the path, gravel flying from the pounding hooves.

Shawn fumbled for the reins, but they slipped from his shaking hands. Was this some cruel joke to frighten him? *Or*, thought Shawn in horror, *is this a horse version of the game chicken?*

At the last second, Len pulled to the side. Both the horse and the man gasped for breath. "For the love of Drake, let's get out of here!" Len cast a horrified look down the path. "There's mortal peril ahead of us, I tell you."

"Huh?" Shawn almost laughed. "Whatever happened to your reckless bravado and mindless courage?"

"Oh, hang it all, Shawn! Whatever happened to your self-preservation?" Len hissed. He lowered his voice. "There's a *woman* on the path ahead."

Shawn gasped. "You don't mean—"

"Yes, he does," a voice spoke from behind them. Both men whirled. A woman stood alone on the path they had taken to escape the castle. At the sight of her, Shawn felt he was back in the queen's clutches again. *Did she chase us down on foot? She would do it. But no, this woman is much younger than the queen.*

Len dismounted from his horse to stand between her and Shawn. After a moment's hesitation, Darth dismounted as well. The prince bowed. "Greetings, Sylindra."

"Gilen." She dipped her head just like her mother.

At his grimace, the princess hid a smile with her shell-like fan. Her gaze drifted past him to Darth. Half-hidden behind his horse, trying to make himself as small as possible, Darth still felt the intensity of that look. *So this is Len's sister.* The thought was accompanied by stab of terror. *Sylindra.*

Knowing that he must meet her eyes, scarcely daring to, Shawn lifted his head. Hers was the most beautiful face he had ever seen. Her face was at once narrow and soft, a perfect oval. Her nose was sharp and obstinate, her full lips parted in a slight smile. Long bangs covered part of her forehead. The rest of her dark brown hair, wavy and thick, tumbled past her shoulders. Her skin shone like marble in the ghostly light. Fringed by lush eyelashes, the lady's dark eyes captivated him. They seemed to look straight into his soul.

The princess's dress was finer than any Shawn had ever seen. What first grabbed his attention was that the dress was blood-red. Trailing at her feet, the dress darkened to crimson before melting into black. Around her waist hung two leather belts. One hugged her waist and the other hung at a slant to her thigh. Various weapons hung from them. Like the Fox soldiers' outfits, two belts formed an "x" over her chest. The reporter wondered how on earth she had managed to sneak up on them wearing such a bold dress.

The prince cleared his throat. "Shawn, this is Sylindra. Sis, this is Shawn Rossow." Shawn nodded, speechless. Sylindra curtsied in the Fox style: crossing a hand over her heart before dipping one knee gracefully. Then all semblance of polite conduct fled. Len and Sylindra stepped nose to nose, neither backing down an inch.

"Look, Sylindra, I know you're jealous that I found him first—"

"You *found* him? More like stumbled over him by luck."

"What do you want?"

She picked a piece of grass off his shoulder. "What do you mean? I am simply on my way home to see Mother and Father and tell them what good fortune it was that brought our paths together."

"No!" Len cried. "By Mordoom's Peak, Sylindra, you can't do that to me!"

"Why not? *Please* tell me you're not going on another fool-mission in the Crow region."

"Fool-mission? That was an honorable cause! Lord Galvorm needed to be overthrown. He was simply crowing for it."

Sylindra rolled her eyes. Shawn would have chuckled if he wasn't still afraid for his life. Len paced to the edge of the forest, running his hands through his hair. "Let me spell this out for you. Don't tell our beloved parents where we are."

"Your request makes the telling all the more desirable," she laughed. "Perhaps I could keep it to myself for two or three days but…"

"I need at least a week. Again, what do you want?"

"Well, you know I've always admired your Sea Dragon dagger. The one you keep in your front pocket?"

Seething, Len pulled it out from a hidden pocket in his tunic and tossed it to Sylindra. She examined it and nodded in approval. "Your secret is safe for three days."

"What else do you want?" he asked, exasperated.

The princess brushed back her bangs, taking her time to respond. *Dang, she's enjoying this,* Shawn thought.

"Remember when you carved a harp? That lovely instrument was utterly wasted on a certain slinky vixen."

Len groaned. "Sylindra, why can't you let that go? Almost two years have passed since Ullia and I stopped seeing each other. Come on, I was eighteen and crazy. Yes, you warned me, and yes, I didn't listen to your superior vixen intelligence. Ullia is history, and so is that harp I made for her. Yet, after all this time, you still bring up that pathetic drama in the middle of the Ranjin Forest as I am trying to flee Castle Fox?" His voice rose until it cracked.

"Well, while you are fleeing, could you make another harp?"

"I'll start one as soon as I can," Len promised. "You will have it."

Finally, Sylindra nodded. "I will tell no one of our meeting."

"Or show any indication you've seen us."

"Of course."

Only then did a grin break through Len's serious countenance. "This is going to be so fun!" He snatched his sister's hand, smooched it loudly, and was rewarded by a stinging slap from her fan. With a running jump, he leapt into the saddle. Shawn mounted his horse with more difficulty.

Just before the two cantered away, Sylindra raised her voice. "So Len, I see that you intend to make a fighter of him. As you know, our dear parents are planning a certain tournament to be held at our castle this autumn." Her dark eyes met Shawn's. "For the honor of our parents as well as for the Foxes, you two will be there, aye?"

"We wouldn't miss it," Len murmured.

It was now or never if he didn't want to come off as a dumb fool. Shawn plucked up his courage. "My lady, er, your highness," he began to stammer while Len stared at him. He recovered himself and declared in the most confident voice he could muster. "Honestly, I know nothing about fighting or your island's customs. But I'll try to change, if I can."

Sylindra gave a slight nod, and shadows danced across her face. Feeling warmer than he'd been the whole night, Shawn nudged his horse forward. Together he and Len entered the dappled darkness of the Ranjin Forest.

* * *

Several hours later, Shawn fell asleep in the saddle. Len didn't even notice until Shawn slipped right off the horse's back and tumbled to the ground. "Mmmm," he moaned, still sleeping like the dead, per the norm.

"Eh?" Len looked back to see a lone horse staring back at him. "Shawn?"

The prince jumped down and found his companion curled up on the forest floor, sound asleep. With a world-weary sigh, Len pulled the reporter to his feet and slapped his face until Shawn finally woke.

"Leave me alone," he mumbled. *Slap!* "Ouch! What was that for?" he whined, now fully awake.

"For trying to desert, that's what!" growled Len. "Now get back on your horse." Utterly confused, Shawn obeyed, wincing at his sore muscles. Before they continued, Len instructed him to wrap the reins around his wrists. On they went, but Shawn forced his eyes to stay open.

Later that night, or very early the next morning, Len stopped the horses. He turned to Shawn and whispered, "From now on, I need absolute silence. Even if you're being attacked by a rabid beast, or get hit by lightning, or the queen arrives, not a squeak!"

Nothing could be worse than the queen, Shawn thought, but he nodded anyways. "Why?"

"We are passing the border from Fox into Sea Dragon," Len replied. When he saw Shawn's confused look he added, "We've been at war with them for years. A blood-war."

"Wait, you're at war with another region?"

"That's what I said."

Shawn was confused, as usual. "But when we were at your father's castle, well, it didn't look like there was a war going on. Fox was peaceful." *As peaceful as anyplace on this crazy island,* he thought.

Len pulled his horse to a stop and met Darth's gaze. "Listen. A hundred years ago, there was another region called Wolf. They lived on and around Mt. Mordoom, just above the Stallion and Crow regions. The wolves were a tall, powerful, and noble people. They were famously wealthy on account of discovering gold under the mountain. Then an accursed sickness overtook them. It caused them to go mad and rampage like wild beasts, killing everyone in their path. The sickness was passed down to the next generation. Werewolves, we called them. Not every wolf had the sickness, but there was no way to know for sure who would become a werewolf and who would not. Fearing Island-wide extermination, all the regions' armies united to drive the wolves down into the Mordoom Mines. They were sealed inside and left to die."

"That's... that's—" Darth struggled to find a word.

Len lowered his face so Darth could not see his expression. "Yes, I know," he said in a low voice. "The wolves were our brothers. The foxes should have fought to protect them. Instead, we were the first to attack and the first to leap on the spoils."

Len was silent, brooding. Darth asked in a whisper, "Didn't any escape?"

"I am certain of it," said Len. "But they lived with a death warrant hanging over their heads. Werewolf hunters were fanatical about hunting down every last one." He shook himself. "Anyways, I tell you this to explain about our wars. After wiping out a whole region, fear seized the whole island. For if one region could be massacred so easily, what would prevent us from killing each other until there was no one left? And so our ancestors took the Oath of Life and Death. They vowed that never again would there be a war of killing. The price for killing another is death, unless the deed is done in self-preservation or by accident."

Len grasped the reins and moved on. Shawn followed as close as he could. "In that case, what's a blood-war?" he asked.

"A blood-war is more than a fight over territory or disagreements," Len explained. "It's a war for the region's honor. Most of the time regions are peaceable towards each other. Sometimes one aggravates another and a scuffle breaks out. The only thing needed to break it up, usually, is an intervening of the royalty. The real trouble happens when the royalty get involved in the quarrel, and somehow, *somebody* gets killed."

Len raised his voice, shaking his fist dramatically. "The atrocity! *Revenge* on every tongue! Blood-wars often last even after the original rulers are dead. Two regions can share a mutual hatred for many seasons to come. The people refuse to even speak to each other. They raid each other's merchants, burn each other's fields, and otherwise work up a storm of mischief."

"I guess that explains why there were so many people in Thonfirm."

"Precisely. Thonfirm's population has doubled, almost tripled, since the blood-war began again. The Sea Dragons have raided and burned almost all the villages close to the border. It's a mess." Pausing for a moment, Len added in a lighter tone. "I think people don't like wars because they cause simply too many weddings."

Shawn jerked his head up, certain that he had misheard. "Weddings?"

"Yes. Funerals cause weddings. Didn't you know that?" Len chuckled.

Shawn shook his head. *I'll never understand these people.*

The night seemed endless, as if the shadows were unwilling to loosen their grip on the island. After they crossed the border, Len became alternately snappy or dreamy. Shawn caught him once murmuring to himself until he lapsed back into his own secret thoughts. Shawn shivered and wrapped the cloak more tightly around his shoulders. When the moon was at its zenith, Len turned off the trail they had followed thus far and plunged right into the forest. Shawn struggled to lead his horse through the thick trees. Thorny branches clawed at him from above. Roots and holes made the terrain treacherous and the darkness even more so. Their horses could only manage a walk.

Creatures shuffled in the undergrowth, and Shawn prayed that there were no bears or panthers. Once he heard a drawn-out shriek. It made his limbs stiffen and his teeth chatter. The second time the creature screamed, it sounded even harsher. "Len, is that a bird?" he whispered. There was no answer. Shawn jerked his head forward and smiled in relief. Len was still ahead of him, either ignoring him or too far to hear his question.

"*Shrreeeak!*" went the "bird" again. Shawn urged the horse into a quicker pace to catch up with Len. He opened his mouth to ask about the sound, but Len hushed him. Stifling the question, the reporter let it out as a sigh. He suddenly realized how utterly exhausted he was.

Len went still as a rock with his head cocked to hear every noise. Shawn listened too, but all he heard was the cry of that wretched creature. He really hated that... whatever it was. Len didn't seem to mind; in fact, his expression brightened. He dismounted and tied his reins to a tree. "You can stay here and take a nap if you like."

"What? You're not leaving me behind." Even as the reporter protested, he yawned.

Len waved. "Watch the horses." He drifted away with cat-like silence into the darkness.

Shawn yawned again, but he was too curious to sleep. Anyways, he didn't want to sleep if that nasty bird turned out to be a panther instead. Slipping from the saddle, Shawn followed after Len. At first, there was nothing to see but the endless forest on all sides. Weak moonlight guided his way. Soon the ground sloped upward so steeply that Shawn had to zigzag to climb up. The thought that he'd gotten off-track bothered him until he reached the top. The trees broke into a clearing where a great table of stone lay in the center. Whether the table had always been there or had been placed there was a story long lost to antiquity. But all the islanders had their theories.

Most agreed that the rock had fallen from Mt. Mordoom. One legend said it dropped from the mountain right on top of the king as he rode past with his hunting entourage! Others believed that it was a message of doom to two lovers from different Islands that met there. Still others think it had fallen there as a sign to retreat when the combined armies of Hawk, Cobra, Sea Dragon, and Crow met with the armies of Fox, Stallion, Lion, and Stag for a huge battle. This theory, though seemingly the most unbelievable, was the one most commonly accepted. Therefore, the stone became a neutral meeting place for people of different regions.

Of course, Shawn knew none of this. To him the stone looked more like an altar for sacrifices, which by no means is what you want to find alone in the middle of the night. He was just about to step closer to study it when he saw a man sitting cross-legged before the rock with the light reflecting off his dark hair. Shawn recognized Len at once and ducked behind a tangle of trees before the knight could see him. He had a feeling that Len would tell him to go back to the horses. Not that he even knew the way back. Shawn shifted further from the moonlight, and the dried leaves crackled under his feet as if to say, *"Hey! There's a spy over here!"*

Len was on his feet in a moment. "Who's there?" he called.

Shawn held his breath and clenched his teeth to keep them from chattering. Len stepped towards the forest, his hand gripping the sword hilt.

Something flashed through the air straight towards Len, and he lurched against the tree. It happened so fast that neither Shawn nor Len saw the dagger until it seemed to sprout from his shoulder. But the blade had not pierced him—miraculously, it had only pinned his hood to the tree. Shawn let out the breath he hadn't realized he was holding.

The prince touched the dagger. "The eighteenth attempt on my life, eh? Your father will be most disappointed to hear that you missed."

A shadow seemed to move on the table of stone, but Shawn thought his eyes were playing tricks on him. Then the shadow spat three words as a snake spits venom: *"I never miss."* The trees stirred around Shawn, like hundreds of voices whispering in unison. The whispering turned into a thunderous song, and the song into a keening scream. The woods blackened, as if someone had put out the moon. Thunder cracked like a giant's clap, and lightning lit up the faces of Len and the shadow—and it was a woman.

All at once, the storm unleashed itself on the forest. Shawn ducked and covered his ears as peals of thunder shook trees down to their roots. Lighting flashed, wind threw the forest into a dancing frenzy, and needle-like rain pierced Shawn's bare face. The woman jumped down and approached Len. As fast as it had begun, the storm lulled and faded away. Shawn lifted his head, still dripping rainwater, and stared with awe at the sky. The black clouds rolled away before his eyes, revealing the crescent moon. *This island must be the center of the Devil's Triangle! These storms are supernatural.*

A weapon flashed in the woman's hand, but Len made no move to free himself. Instead, the prince chanted in a tender voice,

Two Sides of the Coin

"Maiden of the Night, thy brow so pale,
Thy hair as dark as a sea dragon's scale
Maiden of the Night and Thief of Hearts
With eyes like ice, how striking thou art!"

The woman flung her second weapon at Len. As if he were merely brushing away a fly, Len unsheathed his sword halfway and deflected it with a metallic *clang!* The object landed a few feet from Darth's hiding place. It was a throwing star, gleaming with deadly beauty. To Shawn's chagrin, Len merely laughed.

"I have missed you, my eternal beauty," he declared.

The woman seemed to float across the ground towards Len. All her movements were graceful and deliberate as a ballet dancer. She stopped a foot from Len. All the venom was gone from her voice now as she whispered, "And I you."

Their eyes met. She melted against him and kissed his mouth. Shawn stood up to get a better view, hardly believing his own eyes. In one light-speed motion, the women spun towards his hiding place and whipped out an egg-shaped rock. Pain exploded in Shawn's head. He was barely aware of screaming, of falling face-first to the ground, of the smell of decomposing leaves. Then blackness consumed all.

Malia Davidson

Bridge: In Shawn's Absence

Honest Erwin puttered about Matilda's stall with his broom swishing the dust around. Beside him, the fat, little donkey Matilda watched with doleful eyes. He stopped and rubbed her floppy, rabbit-like ears. "There ya go, darlin'. Good as new! I ah- ah-*Achooo!*" He sneezed so hard he stumbled right into the stable door which delivered Erwin into a pile of... well, you don't want to know. He sat up, dazed, and the donkey brayed in amusement.

Nearly hopping with rage, Erwin coughed, sneezed, and shouted, "Gah! Ungrateful critter! I oughta have—*Achoo!*—let those nasty Stallion merchants beat ya 'till your bones showed. *Hack, hack!* Is that the way you treat your unfortunate master? *Achoo!*"

If Erwin's little friends had seen him in this state, they would've been shocked at his words. But when the children peeked into the stable later, they found Honest dumping buckets of water on himself, scrubbing at his dirtied pants, and laughing as Matilda stuck her tongue in his ear. The children giggled at the comical scene. Erwin whirled to face them, bucket on head and broom in hand. "Yaaah! Little rips! Haven't your mothers ever told you not to peek at bathin' people?" he cried in mock astonishment.

The girls blushed, but the boys laughed so hard their sides ached. Erwin removed the bucket from his head and winked at the kids, "Run along to the shop now. I'll make my grand appearance in a few minutes."

The children ran through the alley into the back door of Erwin's shop. It was a wonderful place, full of odd, interesting things. Everywhere you looked, stuff hung from the ceiling and filled the shelves and spilled over the shop counter. The large, glass windows were stuffed with every thingamabob and doohickey you can imagine. On the shop's counter was a bowl of assorted candies. Behind the counter was a huge wooden storage-case that ran from the back door to a flight of stairs in the far wall. None of the various items on the shelves had price tags on them.

Whenever someone asked him, Erwin would answer promptly as if he'd always known it.

The children who came to Fable Friday were all different in many ways, but they were united by their love for Honest Erwin and his stories. They were as young as eight or as old as thirteen. Most of them were children of regular customers. Others, known in town as "street rats," were unknown to anyone. Erwin greeted them all by name. One street boy wouldn't tell anyone his name, so Erwin called him by a different one every time he came in for Fable Friday.

Inside the shop, the children's voices rose in excitement. "It was awful for Honest to leave off last Fable Friday just when it started getting good," said one boy.

An older girl, who was protecting the candy jar from the younger ones, shrugged. "Honest said that that was as far as the story had gotten. What do you think that means?"

Nobody answered, for they were too busy investigating a vicious-looking animal trap hanging in the corner. They debated whether it was real or not, and the boys dared each other to put their finger on the spring. Just then, the door blew open, and a dark figure stood in the doorway brandishing a torch in one hand and a dagger in the other. Several girls screamed. But Erwin (for Erwin it was) lowered his arms and walked in without further grandness. He handed the torch to the children, who realized it was only a clay statue. The dagger was a fake too, but the boys still had fun playing with it (aka, stabbing each other with it).

Finally, Erwin called them together. Like a magnet switched on, the children dropped whatever they were doing and came running to the rug. There was a moment of scooting about before everyone was comfortable. When the room was quiet, Erwin spoke, "I'm afraid we will have to take off another week on the last story."

A universal groan met his words, but a stern look from Erwin and a "Do I have to call Mathilda?" soon quieted them. "What kinda story would you like to hear about?" he asked.

"A war story!" was the boy's immediate response. "Tell us about a great knight."

"Can we have a story about a princess?" begged the girls.

The nameless boy (whom Erwin had dubbed Archimedes today) held up the torch. "I want to know about the torch and dagger. What are they for?"

Erwin patted his head with a fond smile. "Wonderful ideas, children. As a matter of fact, I have a story for you that includes all three ideas." The storyteller placed his wrinkled hands on his knees and began, "Once upon a tragedy, there was a beautiful princess, the only daughter of King Sind of Sea Dragon and his late wife, Queen Eingana."

The girls grinned in delight, while the boys muttered. Erwin wriggled his eyebrows and raised his voice. "Now this princess was very different from others. Different how? Oh, from the moment her little hands closed on the hilt of a dagger she knew that she wanted to be a fighter. At first no one liked the idea. I mean, she was the crown-princess! But eventually even the people who disliked the idea couldn't see any better way."

"From the time she was a child, the princess was graceful, smart-like, and pretty. However, the girl was hostile to almost everybody but her closest servants. Her teachers tried *everything* to help her make friends: sending her around the island, inviting other princesses to the castle, even letting her run free around the city like a common girl. For all their best efforts, the result is that she became good friends with the daughter of King Rubin of Fox, her father's worst enemy." The audience giggled. Erwin laughed along with them, slapped his knee, and declared, "What a gal!"

When it quieted down, he continued, "The princess's teachers were at their wit's end. They presented all their troubles to the king. King Sind considered everything they said. The father realized that his daughter would be much more useful to him as a fighter than an unhappy princess, so he agreed to let her train as a warrior. He found the most skilled swordsmen, archers, and many others to teach her what she needed to know. It wasn't long before she exceeded them all."

"The king's daughter became his tool for dangerous missions. When their region and the Fox's declared the Fifth Blood-war, she became the leader of a group of raiders. She took for herself the symbol of a torch and dagger. Some say her name, Amara, means eternally beautiful. Others say it means eternal wrath. People whispered in the shadows that she had no love in her heart. She was admired by her people and feared by her enemies, and the people called her, 'The loveless one'. But..." Erwin tapped his nose, "little Cupid's arrows find their ways into the coldest of hearts and in the strangest of ways." The children blinked in bafflement.

Erwin lowered his voice. "One dark and stormy night, King Sind called for his daughter. She came into his throne room and knelt. 'Amara, my torch and dagger of wrath,' he said." The children shivered as Erwin's voice changed to imitate the deep, scary voice of the king. "'You are they only one I can trust on such an important mission.' She looked up quickly; her ice blue eyes gleamed with anticipation. The king said, 'The time has come. Those accursed Foxes owe us a blood debt, and this war shall not end until it is paid in full. I send you, daughter, to Castle Fox. This is your mission...'"

* * *

It was as hot as any midsummer night could be. Sleep fell over the whole castle, and even the shadows lay heavily upon the world. In his room in the castle, Len slept deeply with his covers tossed to the side. That evening, he had arrived back home from an exhausting journey. It was so good to be back in a real bed after days of the hard, cold ground.

A shadowy silhouette appeared on his window, blocking the moonlight. Undisturbed, the prince slept on. With great care, the dark phantom cracked each lock on the window. There was no hurry, but as each lock was broken the shadow moved onto the next with steady efficiency. Finally, when all the locks lay scattered over the window sill, it was time enter. Time to kill.

Len did not stir when the window opened. Nor did he awake when the assassin entered his room on cat-like feet. The assassin gazed around Len's room, taking stock of the surroundings. Every piece of furniture, every nook and cranny—nothing was insignificant. Len's bed lay in the corner to the right. The bed was raised off the ground on four legs, and it was a comfortable size for Len even when he stretched out. He looked rather ridiculous, in fact, lying on his belly with one hand drooping over the side. His hair was a mop of bed-head gone wild.

To the assassin's left was a tall mirror. Beside it, hanging from a coat rack, were clothes of all regions: a Cobra-hooded cape and snakeskin belt, a black vest with a crow-feather hat, a coat of thick fur around the collar like a lion's mane, Stallion's loose-fitting pants and tunic specially designed for riding, a deerskin suit and moccasins from Stag, an outfit of perfect camouflage from Hawk, and even a long sleeved, baggy shirt with black leggings, the typical Sea Dragon sailor clothes.

Hanging off the walls was a number of masks. Some seemed overjoyed to see the stranger. Others looked angry enough to bite. One had a comical look of amazement. Another was shedding black tears from its eyeless face. A war-sword, hung on the opposite wall, demanded the stranger's attention next. The sword was double-edged, longer than a person's leg, and the handle was cross-shaped. It was beautifully crafted, but the assassin gave it no more interest than a passing glance. There were two doors. One led to an empty guest room, covered in dust. The other door, of course, adjoined the main hall. There would be no problems as long as everything was done without noise.

The only other furniture was a writing desk near the door, a small table with a stool, and a closet next to Len's bed. *Good,* thought the assassin. *Hardly anything to get in my way.* The midnight attacker stalked back to the window and breathed the biting air. Placing one foot on the window sill, the assassin drew back on the string. Even while training the arrow on Len's head, the assassin mused, *What kind of name is Gilen? It's not even a bit scary.*

It was the sound of the arrow on the string that penetrated Len's senses. He had heard that sound countless times. Every time he drew back the string, always that distinctive sound. Why was he hearing it now? In his room? Nothing else could make that noise! That could only mean... Len came awake the instant the arrow was released.

Sssst—Thwack!

In that moment of realization, Len tucked his head under and somersaulted off his bed. When he came up, he held his hands open defensively. For a second, he was confused by a cloud of white floating about his pillow. It looked as if someone had killed half a dozen birds, there were so many feathers. *Am I dreaming?* He asked himself and found the answer in the unmistakable black line of an arrow sticking out of his pillow. And the source of the arrow… a tall figure halfway out the window.

Len found he was trembling. His first encounter with a midnight attacker, and he wasn't even wearing his boots! "What do you want with me?" he barked.

In reply, the assassin shot a second arrow. Len threw himself to the floor. "I see." He pulled a dagger out from under the table, "You want me *dead!*" He flung the razor-sharp dagger at the figure's head. As if it were nothing but a pebble, the assassin flicked his head to the left. The dagger fell into blackness and a muted *clang* followed its flight.

Furious, Len's attacker pulled three flashing shapes into his fingers and flung them at Len. The prince knocked aside the one aimed at his face, gasping as another sliced his arm. He stumbled against his dresser. In the blink of an eye, the attacker threw another two which pinned Len's tunic to the wood. *Blast!* he thought. *The fiend would have throwing stars!*

The assassin leaped down from the window, drawing a thin, one-edged sword. It was in this motion that the hood fell back. Long, dark locks fell down her back in graceful curls. She had a proud, exotic face, with a tall forehead, sharp chin, and full lips. One of her ears was pierced with a jinx earring in the shape of a crescent moon. Everything about her was sharp, striking. The woman was exactly Len's height, but she seemed to look down on him. All this Len saw in one glance and hardly noticed afterwards. It was the lady's eyes, reflecting the moonlight, which captivated him. They were an impossibly light blue, like a winter sky.

He heaved a world-weary sigh. "Just what I need, another lady out to kill me. Oh why? Why did it have to be a *woman?*" He flopped his free arm dramatically.

"A woman? Is that all you see me as?" the assassin murmured, examining her sword's edge. Her voice was husky and rich as foreign spices.

"I haven't seen much of you at all, really," Len replied. Hidden in the shadows, he inched his hand behind the closet. "Which is what makes it somewhat surprising that you're out to kill me." He searched for it, panicking, until he touched the hilt of his spare sword. Len looked up, grinning, "You wouldn't happen to be related to a certain crow lord, would you?"

She stepped forward and slashed upward at his throat. *Shhink!* Len drew his sword and deflected the strike before it cut him. Without pause, she followed up with a backhanded swing at his legs. Again he moved the sword to block it. This time, however, she twirled her sword in a peculiar motion that resembled a snake curling around its victim. Len's sword clattered to the floor, and she drew back for the final strike.

Hisssss! An arrow whizzed past the assassin's face. She gasped and whirled around to face the doorway. There stood Sylindra.

Never had Len been more delighted to see her. Longbow at ready, she pointed the arrow at the blue-eyed assassin. "Get out."

Keeping her eyes on Sylindra, the assassin slunk backwards with her hand outstretched until she reached the window, where she climbed onto the sill. Before she left, her icy gaze focused on Len. Standing tall, she pointed a finger at him. Her words rung like a bell inside of him, chilling his blood:

"Mark my face clearly. For it will be the last thing you see before you die."

And with that, the night swallowed her whole.

* * *

"Wow," chorused the children, their mouths shaped like O's.

Erwin chuckled at their astonished faces. "I know what you're wondering, now. I'm sure poor Len was wondering the same thing. How on earth had she broken his special, hand-made locks?"

The children laughed. "No! No!"

One boy held up his hands. "Why on earf did she want to keel him?"

"Hmm," Erwin stroked his chin, his eyes twinkling. "Prince Gilen was probably wondering something like that too. Anyways, when the mysterious stranger jumped out the window, neither the prince nor princess relaxed a muscle until they both checked outside. Len could just barely see her flying gracefully away from the castle until the darkness covered her. I gotta tell you, boys and girls, the prince was no coward. He feared no man or beast on this island. But on that fateful night he found himself shaking... not in his boots though, which made it even worse. That very hour he went to see the queen and king."

* * *

Len fidgeted outside his parents' room. When he had asked a servant to go awake them, the servant's expression became the picture of horror. "N-now?" he stammered. "B-but I can't! Begging your pardon, sir prince—that is *quite* impossible for me!"

Len grabbed the unhappy servant by his shoulders, raising his voice. "Impossible? This is a matter of life and death. Have courage, man!" He added in a gentler tone, "Anyways, my father has a policy about not killing the messenger. As long as you stand behind the door, I'm sure you'll survive." Giving the man an encouraging pat, he sent him off.

Now here Len stood. He had pulled a robe over his nightclothes and finally got his boots back on. In his mind, however, he was still replaying the past hour in his head. The memory of when she arrived and left was foggy, like a photograph blurred around the edges. But those amazing, terrifying moments when they were close enough to touch were crystal clear.

Len remembered gripping the sword hilt in his hands and the numbing shock when they had clashed blades. He could hear them grunt in exertion, see her flashing eyes, feel her breath on his neck. Gazing into her face as her blade whipped around, he had never seen anything more terrifying... or beautiful. The whole time he relived the scene, her final words repeated in his thoughts.

Mark my face clearly.

Len wanted to scream, "*I have! And now I can't get it out of my head!*"

The door opened, rousing Len from his thoughts. His father, King Rubin, stood in the doorway. He was dressed in a rich purple tunic with gold around the collar and sleeves. The king looked as though he had not been sleeping at all. Len wondered what they'd been doing. Then again, some things are better left unknown.

Rubin nodded. "Gilen, you may come in." Len followed him inside.

The room was simple yet elegant. In the middle of the room was a table with three tall chairs. To his left was their large, sink-into-the-mattress-O-so-comfortable bed. There was a pitcher of water in the corner for washing, and a goblet of wine with two cups of the purest silver.

Rising up to the ceiling in the middle of the back wall was a great, tall door of clear glass. Len could see nothing but black outside. The door led to a small stone balcony. On either side of the door were two old lanterns. The glass of the lanterns was dyed such a dark blue it appeared black, but with a flame inside the lanterns glowed with a ghostly light that would give you shivers. To Len's right were two walk-in closets for the king and queen's wardrobe, and between the rooms hung a double-edged battleaxe.

His mother was curled up in one of the tall, plushy chairs. Like the king, she appeared perfectly awake. Unlike the king, she was anything but calm. Len could sense her emotions like boiling water under a lid. Len and his father sat down.

There was a moment of a silence as Len gathered his thoughts. He took a deep breath and stated, "An assassin broke into my room tonight."

Queen Alexi let out her breath. "Is that *all?*" Both men stared at her. Rubin leaned back in his chair and laughed: not his typical evil laugh, although Len certainly felt victimized by it. The queen rolled her eyes.

"Did you even hear me?" Len cried. "A woman broke in and tried to kill me!"

That silenced them. "You didn't mention it was a woman," said the king. "That changes things."

"Tell us everything, Gilen," said the queen.

Two Sides of the Coin

Len told them what had happened from the moment he fell asleep that night to when he ordered the terrified servant to wake the royalty. His parents listened without interrupting, their faces unreadable. When he finished, Rubin spoke first, "It sounds like the assassin meant what she said. It is strange... Are you sure did not recognize her?"

"No, not really," Len frowned in concentration. "Come to think of it, her face was familiar somehow. Maybe I could've gotten a better look if Sylindra hadn't chased her—Oh, Sylindra!" He snapped his fingers. "That it! I saw her once at one of Sylindra's parties."

Len recalled the day very well. After all, his sister had all but banished him from the castle while she prepared the party. He was around sixteen, but fifteen-year old Sylindra acted like she was years older. She would've liked him to stay away entirely, but he was curious to see what sort of people could be friends with his sister.

Some of them he recognized as various princesses of the other regions, but there was one girl who arrived later than the rest that he didn't recognize. She kept to herself and said little the whole party. When Len tried to go make her acquaintance, she turned her back on him, not once, but three times. Finally, Len shouted after her, "What are you, deaf? You might just let me introduce myself before you decide to hate me."

She faced him. "Oh, were you talking to me? I thought that was an *insect* buzzing about the room. It seems I am not too far off." At that, Sylindra's party guests hid smiles behind their fans, although a good deal of them didn't even try to hide giggles.

Len wanted to say something clever, to make the perfect comeback. Yet he found himself, for the first time in years, completely lost for words. He stalked from the room. An explosion of laughter could be heard as soon as he slammed the door shut.

Three years later, the prince was a knight. He had been given his wings, made his own sword, and traveled across the island from the crags of Mt. Mordoom to the wave-beaten shore of Cobra. Through the treacherous Stag forest, into the western regions of Lion, Stallion, and Hawk he had lived. Len had passed through Sea Dragon several times (each under a different name) and toured the Crow's capital city. He had watched the seasons pass, the moon wane and rise. Then, the full moon. Oh, the full moon! What joy was his the first time he flew across the ocean and kidnapped his first "damsel in distress."

It seemed so long ago that an arrogant teen had taunted Len to his face. Now it was worse, much worse. *Goes to show that people who don't respect you won't mind killing you as well,* thought Len. He leaned back in his chair. "So, O wise parents of mine, what should I do?"

Alexi looked at Rubin. The king looked back at her. It was like they were communicating with their eyes. Then Rubin folded his hands on the table. "It's quite simple really. You must try to kill *her* before she kills *you.*"

* * *

Erwin got to his feet and stretched. "Oofta! Time for a break."

Immediately, all the children set up a chorus of protests. "Awwww! No, no, you can't stop there! Hon-est!" Without blinking, Erwin shuffled behind the counter to assist a customer. They began to chat, while the children squirmed. In all, there were around twelve of them. It was a miracle they could all fit on the bearskin rug.

Several of the children got up to look around Erwin's shop, and the others soon followed their example. The atmosphere in the shop was as cozy as a rat-nest. There were always wonderful, bizarre things around Honest Erwin's place. First, they went to examine the puppets hanging in the wide, glass window. Some were the type that could dance around on strings. Others would fit on your hand so you could mime all the actions. Giggling, the children began a game of their own with the string puppets.

"My boots! Where are my boots?" squealed a boy, dancing his puppet on the floor.

Another girl pranced her doll beside him. "Well, hi, brother! Do you need help finding your boots, or should I release you from the wall first?"

The woman who came into the shop was a regular customer. She carried with her a few jars of spiced-apple jam and fresh bread. Erwin laid out his goods, and they began to barter back and forth. The woman was alternately sweet and sour with Erwin. Several times she called him a thief, to which Erwin would hold up his hands and say, "Now, now! We mustn't get insulting. Erwin's *always* honest with his friends, see?"

Finally, they made the trade, though the woman's face showed that she was not altogether pleased. As she left, Erwin called after her, "Thank yew kindly, my most wise and ahem, *beautiful* customer."

"Oh!" She slammed the door behind her. The children looked up from their game in surprise.

One little girl with two black pig-tails asked. "Why is she so mad at you, Honest?"

Erwin rummaged underneath the countertop, making quite a clanging, crashing racket. He hollered over the din, "Heh, she always pretends to be mad—" *Crraaash!* "—when she knows she's got a good deal." *Clang!* "But she adores me, truly." *Thump!* "Ow!"

Honest Erwin said this of all the women who entered his store, though he claimed that the women themselves would never admit it. Erwin was not exceedingly vain, but modesty obviously wasn't his strong point either. It was true that the storekeeper/storyteller was rather handsome, as older gentlemen go. He was simultaneously a lovable gentleman and an outrageous flirt. Whenever the older women of the town got together for their quilting parties, they would gossip and shake their heads at Erwin's strange ways. "Oh, dear Honest," they would say. "He's a darling, old bother, isn't he?"

Erwin stashed his goods safely away before seating himself once again on the little plush stool. The children flew from all directions to sit down as if there wasn't a moment to spare. Honest cleared his throat and began again, "Now where were we, children? Ah, right. The king had told Len that the only way to resolve this problem was to fight fire with fire, as it were. Now of course, the prince didn't like this idea much, no siree. He'd never killed a person before, and to go after a woman, well, it seemed to him like the opposite of all he'd ever been taught. Luckily, Len didn't have to make that decision right away. For the next few weeks, everything was peaceful, as if there had never been an attack.

Of course, the castle servants discussed the rumor of it in whispers. They didn't dare breathe a word of it outside the castle, for fear of the royalty."

"Then how did you learn about it if them servants didn't breathe a word?" Archimedes pointed out.

Erwin cackled and slapped his knee. "Bright one, aincha? That's a good 'un, boy! Don't you worry about how I know it. Doesn't make much difference, does it?"

Whether it made a difference or not, Erwin quickly moved the subject away. "Well, as I was saying, Len didn't like the idea of trying to assassinate the assassin. But when a month passed and no phantom of the night arose to strike again as she had promised, naturally Len began to wonder. Then one day his parents announced that they and their royal guard and servants would be going on a diplomatic visit to the Stallion region. Everything went smoothly until the night before they would arrive back home." Erwin dropped his voice to a whisper, "That night, when the whole party was asleep, a shadowy figure strode into their camp, torch in hand."

"Ohhhh!" gasped the children.

"Well, let me tell ya, they must've been sleeping like babies, for not one person awoke when Len's tent was set on fire. Ironically, what saved their lives were the horses they'd just bought from Stallion. Yeah! Them horses went wild of fright from the fire, all rearing and screaming so as to wake the countryside for miles around. Of course, all the servants were runnin' willy-nilly with buckets of water, but the fire was so out of control they thought Len was a goner!"

Erwin's voice rose, and the children all leaned forward, their eyes round as shekels. "Meanwhile, Len awoke to an inferno of heat and smoke. At once, he grabbed his sword and began to slash the burning material away. Oh! Hardly had he begun to do so when he heard the sound of the wooden props of the tent crack. The fire was about to fall right on top of him! With one last slash, he cut off a square of the tent wall. He dove out of there just as the tent collapsed and was unceremoniously dunked with a freezing bucket of water."

The children laughed and sighed in relief. Erwin wiped his brow as if he could still feel the heat of the fire on his face. "That wasn't the only

Two Sides of the Coin

close call Len had. The assassin simply would not give up. Sometimes she attacked him within a week. Sometimes she waited several weeks, even a month. Each time she slipped away before Len could so much as look at her. Len's parents put restrictions on him for his own safety. He was not supposed to leave the castle without a guard, and a knight always slept outside his door. Of course, this rankled with the prince. He was a knight after all, not a boy! So one day he ups and sneaks out of the castle for a hunt in the forest. After so many attempts on his life, it was pure foolishness, of course. However, it was then that strange things began to happen..."

* * *

Len marched through the thick undergrowth, spirits high. He was free! He cared not that he made a horrendous noise. In fact, he wanted to perform the Crow's Concerto right there, a spirited dance that involves a great deal of leaping and flapping your arms in the air. After he had so cleverly lost the guard assigned to him, he had succeeded in slipping from the castle without hindrance. Now he was free as a bird, and the sky had never looked so beautiful.

The prince stopped to take a deep breath. Enough gloating. It was time to come back to reality. He had brought no food except for a skin of wine, no flint stones, no blankets, and no money. His plan was to shoot some animal, preferably a buck, and smoke the meat. On that alone, he might live away from the castle for at least twenty days. Len's mouth watered. He would need more than meat though. He made a mental note to check on that huge, wild grape orchard he'd found last year for ripe fruit. The prince could hardly wait to get started, but first he had to get a safe distance from Castle Fox. Len looked over the map in his head. He had departed from the west wall and traveled several miles at a near run, so he must be in the Faegan Forest. If he continued in this direction, he should soon hit Fox Run Brook. Len increased his pace, his boots crunching the fallen leaves.

The late summer air was heavy with moisture. The terrain, like most forests, was difficult and uneven. Fallen logs, low branches, and thick vines created a veritable obstacle course. Up ahead, the ground rose steeply. Len didn't mind the tough traveling; it allowed him to think more deeply as he ignored his body's complaints. The sound of water tumbling down stones awoke Len from his reverie. Grinning, he trotted through the trees to the brook's edge. Oh, how inviting the water looked! The prince dipped his hands in the water, but didn't drink. This stream was flowed from a lake rather than an underground spring, making it unsafe to drink. That didn't stop him from dunking his head once or twice.

Refreshed, Len murmured, "Time to tighten my belt and get to work." He knew that his best chances of finding a deer nearby would be to discover tracks in the mud where it had come to drink. From there it was only a matter of tracking, which Len was an expert at. He shuffled along the brook side, bent over like an old man. Tracks of raccoons, opossums, squirrels, rabbits, skunks, and foxes crisscrossed like a puzzle. Seeing the fresh tracks of a grizzly bear, Len froze. He became part of the stillness, until even the shyest birds emerged, played in the brook, and sang. Reassured by their carefree conversation, Len resumed his hunt. He found several deer tracks within half an hour, but beside the tracks of every adult were the smaller prints of a fawn or two. Although it would be very tasty, a fawn didn't have enough meat to satisfy the hunter. He was intent on finding a buck, or perhaps a young doe.

Finally, after about an hour of searching, Len spotted a lone pair of fresh deer tracks. He followed them away from the water's edge until they disappeared. Still the prince kept following a trail invisible to all but him. Faster and faster, the prince strode on, silent as a forest spirit. The trail led him to a small clearing, the buck's final destination. Without breaking his step, Len pulled the long bow off his shoulder and set an arrow on the string. The cautious animal continued to graze, his magnificent rack of antlers bobbing. Len stole to a hiding place behind a wall of thin trees and knelt there. For a minute, he waited for the deer to get closer.

Len wasn't the bragging sort of person. Therefore, before we go on, I must brag a bit for him. Len was a dead shot with both the longbow and the crossbow. Years of pulling back the string, (if you have never pulled back a bow string, you wouldn't believe how hard it is) had strengthened his arms and shoulders. He could shoot while running and riding a horse. Len was very confident about his ability. Thus we may forgive him his moment of quiet triumph, as he held the arrow ready to shoot down the buck. He could already taste the delicious steaks of venison.

Unfortunately, that moment of hesitation was all that was needed to ruin his happy dream. With a hiss like a giant wasp, the buck toppled to the ground with an arrow in its neck. Len's mouth fell open. He checked the weapon in his hands to make sure the arrow was still on the string. Someone had killed *his* buck! The thought made Len close his mouth so he could clench his teeth. How dare they steal his lunch? Although Len hated using the royalty card, he did have the right to take the deer from anyone who was not royalty or a knight. Having come to this conclusion, Len was about to step out and call for the person to show himself. Once again, he was beat to it by a moment. Also once again, Len was left speechless. The person who stepped out was *the woman*.

In the daylight, she was no less lovely. She wore a tunic of deep blue with embroidered dragons on the sleeves and around the collar. Her legs were covered by black leggings and a short, brown skirt that fell to her thigh. Over her shoulders she wore a black hoodless cloak with a silver clasp. She carried a knife in one hand, and a bow in the other. Her bow was half the size of Len's, used for hunting at close quarters.

As before, Len was transfixed by the woman's face. It was she who had once said, *"Mark my face clearly, for it will be the last thing you see before you die."* Though he had never glimpsed her since that fateful night, he remembered. As much as he wished, there was absolutely no mistaking those ice-blue eyes. She was the assassin. While Len's mind whirled, the woman strode to the deer and nudged it with her bow. Satisfied, she knelt beside it and set to work cleaning the carcass with her knife.

It took a whole minute for Len's hazy mind to grasp that she didn't know he was there. Len felt absurdly proud about this, until he realized his precarious position. All it took was a mere glance in the right direction, and she would see him kneeling behind the trees. There was no way he could sneak away without detection. Only three choices presented themselves: escape by running or flight (and show himself a coward), step out boldly and challenge her (although he knew her knife throwing skills quite well) or, worst of all, use the arrow meant for the buck to finish this once and for all.

The maiden continued her gruesome work, unaware of any danger. She began to sing an old sailor song which she had known since she was a little girl. Len, in an agony of indecision, found himself lifting his head in a soundless gasp as the lady burst into song. If her normal voice sounded like exotic spices, then her singing sounded like rich wine. When she sang, the woman smiled and half-closed her eyes. With every word, Len was entranced by the Sea Dragon accent. It lent a rolling, passionate feeling to the otherwise simple song. The song created a picture in Len's mind of a ship sailing on and on across the restless waves. He tried to turn his mind back to reality, but in the end he merely listened.

Waves crashing, calling, crying
A heartbeat that knows no end.
My first love was she
The beautiful, endless sea.

Then I met the North Star
And I fell in love a second time
Her eyes were sapphires
Her heart the ocean I drowned in.

Shall I be a lonely albatross
Forever to fly the seas alone?
Or forsake my first love
And furl my sails forever?

But when the tide came in,
My Star was swept away.
I sail in darkness now
Wondering what might have been.

As gently as the wind in the trees, she sang.

*Waves crashing, calling, crying
My love's eternal heartbeat*

The silence after she had finished was complete. Even the birds seemed afraid to sing. The trees rustled in unison, as if to say, *"shhhhhh"* to Len's pounding heart.

Then, like a discordant instrument in an otherwise perfect orchestra, a twig snapped in the woods to Len's left. At the wink of an eye, the lady jumped to her feet, drawing an arrow taut on the bow. She waited there for half a minute. Only when a squirrel went scrabbling up a tree did she return to her work. Len knew he could not wait any longer. Raising the bow, he eased back on the string so it made no noise. He took aim, closed his eyes, and released the arrow. The string twanged.

There was a sharp gasp. Following that was a silence even worse. With self-loathing aching in every bone of his body, Len forced his eyes open. There was a limp bundle lying on the ground underneath the lady's cloak. The prince stumbled out of his hiding place. "No... What have I done?" He lifted the edge of the cloak and saw... a deer carcass.

You can breathe again, reader.

For being fooled so easily, Len caught on at once. Without hesitation, he drew his sword. Like an echo, another sword came unsheathed. Len spun on his heel. Charging at him out of the woods, clenching the hilt of the naked blade with both hands, the assassin screamed a war-cry. Len jumped over the deer's body, followed by the lady. They faced each other. The sky darkened, and the wind sounded harsh now as it rattled through the trees. Len and the woman circled, bouncing on the balls of their feet. At the crash of thunder, she attacked.

This was a confrontation Len had looked forward to for months. The assassin was a worthy opponent. She wielded her sword as if it weighed as much as a stick. Attacking and defending are two sides of the same coin, and this lady carried that coin in her pocket. Whenever an obstacle appeared, she didn't just avoid it but used it to her advantage. Her only struggle was to mask her emotions. Strike for strike, block for block, insult for insult, they asked for no ground and gave each other none. Sometimes they clashed head on and exchanged so many blows it seemed impossible that neither of them were killed. Mostly they circled, eyes locked. Len was drenched in sweat after only a few minutes. Every lesson he'd ever learned during his training, every move his father had taught him—it all came back with clarity. He would not be beaten.

Pain shot up from their hands at every sword-clash. For every three beats, their heart skipped a beat. It was pure madness, and they loved every moment of it. If any commoner or even you or I had seen these two, we should surmise instantly (and correctly) that the prince and the woman were intent on destroying the other. If a knight's apprentice saw them, he would be awed by the sheer grace of their sparring. Indeed, the prince and the assassin moved as one. He might guess that these were close friends practicing their swordsmanship. However, if an experienced knight could see them, he would say with certainty, "These two have become more than enemies. Now it seems one cannot do without the other. They aren't merely fighting. They're *dancing*."

After a particularly fierce exchange, the two pulled apart. They panted for air, and both were wounded—but nothing too serious. The woman let the tip of her sword fall for a moment. "You remember the night we first met?" she asked breathlessly, her cold gaze drilling into Len. "I could've killed you right away, but I didn't." She lunged forward with a backwards swing at Len's neck.

He ducked and came up beside her. "Well, why didn't you?"

They exchanged a few blows before she responded, "It was too easy."

This time he charged at her, sword outstretched. She deflected his sword and spun to the side. Suddenly they were back to back, twisting their sword to strike, staying close against each other, and moving, always moving. The lady landed an elbow in his ribs, and Len used the momentum to roll forward. When he came back on his feet, he blurted out, "Remember when you were singing as you cut up the deer? I could've killed you then too."

She raised an eyebrow. "Why didn't you?"

Len didn't have an answer for that, so he used hers. "Too easy."

For the next countless minutes, the assassin fought with more fervor than ever, as if to make one last, desperate attempt. Not until they were covered in wounds and could hardly lift their swords did they draw back again, gasping. The woman paced a few feet away to catch her breath. "You know," Len grunted, "there's a danger to waiting to strike each down simply because it's too easy. By engaging each other, we risk becoming friends." He chuckled at his own joke.

With her back to Len and her long, black hair creating a wall between them, the woman glanced at him from the corner of her eye. He thought he had never seen anyone look so beautiful, smudged with dirt and sweat though she was. A feverish shiver overtook him, starting at the tip of his scalp until it reached his toes. The lady faced him, both hands grasping her sword. The look on her face was as innocent as a baby. Cocking her head, she murmured, *"Just* friends?"

Len gulped. Twirling her sword in one hand, the woman sheathed it at her waist, raised a hand to her mouth, and giggled. To add to Len's confusion, she bounded into the forest from whence she came and disappeared. It took him a full minute to hear the sound of hoof beats, shouts, and whinnies in the distant woods. Len sighed at the sudden emptiness he felt when the presence of the blue-eyed assassin was gone.

The search-party discovered the prince seated by the carcass of the buck, cleaning it and humming to himself. The soldiers thundered out of the trees to surround Len with their stomping horses. He grinned. "Anyone for an early dinner?" In reply, a row of arrows pointed in his direction. He ignored the weapons and continued chopping up the deer. The captain, a stout man with an impressive, black goatee, growled at Len, "Sir, with all due respect, cease that idiotic humming and mount your horse this instant."

To everyone's open-mouthed surprise, Len did just that. He stood up, threw the bag of deer meat in the saddlebag, and hopped onto the horse faster than you can say, "That's it?" As soon as he was in the saddle, he was flanked on all sides by the soldiers. The captain took the lead, glancing over his shoulder at Len and the soldiers every so often. Together they trekked back through the woods, over the Fox Run Brook, and across the western field to the castle. All the time they walked, the soldiers were on edge, convinced the prince had something up his sleeve. Even the captain was nervous. The prince said not a word the whole journey. The expression on his face was not one of resentment, boredom, disappointment, or even that smug I-can-escape-any-time-I-feel-like-it look. Instead, he smiled in a dreamy sort of way.

It was just too easy...

* * *

"And that is that," proclaimed Erwin. He slapped his hands against his knees and pushed himself up with a huff. The children watched him like vultures, knowing what always came after the story. Erwin crouched behind the counter, fumbled around, and cried in horror, "Oh, no! *The snacks!* Matilda, how could you?"

Half the kids came running. The other half echoed Erwin. "Oh, no..."

"Surprise!" Erwin popped up like a jack-in-the-box. "I hid an extra plate of gingersnaps since I knew how much Matilda likes 'em!"

The children laughed, suddenly aware of how silly they must have looked. Soon Erwin was swamped with children scrabbling for the cookies. They had no reason to fear though, for Erwin made enough for them all to have three of the sweet, spicy, little cookies. Amid the contented munching that followed, they drifted back to the rug.

Archimedes asked around a mouthful of cookie, "Aren't chew supposed to," he paused to gulp, "say 'The End' at the end of a story?"

"Of course, of course. But this particular story has no end yet," Erwin replied.

"What happened afterward with Amara and Gilen?"

"Did they stop fighting and be friends?" questions popped up all around.

Erwin held out his hands to quiet them down. "Well, children, I cannot answer all your questions. But I will say this: Amara and Gilen will never stop fighting each other. Never! They're born rivals. Heheh, but who said anything about being enemies? Naw, they just can't help liking each other. How different they are, and yet they fit together like a glove," Erwin intertwined his fingers. "At this point, it seems impossible for them to ever be together." He grinned, "*That's* why I said the story is not over! Nay, it continues to this day. Heh, that rhymes."

"Good one, Honest!" laughed the children.

As each child left the shop and went to their respective homes, they couldn't help wondering. Wondering what was happening in this story at that minute. Perhaps they will find out next Fable Friday. However, reader, we are bound by no such lines of time or distance—all it takes is the turn of a page.

CHAPTER 10

Rocks, Love, and Other Dangers

Shawn's first thought when he woke up was surprisingly not a question but an observation: *There's a bug crawling up my back.*

Shawn sat up, cried, "Eck!" and batted the huge bug off. It was the kind of bug one would see only in pictures: a rhinoceros beetle. The bug's black armor flashed in the sunlight. It had six long, grotesque legs with hooks at the end. The scariest thing of all, of course, was the hideous horn on its head that extended at least three inches.

The bug stared at Shawn. The reporter stared back. Slowly, he grabbed a thin stick and poked it. The rhinoceros beetle jerked towards the hapless reporter and hissed. Shawn dropped the stick with a scream. "Gyahh! It hissed at me! Len!!!"

Just then, the enormous bug turned around and waddled into the tall grass as if to say, "You're not worth my time." Shawn was safe, for the moment.

Lifting his head, he looked around him for the first time. Tall grass, dry and wispy, surrounded him on all sides. One of his boots was buried deep in the grass, and his other pressed down on his cape and saddle which had been made into a makeshift bed. A little ways away the two horses grazed together, their tales swishing back and forth. In all directions of the field, it ended where the ground rose until it was nearly vertical. *We're in a valley,* Shawn realized, *and I have no idea how we got here.* As far as he could see was golden grass, rocky bluffs, and beyond those more forest. There was no sign of human life... except perhaps for that lump of blankets snoring a yard or so to his right.

Shawn took in all this at a glance. Out of the corner of his eye, he was blinded by a flash of sunlight. Awoken by the light, his forehead suddenly throbbed with pain. Shawn reached up and brushed his fingers against the rough bandage around his head. "What's this?" he asked aloud. To add injury upon injury, his whole body complained of the long ride he had apparently taken, though Shawn could hardly summon up the memory of last night at all. He lay back down on the blanket and squeezed his eyes shut against the persisting sunlight. *Of course, on the very day I have a headache the size of Texas the sun decides to shine. Typical.*

Wondering where he had gotten such a voracious headache, Shawn tried to pull together his befuddled thoughts. The memory hit him like a second ray of light. He jerked upright as everything came back to him: traveling through the forest, meeting Sylindra, following Len into the woods, and then... that woman had knocked him out with a rock! This explained the splitting headache.

In Sanfran Cisco, a realization like that would've made the reporter almost lose his wits. Here on the Island of Darkness he did not react beyond a shudder. Still, he had a lot of questions for Len. It was quite an odd feeling, going to wake up the prince. Usually it was the other way around. Shawn nudged the prince and was rewarded by a muted growl. "Len, wake up! It's morning. Don't we have to get going or something?"

Len's head appeared from under the blanket. His tangled hair was full of dirt and grass. There were dark lines under his eyes, and his chin was bristly with unshaved hair. Shawn however, was not one to judge. He probably looked just as bad. Len sat up and yawned, rubbing his eyes. "Blasted sunlight," he muttered.

"Good morning to you too," said Shawn with a grin.

Len gave him a look that wiped the grin from his face. Grumbling, the prince got up, waded through the grass to the horses, and rummaged through their packs. "Rossow," he called, "make yourself useful collecting some wood. A good fire and some breakfast will give us a better start to the day, eh?"

Thirty minutes, five tries with the flint stones, and a few sharp arguments later, Len and Shawn sat eating biscuits, cheese, and coffee over the meek fire. Despite the grim beginning, Len's words proved true. Breakfast lightened their moods considerably. Shawn cleared his throat. "Sorry about last night. It was pretty stupid to follow you after you told me to stay."

Len stopped eating and blinked at Shawn. "You are a strange fellow. Yes, it was stupid to follow me, but I would have done the same thing. On the whole, I am actually rather proud of you. It is your own self you should be apologizing to for getting yourself caught." He licked his fingers and added, "Not like you had a chance anyway."

Shawn didn't know whether to smile or frown. He asked the question that he'd been dying to ask for the past half hour, "Who was that woman?"

Len said nothing for a bit. Stuffing the last bit of food in his mouth, he continued to stall by stirring the fire's embers. Finally he spoke. "Many years ago, before I was born, a grand ball was hosted by one of the crow-lords, who are richer than kings. It would take me days to give credit to the glory of that ball. There was an orchestra with one hundred players, a ten-course banquet, lords and ladies garbed in dresses made purely of gold, and thousand other distinguished guests. This was a party to remember. It seemed every region tried to outdo the other in extravagance."

"Such dancing you could hardly imagine! The dance floor was larger than an arena, with diamond chandeliers dangling high above. They played a famous dance from every region except Stag."

"Why not Stag?" Shawn asked.

Len chuckled a bit. "Well, Stag's most famous dance involves jumping over a bonfire."

"Oh."

"Continuing with my story... to look into that ball room was almost overwhelming. The ladies' dresses shimmered and sparkled with jewels as the men spun them around. Music, rich and dreamy, swelled in the air. Delicious smells drifted from the kitchen to set your mouth watering. Amid all this cacophony of sights and sound, *it* happened. A woman sauntered up to a table where the new king of Sea Dragon sat drinking his punch with a solemn face, as if in quiet defiance of the festive mood. His attention was pulled to where she stood, and no one could blame him for noticing the lady. Her dress was the color of fire; indeed, it was made to look like leaping flames. The sleeves were long and thin, with a train of scarlet falling from her wrists. Mostly made up of reds and oranges, the front of the dress was embroidered with a golden phoenix."

Scribble, scribble, scribble... Shawn wrote as fast as he could to catch all these details. In full story-teller mode, Len used different voices for the woman and the king.

"The woman had a hand on her hip, and a smile tugged at her lips. Sind turned in his chair to address her. 'Is there something you wish of me?'"

She laughed. 'Nothing escapes you, does it, my lord? I am in need of a partner for this next dance. It is the dance of the Fox and Hunter. Do you not know it?'

'Aye, that I do. However, I have no wish to participate in anything from the *Fox* region,' the way Sind said it made it seem like a curse word.

'Ah, I see,' said the lady. 'In that case, you may be the Hunter, determined to hunt down the Fox and take his life. You are a mighty hunter, a great warrior, and a leader such as this island has never seen.' Her voice was gentle, and her manner almost playful.

Sind, unmindful of her compliments, caught her wrist in a crushing grip. 'I *will* hunt down the Fox,' he vowed.

She bared her teeth. 'Catch me if you can.' With a fierce twist of her wrist, she broke loose and ran to the dance floor as the music rang out through the hall. Sind took his place beside her, and the dance began."

"Now, this dance starts the same, but the outcome is always different. The man and woman who dance it together are dancing a story. It begins with the Hunter, strong and proud, who swears he will chase down and catch the legendary Silver Fox. So the Hunter leaps and twirls, stamping his feet and clapping his hands. The music rings forth triumphantly with the sound of horns and drums. At the end of his solo he poses with his arm pointing to the Fox." Len stretched out his hand and made a surprised face. Shawn had never met a more eloquent, in depth story-teller.

Len continued, dropping his voice to a murmur, "Then the Fox comes to life. She does the same dance, except with all the grace and silence of a forest nymph. Now the music is gentle, patient. A flute plays the leading melody, with mandolins plucking the strings at each step of the Fox. Having finished her solo, the Fox freezes to the sound of squealing violins." Len's voice sharpened. "The Hunter and the Fox look face to face for a tense second, and it seems as though the world has stopped breathing. At the sound of a symbol crash, the chase begins!"

"What do you mean, the chase? I thought this was a dance," said Shawn.

Len rubbed his chin. "How can I explain it to you? Tell me, have you ever played a game called barbarians?"

"No."

"Well then, I will describe it to you. What you must do is grab hands with another person and, without letting go, try to touch their toes with your foot without getting tagged yourself. You soon find yourself jumping about like a maniac, trying not to get touched, and moving your feet as fast as any crow dancer could go. Besides making you look like a fool, it is a dreadfully fun game."

"The chase is somewhat like that game, except different in every sense. The Fox tries not to get touched by the Hunter, nor the Hunter by the Fox. However, every leap, gesture, and dodge are made to look like part of the dance. During this part, the music now is a mixture of the triumphant horns and the beautiful flute, but both are now played at a breakneck pace against the thundering beat of the drums. Faster and faster, this beat grows the whole time."

"Finally, the end is near," Len lifted his hands. "The music comes to a climax, and the Hunter has one chance to catch the elusive Fox. If he touches her, she will fall to the ground. But if he does not touch her, he is the one who falls to the ground in defeat. After the crash of cymbal," Len clapped his hands together, "the music ebbs away into nothingness.

That, Rossow, is my region's dance, and a more challenging one you would have a hard time finding."

He took a deep breath and continued the story, "With the dance ended, no one dared speak at first. A loud, angry voice shattered that stillness. *'It was you the whole time!* The betrothed of King Rubin, soon to be Queen of Fox! How dare you, vixen?' The king of Sea Dragon shook his fist at the woman, Alexi herself, who had escaped his hand.

'Yes, I have won, Sind,' she declared. 'I am the vixen you were unable to catch.'

He took a step towards her. 'You'll pay for this!'

'How do you plan to do that, Sind?' A voice shouted from the crowd. 'Will you poison her, like you did my father?' A man burst onto the floor, fury written all over his face. He stepped between Sind and his betrothed. The crowd buzzed with excitement. It was Rubin, newly crowned King of Fox.

'You think I did that?' Sind scoffed and unsheathed his black sword. "You lying fox!' Rubin drew his sword and within the space of a second, they were clashing blades right there on the dance floor. Some of the crowd cheered for Rubin, others for Sind. But they'd only fought for a minute before the fight was broken up by the master of the party. 'Take your battles elsewhere, my lords,' he told them."

"Simmering with anger, King Sind stalked out, but not before calling, 'This is war!'

'To the death,' Rubin agreed. And that is how the blood war began which continues to this day."

"That's it?" asked Shawn, his pencil pausing midway through a sentence. All the questions he had jotted down in the margins throughout the story's telling slipped out of his mind at Len's declaration. The reporter held up his hands. "The war was sparked by a *dance?*"

Len glared at him. "Don't be stupid. Our regions had already been fighting for years. They were just beginning to settle down when my grandfather died of poison, and that was what sparked another war."

"How many wars have there been?"

"Oh, it's just been one continuous fight, really, for the past fifty year."

"That's insane. What happened fifty years ago?"

Len shrugged. "Everybody's been asking those very same questions for years but to no avail. It seems like we have always been enemies of the Sea Dragons, but it isn't so. Why, a hundred years ago, we were allies. That was during the civil war of Sea Serpent, when it split into Cobra and Sea Dragon."

"Alas, something changed," Len explained with a sigh. "It probably started with little misunderstandings, or perhaps someone was really out to make trouble. People who lived by the border found animals missing from their barns or food stolen from their cellars—little things like that. But when the common folk began to point fingers, the dilemma turned worse. A Sea Dragon merchant was robbed by Fox warriors, and his goods destroyed. A group of Sea Dragon lumbermen were found cutting down our trees and hauling them away for ship-wood."

"I see!" Shawn interrupted. "The more problems that happened, the more bitter feeling sprang up between the regions. It's like a snowball rolling down the hill. As it rolls, it gets bigger and bigger until it flattens somebody!"

"Precisely," said Len in a pleased voice. "Once the fighting began, there was no stopping it. It got so bad that when the two kings of Sea Dragon and Fox visited each other to discuss peaceful negotiations, they ended up in a fist fight! Ever since, the regions have been leaping at each other's throats and retreating to lick their wounds. All this trouble came to a climax at the ball."

Shawn scratched his head in bafflement. "I still don't understand why she would do such a thing unless she was deliberately trying to start a war."

"Maybe so, but there is still more to the story. My mother Alexi is the daughter of a great knight who lived in a prosperous town called Gale. One night, there was a raid on Gale by the knights from Sea Dragon, and they were led by King Sind himself. You see, they blamed this city and especially Alexi's father for poisoning the River Dagon earlier that month. Dagon flows right into the capital city and is the main water source for the people."

Shawn whistled under his breath.

"Consequently, they ransacked the town, drove out all the people, and then burned it to the ground. Talk about sweet revenge, aye? In addition, they captured the knight and his wife. His only daughter Alexi, however, evaded capture."

"What happened to her family?"

Len pressed his lips together before replying. "They were imprisoned in Ravenlocke. Only Alexi managed to escape. She led the people of Gale to Thonfirm herself, and there my father met her. He fell head over heels for her, and after many months of wooing, he brought a black rose to her. She—"

"Black rose?"

"Yes, O petrified parrot," Len returned. "That is a story for another time. Suffice it to say that the presentation of a black rose to a lady means you wish her to be your wife."

"Ahh…"

"The first time my father proposed, Alexi utterly rejected him."

Shawn couldn't believe it. "Wh-what? You mean, she said *no* to the *king*?"

"Aye," Len nodded. "Five months later, he asked again, and she said no."

"Ouch."

"After the third time she rejected him, he challenged her to a duel." The reporter's mouth fell open, but Len just smiled. "They agreed that if he won, she would become his wife. But if he lost, he would never approach her with a black rose again."

"And he won?" Shawn asked, disbelief written all over his face.

Len gave him an odd look. "Rossow, how do you think I was born? Of course, he won. She almost killed him, but he won." He peered at Shawn. "Are you trying to catch a fly in that mouth of yours?"

Shawn shut his mouth tight and thought, *I will never understand these people.* Looking down at his notebook, he saw that it was a chaotic jumble of exclamations and side notes. He reread the words of the royalty at the party, and something clicked in his brain. "I see now why the queen danced with Sind! She was the vixen he couldn't catch. And that was why Sind was so upset over losing her, and the King of

Fox furious at both of them." He slapped his forehead (and winced). "It makes perfect sense now!"

Len stretched, yawning. "Took you long enough." He stirred the embers again. The fire crackled, the birds twittered among the trees, and the horses nickered to one another. A fresh breeze blew down through the valley. It rustled the golden grass and eased the pain in Shawn's forehead.

Once again, it was the painful goose egg that brought Shawn back to his first question. "So what does that woman last night have to do with this?"

Len jumped to his feet. "First, we break camp. We've already wasted enough time. Then when we've gotten back on the path, I'll tell you more... possibly."

* * *

Shawn and Len bustled about the campsite. The fire hissed and sizzled as Len tamped it out, filling the air with a lingering aroma of campfire smoke. Shawn gathered his few belongings: a thick, woolen cape, the skin of water, his notebook, a change of clothes, and the small dagger Len had given him. As he bundled these into his horse's saddle bags, something fell to the ground. Shawn stooped to pick it up and froze when he saw it.

It was his razor.

Looking down at the tiny object from another world, Shawn thought about how luxurious it would be to shave over a sink with warm water and a soft towel. The reporter felt his face and frowned. *I feel like a cactus.*

"Hey, Rossow! What are you mooning over?" Len called from his horse.

Shawn sighed. He would have to shave later. Lovingly, he placed the razor in his saddle back and strapped it closed. Lifting his foot into the stirrup, he hopped once or twice before throwing his leg over the saddle. The soreness, a dull ache before, now became a fierce pain. "Oi, it feels like I'm sitting on a spear instead of a saddle," Shawn hissed under his breath.

At Len's mocking, "You look like an old man!" he straightened his back. Len slapped his reins, plunging into the sea of tall grass, and Shawn followed in his wake. Soon the horses made it out of the grass, leaving a road of flattened grass behind them. The hills looked steeper the closer they got, but without hesitation Len directed his horse forward. They loosened their reins so the horses could lower their heads to scale the rocky bluff. The sun was hot on their heads, and within a few minutes all of them were sweating. Halfway up, the ground broke away under Len's horse and they began to slide down the hill right towards Shawn. Just in time, the horse recovered its footing. Len kept them at a careful speed after that. At last, they scrambled onto level ground and were out of the valley.

Len let out his breath. "That was an adventure, eh?" The prince dismounted. "Wait here." Before Shawn could protest, Len plunged into the forest.

The reporter was left with the horses, the singing birds, and the wild creatures stirring in the forest. In the shade of the trees, his head didn't ache so badly. Shawn sniffed the air and smiled. The forest smelled like life itself. Shawn thought he could even feel the plants pushing out of the rich, moist earth. He tilted his head back and was delighted to see little patches of periwinkle blue. *They actually do have sunshine and blue skies here.* Shawn quickly pushed away the thought. He feared that it would somehow jinx the beautiful day.

When Len arrived again, he was behind Shawn. "I knew I'd find it," he said.

"Find what?" Shawn asked. "A hidden chest of money? A map of the area? A restaurant for lunch?"

"The path, you fool." Len swaggered to his horse and swung into the saddle with one smooth motion.

Shawn watched enviously. "You have to teach me how to do that."

The prince chuckled. "The key is practice, allowing yourself to look like an idiot, and more practice. Don't worry though. No one is here to make fun of you but me."

"How comforting."

The men spurred their horses. They cantered along the line of trees, and the hoof beats sounded like three beats on a drum: *Thud, thud, thud. Thud, thud, thud!* Shawn felt like he could ride like that forever, with the wind blowing in his face, the trees rushing past him, and his friend riding close beside. Soon, they both had to slow down to enter the forest. The horses also seemed reluctant to enter the forest. Len turned in the saddle to explain, "I had to stray from the path last night to get into the valley. But, clever fox that I am, it was child's play to retrace my steps."

As always, it was rough going. However, riding through the woods in the daylight was definitely easier than in the middle of the night! Shawn looked back on that scared Shawn the night before and smirked. Len had spoken truly; it wasn't long before they reached the path. The horses nickered to each other as if to say, "Thank goodness, a real road!" Side by side, the prince and the reporter rode down the gravel path.

There was no sound for a minute or two except the clopping of the horse's hooves, and the wind pushing its way through the trees, the heather, and the men's hair. *Should I question Len more now or wait for him to tell me?* wondered Shawn. He glanced over at the prince. Framed by dark, windblown hair, Len's face looked serious. He sat straight as a spear in the saddle. His eyes were fixed on the road ahead of them, and they did not waver as Shawn's eyes did when twigs snapped in the woods. Shawn wondered how so ordinary a posture could look so intimidating.

Eh, I've had worse. Like when I had to interview the manager of the Sanfran Cisco Boxing Club! Shawn smiled, recalling that day. The interview was for a paper about the showdown between the boxing teams of Sanfran Cisco and L.A. Shawn did not follow the sport, but even he knew it was a big deal when the teams tied off for first. There was to be a rematch soon, so Morri's Magazine gave him the assignment to interview the boxing manager in Sanfran Cisco. So there he was, little ol' Shawn Rossow the Rookie Reporter, to interview the big guy himself: Ivan Tanner. From stories he had heard about Mr. Tanner, Shawn knew he was not a man to mess around with. When he entered the boxing school to see gigantic men with bulging muscles lifting weights, exercising, and sparring, you can imagine how poor "Tubby" felt. He was quite ready to run the other direction when he went to meet Mr. Tanner.

Several days later, in a small editorial near the front of the magazine, Rossow had this to say,

In light of the astounding tie for first between the long lasting rivals of Sanfran Cisco and Las Angeles, many fans of both sides ask, "What does Mr. Tanner think of the upcoming rematch between his team and the team coached by his arch-enemy Ronald Richardson?"

Mr. Tanner answered, "I am so pumped I could throw the nearest reporter through two walls, and still have enough energy to fight off the rest of the press." Obviously, he is quite confident in his team and very excited to prove it.

Len interrupted Shawn's thoughts. "You have been quiet, Tubby. I'm impressed with your patience."

Shawn shrugged. "I wouldn't dream of rushing you."

Len's face was the picture of devious delight and smug satisfaction. "Of course." He gestured to their right, where they could barely glimpse the ocean many miles away, "Sometimes I forget that you are not one of us. You know so little, yet you have survived for a surprising amount of time here."

Shawn bristled at Len's patronizing speech. "Hold it there, Len!" he growled. "I'm not an absolute idiot. I've taken care of myself for quite a long time before I came here. Sure, I might be a little out of shape, but that's America! Anyways, Sanfran Cisco wasn't exactly a haven of peace. And you know what? I'm not such a bad fighter. Stop treating me like I'm completely help-"

The reporter never saw the kick coming. One moment he was in the saddle, and the next he lay on the ground, groaning in pain. Drawing his sword, Len got his other foot out of the stirrup and leaped from the saddle. He charged at Shawn with a fierce war cry, brandishing the blade over his head. Shawn rolled over just in time as the sword came down. *Shinkk!* It pierced the rocky ground. Shawn tried to rise, but his legs were all tangled. Len left the sword sticking up from the ground and drew a dagger instead.

Without thinking, Shawn unsheathed his own dagger. Len struck at his arm. Shawn barely blocked it, gasping as the blade nicked his knuckles. Len kicked Shawn in the belly, driving all the air out of him. *Ouch,* was all the reporter could think as he struggled to his feet. Hardly was he up before Len lunged again. Shawn tried to defend himself, but Len was so quick it was all he could do to block, let alone go for an attack. Once or twice as he flailed in vain, Len nicked his wrists with the dagger.

The prince drove him backwards. Shawn knew he was losing his balance, but he couldn't stop. Len brought the hilt of the dagger down on Shawn's wrist, and the reporter's dagger fell to the ground. Shawn followed a moment after. The fight, if you could call it that, had hardly begun when Shawn was pinned to the ground thirty seconds later. Shawn lay there, panting and wide-eyed. The prince posed with his blade pointing at Shawn's nose. His expression was not hostile but deadly serious.

After a few seconds, he sheathed the dagger and stalked away to catch the wandering horses. Shawn sat there for a long minute. Many thoughts went through his head, but the one that kept coming back to him was, *I'm bleeding.* Indeed he was, and it seemed like a lot of blood. They were only small cuts, but they stung like nettles. Ironically, it was the pain that forced him to get back up. He approached Len cautiously, but the prince ignored him. It dawned on the reporter that he would have to bandage his own wrists.

But how? I don't have any bandages, and I'm certainly not asking him for any! Shawn thought. Then he got an idea. He trotted back and found the discarded dagger lying amidst the weeds. After a moment's hesitation, Shawn sawed off a long strip of fabric from his own tunic. He ripped it into two pieces before winding them around his wrists. *Just wait until they get infected,* snickered a mean, little voice in his head. Shawn only shrugged. The bandages would have to work until later. The two men mounted their horses and led them back onto the path. They continued their journey in thick silence. Len didn't look at him once, yet he seemed neither angry with Shawn nor sorry for him. He did not need to speak to get the point across.

It was nearly an hour later when Shawn held up his hands. "I am *thoroughly* and *utterly* chastened, Len. Now will you *please* stop giving me the silent treatment?"

Len let out his breath. "I was wondering when you were going to ask." He chuckled. "You look so funny when you're surprised, Rossow. I quite enjoyed that."

"Well, I'm glad somebody was having fun," Shawn grumbled.

Len sighed. "I hope you understand now how inexperienced you are in the face of a knight… or worse. Although you are endowed with more than your fair share of luck, it's only a matter of time until it runs out, and you find yourself up against an enemy who really means to destroy you. You're not ready to defend yourself. However, I plan to remedy that as soon as we reach Strothar Canyon."

The reporter said nothing, but shook his head just the slightest. *Len can train me, but he can't possibly make me one of them. If someone ever really means to kill me, I might die solely of fear.*

CHAPTER 11

Close Shaves

The two travelers hunched like old men over a pot of water, their faces dripping. With as much care as a sculptor, the two men, armed with a knife and a razor, shaved their bristly chin and cheeks. Soon Len finished while Shawn went on meticulously shaving. His razor was getting dull, and unlike Len, he disliked leaving a few hairs. He was a reporter after all. Len sat back and watched him. "Careful now, Rossow," he said. "It would be an *awful* shame if you cut yourself..."

Shawn, in an attempt to change the subject so he could have a little peace, asked the prince, "Since the sun's going down, and you obviously have nothing better to do than torment me, why don't you tell me more about last night?"

Len rolled his eyes. "You are so aggravating when you plague me with the same question hour by hour."

"It's my job to be aggravating."

"Fine." Len held up his hands in surrender. "I'll get it over with. Remember yesterday when we abandoned the path and headed through the forest instead?"

Shawn nodded. Len scrutinized the reporter's face, but only saw a blank, expectant look. He shook his head. "For a spy, you sure don't make connections very well." Shawn snorted. "If you had been paying attention to our direction, you would see very clearly that turning off the path at that point and continuing due northeast as we were would take us right onto the western boundary of Sea Dragon." As if he had said nothing out of the ordinary, Len reached into his pocket for his wooden figurine and shave away tiny woodchips.

The reporter, on the other hand, nearly cut himself in his surprise. "You mean, we were traveling in *Sea Dragon* last night? Enemy territory? Why?"

"Why do you think, Rossow? We had to escape from Fox soldiers." Len looked smug. "And due to my *brilliant* plan, we succeeded."

"Wait a second," interjected Shawn. Setting his razor aside, he fumbled in his saddlebag and returned with the map. Unfolding it with a snap, Shawn traced their pathway with his finger. *So here's Castle Fox,* he thought. *And here's the path we took through the Ranjin forest where we met Len's sister.* Just thinking about Sylindra made Shawn shudder. Looking about in the upper left-hand corner of the Sea Dragon region, the reporter noticed several black markings dotted here and there which read "Guard Towers." He turned to Len, whose narrow, tanned face was scrunched up in concentration as he carved his wooden statue. "What's with the guard towers?"

Len made a face and drawled, "Well, considering how the Royal Summer Palace is situated somewhere in the forest there, they've surrounded it with guards so there would be no surprise visitors."

Shawn put his hands on his hips. "So you're saying while I was out cold on the horse's back, we *skipped* across Sea Dragon, moseyed on through the guard towers, called a good evening to King Sind, and made it out again?"

Len laughed. "I love it when you get yourself all worked up. You are too funny. Now do shut up and finish shaving while I finish the story. Ha, you think *I* got us through Sea Dragon's nightly patrols? You flatter me. Listen first, and it will soon make more sense, O Excitable One. You may or may not have noticed a place on the map called Mordoom's Truce Table. This stone table, said to have fallen from the mountain, serves as a fighting free zone for all regions. And so, the visitor last night that you may or may not have seen was indeed a... friend of mine from Sea Dragon."

Just friends, huh? A memory of last night flashed through Shawn's mind: the woman leaning forward to kiss Len with all the tenderness of an angel... a very dark, dangerous angel.

The reporter shook his head and tried to focus on what Len was saying. "Like me, my friend thinks the fighting is stupid. That person has some connections in high places though, so he, or she-"

"You don't have to talk like that," Shawn interrupted. "I know your friend is a girl."

"Oh, darn," Len said in a wry voice. Running a hand through his dark, scraggly hair, Len sighed. "No, I'm not even going to ask how much you saw. All that I can say is... lackaday, she is the fairest of the fair!"

Len rocked back against the tree, and his face was the picture of idiotic bliss. Shawn dropped his head in his hands as if to say "Oh brother," but it came out as "Ouch!"

"Ah, I was just getting to that," Len said. "You may or may not have guessed that my friend and I are—er, intimate. With her being a siren—that's a lady sea dragon—and me a fox... well, I'm sure you can understand why she was so quick to kill the proverbial Christmas goose."

Is he calling me a goose? Shawn wondered.

"She was sorry about it afterwards," Len added. "Sort of."

"Smmack!" Whizzing through the air, Amara's stone hit a bulls-eye on its intended target. The reporter, knocked airborne for a moment, was out cold before he landed. Len tried to move towards Shawn but was held in place by Amara's dagger. Its owner glared into the woods. "That poor creature shall not bother us again," she said.

"Amara, that poor creature was *my companion,*" Len complained. "He's the stranger who came to our Island almost a month ago."

"Oh, yes. I heard you caught him in your bear trap." She sounded amused.

"How did you—" Len raised his hands in surrender. "Well, it doesn't matter. I may have caught him in a bear trap, but that unfortunate fool knocked me flat after hanging upside down for hours. That's when I knew there was something special about him. Call me crazy, but I'm going to *train him. In fact, that's why we're here now. At least, he wasn't supposed to be here. Poor fool. I left him with the horses."*

Amara tugged the dagger from the tree, and together they knelt beside the unconscious man. The lady leaned her head in one hand while she gazed at Shawn. "Hmm," she said without a hint of emotion in her voice. "That's a shame. We'll have to go extra slow with this dead weight holding us up. Are you sure we can't leave him here?"

Len went on to explain how his friend had brought them through the guard towers, dodged patrols, even brought them within a stone's throw of the royalty's summer castle, and showed them the safe way out. By the time Len was done, the sun had slipped beneath the horizon. Shawn dunked his face one last time in the water, and a small cut on his cheek stung. He had a shaved a little too close in one spot… probably when he was trying to take notes and shave at the same time.

* * *

Their journey continued uneventfully for several days. During the day, they darted on and off the trail, pushed through dense forests, splashed across wide streams, jumped across narrow ones, and hiked through the hills, only stopping once or twice for Len to add extra resources to their food stores. Shawn tried hunting with Len's bow a couple of times, but forsook it for the easier task of collecting raspberries, mulberries, and wild grapes. Headaches plagued Shawn on the first full day of riding, especially when the sun showed its face. True to Len's prediction, Shawn had come to appreciate the island's darkness. The first time Len changed the bandage on his head, Shawn felt faint and dizzy. Len reminded him to be grateful the stone hadn't been any larger.

It still hurts like blazes, thought Shawn, *and Len only makes it hurt more.* It was true, for each day when the prince changed the bandage he cheerfully described the colors forming on Shawn's wound. The goose egg first turned a greenish, black hue. The next day, it was purple and blue. On the third day, it was a yellowish mustard color. By the fourth day, when it had turned a healthy pink, Shawn took the bandage off for good.

They rarely met travelers on the small stretches of road they used, but Len still tried to stay off trail so as to leave no scent for Fox soldiers to follow. "You still think they're after us?" asked Shawn. He leaned against his horse as it drank from a creek. "I mean, we haven't had a glimpse of them since we left Fox three days ago."

Len took a long swig from his water skin before responding, "Cockiness, Rossow, is the downfall of a knight. Most likely, we lost them after we cut through Sea Dragon. But, although there are a number of different ways we could have gone, it's only a matter of time before they discover ours."

Evenings found our travelers sitting by the fire in the midst of their newest campsite, their belts loosened and their face and fingers greasy. Shawn would beg a story about the Isle of Despair from the prince. Shadows flickered and danced across Len's face, and his eyes gleamed as he gazed into the leaping flames. He filled Shawn with epic stories about famous knights, kings, queens, and exceptional common folk. Using his hands as well as his voice, he painted vivid pictures in Shawn's mind of the legends of the island.

"Once upon a tragedy," Len would always begin, "the waters of the White Sea were bare, the waves unbroken upon a solitary shore. Only currents ruled these seas. And what currents they were! There were two waves, strong and stubborn, that for years and years traveled in opposite directions in a wide circle to crash against each other in the center. It is thought that this constant battle between the currents is what caused the upheaval of the earth. Some believe it was like this: from the heart of the sea, there came a great roaring, bubbling, crashing. The quaking went on like this for many days—until, as if brought up by the warring currents themselves..." Len raised his hands. "Two towers of steaming earth arose from the depths of the ocean."

"Immediately, from the one of the west, a hellish combination of smoke, lava, and flaming boulders spewed out of the gaping volcano. The land formed below was rocky in some places; mountainous, flat, and low in others. Black smoke shrouded this newborn island in darkness. Comparatively, the volcano to the east was tame. Lava flowed down its side to harden into gentle valleys and plains. All through this marvelous catastrophe, the currents continued their endless battle of power. Amazingly, these newly formed islands did not obstruct their paths. At last, the war between land and water ceased." Len let his breath out and spread his arms, "Where there once was nothing, there now were some things."

"Gradually, a sort of peace returned to the White Seas. Along with it came seeds borne on the wind, the waves, and the fur of wild creatures and the beaks of birds. Both islands' soil was rich; therefore, it wasn't long before they were filled with growing plants. Springs of freshwater burst up from places where lava once flowed. One such spring of water formed in the belly of the dead volcano on the east island. The river became a waterfall as it cascaded down the side of the mountain and drained into a basin to form a large lake. However, the volcano on the other island did not die so quickly. Smoke still seethed from the sleeping monster's nostrils. There was always a cloud hanging about that island, while the other became more saturated with light every year."

"It was around this time that people first came to the islands. No one knows where they came from or where they had intended to go. They say one group wrecked on the rocks of the hostile island, and the other ran aground on the sandy shore of the other. The people who arrived became very different... as different as the islands themselves."

Shawn blurted out, and for a moment seemed almost like one of Honest Erwin's children, "From the beginning, were the people distinguished by dark and light?"

The prince moved to pile some more branches on the dwindling fire before answering, "Many people believe that. It makes sense that they would be different. Otherwise, why would the people on the... *Island of Joy*," he shuddered at the name, "stay there in that blinding, intoxicating place instead of coming here?"

Len looked left and right, as if to make sure no one heard him speak the name of the other place. Then he turned back to Shawn, whispering, "Others think that when they came to the islands, the people were the same... neither dark nor light." Len fixed Shawn with his keen gaze. "Kind of like you, Rossow. But over time, the islands *themselves* changed the people." Len jerked his head to the right. "*That other place* changed them into a group of crazy, butterfly-chasing nuts. *This place* changed us into to a dark and dangerous people, a people as mysterious as Mt. Mordoom's peak."

Shawn felt the hairs on the back of his neck prickle, and he shivered. Maybe what he felt was concern: *Could Steve turn into a tree-hugging lunatic?* Maybe it was confusion: *What is it about these Islands that changes people?* But maybe, just maybe, it was curiosity: *What if I became like them? What if I became dangerous?*

One evening, Shawn lifted his gaze from the road ahead and saw, scarcely a mile away, a little village. It looked very safe and cozy, with tall wooden walls surrounding the place and lights shining from within. Len noticed Shawn's excitement at once. "Behold, Tubby," he said with a gleam in his eye, "civilization, though I don't quite know anything civil about the place. There are hardly any civilians, for one thing, it being a border town between Fox and Crow. The types of people come in pairs, you see. There are travelers—people trying to sell stuff to the travelers—and innkeepers. There are criminals, escaped bond servants, pickpockets, and the soldiers from numerous regions after their bounty. Finally, there are people who nobody knows or likes who pass through, and those who stay on just to make themselves invisible in this wondrous tangle. People like us."

"Fine with me," Shawn grinned. "I'm used to crowds. I've even missed them. That and sleeping in a cushy, warm bed!"

"Amen," intoned Len. The travelers spurred their horses, and they sped along the dusty road. Bouncing up and down in the saddle felt almost natural to Shawn now. He brushed a hand over his forehead, sticky with sweat, and thought about how heavenly it would be to step from the muggy, hot afternoon into an air-conditioned building. Even the bird calls seemed muted by the heaviness in the air. The reporter consoled himself with the thought that he could soon get off the warm horse, and they could both cool down. Len had taught him how to take care of his horse after a hard ride. Many of the instructions, like putting a blanket on them when the horse was sweaty, and not giving them a big bucket of cold water, seemed very strange.

At last, they were within sight of the village gates. It was indeed a small place, but still a trickle of people flowed in and out. Shawn noticed at once that before anyone could go in, they were questioned by two burly soldiers at the gate. Len and Shawn dismounted from their horses to lead them into the line of people waiting to go in. Most of the people ahead looked just as haggard and road-weary as them. There was a lone man with his handsome black horse, a small party of merchants dressed in richer clothes, two young women with arms full of laundry, and an old man on a donkey with the floppiest ears Shawn had ever seen.

The bubble of conversation reminded Shawn of Sanfran Cisco. What happened next though, reminded him how different this place was from the modern world. A harsh voice called out, "Hey, you! Haven't I seen you before?" Everyone's attention was diverted to the gate, where one guard had caught hold of a scrawny, dirt-smudged boy.

"G-good sir!" the boy stammered. "I pray your mercy, I've never seen you before in my life!"

"Aye, but your face is very familiar—on this wanted poster," the other guard chimed in. He held up a paper for the crowd to see. "An escaped bond servant, that's what ye are, boy!"

Fast as a rabbit, the boy twisted from the guard's grasp and darted into the city. Shawn could have been looking the other way and not seen him vanish. The man on the black horse barreled past the guards, who called after him, "Good luck with your quarry! Rid our town of the pest!"

I hope he got away, Shawn thought and glanced at Len, who showed no surprise whatsoever at the incident.

With the excitement over, the guards went on passing people into the city. It was then that Shawn got a bad feeling in the pit of his stomach. He sidled over to Len and asked him in a whisper, "How are we going to get past them without giving away who we are?"

"Have no fear," Len answered with a yawn. "These are not the vigilant type. I can feel it. They will not bother us any more than they have to. Even our hunter, Commander What's-his-face, wouldn't be stupid enough to send out wanted posters and give away that I'm missing."

Shawn smiled. "So there are advantages to being a prince, after all."

He regretted the joke at once, for Len shot him a murderous glare before raising his voice, "It would be nice to be a prince, wouldn't it? No soldiers always on your tail, or nosy, old men trying to eavesdrop!" With that, Len whirled on the little man behind him. "Get away from us before I give you the boot!"

"Eh?" the man peeked over his shoulder. The only part of him visible was his twinkling blue eyes, hiding underneath white eyebrows so bushy they looked like caterpillars. The caterpillars wiggled up as the man cried in self-righteous anger, "What? Eavesdropping? Where did you get that idea?" The man had an odd voice that dropped from squeaky to deep like a parrot. "Heh!" he grunted and hobbled away on a little crutch, "You can keep your boots, I haven't any need for 'em. Honestly! C'mon, Matilda, darlin'."

At that, Len's face change from anger to amusement. "Well, whether you need boots or not, I suggest you clear out, you rascal. This isn't a good time for stories." The man grumbled to himself as he mounted the donkey, and the odd pair road back down the road our travelers had just come.

Shawn stared after them. "*Who* was *that*?"

"Just what I said, a rascal. Nevermind him, we draw close to the soldiers, so please keep your mouth shut from now on and let me do the talking."

Most of the travelers had already been let in. When the two young women passed through without a question, the guard beckoned them closer. The other guard leaned on his spear and grumbled, "Let's close the gate after this lot."

Shawn's heart pounded in his chest, but he tried his best to look unconcerned like Len. The first soldier, who had a rather impressive beard and moustache, glanced over the travelers without interest. "Name and business!" he rapped out.

Two Sides of the Coin

Len struck a pose with his hand on the hilt of his sword and his eyes narrowed. "Our names are our own, and our business is to rest this night in your fair village."

Before he had finished this declaration, Len snapped a golden coin into the air. The soldier caught the coin, pocketed it, and stepped aside. "On your way, Master Drake, and enjoy your stay."

As Len stepped forward, the second guard blocked the way. "I don't know. You seem a little suspicious to me." Shawn gulped.

"Suspicious in what way?" the prince toyed with another coin in his hand, which soon passed into the guard's hand.

"No way at all, friend," the guard slapped Len on the back. "Safe travels."

They strode into the town with the cranking of the closing gate in their ears. "That… was… so… cool!" breathed Shawn when they were out of earshot. "Do you always do that?"

Len strutted down the street, a very pleased expression on his face, "I wish! But you have to pay attention to the guards. With some, orders are orders, and I have to make up a name to please them. Some, like those two, couldn't care less about a name, as long as it wasn't on a wanted poster. If only they knew!" Right then, walking down the dirt road with Len, passing little shops, with the sun sinking on the horizon, and the two friends laughing together like a pair of college kids, Shawn felt there was nowhere he would rather be.

* * *

Len took Shawn to the stereotype of all inns: crowded, smelly, and loud. An innkeeper, stout as a barge, served drinks at the grainy wood counter. The cook was a woman whose singing in the back room made a yowling cat sound musical. A fire crackled in the corner where a few travelers sat eating. Several maids darted in between the tables to dish out semi-recognizable food. Straight ahead, Shawn could see a flight of stairs which must lead to the rooms. He couldn't help smiling at the scene, so familiar in a strange way.

Len had a word or two with the innkeeper, who told them that if all these other men stayed the night the inn would be out of room. There was a chance that some people would leave after dinner. He suggested they make themselves comfortable, order some food, and he would throw in a free slice of pie if they had to sleep in the dining room.

Meanwhile, Shawn kept stealing glances about that place. He stopped mid-glance when a hooded traveler slouched at a table met his eye boldly. Shawn avoided the scorching gaze which made him feel very much like a fish under an eagle's eye. A crazy thought popped into his head, *Does he know who we are?* He scolded himself at the idea. *Stop being so paranoid. The only one who might know who we are in this town is that weird, old man on the donkey, and Len didn't seem worried about him.*

"What do you say, Rossow?" Len asked, interrupting Shawn's thoughts. "Shall we have kidney pie, roast boar head, or—oh! how about some genuine Cobra soup, aye?" The prince winked and elbowed him.

Shawn regretted telling him that story. His stomach, which had been growling for food, now felt a bit queasy. "Those sound like pretty expensive meals, don't you think?" he asked, a little too hopefully.

"Don't worry about that," Len laughed. "Come on, I will pay for all expenses just this once. Don't be shy— I've heard the cook's eel stew is famous."

Famous for killing someone, maybe? Shawn wondered. "Umm, no thanks... I think I'll stick with a loaf of bread, maybe some cheese, and some ham slices."

Len gave Shawn a look that probably meant, "How dare you not take advantage of me?" but didn't harass Shawn with any more exotic food choices. The two men went to sit down. As there were no tables open for them, they slid into the two seats with the lone traveler Shawn had dubbed Eagle-eye.

Plopping down with an enormous sigh of relief, the prince exclaimed, "Ah, to feel solid wood under my bum after perching on pointy stumps, the wet earth, and rocks swarming with lice!"

Exaggerating much? Shawn thought.

Eagle-eye raised an eyebrow. "So, the road hasn't been kind, has it?"

"The road was kind enough," replied Len. "The saddle, not so much."

The fellow travelers started an animated yet empty conversation. I say empty, for neither of them gave away any information on their actual journey, nor did they ask. Len complained of the blasted clear weather they'd been having, to which Eagle-eye sympathized.

"Tis a bad omen," the man declared. "Sunshine on the Island of Despair? Unnatural!"

The two were in a heated debate, something about Hawk and Lion politics, when a maid swept by, dropping their food with a heavy thud that made all the food jump as if it were alive. Shawn was not at all convinced it wasn't, for that matter. He snatched up his loaf of bread, which was being invaded by a tidal wave of gravy from Len's fried… something.

Whilst the men continued their heated argument, Shawn split open his loaf to construct a thick sandwich. He had missed his lunch stops at Subway every Sunday afternoon. Len blinked at the strange food he had creatively put together. Instead of asking, he diverted his attention to his own food. However, the other man, whose food had not yet arrived, stared under his hood at Shawn. "What on Mordoom's peak is that thing you're eating?"

Eagle-eye had caught Shawn mid-bite, which gave him time to come up with a good reply. "Well, good sir, this thing, as you call it, is a delicious combo of bread, meat, and cheese. A nobleman invented it so he could gamble and eat his supper at the same time, not that I gamble or anything! He was called the Earl of Sandwich, so that is why they were henceforth dubbed sandwiches."

Eagle-eye looked away, obviously having lost interest after Shawn's monologue. Len coughed to hide a snicker, and Shawn felt pretty proud of himself. Before Eagle-eye could ask another question, the maid practically flew past them and landed his bowl of eel stew so hard it spattered over him. He turned to bellow at the maid, but she had already fled back to the kitchen. Eagle-eye excused himself to wash, swung open the door, and came face to face with a whole troop of soldiers in gleaming armor.

Time seemed to stop for a moment. Then, as if it had to make up for lost time, a breathtaking moment flew by. Len jumped from the table, snatched up his packs and strode towards the stairs. He left his plate behind, but who would want to eat that, anyways? The reporter followed as quickly as he could without drawing attention; luckily, everyone's attention was diverted to the soldiers entering the inn.

They were dressed in light armor, silver and radiant. All wore a scarlet tunic on which there was the symbol of a blazing white fox. Shawn felt the foxes' eyes even before he saw them: a sixth sense he had picked up at Castle Fox. It made his heart jump so high it collided with his lungs. The reporter turned the corner and breathed deeply to get his breath back. Len was beside him doing the same thing. Grabbing Shawn's arm, the prince dragged him upstairs.

Below them, Fox soldiers barked orders. There seemed to be one in charge, a man with a deep voice that might have been more intimidating had it not sounded like his nose was all stuffed up. "You, you and you, question all the travelers if they saw where the two men went. You, soldier—check the kitchens … What? Oh, fine, take a shield so the cook doesn't batter you to death. Sir Wilfred, guard the stables. Now what? … Does it matter if the cook makes eel soup? The rest of you, follow me up the stairs and— Man, I don't care whether someone died from it—go, go, go!"

As soon as the hunted pair reached the top of the stairs, they tried the door handle: locked. They tried the next and O huzzah! it opened. The two rushed in, and Len shut the door just as the chief commander's head was visible on the stairs. He shot the bolt home and brought a chair over to prop against the door. Shawn stood there, trembling, the sandwich still clutched in his hand. "What are we going to do?" he whispered. The room they were in had no doors except the one the prince had blockaded, and only one window. Among the scanty furniture was a bed in the corner, a table, a chair, and a desk, all in desperate need of dusting. The whitewashed walls, soaked with moisture, were cracking along the edges. It was not a nice place to be trapped in, but then, is there any?

Two Sides of the Coin

"The window, of course!" said Len. He crossed to the other side, gripped the window so hard his fingers turned white, and pulled up. There was not the slightest movement. The window was locked.

A heavy pounding sounded from the first door they had tried, "Open up! There are soldiers of Fox searching the inn for two wanted men." Frantically, the fugitives flew about the small room, trying to find the key to their fate: namely, the window key. Whoever was staying in this room was not a neat person, much to their dismay. Clothes were strewn all over the floor along with several traveling packs which seemed to have a hundred pockets each.

Hardly had the search begun when a soldier pounded at their door, shouting, "Open up in the name of the King of Fox!"

Len and Shawn froze. There was a long pause.

"If no one answers within ten seconds, I will bring the door down!" shouted the soldier.

"He can't do that, can he?" mouthed Shawn.

"Of course, not," Len whispered. "Unless he has an axe."

Crack! The door shook under a shuddering blow.

Len winced. "Oh, look, he has an axe."

"That was a warning," growled the soldier. "I'm giving you five seconds to open this door."

The prince rubbed his forehead, thinking, as the soldier began to count. A light-bulb seemed to appear over his head. "Keep looking for the key. I'll buy us some time," he whispered.

"Three..."

Shawn went back to tearing the room apart.

"Two..."

Len padded over to the door, lifted his head towards the ceiling as if to say "Forgive me" and braced himself.

"One!"

"EEEEEEEEEEEK!"

Shawn nearly jumped through the roof at the high-pitched squeal. The soldier on the other side leapt back from the door. "Who's in there?"

"You brute! You beast! How dare you break the door down while I'm changing—you evil fox! My father will have you horsewhipped. My

187

beau will slice you to ribbons. My mother will see you *hanged!*" Len spoke so fast the sentences melded together, and the voice, if not very feminine, was passable for a girl's voice.

Searching under the bed and trying not to sneeze, Shawn knew he would have died of laughter under any other circumstance. He searched all the while the make-believe girl and soldier conversed in the background. At first, the soldier was lost for words. Nothing at all in his many years of training had taught him what to do with a frazzled woman. "I'm sorry, madam, I had no idea anyone was in there."

"Ha! Your own lies trap you, indecent monster. Why would you break down the door if no one was there?"

While the poor soldier went into a stumbling recitation of the reason they were searching the inn, Shawn groaned in despair. The key must be lost or in the owner's possession, for he felt he had checked everywhere. Then three things happened at once. The general arrived to tell the hapless soldier all the other rooms had been checked (why wasn't this one?!). Shawn saw a shiny bit of metal sticking up out of the layer of dust on the desk's ink stand (the lost key!). The person who's room it actually was arrived at the scene (with a key to get in).

Shawn pulled the key from its dusty abode and cried like a prospector who had just discovered gold, "Len, I found it!" No sooner had he said those fateful words when the two men heard very clearly a sound that made their blood run cold. It was the turning of a key in the latch.

Dear reader, I must interrupt this perilous scene for a minute. Please bear with me. If you are an older brother or sister, and have had experience of holding the door against some younger sibling, then you will understand perfectly what our prince and reporter experienced here. If you've never had the chance for this, then you'd better put the book down right now, find yourself another person, preferably bigger than you, and instruct him to try to get in the room while you hold the door shut. No locking the door, mind you!

... Done yet? I'm serious, reader. Just because it's a command in a book doesn't mean you can shrug, adjust your position, and keep reading. I'm counting on the fact that most people have held the door from someone in their life. But if you haven't, that is a terrible shame. Come on, you only live once!

Tell me, how did that go? Perhaps you leaned into it with your shoulder against the door. The problem in that stance is evident when the pusher throws his whole weight against the door, causing the pushee to get knocked aside. What if you switched to putting your back to the door? Ah, but then if the pusher is strong enough, he could give enough pressure to move the door, and your feet would keep sliding. How do you keep them out then?

For those of my readers who are veterans at this sport, you know that the most effective way to stop the door from moving is to brace your foot right against the bottom of the door. It seems odd that your foot could hold the door, considering that neither your shoulder nor your back could hold it. But your foot against the door works almost like a lever to hold the door shut. No matter how big or how strong the pusher is, you are rather safe with your foot on the door. Doesn't it give you a very satisfied feeling?

It is so much easier now to imagine Prince Gilen trying to hold the door against the soldiers. There was no doubt in anyone's mind that their quarries were trapped in this room. Soldiers came from all parts of the inn to break in, no pun intended. By the time they arrived, Len had piled up every piece of furniture in the room against the door. One would think he was trying to keep a flood out. He had the heavy wood desk in the corner of the door, the bed propped up against it, and the chair under the handle. Finally, he had his foot at the door in our famous lever-stance. Considering the circumstances, he was doing fantastically.

Shawn, meanwhile, had fitted the key into the keyhole, but alas! he could hardly turn it. "It—won't—move!" he grunted between gasps for breath. Len couldn't hear him over the din outside, but he guessed the problem.

"Rossow!" Len barked. "Hold this door just like I'm doing—no Tubby, with your foot like this."

Shawn grimly changed places with Len. Brandishing the key, Len fought against the lock, coaxed it, and forced it to move. Shawn started to cheer from the door, until a shocking bump from the other side cut him short. It caused the bed to fall over with a great crash, missing Len by a hair. The soldiers were battering down the door!

"Len!" screamed Shawn as the blade of an axe came through the door not a foot from his head.

"Leave it, and come help me with the window!"

Shawn rushed to Len's side. They placed their hands against the bottom of the window and pushed with all their might. Shawn panted. "Why would they use axes against the door if they knew you might be holding it? I mean, these are Fox soldiers, so they wouldn't kill us, right?"

The window ever so slowly started to slide open. At the same time the door cracked from another heavy blow. Len flicked his dark bangs from his eyes and grinned as he said, "Wrong! They wouldn't *try* to kill us."

Shawn knew he would always remember that time: he and Len covered in sweat and dust struggling with the window; the reporter's heart still jumping from his near-demise. Len's lighthearted response while the soldiers' voices came louder and louder at them, mingled with the sound of splintering wood. Finally, a breath of fresh night air blew into their faces. The space was only big enough to fit their shoulders through, but the sight of freedom was motivation enough. Agile as a cat, the prince slid through the opening. He crouched for a moment on the window frame before jumping down out of sight.

Shawn put one leg through and began sliding his shoulder under the window when a section of the door gave way to reveal the faces and shoulder of the furious soldiers. He tried to pull himself through and panicked when his back got stuck against his belly. *Oh no, oh no, oh no! Stupid McDouble Cheeseburgers!*

The reporter gave himself a hard push and almost fell out the window sideways. He caught himself just in time in a position even worse than the first: with one foot still hanging in the room, his hands gripping the window sill for dear life, and the rest of his body hanging out. Like an avalanche, the furniture, the door, and the flood of soldiers burst forward at little ol' Shawn. He wasn't thinking at all now. He removed his foot from the room, stretched out his arms as far as they could go, and dropped.

For the second time in Shawn's stay at the island, he escaped via window. This time, Len wasn't there to catch him, nor was there a convenient hay pile to break his fall. Luckily, the teensy inn was much closer to the ground than his room at Castle Fox. When his feet hit the ground, Shawn collapsed in a heap on the grass. The breath was knocked out of him. Relief—wondrous, enormous relief—nearly drowned out the pain. He was alive, and he had escaped that horrible room. Len was not too far ahead, beckoning the reporter as he sprinted across the courtyard to the stable. Shawn stumbled after him. He caught up to Len at the doorway, and the overwhelming smell of horses hit him. The prince had stopped frozen in his tracks.

In the middle of the passage, a Fox knight towered over them. A broadsword with a cross-shaped handle he clenched in both hands. He was taller than the prince, broad-chested and bulky as a bear. His bright armor made him seem even larger. He didn't look frightened, though his bald head already gleamed with sweat. Despite not having any hair, he appeared middle-aged, with a thick, brown beard and a double chin.

Surprisingly, Shawn did not feel intimidated. *What a brave man!* he thought. *I would be shaking in my boots if I were him. Doesn't he know who he's up against?*

Len whispered to Shawn, "When I give the signal, you run and find the horses." Shawn nodded. With that, the prince strutted forward and called a cheery greeting. "Wilf, my friend, you're looking well."

"It's time you came back home, Prince Gilen," rumbled Wilfred. "You have some explaining to do."

Len unsheathed his sword. "Sorry, I'm a little busy." He leaped forward to strike at Wilfred's sword arm. The knight blocked the attack and circled around him, striking at Len with his impressive sword. Len parried with the side of his sword and countered with a kick at Wilfred's shin. As soon as their blades clashed, all the horses began to neigh and scream. The stable boys came running from all directions to stand openmouthed and wide-eyed before the fighting knights. After the initial shock, they cheered Len and Wilfred by turns. Most sided with Len, partly because he was smaller and wore less armor, and partly because they could already see his superior skill.

The prince knew he had little time before the soldiers would reach them, so he went at the knight with everything he had. Using the same method that he had used with Shawn, he tried to put the man off balance and drive him back. But Wilfred was unusually nimble, given his size. Whenever Len came after him, he dodged to avoid the charge. Len kept him on his feet though, and within a minute the man's whole head was red as a tomato. Again, Shawn thought he might have laughed if the situation was not so urgent. At last, Len maneuvered Wilfred into a corner and shouted, "Go!"

Shawn took off past them. Before Wilfred could do anything, Len was on him again. Shawn cut right through the crowd of stable boys and might've kept running when he realized that he had no clue where the horses were stabled. *Think, Shawn, think! What would Len do?*

The memory of Len's coin flicking up into the air and into the guard's hand appeared in the reporter's mind. He turned around to face the crowd of boys. "Hey, boys!" he called, pulling a golden coin from his pocket. They looked over their shoulders and gasped at the gold in his hand. "This coin to whoever brings our horses the fastest!" he shouted.

Shawn could have turned into a werewolf the way those boys took off. They raced past him down the aisle, pushing and shoving to get in front. No sooner had the sound of their pounding feet diminished when it appeared again. It was accompanied by the clopping of hooves. Never did those horses look so beautiful to the reporter. He grabbed hold of the horses' reins and tossed a handful of coins amidst the boys. Taking hold of his horse's saddle horn, he mounted in one smooth motion. The stable boys murmured in admiration as Shawn wheeled the horses and thundered towards the knights. Wilfred saw him coming but fought all the harder, turning Len right into the horses' path.

Shawn let Len's stallion move behind him and shouted, "Look out below!" Len whirled around and jumped out of the way. The other knight seemed rooted to the ground, paralyzed. Shoving him out of harm's way, Len threw himself onto his horse. They tore out of the stuffy inn, whooping at the top of their lungs. The horses' hooves clattered on the stones of the courtyard. They left the inn behind in short order: soldiers pouring from the building, Wilfred tumbling out of the stable, and the stable boys cheering at the top of their lungs.

Everything had happened so quickly, time itself seemed to be acting funky that night. The whole escaping ordeal had taken place in minutes, but it felt longer. Still, the madness didn't stop. The fleeing pair could hear their hunters behind them like a pack of blood hounds. Shawn stole a fleeting glance over his shoulder and nearly had a heart attack. Up in the air, several yards behind them, flew a monstrous bat-creature: Wildfred!

Len shouted over his shoulder, "Scared you, did he? Well, he can't keep up for long!" So saying, he turned the horses into a tight alleyway. Like a bloodhound, Wilfred yelled to point out their escape and flew over the houses to watch for the runaways. Shawn couldn't lose concentration for a moment. He followed Len left and right through a tangle of side streets and alleyways, over shop courtyards, and back onto the main road. Wherever they went, their pursuers always sounded close. Shawn was sure they were going in circles. Every time he heard the sound of heavy wing beats, he shivered. But as Len promised, Wilfred could not keep up with them.

When at last the sound of pursuit grew quieter, Len brought them back to the main road. They flew past the little sleepy buildings that they had passed earlier at such a carefree pace. Soon, Shawn looked up to see the wall rising up, silhouetted against the black sky. *The gate must be closed,* Shawn thought in dismay.

It *was* closed. However, when Len cried, "Master Drake wishes to depart from your fair town!" the gate mysteriously came open. The bars seemed to take forever to rise, and they rode out before they had fully come up, but that was one thing Shawn could do. The gate began to slide shut behind them, and the men's hopes rose that they would make good their escape.

Shawn jumped as a scream followed them. He looked back. The gate stopped its downward plunge and began to rise again at an incredible speed. In a minute, the horsemen would soon be upon them again. Shawn wondered how long they could ride that night before their exhausted horses collapsed. At that moment, Len veered off the road into the thick undergrowth. The horses neighed in confusion, but Len quieted them. Both Shawn and the horses watched Len, wondering what he would do now.

Len motioned for Shawn to dismount. When the reporter had hopped off, he moved behind the horses, raised his hands high as if in blessing, and brought them down with a stinging slap on the horses' rumps. Immediately, the horses galloped out of sight into the dark woods. Shawn opened his mouth, but his question was stifled by Len's hand. The sound of stamping horses, jingling reins, and the commander's gruff voice came at them from the road.

"Move," whispered Len. So move they did, deeper into the woods. Len pointed to a fallen pine tree, and they crawled underneath like a pair of lizards under a rock. No sooner had they hidden themselves when the thud of the horses' hooves and the soldier's shouting filled the forest. They waited for what seemed like an eternity.

In reality, it only took the general a couple minutes to pick up their horses' trail, and the party moved off as quickly as they had come. Only when all around them the crickets began to sing and the frogs croak did the prince and the reporter crawl out. Brushing the itchy pine needles from his clothes, Shawn asked the question that had been burning on his tongue the entire time, "Why on earth did you let our horses go?"

"The first lesson in escaping, Shawn, is that the less you take with you, the easier it is to hide," Len answered. "Not to offend you, but it would've been far smoother getting out of that inn if it was only me."

Shawn hung his head like a chastened puppy. Len ruffled Shawn's hair. "But where's the fun in that, eh? You did well, Rossow." And with those simple words, Shawn felt his heart expand.

Continuing his midnight lecture, Len pointed out how much easier now it would be to travel and stay hidden. "And I haven't even gotten to the best part," Len said with a wicked grin. "Think a moment, Shawn. Those were castle horses. Now that we've released them, where do you think they'll go?"

Shawn laughed. "Why, they'll make their way back to Castle Fox, all the while leading the soldiers away from us! Or, if the party finds them first, imagine their faces when all they find are two free horses." He declared, "Prince Gilen, you are a real fox!"

"Ah?" Len's face brightened. "You're finally catching on, Tubby. Don't ever forget it." Shawn nodded, and they pushed their way out of the woods. Len wanted to get some distance between them and the village in case the soldiers came back. With the moon lighting the way, they found their way to the path and resumed the journey.

"I guess this means no warm beds after all," Shawn mourned.

"Nay," said Len, "nor a hot dinner. When I think of that gourmet dish I had to leave behind, now growing cold and congealing, why, 'tis enough to break your heart!"

Digging in his tunic pocket, Shawn pulled out a squashed lump. "Anyone for a sandwich?"

CHAPTER 12

A Perfect Day

Sunlight beamed down from a rustic, wooden window to illuminate a host of dancing dust motes. The ray of light fell down from the heavens to rest at last and breathe its warmth onto a little, red handmade rug which lay beside a bed in the corner. The bed was made of the most beautiful wood you could imagine. The wood shimmered as if it had a life of its own. Indeed, the trees and flowers carved on the headstand appeared to wave when a sweet breeze trickled into the house.

The man who slept in that lovely bed had the look of one who was under an enchantment; his breathing was so deep and even. His face was tan and handsome, and his blonde hair lay as if a hairdresser had done it while he was asleep. A tinge of a smile lifted the corner of his lips. With a flutter of wings, a gold bird perched on the sill of the open window across the room. Raising her head, she trilled to the sleeping man, the sweetest alarm clock that could exist. The spell broken, he opened his eyes slowly. He took one last deep breath, stretched out his arms, and released a contented sigh. Throwing back the thick quilt, he sank his feet into the warmth of the red rug, smoothed back his straight, blonde hair, and smiled at the sunlit house as if it were a good friend.

How will I describe that little cabin? It was the sweetest, quaintest, most cozy house you ever laid eyes on. The walls were made from brick that fitted together like a puzzle. The floor was marble, a rich brownish color, like dark honey. In the center was a large oval carpet covered with rainbow hues. Over it stood a table with a pure white tablecloth. Two chairs gathered around it. A yard ahead of the bed sat a round, stone fireplace where light still glowed from the embers. Beside the fireplace was a cupboard overflowing with homemade food: a round loaf of bread, cookies, and biscuits on the top shelf; butter, honey, grape jelly, cheese, and milk on the one below that; the third shelf overflowed with fresh fruits and vegetables; and all sorts of canned food were on the last shelf. In the opposite corner from the bed was a tall wardrobe, and it too had a mysterious life about it. A desk stood beside it, stocked with sheets of parchment, ink, and feathers.

The man walked to the wardrobe and pulled on some white leggings, boots, his white cape, and a tunic of vivid green. *Like Melody's eyes*, he thought. As he dressed himself and ate a light breakfast of biscuits, honey, and fresh milk, he hummed a tune to himself. He strode from the house with no destination in mind. The morning was too delicious for words. Dew sparkled on every blade of grass, flower petal, and leaf. The man laughed when one of the trees shook itself like a big, wet dog, exclaiming, "Brrrrrr! Good morning, stranger."

"It is a good morning indeed," he responded. He decided not to go through the woods, or else he may be soaked by shaking trees. Instead, he climbed up the grassy hill until he stood at the top with his head tipped back to view the rosy pink and purple sunrise. Gazing below him, he saw his roof of his cabin with its chimney peak trailing smoke. Further on, Sparkle River meandered through the valleys until it poured into Lovely Lake. And it was there, on the opposite shore of the lake, the Joyful Village and Melody resided. The man thought of how kind they had been to him to give him the cabin for his home, supplying him with food, and even giving him his very own ground to farm. He reflected upon yesterday.

Steadfast led him through the perfectly straight rows of corn, wheat, and other vegetables. All around, the people lifted their hands to salute their leader. The stranger tried to peek ahead from behind Steadfast's broad back, but with no luck. Instead, he glanced over his shoulder and smiled from ear to ear. Melody followed close behind him, her bare feet making no sound on the black earth. With her sky-blue dress, her golden hair spilling free over her shoulders, and her emerald eyes turned to the heavens, Melody truly looked, as the stranger first thought, like an angel.

He reeled back as he bumped right into Steadfast, who'd stopped ahead of him. Melody lifted a hand to hide her smile, but couldn't hold back a giggle. The other people laughed too. "Caught staring again, aye, friend?" Steadfast elbowed him. The stranger blushed, but it was true. Whenever he saw Melody, he felt like a deer caught in the headlights. Sometimes he quite forgot where he was, but no one here seemed to mind.

The stranger glanced up at the empty plot of plowed ground. The soil, rich and dark, was well stocked with dandelions and little else. Steadfast began to explain about how they kept this field set aside in case someone needed it. While he spoke, Melody crossed to him and intertwined her fingers with his, smiling up at him. The man was so enraptured he hardly heard what Steadfast said, until Melody gasped, "Goodness gracious! A farm of your very own. Why, it's just the thing you need!"

The man blinked at the field dubiously. "I don't know, Melody... I've never farmed before. At least, I'm pretty sure I've never done it."

Steadfast spread his hands. "No worries, friend, we are all here to help."

"All?"

As if the stranger had given them a cue, people suddenly appeared from the woods, the fields, and the village. Little animals bounded in between their feet: chipmunks, squirrels, rabbits, mice, a couple foxes, and badgers. Whole flocks of birds alighted on the trees and whistled a tune in unison. Everybody got in a circle around the field and sang:

O—Oh—Ohh—Ohhh—Ohhhhhhhh!
Look out, you grass, move out you trees, it's time to plow the field
And when that's done, you've finally come,
To find what seeds will yield!

Apparently, everyone knew this song but the stranger. As they sang, the people and animals danced about, brandishing seed packets, shovels, and hoes that seemed to appear like magic. Oddly, the man did not feel overwhelmed; on the contrary, he was enjoying himself. After each line of the song, the people showed him how to do it.

Two Sides of the Coin

You poke a hole, you take a seed, you drop it down inside
Don't forget, to cover it,
With soil so it can hide!

The rains will come, the sun will go, to give your seeds a drink
But when they don't, you take a cup,
And water 'em before they shrink!

So rich and dark, so cool and clean, the weeds just love this place!
But cross your arms and STOMP YOUR FEET!
And they'll run with all haste!

This was the children's favorite part of the song, the man could tell. Adults laughed as the kids shouted and stomped their feet very with fierce expressions. Sure enough, all the dandelions that had sprouted up moved out of the plot. It was fascinating to watch them, for the plants could wade through the soil just as someone wades through water.

The plants will grow, though they seem slow, higher than your head!
So take a post for the climbing host,
Before their leaves they shed!

And when the corn and the wheat too are ready then to pick,
DON'T EAT THEM YET, but grind them up,
For flour so you won't get sick!

The ground may try to toughen up, but keep it nice and soft
Take your hoe, and use it so
And make sure you do oft!

And when at last, the harvest's past, you cover the field with leaves
You leave it there, through winter's spell
So they're ready on next summer's eve

By the time the song was finished, the man's garden was ready. As everybody left one by one with encouraging and helpful remarks, he thanked them again and again. Several ladies conversed as they went home, "Such a nice, grateful man, isn't he?"

"Yes," replied another, "one would think he'd never been to a public singing before, the way he was trying to thank everybody. You'd think he's never had a nice thing done to him in his life."

It was a sobering thought, soon broken by a cheery, "Well, now he has!"

As he looked back on the memory, the man felt a great excitement welling up within him. When he'd gone to bed yesterday night, he felt pleasantly tired and was now refreshed after a good night's sleep. Never had he experienced such a thing. Instead of typing on a computer all day and wracking his brain, he indulged his mind in simple, wholesome work. No longer was he brooding on the subject of his next issue. Now his thoughts were care free ones, such as, *I wonder if any plants have sprouted yet.* He would check the plants later. First, he'd visit Melody. The sun was already high in the heavens when the man came jogging into the Joyful Village.

I will sparingly describe the village, for to paint it out in detail would take up the whole chapter. The place was unlike any city, town, or village, which one would find back in the place the stranger came from. There was no telling how many people lived there, somewhere in the thousands, and yet it didn't seem crowded in the least. It sprawled in a manner some would consider unorganized, yet it was easy to find your way around. The lake was to the east, the forests to the west, the fields to the south, and the majestic peak of Rainbow Summit to the north.

In the very center of the village was a lovely, round boulevard—a market-place that always seemed to be buzzing with energy. It was here that the people opened their stalls and sold goods of all types. Well, perhaps *sold* is not quite the right word for it. Oh no, the people of joy didn't use coins of gold, silver, and copper. Instead, they traded their own goods for the things they needed, and everyone went away happy. The market was full of pleasing sights, scents, sounds, and sensations. The farmer's stalls were like a rainbow of food: plump apples and

Two Sides of the Coin

beets, huge pumpkins, bananas and corn, cucumbers and zucchini, blueberries, purple plums, and peaches that could shame the pink of dawn. Colorful cloth fluttered in the breeze from the tailor's stall. The aroma of freshly baked bread, pies, muffins, and other delicate pastries made even the most content stomach rumble with a new-found hunger.

A motherly woman and her daughter with their best milking cow called out, "Soothe your soul with warm milk, fresh from the cow!" Their cry was interrupted by the pounding of an anvil against metal, which rang strong and clear like a bell. A crowd of children watched from the sidelines as the village blacksmith shaped a shovel out of the red-hot metal. All the while, there was the beautiful murmuring sound of running water in the background, coming from a tall fountain in the center of the marketplace. The place was loud enough to be heard many streets down, yet the noise was never aggravating. The market-place was only open a couple hours each day, and after that everybody left the main square in peaceful silence until the morrow.

The main square was not only a place of good-natured bartering and business, it was also the location the villagers held their monthly festivals and all other holidays. It was located at the exact middle of the village: around the boulevard, the cottages expanded in circles with four main streets leading back. Each street had five sub-main streets: for example, the North Road would have five North-East Roads, each labeled with a different number, and number 1 was the road closest to the center place. Every time the stranger entered the village, he marveled at how easy it was to find his way.

Melody and her family lived on 3rd Southwest Street in a little cottage covered with climbing ivy. Every morning, she awoke before her family and crept from the cottage. Since she was a little girl, Melody always wandered the dew-laden meadows at sunrise. When the village stirred awake an hour or so later, she flew back to her house, more often than not bringing a basket-full of berries or apron-full of apples for breakfast.

Melody's father, named Mathias, was a retired swordsman who now spent his days at the most tedious task of stone-crafting. Mathias's work was renowned, and his customers joked that the stone itself softened for him. That rumor could almost be true, for he had the firmest hands in the whole village. The stranger found this out the first time he shook hands with Melody's father and felt it for five minutes afterward. Like his daughter, her father had green eyes, although they were more of an olive green. She had also inherited his height, and his high, ringing laughter. The man was considered quiet, and some thought he was perhaps more serious than he should be. But that didn't matter, for the man's wife was loud enough for both of them, and her constant talking made up for his silences.

Her name was Rosie Ann Milibeth or Millie for short. She was the stereotype house-wife: small, round, and rosy-cheeked, just like her name. She always had something baking and took pleasure in watching people eat with a good appetite. The man, expecting as much, made sure to eat light before going there. The goodwife was convinced that he needed fattening up. Whenever he walked into the house, she would bustle over to him, exclaiming, "Me oh my, you're as thin as a post! Poor boy, would you like a little something to eat?" And who could argue with a hot cinnamon roll or a bowl of homemade chili sprinkled with cheese? The man vaguely remembered being a picky eater, but everything he tasted here was delicious. It was from Millie that Melody got her wavy hair and brilliant smile.

With all the work in the fields, the good food, and of course, the magical air of the Island working for the stranger, he grew less strange every day. The man no longer tried to be dignified: he ran about like a boy, reveling in his new-found strength and endurance. His skin was tan from being outside, and a healthy glow showed in his face. He put on quite a few pounds what with all the eating and growing new muscles. All these things could be attributed to just being outside and Millie's nutritious food. But perhaps the most remarkable outward change was his hair. For like a fire creeping over the surface of paper, a streak of gold had started at his part and begun to spread over his dish-water blonde hair. With so much else to occupy his mind, the man hardly noticed. One of the biggest things (almost a concern but not quite) was the question: *What do I call myself since I can't remember my old name?*

The people of joy didn't seem to mind the namelessness at all. When they greeted him, they called out, "Good mornin', sir," or "How's the farm going, friend?" It was only the trees that sometimes called him stranger, which is evidence of their longer memory. He tried thinking of new names, but nothing fit. Melody and her family helped him come up with names as well. None of those stuck either. It probably didn't matter to the parents if he did come up with a name, for that matter. They would still call him son. But most of all it bothered him that the creatures of the island would say Melody's T.L was nameless.

The man mused on this as he made his way to Melody's cottage. The feeling could not be called depression by any stretch, but he certainly didn't feel joyful at the moment. Then he remembered what Millie had told him the other day, "It must be hard, movin' in all of a sudden like that. There's so much to learn! But remember, if ever you're feelin' down, just make up a song, sing it out, and you'll feel better, I promise."

The man stopped. Him, make up a song? How? He rested his chin on his hand, narrowing his eyes in concentration. Within a few seconds, an idea sparked to life. Humming, he continued on his way. Once he began, the verses seemed to line themselves up for him. With every step closer to the village, the more excited he became. *I'll sing it to Melody today. Oh, I hope she likes it!* he thought.

At last, he came into the village. The sun was already high in the heavens, and the people of joy were making their way to the marketplace. A random man burst into song, *"What—a beauuuuuutiful mooooooorning!"*

In the crowd, a woman responded, *"The likes you've never seen."*

The whole crowd lifted their voice as the song picked up in tempo,
"Oh, what a beautiful morning, the likes you've never seen!
The sun is in the heavens, and all is right in the world."

There wasn't any solid beat in the song, and neither did it rhyme; in fact, one would think they had made it up on the spot. How then, you ask, did they all know how to sing it?

...*I* don't know. Do you?

Anyways, amidst much singing, the man found 3rd Southwest Street, which was very calm compared to the main street. He skipped down the road until he came to Melody's house. An enthusiastic hug from Melody, a quiet greeting from Mathias, a hot muffin from Millie, and the T.L's were on their way hand in hand to Rainbow Falls.

Rainbow Falls was indisputably the most beautiful, romantic, and "wonderfullest" place on the Island of Joy. The majestic roar of the falls could be heard far away. Shining in the sun, taller than the trees, the waterfall had graced Rainbow Summit longer than anyone could remember. Yet the falls were not at all like a raging giant. Neither was it a pathetic trickle down the hillside, with moss growing on the bare rocks. This was the mother of waterfalls, perfect as a fantasy. At the top of the falls to its right side, a sheer cliff rose up. Melody and the stranger climbed up the gentle slopes on the other side. A simple bench carved from marble sat at the top of the path. It was damp from the waterfall's spray, so the man shed his cape to fashion a cushion for Melody. As she sat down, surrounded by the beauty of that place, she had eyes only for the stranger.

Since the moment Melody had kissed him, a flower of deep love had blossomed in her heart. All the doubts had vanished from her mind that this man, though a stranger, was meant to be her True Love. When he in turn had responded with genuine affection, her joy was boundless. What did it matter if he didn't know anything, let alone his own name? At that, Melody clasped her hands together, her heart fluttering. "Have you found a name for yourself? Is that what you brought me out here for?"

The man shook his head. "I'm sorry, Melody. I still haven't thought of anything. I was actually pondering how sad it was that such an extraordinary woman would be with a nameless man…"

"It's not sad, it's exciting! You're like a newborn baby," she pointed out.

Taken utterly by surprise, the stranger laughed and almost forgot what he was going to say. He lifted a finger. "Well, that's when I remembered what your mother said to me. If I was ever feeling down,

I should make up a song. So I did." He stood up and paced away from her. Taking a deep breath, he turned to her, "Ready?"

Her smile said yes. Consequently, just as the water poured from Rainbow Falls, a song poured from the stranger. It was his First Song—one of the most precious things on this Island. It is said that love is blind, and I wonder if love is deaf as well. For I must be honest with my reader, even the Island of Joy cannot make good singers out of tone-deaf people. Neither can it inspire revelation from an imagination dull with ill use. In short, the song was awful. The melody was repetitive, the cliché lines would make a poet grind his teeth, and the rhythm was nonexistent. So far I've recorded the songs of the Island faithfully, no matter the cost, but this monotonous song I will leave out.

It is difficult to tell whether Melody knew this just as any other sane human being would know this. However, though the weeds themselves ran for cover at the man's voice, Melody's eyes shone, and she looked perfectly relaxed. When the song finally came to a lame end, she sprang up to hug him. And even if the song didn't erase the would-be depression from his mind, the words she whispered in his ear, "No simple name could describe who you are to me," effectively lifted the man's spirit to the high heavens.

* * *

They sat by Rainbow Falls and talked until the sun hanging directly overhead told them it was time for lunch. Millie was just putting the finishing touches on a beautiful white cake when they walked in. She jumped at the sight of them and tried to shield the cake from view. Melody giggled. "Mother, what celebration is this?"

Millie sputtered a few incoherent sentences before they could understand, "My, my! No good—you weren't supposed to see, why, we meant it to be a surprise for him—I thought you'd be late for lunch and, oh dear, that soup must be near burnt by now!" She bustled away, leaving them to admire the cake.

"Wait, she made this for me? Why?" the man asked. Melody echoed his question.

Mathias, seated at the table with a thick book in his hands, responded, "Melody, dear, I would expect you of all people to know. Today is our friend's month long anniversary of coming to our island. Congratulations, son."

The man didn't know whether to feel more shocked or pleased. Shocked, for he'd never heard Mathias speak more than a couple words at a time. Pleased, because Melody's parents had kept track of the time. It was a shame that Millie's surprise party never happened. Over the course of a half-hour, many friends of the family arrived shouting, "Time to get a party ready! Boy, he's going to be so surprised!" They walked in only to be surprised themselves with a party in progress. Melody, her parents, and the man couldn't stop laughing at their guests' befuddled faces.

The atmosphere was as festive and crowded as a graduation party. Millie brought many dishes out that she'd stashed in preparation of the party. Mathias pulled several extra tables into the dining room so everybody could eat together. After they'd feasted until they couldn't eat another bite, they leaned back from the table in satisfaction and conversed together. Their talk centered on the stranger's farm and the preparations for the next festival. However, as Millie cleared away the dessert plates, the conversation took an unexpected turn. A husband who looked about in his forties spoke, "I wonder when those evil creatures from the other island will strike again."

Silence fell over the table like a heavy blanket. The stranger looked left and right at their grave faces. Though he had never seen anything from the Island of Despair, the man felt a cold dread creep into his heart whenever the place was mentioned. Millie invited the ladies into the next room to knit with her. When the last woman left, the stranger leaned forward, "I have heard of these creatures before, but I don't understand what goes on whenever they come."

"The devils!" the older man growled. "They fly here at night on their fiendish bat wings and snatch up many of our young women. But, by Rainbow's Summit, we don't let them get away with it."

One young man named Christopher pumped his fist. "You've got that right, Brunden! We give those blighters a taste of our steel, and they always run like the coward they are. You saved your wife Hilda from one of 'em, didn't you?"

This led to an exciting tale of horror, bravery, valor, and intrigue. Brunden was a very good orator and held his audience spellbound by the tale. When he came to the climax, the man who was usually so mild-tempered jumped to his feet and waved his arms to emphasize his words. "Having found the kidnapper, with my dearest Hilda unconscious at his feet, I shouted, 'Come and fight like a man!' Then *it* grinned horribly, and I could see his fangs as he growled, 'A man? Are you sure that's what I am?' I unsheathed Courage from its sheath and charged the creature. Oh, he was a tricky one! He tried to slip past me, but I didn't let him get away. We fought all through the night, until I had at last exhausted its strength. Vanquished, the creature fell to its knees, begging me to spare its life. I was disgusted but granted its request and tied the creature to a nearby tree. At last, with my bride Hilda in my arms, we fled from the land of darkness. When we came home, we were wed that very evening, so that never again could the evil creatures steal her away."

The men cried, "Bravo!" and applauded Brunden.

He bowed and murmured, "It was really nothing. Mathias rescued Millie from a whole score of them, didn't you, Mathias?"

Sitting back in the chair with his hands folded over his stomach, Mathias smiled. "Not really." The men looked at each other in puzzlement. Mathias leaned forward with the expression of a little boy telling a secret. "It was I whom they captured and carried away," he whispered. "Then Millie came and talked them to death."

All the men burst into loud guffaws. Millie poked her head into the kitchen. "Mathias!" she snapped. "Are you telling stories about me again? Ooh, you are a frustrating old man. I'll have you know I've never talked anyone to death yet. I may be a bit of a talker but that's no call for making fun of me. No sir, no one's ever gotten away with poking fun at Rosie Ann Millibeth. Why, right in front of all the guests too, I oughta—Oh!" For at that moment, Mathias rose and kissed her before she could get another word out.

With a chorus of "Awwww," and "Nice one, Cap'n Matt!" the stranger couldn't help thinking that in some other place and time this would be awkward, but not here. He was just fine with that. Millie returned with the women in the other room commenting that she was more rosie-cheeked than ever.

Leaning back his in chair, Christopher flipped his long hair from his eyes. "I'm never going to let one of those filthy things touch my Penelope. If any of them tried to take her, I'd slice them to ribbons with good, ol' Triumphant." He patted his sword and winked at the stranger. "I wager you'd do the same for Melody, aye?"

The man looked down at his hands. He shrugged. "I would, but I don't know how to fight."

Christopher jumped to his feet. "Then there's no time to waste!"

"I can't believe we hadn't thought about it before," said Brunden.

"I'll teach you," rumbled Mathias, and at that everybody cheered.

Thus, a spontaneous sword lesson followed in the backyard of their cottage. Even the ladies came out to watch. Mathias started out by teaching the stranger the eight points of striking. All the others immediately set about swinging their swords, while the stranger went through the motions with painstaking care. The sword Mathias had given him was quite heavy, and soon he was covered in sweat. It relieved the stranger that his sword was blunt, so there was no fear that he might hurt somebody. Mathias continued to teach him the forms, but the other men soon lost interest and began to show off their favorite moves. The training session lasted about half an hour, until the women called their T.L.'s and left in pairs.

"Ooh, my muscles are aching!" complained the man as soon as the last person had left. Mathias smiled, Millie shook her head, and Melody gave him a hug.

"You sure worked hard out there. I just know you'll be the best student Father's ever had!" she murmured.

"You did well, son," Mathias agreed. The man felt bashful at the praise. Somehow his sword didn't seem so heavy now. He held it out to Mathias, but the retired swordsman said, "No, that sword is yours now."

"Really?" he cried. All three of them beamed at him. The man shook his head in wonder. "How kind it was of you to think of me and prepare this party. I can hardly believe your generosity to me, though I'm a stranger. This is probably the nicest thing anyone's done for me."

Millie snorted and waved it off. "Oh, it was nothing, really nothing. You deserve something nice for all your hard work. Heavens above, I won't ever forget when I first saw you, sitting by Sparkle River with my baby. It was the happiest day of my life." Her voice cracked, and she dabbed her eyes with the corner of her apron.

Mathias put an arm around her. "None of that now, mother."

"Anyways," added Melody, "you're not a stranger anymore. You're one of us."

There was a minute of silence as the man admired his sword. "It needs a name... just as you do," Mathias commented.

A needle of sadness pricked the man's happiness. He pushed it away and concentrated on finding a name for his sword. It came easily. Laying his hand on the blade, the man declared, "I dub thee Harmony, after Melody. You will bring harm to any that would hurt her."

The little family gasped in delight. What a marvelous idea! Reverently, the man sheathed Harmony. Millie smiled, rocked back on her heels, and clucked, "Mathias! Where did you put those sheaves of wheat from the field?"

The man's head snapped up. At the word "sheaves," he looked like he had been hit by a sledgehammer, and Mathias's reply was lost to him. Out of nowhere, it came back: STEVE. That was his name. In the past, before he had met Melody. He was not Steve any longer, but at last he had an idea for a new one.

CHAPTER 13

Strothar Canyon

How many miles had Shawn Rossow the Reporter ever walked at one time? Back in Sanfran Cisco, he prided himself that he was a good walker. Considering that he hardly earned enough money to pay all his bills, getting rides from taxis was out of the question. It was hard, but Shawn had tried to make the most of it. The length of the walk from his apartment to his job was around a mile and a half. From there he would pick up his daily assignment at the desk. After that his schedule varied.

Sometimes the place or person he was supposed to see was close enough to get there by walking. Or, if he was lucky, he would be assigned with another reporter. Between the two of them, there was always a way to get there. Other days he was not so lucky… and those days happened more than Shawn would care to admit. Oh, they always started out full of hope, just as Shawn's last normal day at work had been. The sun shone off the windows of skyscrapers, the birds sang in the city park: all in all, a perfect spring day in Sanfran Cisco. Shawn reached Filtzine's HQ at precisely 8:00. Exchanging greetings with the other reporters, he had the good feeling of being known.

Shawn strolled to the main desk where the clerk Mrs. Andrews made her appearance each day with not one hair out of place. Indeed, it was a joke among the reporters that she was made of plastic and therefore never got sick. That also would explain the scowl frozen on her face. The reporter put his elbows on the glass counter. She kept her spectacled gaze fixed on the computer screen, jabbing the keys at fifty words per minute. "Good morning, Mrs. Andrews!" Shawn said with a grin. "You look lovely as always."

The woman glanced up at him but showed no hint of returning his smile. "Mr. Rossow, what do you want?" she stated, as always.

Shawn liked to come up with stupid responses to that question such as, "A life," or "Oh, just a smile to grace your beautiful face," or "A car." He laughed at his own jokes, but almost always lost the nerve to tell them. "A schedule, please," he said.

Mrs. Andrews was the type that would rather gratify your request right away to get you out of her hair than have you wait around. So on this unlucky day, she sealed Rossow's fate very quickly. He took the schedule from her, looked down, and saw that crucial sentence at the bottom of the page, *Mandatory meeting at 12:00 at Morri's HQ2.*

The statement was cold, it was cruel, it was business. Shawn looked from Mrs. Andrews to the schedule, to the woman and back to the paper. Finally, he shrugged and trudged from the building, his previous good mood absolutely thwarted. Morri's HQ2 was on the other side of the city, and usually there was nothing for it but to walk or run. On that day, however, he had to use his lunch money to pay for a taxi. That was life in Sanfran Cisco.

This was the Island of Despair, and no amount of walking around the city could prepare Shawn for this: the faint sensation that washed over him when three days after their night run, he pulled off his boot to behold his foot, bloody from popped blisters. The first day, when the blistered appeared, he thought it was horrible. By the second day, the blisters had begun to bleed. And now this: he had blisters on his blisters! "Oh no…" he moaned.

Len looked up from the half-cleaned fish. The prince had been in an unpredictable mood all day. Although he still seemed proud of his deception in leaving the horses behind, Shawn could sense a change of attitude in the prince. On foot they had to move at a slower pace, and Len's normal walking pace was far faster for the reporter. The prince hardly spoke, bolted down his food, and woke earlier in the morning than he had before. He was, in a word, restless. Like a horse who knows he's nearing home, he chafed at their slow progression. In response to Shawn's complaints yesterday, he had replied, "A knight must be able to walk all day and hardly feel it the next."

Today, however, Len grimaced, "Apologies, Rossow. I didn't realized how tender your feet are. Why, one would think you hadn't walked more than five miles in your life!"

"Eight actually," he muttered.

"What's that?"

"My old record for walking in a day was eight miles. I was very proud of it... before today, that is." He paused, prickled with curious. "About far have we walked today?"

Len heaved a despondent sigh. "In the general vicinity of twenty-five miles."

The reporter's mouth dropped open. He pushed back his dark hair with a grunted exclamation. One part of him felt that his pain was justified, as if he'd just been awarded the Purple Heart. The rest of him, however, couldn't care less about his record, he was in such agony. It didn't get better all through that evening. Even when he was asleep, the pain came and went in waves. He woke early and lay watching the sky turn from black to grey streaked with pink. The sky promised rain, the wind shook the canopy of groaning limbs, and the air smelled damp and heavy. Indifferent to the threatening storm, a flock of chickadees played overhead while the bullfrog's song harmonized with the crickets. Yet in the midst of this peaceful morning, Shawn's mind was fraught with worry. For he was anticipating, yea, dreading the minute when he would have to pull on his boots and walk again.

Little did he know that while he lay awake wrestling with his worry, Len too was awake, worrying. His mind was far from Shawn's blisters though. His worry was the same that had been plaguing him long before their arduous journey began: *Say the reporter is only going along with this so that he can learn more about the island. Say he really is a spy. Say, after I've taught him all these things, he leaves the Island... and betrays our secret life. What then? It would be the end of the Islands.* At that final thought, which would make even the bravest villain shudder, Len resolved to himself, "The man must not leave."

One idea after another presented itself how to accomplish this: sink his boat, sell him to the Sea Dragon pirates, throw him in Castle Fox's jail, or expose him to the regions and leave him at their mercy. But, no matter the black-hearted villain he was, he couldn't in cold blood end the project he had begun. Oh no, he couldn't kill the fellow, heavy sleeper that he was. Or perhaps there was another way? Maybe he could make Shawn swear not to tell anyone about them. That solution begged the question, could he trust Shawn?

People here had a hard time trusting anyone. Knights weren't *supposed* to trust anyone. Princes couldn't *afford* to trust anyone. *Shawn is different though*, thought Len. *He's the trusting type. Foolish, but oddly endearing. He's not tried to escape from me since that time the Cobras put him in the stocks.* Len would always have that image in his mind of the reporter hanging from the stocks, hair covered in rotten egg. Len chuckled at the memory.

From a couple feet away, Shawn stirred. "Len? You awake too?" When Len kept quiet, he sighed and turned over on his belly, muttering something about infection, amputation, and, "Most likely be dead by morning."

Len couldn't help it; he *liked* the man. He enjoyed his sarcasm, his strange speeches, and his ridiculous exaggerations. Plus, he had a great sense of humor even when he was the butt of the joke. Shawn had proved his mettle first escaping from Castle Fox and later the inn. He was rather predictable, which made Len feel a step ahead. At the same time, he was constantly doing things that surprised the prince. *Whether Shawn stays, or whether he tries to leave, he deserves to have a fighting chance.* Len concluded.

When at last the night was assuredly over, and both men made a show of yawning and stretching, they both pushed their worries aside in preparation of breakfast. Truly, there's nothing like good food to raise one's spirits. Len brought out sausages, a treat he'd been saving. Shawn also brought out some sweet honey buns from the last town which he'd hoarded for a special occasion. They had a merry breakfast, celebrating not only their escape, but also Shawn's month-old anniversary for arriving.

A month, huh? thought Shawn. *I can hardly believe it. It seems as if I've been here for years.* He smoothed his wavy hair back, a habit which he'd picked up since his hair had started to grow. Along with its length, the color had changed. Just as Steve's once-dishwater-blonde hair became more golden every day, Shawn's brunette hair became darker, as if he had begun to wear the shadows of the island on his head. It was such a slow change, however, that he didn't notice. It was Len's cheerfulness that Shawn noticed, and he hoped to take advantage of it while it lasted. He let Len take the last sausage, and as the prince popped the tasty morsel in his mouth, Shawn blurted out, "Could I ask you something?"

Len took his time chewing the sausage. "You needn't speak, Rossow," he said. "You're wondering whether we could take the day off, am I correct? So that you can rest your poor, blistered toes."

Len's tone was so discouraging that Shawn's hopes sank like a ship with a hole in its bottom. How had the prince known? "And now you'll say 'Absolutely not!' am I correct?" he retorted.

"Absolutely not!" protested Len. "I think today would be perfect for a rest."

And so began Shawn's unexpected vacation.

* * *

Nothing is so delightful as waking up on a dreary winter school morning, turning on the news, and hearing that the school officials were too wimpy to make it through the ten-foot snow drifts, declaring a SNOW DAY! And suddenly the world seems like a brighter place where dreams still come true. It was like that for Shawn this morning. Upon hearing Len's proclamation, he cheered and hugged Len. The prince yelped like an animal being pounced on. The next moment, the point of Len's knife prodded his stomach, but Shawn was too happy to care. He let go of Len and went back to bed.

How long he slept he had no idea. When he awoke, the sky was dark, sprinkling tiny raindrops. Shawn didn't mind; living outdoors had become second nature to him. Len had left camp. Shawn sat up, stretched, and immediately started looking for food. He spied some rabbit stew leftover from last night in the tin soup bowl. Eating with his knife, Shawn noticed a scroll of birch bark sitting on Len's pack with words scribbled on it. The reporter picked it up, caught a whiff of smoke from the charcoal lettering, and read,

Tubby,

I went back to erase our tracks. Don't make new ones. After you finish reading, eat the note. It's very filling.

~Len

Shawn liked Len's first bit of advice but decided to ignore the second. Instead, he tossed the piece of birch bark into the coals and watched it go up in flames. He spent the next couple of hours resting on his bed while recording the inn adventure in his notebook. By the time he finished, he had written to the very last blank page. Rereading his first experiences on the Island, Shawn shook his head at the dreadful problems his questions had landed him in. Then he went back even further to read the entry from that historic, record-breaking day:

> I'm the most unfortunate reporter that ever lived. I don't have a car, and this measly paycheck just isn't doing it for me. Today I walked eight miles! I bet Steve has never walked that much in his life. My feet ache.

Shawn laughed out loud at himself. He turned page after page, forgetting all about his feet as he remembered the past. It was his impatient stomach which awoke him. The shadows of the trees had grown long, but Len still wasn't back. "I suppose I should have dinner ready for him," mused Shawn. "And anyways, he might not come back tonight, so I might as well feed myself."

Shawn was no cook by any stretch of the imagination. Making macaroni and cheese was the extent of his culinary skills. But camping was a different matter. He could make masterpiece hot-dogs and the most golden, gooey marshmallows you've ever seen. Never before did Shawn miss modern food so much! He crawled over to the food pack and rummaged through it. "Let's see, we've got cheese, two loaves of black bread, and, ooh, beef jerky! Some wild apples, and... leaves? Ewww, nope, it's the *other* rabbit all wrapped up. And what are these dirty things? Onions?"

Shawn cut off a small bit of the mysterious, white bulb with his knife and tried it. It had a mild taste, like a cross between a potato and an onion, and something else... pickles? "Good luck finding a recipe for that," Shawn grumbled, setting it aside.

Surveying his ingredients, Shawn felt his heart sink. Or maybe that was his stomach. No macaroni or marshmallows this time. "Well, I suppose we could always have sandwiches," he murmured with a smile. He brightened. "Of course, we've got rye bread, white cheese, and beef. I can make Reuben sandwiches! No sauerkraut, but this should do." Brandishing the mystery bulb, Chef Shawn got to work right away.

Evening was Len's favorite time of the day. The sun fell behind the horizon so that only a thin wash of light could paint the bellies of clouds scarlet and sea-blue. It was neither day nor night, but somewhere in between. The world was quiet, as if holding its breath for the sun's plunge into darkness. Len breathed deep of the sleepy, woodland smell, and detected a mouth-watering aroma. Urging his tired feet to a faster pace, Len soon saw the twinkle of the campfire up ahead. Silent as a ghost, he crept up and reviewed the battleground.

The food pack was turned on its side, apples spilling out. Bits of food littered the ground. Shawn's blanket, charred and dripping wet, hung from a tree branch. Perhaps the oddest thing was the dead rabbit from last night, suspended on his sword like some gruesome, savage decoration. In the center of all the chaos was an elegant birch-bark dish graced by two thick, steaming sandwiches... perhaps a little blacker than the usual rye bread color.

The reporter himself sat on the ground on the other side of the campfire, muttering to himself as he tied rags around his hand. "—never made out to be a cook, and now I know why. The stars in their courses strive against me. If it isn't evil squirrels, then it's bed-eating campfires, and if it isn't bed-eating campfires, then it's stupid knives which refuse to cut, or rather, cut the *food*. No wonder cooks hate me. I'm never going to set foot in a kitchen again as long as I—"

"—Is this one mine?" Len asked.

Shawn jumped and looked at Len a sheepish expression. "You're back."

"Did you think I'd let you have dinner without me? I see you've been experimenting with sand-wizards again."

"Sandwiches," Shawn corrected with a sigh. "Reuben sandwiches, actually. The burnt one's mine."

The men sat down together, and Shawn watched nervously while Len raised the sandwich to his mouth and took a huge bite. His eyes widened. Shawn gulped. "Oh no, there wasn't a grub in yours, was there? Or maybe—"

"Shawn, this is pure genius. I've never tasted anything like it!" Len exclaimed. He took another large bite, convincing Shawn of his sincerity.

The reporter let out his breath in relief. "Amazing. They turned out alright after all."

"Oh? Had some trouble, did you?" Len asked casually.

Shawn bent over his own sandwich, avoiding Len's gaze. "Just the usual." Len pointed to his bandaged hand. "The knife slipped," he explained. The prince raised an eyebrow at his burnt blanket. "Umm, I built up the fire a tad too much," Shawn mumbled.

"Dare I ask about the rabbit?"

"Nope." There was a minute of silence as they enjoyed the sandwiches. Then Shawn confessed, "The campsite was attacked after you left. I'm sure those squirrels were rabid. Anyways, I had to resort to terror tactics."

"I see. Did you get *any* rest while I was gone?"

"Oh sure, but…" Shawn dipped his head. "I'm afraid today won't be enough for my feet to heal. I mean, if I tried to walk another day like yesterday, they'll start bleeding again."

Len stayed silent for a long time, while Shawn hung in suspense. Finally, when he'd finished his sandwich, Len wiped his greasy fingers on his pants and declared, "I'll give you another two days on one condition."

"Okay?"

"You have to make dinner." At Shawn's horrified expression, Len threw back his head with a deep, evil laugh, "MWAHAHAHAHA!"

Within a few seconds, Shawn began to laugh with him, and they couldn't stop after that. Every time one of them would start to sober up, they'd catch a glimpse of the speared bunny and start up all over again. Finally, with aching bellies and teary eyes, the two men sat back against the trees to catch their breath. "If you teach me to throw knives," said Shawn. "I'll make dinner."

Len put his hands behind his head and gave one last chuckle. "It's a deal, Rossow."

The next day flew by. Once Len gave him the general instructions, Shawn practiced throwing his knife at Len's squirrel carved into a nearby oak. When he didn't miss the tree altogether, the knife merely bounced off and thudded to the ground. Time after time, Shawn crawled over to retrieve it and try again, only to have it fly back into the woods like an escaping bird. Len raised an eyebrow over his figurine, but he didn't laugh, and Shawn didn't complain. After hours of practice, when the sun began its downward plunge, Len spoke for the first time since his instructions that morning, "You have to *believe* you can hit it."

"What?" asked Shawn, pausing mid-throw.

"You can have all the patience in the world, but if you tell yourself before every throw that you won't hit your target, believe me Tubby, you *won't*."

"I haven't been doing that!" scoffed Shawn. "And don't give me that wise, mentor-ish look."

Len shrugged and went back to carving in silence. Shawn rubbed his hand. *That's what I get for wanting a day off to heal my blisters. I just get more while I'm waiting!* The reporter stared at the squirrel, which grinned back at him. He thought about each throw. Alawys, there was a moment of hesitation and Shawn would think to himself, *You're a beginner. Don't be surprised if you don't hit it this time.* He never surprised himself. He wasn't even disappointed. But then, he hadn't hit it once either.

Shawn raised the knife again. He thought about his technique, and he knew the moment he would have to release the knife. Most of all, he thought about hitting the target. He threw open the cage bars and let his imagination run wild. In his daydream, he sat on the same stump with the same knife, but this time as he whipped it out flawlessly, the knife spun in slow motion, and hit a bull-eye… or squirrel's eye, rather.

The reporter opened his eyes, shattering the daydream, and glared at the squirrel, *Yes, I can hit it.*

Whizzz! The knife turned end over end in a perfect arc and… *thunk!* The knife stuck into the tree, quivering. It missed the squirrel by at least a foot, but to Shawn he may as well have scored a winning touchdown or home-run. "YES!" he screamed, almost dancing with joy. "I hit the tree! Look, Len, I finally did it!"

"Excellent, Rossow. Now make me a sandwich."

Shawn was too happy (and hungry) to argue. With Len to fend off inquisitive woodland animals with fluffy tails, Chef Shawn was back in business. Within fifteen minutes, he had two more beautiful Reuben sandwiches, and no more scorched blankets. By the time they finished their sandwiches, the flames had consumed the firewood and it was time to crawl into bed.

"I think I could walk tomorrow," the reporter offered, glancing down at his bandaged feet.

The prince shook out his blanket, plopped down, and grunted, "One more day. I'm still building up our supplies."

Comforted, Shawn snuggled down into his blankets and fell asleep at once.

A fat raindrop diving off a leaf spattered on Shawn's forehead, bringing him awake. He yawned, stretched, and wiggled his toes. Only a faint sting remained. The aroma of cooking meat filled the air. "Rabbit for breakfast, Len?" Shawn asked. There was no reply. The reporter looked around the vacant campsite for another birch bark scroll, but this time Len had left no explanation. Shawn shrugged and had himself a laid-back breakfast. *Vacationing in the woods is great,* he thought. *No alarm clocks, nobody telling you how much time you've wasted, nothing!*

The reporter sat there for awhile, listening to the birds and the wind in the trees. Then he wondered, *What else does one do in the woods?* Not much, he found out. For an hour or so, he poked about the campsite, washed his feet, and wrapped them up with some cloth he'd bought at the last town. The clouds, getting darker by the minute, sprinkled raindrops absentmindedly. This sent the reporter dashing hither and thither, stowing their supplies under the cover of the trees. Shawn curled up in his cape under the trees as the sprinkling became a pattering, the pattering a shower. Despite the relaxing voice of the rain and the warmth of his cape, he didn't feel drowsy at all.

Shawn knew he should be overjoyed right now at his peaceful rest. But to his dismay, an edgy boredom was casting a cloud over his last vacation day. How could this happen? He had longed for a free day like this for weeks. Now that he was here, surely he could find *something* to do. At last, when the rain began to slack off, Shawn decided a little walk wouldn't hurt his feet too badly. Hobbling along like an old man, he left the campsite. His boots sank into the wet earth; it smelled better than perfume. The forest was like a patriarch: tall, solemn, and wise. Shawn saw its age in the towering birches, the wide oaks, and a brook sunk nearly three feet from the rill. There were still a couple trees here and there with budding flowers sprinkled among their new leaves. He

Two Sides of the Coin

passed by a grove of willows, truly weeping raindrops from their draping branches. Everything seemed to murmur rather than shout. Thunder growled, but even that sounded muted.

While the reporter enjoyed the fresh rainstorm coming down on the ancient trees, he reflected over all the things that had happened to him since the day he left Sanfran Cisco. He could taste that morning's coffee on the way to *Morri's HQ*. He could smell that trashed apartment, room 66. He could hear the sounds of the ocean: seagulls crying, surf rolling, the boat engine's roaring. He could picture the very moment he'd laid eyes on the Island of Despair. He could feel the rope around his ankle, the heavy wood against his neck, the sharp pangs of hunger in his belly.

Remembering the queen's discovery of him in her special room, Shawn grimaced. His grimace turned to a smirk as he recalled his first encounter with using a dagger, and his idiotic scream, *"Get out of the way, I don't know how to use this!"* His spirits lifted when he saw himself whiz past the queen's soldiers and away from the gate. Chills went down his spine at the memory of meeting Sylindra. He reviewed all the adventures he'd had, stories he had heard, lessens he had learnt. The Shawn he saw here on the island was different from the Shawn of Sanfran Cisco. And he thought, no, he *knew*, with some measure of fear, that he liked the change.

"Don't think like that," he spoke aloud. "I can't stay!"

"Why not?" a voice spoke, so softly he could hardly hear it.

"Because—because..." he searched his mind for one of his thousand excuses. Yet all he could see was a scene playing out in his mind's eye:

As Sylindra turned to leave, Shawn spoke out hesitantly, "My lady, er, your highness. I confess I know nothing about fighting or your islands customs. But I'll try to change, if I can." Sylindra nodded slightly, and shadows danced across her face.

Shawn let himself sink against a tree's wet trunk. "Because I promised myself I would never understand these people," he murmured. "But I also promised Sylindra I would try."

"What's to understand?" This time the voice was much louder and sounded uncannily like Len. Shawn looked to his left and came nearly nose to nose with the prince. Before he could speak, Len declared, "You think you can win my sister over with a promise? Bah! You haven't even won *me* over yet."

Shawn got to his feet. "I don't belong here, and you know it! Seriously, what do you want from me?"

"A good fight!"

Smack! Len rammed Shawn faster than you can say, "I'm a pacifist!" Shawn hit the ground hard with the prince's weight on top of him. Grunting, he grabbed hold of Len's shoulder to twist him off. Len caught his balance just in time. Each of them strained their muscles hard. Finally, Len pinned Shawn's arms at his side. The prince grinned—too soon. Shawn rocked forward while bringing his legs up. He got one around Len's back, pinned his hand and foot on one side, and with a quick flip, found himself on top of the prince. Len didn't hesitate. He bucked underneath Shawn, and the reporter pitched forward off him. When Shawn turned around, the prince was on his feet, crouching with his arms spread out. The sky began to pour down rain upon the two.

As they circled, Shawn thought, *It was a good thing after all that I became friends with that manager of the Sanfran Cisco Boxing Club.* It wasn't really a choice, attending those first few classes. But after the interview, and a coffee break with Mr. Tanager, Shawn felt that it would be unwise *not* to go.

However, he had hardly begun his lessons when the big guy pulled him aside, drawling in his southern accent, "Naow you leesen good, Rossow. Some men are built for this kinda sport. Some ain't, but that don't stop 'em."

Shawn nodded, the beginning of a smile already growing. It was wiped from his face as Mr. Tanner stated, "You haven't got a chance no how! I can see this sport ain't for a lil' reporter like you."

Deeply offended, Shawn snapped, "Hey, it was you who suggested it in the first place. Were you hoping to get a punching bag or something?" Immediately, Shawn wanted to clap his hands over his mouth, but the words had already flown the coop.

Luckily, Mr. Tanner was not insulted in the least. He chuckled, "Naw, there's shore to be an ordinance somewhere against usin' a human punchin' bag. Don't let it get you down. I was just saying this to point you in a different direction. A boxing reporter? Fail. You ought to try some wrestlin' classes though."

"But if I'm no good at boxing, what makes you think I could wrestle?" Shawn protested.

Mr. Tanner slapped Shawn's back. "You've got guts, kid." They had been good friends ever since.

Now Shawn found himself embroiled in fight with one of his good friends; that is, if Len was a friend. Right now, at least, he was the enemy. The two men wrestled as though their lives depended on it. Shawn found speed and strength he didn't know he had. Len found a cunning in him he didn't know he had and was very pleased to find. He was surprised by Shawn's skill, but this only made him more determined to win. Sweat covered their whole bodies, and within minutes they were also covered in mud from rolling on the forest floor. All this time, the rain pounded their bodies.

Just as Shawn staggered to his feet, Len pushed him back against a tree and pinned his shoulders. Shawn pushed his own arms against Len's shoulders. Yet again, they matched strengths. Len was bound to win. Shawn remembered one of his first lessons. In this position, he learned to put his arms on the inside of his opponent's, chop down on them, and before they recover, grip them in a headlock. Just as he felt his strength giving way, he executed the move. Len grunted in surprise as Shawn chopped down his arms. He stumbled forward, right into Shawn's headlock. The reporter had forgotten to make his stance strong though, and when the prince barreled into him, they both fell in a heap. Still, the prince was in no better position, caught in Shawn's arm. Before he could break free, Shawn had already adjusted his grip and tightened the chokehold.

He counted slowly, *One, two, three, four, five...* waiting for the tap. *Six, seven, eight, nine, ten... Good night! Am I doing this wrong or does Len just have an incredible pain tolerance?* He adjusted his position again for a better choke and had begun to count before he realized the prince was out cold. *I won.* Shawn sat up, absolutely dumbfounded. First, he felt like leaping and shouting it out to the world. Second, he felt concern for the prince. Third, he felt dreadful fear of what Len would do to him when he awoke. But nothing could ruin this victory! Oh, how sweet it was.

* * *

Fortunately, Len was only out cold for a couple seconds. When he opened his eyes to behold Shawn peering at him from above, he groaned, rolled over on his belly, and proceeded to utter a stream of curses Shawn had never heard before. He went on like that for a minute or so before sitting up, his face beet-red. When the mud-and-sweat-covered-prince addressed Shawn, his voice was calm. "It seems I underestimated you, Shawn." His short speech even had that royal condescending tone the reporter knew so well.

Just the fact that he said "Shawn" instead of "Tubby" or "Rossow" impressed the reporter. "I didn't mean to knock you out, you know," he said.

Len gave him a dubious look. "Hmm," he scratched his whiskers, "in that case, I did not underestimate you too much." The prince sprang to his feet as if he'd had himself a relaxing nap and declared, "Well, that's enough fighting for now. I'm ready for a bath—a gentleman must bathe at least once a month, you know. I'm sure your feet could use some soaking too. To Barbadensis Lake we go!" And with a whirl of his cape, Len trotted off.

What in the world? I swear that man has multiple personality disorder. Shawn got to his feet, groaning. "I'm beginning to think this vacation business isn't any more restful than a regular day's walk!"

Barbadensis Lake, as Len called it, was much further than Shawn liked. Now that the storm had ended and the sun showed its face to the world, all the dripping plants, the moist ground, and Shawn's clothes steamed. He wished he could go change out of his muddy, uncomfortable clothes. Only the thought of dipping his aching feet in the cool water kept him going. Len kept ahead of him the whole time, swaggering ahead as if he, not Shawn, had won the wrestling match.

Two Sides of the Coin

At last, through a sprinkling of trees, the reporter saw the glittering lake. He came to the edge and gaped at the view. In the middle of its deepest waters rose a giant arch of smooth black stone. Shawn could see more of this stone in varying shades of black in the cliffs surrounding the far side of the lake. According to one of Len's lessons, this black stone was called jinx. The purest veins of jinx on the island were found in Sea Dragon. It was the pride of Sea Dragons' natural resources, Len had said. It surprised Shawn that such a natural monument still existed, for it seems the people would've mined it for jewelry or weapons long ago.

Len, with his shirt off, stopped at the water's edge. "On second thought," said he, "I'm far too hungry to swim. You can soak your feet, but don't scare away all the fish, got it?" Still half-dressed, he marched back into the forest. Shawn wondered why he was being so nice. The reporter stepped closer to the water and grinned. How inviting it looked! Plopping down, he carefully removed the boots from his feet, sat on a rock by the water's edge, and lowered his feet into the water. It felt like putting a smoldering twig into a puddle. He sighed and massaged his tender feet.

Something hard and slippery brushed his hand underwater. He jerked out his hand with a gasp. *Ah, it's only a fish,* he realized. *What kind is that anyway?* It was the strangest fish Shawn had ever seen. It was the length of a small dog, and its sleek body reminded him of a pike. However, instead of a pike's pointy snout, this fish had a stubby snout, large eyes, and what resembled catfish whiskers. Long fins, dark stripes on its scales, and a powerful tail gave it the look of a hunter. All the while these thoughts ran through his head, his hand eased back into the water. That's when he saw *them.*

About seven feet away, a school of the creatures, large and small, had gathered in a semi-circle around him. "Wow, look at all of them!" Shawn exclaimed. "I didn't know freshwater fish swam in schools. I wonder why they're coming so close to the… oh no." Shawn's stomach dropped. The fish were watching *him.* And they looked hungry. Just as he lifted a foot from the water, the fish broke lines to attack Shawn's wounded feet. He tried to scramble back from the water's edge, but they were already upon him, snapping viciously. As Shawn turned to beat them off, a huge one latched onto his hand.

He did what any person would do under those circumstances. *"AHHHHHGH!"* The reporter screamed loud enough to wake the dead, and was not at all finished when someone wrenched him away from the writhing water's edge. It was Len, of course, who yelled something at him Shawn couldn't understand. Screaming and beating the fish against the ground, Shawn had no luck getting it off until Len sat on his arm, took his knife, and it was all over. For the fish that is. Poor Shawn lay on the ground next to it, shuddering.

It took a minute for Shawn to get his breath back. Meanwhile, Len calmly began to scale the fish. At last, the reporter sat up, examined the bite on his hand, and rattled on. "Man, I thought I was a goner for sure. Thanks for saving me, Len. What were those fish anyways? They looked like one of those ancient coelacanth fish except piranha style! I mean, when I first saw the lake, I wondered why there was jinx still left. Ha! Now I know. I'm never going to soak my feet in a lake again…" he trailed off.

Len looked over his shoulder and gave his narrow-eyed smirk. "Put the pieces together."

"*You* were the one who brought me here!"

"Very insightful of you, Rossow. And very insightful of *me*. Tell me, how often can a villain get his revenge and dinner at the same time?" Len cackled.

Shawn jumped up, mad as a bull. "You *planned* this?!"

"Slow and stupid as ever, Tubby."

Shawn's temper rose, hot and acid. His eyes flamed, "You—you are the most evil—" Shawn stopped when he saw Len smile and look down humbly, as if he were receiving a complement. The reporter clenched his fists and paced back and forth, growling between gritted teeth, "I'm so sick of being mistreated by you and everyone else on this stinking island. I never asked to be dragged into this. All I wanted was to find a good story, take some pictures and leave. But oh no, I've been chased, chained, starved, trapped, poisoned, knocked out, humiliated, and put in the stocks. I don't even know why you take me along with you! I guess I turned out to be a human punching bag after all."

Len had stopped laughing. He stared at Shawn, but the reporter didn't care what he thought. He ranted on. "My whole life I've been tossed to and fro like so much useless baggage. I guess in Sanfran Cisco all those people were worse because they were two-faced, pretending to be nice when they really don't care at all. At least here people will tell me to my face what they think... that I'm a nobody. Do you know that if I never made it back, I wouldn't be missed? I'm one of those hopeless cases with no friends and no family. Maybe that's why I left. Maybe that's why I wanted Steve to respect me. Call me an idiot. Call me anything, but I don't care." All the while he spoke, the anger started to seep out of him, replaced by an ugly combination of shame and self-pity. Shawn hung his head, defeated at last by these familiar enemies which pursued him at every turn.

Len reached out and shook his shoulder. "What do you mean, you're a nobody, fool? You're Shawn Tubby Rossow the Reporter Spy! If that's not a title to be proud of, I'm a balmy peasant. It wasn't a nobody that showed his steely determination and didn't give up in the face of humiliation. Ha! It wasn't a nobody who smacked the Prince of Fox, knocked him out cold in a wrestling match, and lived to tell the tale. And not only me, but didn't you also survive those deadly women: Queen Alexi, Princess Sylindra, and Amara, the Eternal Wrath herself!"

"Just think about everything you've accomplished in a single month! Walking, riding, running—you toughened up and bore it like a man. Yes, you've had a rough beginning, but can't you see how you've become stronger? As a hunter expects a rabbit and found a deer, you came expecting a story and found an adventure. Come on! Stop living in the past. Look around you, O Sad Scribbler. Whoever you were before, when you came to this island you became someone. Why else do you think they paid so much attention to you? You've proven yourself over and over. I've never said this to anyone before, (partly because the expression makes me feel ill) but you're a rising star. Aye, it sounds even worse when you say it," Len wrinkled his nose as if smelling sour milk.

He shook himself and continued, "So, you dislike lies? Then don't lie to me now. Who are you?"

"I'm... not a nobody."

"So what are you?"

"A reporter."

"And what, do you report, am I?"

"You're a great friend, Len." Shawn lifted his head at last, scrubbed clean of all bitterness. "I forgive you for using me as fish bait."

Len smiled. "One more question."

"Yeah, Len?"

"Will you please be my bait every time I go fishing?"

They continued their journey the next day, but the taste of that fish and the memory of that day stayed with Shawn. Just like him, the land around them changed over time. They left the leafy forests of Fox behind and entered the land of pines and cliffs. The going became rough, but Shawn was grateful that at least they didn't have to take their horses over the steep passes. After a day of climbing, they skirted the edge of a tall cliff. Len strode ahead while Shawn inched along with his back against the stone wall. He tried not to look over the dizzying edge. Len called back at him. "Hurry up, Ros—Ahhh!" His scream was accompanied by the sound of crumbling rock. Shawn looked up just in time to see Len vanish from sight, leaving a gaping hole in the path.

"Len!" Shawn screamed.

Disbelief sped through Shawn's brain as he crept towards the ten-foot gap, peering down for any sign of the prince. He half-expected to find Len clinging to the rock wall, saying, "Thought you got rid of me, aye?" But there was nothing to see except the last great boulder crash against the ground far below.

Shawn sank to the ground, trembling with horror. He squeezed his eyes shut and willed the nightmare to go away. All he could think of was the scene in *Lord of the Rings* when Gandalf was torn off the bridge of Khazad Dum, leaving Frodo and the others without their greatest helper and friend. But could it be true? Could Len be *dead*? The reporter buried his face in his hands. However, whatever grief that might have followed was stopped short by an idea that came to Shawn like a morsel to a starving man. *Perhaps, like Gandalf, the fall hasn't killed Len! After all, he has wings doesn't he? Could he get them out that fast?*

Shawn hardly dared to hope, in case tragedy was around the corner; or, in this case, lying at the bottom of the cliff. Yet whether he meant to or not, as Shawn looked down again, he did hope. The pine forest below was dark, forbidding, and betrayed no secrets. All Shawn could see at the bottom of the cliff was a pile of shattered rock. *Could Len be under...* but Shawn pushed the thought away before it was finished. Somehow, he had to get down there and find Len.

Shrugging off the bag, Shawn rummaged through it. Besides the food, he had two flint-stones and a tinder box, an extra cape, and his razor—all these he set out on the cliff-side. The only remaining item was a bundle of rope. Shawn reasoned he had three choices: Go back the way they'd come and try to find his way back to the pine forest; try to bridge the gap and then go down; or, worst of all, descend the cliff with the rope. An unseasonably cold breeze swept along the cliff-side, but that was not what caused Shawn to shiver.

The reporter knew he could not turn back. They had spent the whole day on the cliff path. Who knew what was happening to Len at this minute? And once off the trail, how would he be able to find exactly where Len might be? But if he couldn't go back, could he go forward? For all he knew, the ground might slope down soon. Or there might be a path cut into the wall that he could take down to the forest floor. Best of all, there might be a town where he could find help. Shawn shook his head, *Too many "mights"!* There was also the "might" of even crossing the gap, and Shawn was not willing to risk that for nothing. That left only the descent of the cliff, but he didn't know anything about rock-climbing. *Can I trust one little knot with my life?* Shawn wondered. Yet he knew he must.

Shawn rose to his feet at last, feeling like the weight of the world rested on his shoulders. Resolutely, he set out to find an anchor for his rope. He soon discovered a gnarly pine a little down the path by the wall. Using the sailor's knot which his father had taught him so long ago, Shawn made the rope secure. *Now what?* he thought. It occurred to him that he should make sure the rope reached the bottom. He flung it over the side and watched the rope fall twisting through the air like a flying serpent. Soon it lay flat against the cliff-side, and disappointment twisted in Darth's stomach when it brushed the ground. No excuses there.

Next was the problem of how to get *him* down. First, Shawn tried making a loop around his waist like he imagined the rock climbers did it, but it felt wrong. He tried one way after another—wishing with all his heart he'd watched that Friday night rock-climbing TV show. At last, he discovered that if he started by putting the rope through his legs and over his left shoulder, it would hold him securely even when he leaned back with all his weight. He began to slowly back up, looking over his shoulder as he let the taut rope slide between his hands. Shawn knew that if he stopped at the edge, he would not be able to go another step. He would see what a crazy idea it was and leave Len behind. Still, when his heel met thin air, Shawn was paralyzed.

I can't go on, I can't go on! Shawn the Reporter screeched in one ear.

I must go. There is no other way. A calm, clear-headed voice spoke in his other ear.

As much as he hated it, the louder voice overpowered Shawn's courage. He started to pull himself forward to safety when his right boot slipped. Screaming, Shawn fell until his arms hit the rock shelf. Pain shot through his body, but with it a rush of adrenaline. The rope was still wrapped around him, keeping him from falling further. Shawn gripped the rope so hard his knuckles turned white. Little by little, he got his feet under him and began the long climb down. After the initial start and the moment of gutless panic, a strange peace settled over him. Every minute or so, he got stuck, and fear would prick his bubble of calm. Somehow, he always found a way. Holding the rope in a death grip, he let it go an inch at a time.

Shawn kept thinking as he descended how a near-death experience changes things. Perhaps, having seen the worst terror life can throw at you, the present terrors lose their power. Maybe if that happened to him enough, he could be as brave as Len. *However, courage is stupidity when one doesn't use his brain,* he reflected. *On the other hand, sometimes you have to disregard what your brain is telling you and just do it. Good old Nike.* About ten minutes later, Shawn looked down to see the tops of the trees just a couple yards below him! Grinning, he began to bounce down. On his last bounce, he lost grip on the rope, spun around, and fell. He belly-flopped onto the ground, startled but unhurt. The reporter jumped up and pumped his fists in the air, shouting, "Huzzah!" A flock of birds foraging on the ground shot upwards so suddenly that Shawn nearly fell over. He laughed at himself, marveling at how good it felt to be alive.

Len may not be alive. This thought sobered Shawn at once. He set off with the cliff wall on his left, gazing up to pinpoint the gap. The sight of that gaping hole in the cliff pecked away at any optimism he had left. Faster and faster, he quickened his pace until he was at a dead-run. Now there was no time for worrying. He searched back and forth through the trees, listening for any faint cry for help. A family of rabbits were surprised when the reporter came running to them, "Len, is that you?" When Shawn arrived at the gap, he found a pine tree crushed underneath the boulders, with shards of rock and wood scattered over the ground. He scoured the debris, clearing away branches and stone to see if the prince lay amid the pile. There was no trace of him. It was as if Len had been teleported to another world.

As mysterious as it was, Shawn's hope rose again. Surely if Len had hit the ground, there would be some sign of him. He must have gotten away! *If that's true,* thought Shawn with a wry smile, *then I've climbed down here for nothing. Why, he might even be looking for me up there. Oh blast, I wish I could call out to him! But if I did that, even if he was dead, he'd come back to life just to slap me silly for being an idiot. Hmm, not a bad idea at that. I yell, he finds me to shut me up. Then that Fox general and his cronies hear about it and shut both of us up. Well, if he doesn't find me soon, I couldn't care less about those soldiers. For the love of Drake, as Len would say, who made that stupid, old mountain path anyways?*

Putting his back against the cliff, Shawn noticed for the first time that the sun had slipped from its zenith. It bathed the pines with a faint, red light. Although it was a beautiful sight, Shawn closed his eyes and sighed. Exhaustion crashed upon his shoulders like a waterfall. He laid his head against the cold stone and let his mind drift. It floated with the wind over the rustling pines and away to the ocean. The surf moved with it up and down, back and forth, until with the crashing of a wave, it flew up into the blood-red sky. There it spiraled and corkscrewed between the heavens and the earth, a pleasant place of rest. Even up there, however, a whisper of thought broke his reverie.

Where is Len?

* * *

When Shawn opened his eyes, the world had changed. The sun had gone to bed. He shivered, wrapped his cape more tightly around him, and fought to return to the land of slumber. Just then, a delicious smell met his nose, which awakened his stomach. How could he sleep now, with that aroma assailing him on the wind? Up he got and away into the woods. Both caution and curiosity accompanied him on the way. It wasn't until he saw the glow of a campfire ahead did he stop and consider what to do. He was still considering when a song arose from the campfire area, rich and warm,

Tell me, have you heard the thirstin' of the night, lookin' for some wine?
Have you sipped the brew of the wild, I ask
No, I haven't, sir—but if you'd be so kind
Would you sweeten this despair of mine?

Oh no, no, no, no, no-oh!
Despair is plenty sweet here in the shadow

Tell me, have you heard the grumbling of the Isle, hungry but reviled?
And could you feed him please, I ask
No, I could not, sir—and if you'd be so kind
Would you let me go before he bites?

Oh no, no, no, no, no-oh!

Two Sides of the Coin

Despair is plenty sweet here in the shadow...

Shawn stepped out from behind the tree, wanting to sing, wanting to cry. "LEN!"

The prince himself sat back against a stone, his legs crossed before the fire. He strummed a wooden, hand-held harp and murmured, "Took you long enough to get here. Your dinner's getting cold."

"But I can't believe this! I thought you'd—"

"Gone to my rocky grave? Funny. To be fair though, I was starting to think you'd either died or left me to my fate. Oh well, you should eat. Your plate's on that log there."

Shawn took his tree bark plate of roasted meat but kept his eyes on Len as he sat down by the fire. "I take it you got your wings open, then? You didn't get hurt at all?"

"Wings open, yes. I still had a rough landing. I had to swerve into the forest to keep from hitting the rocks, then my wing hit a tree branch, and when I crash-landed I believe I sprained my ankle. Ha! I've had worse from fights with Sylindra."

Shawn laughed. "You seemed to hold your own against her last time you met."

"She was in a good mood," he responded. "She must've been devastating the lives of some poor, innocent creatures before she met us."

"That's the harp she wanted, right? I guess today was the perfect time to make it."

"Yup. Jealous vixen, she never forgave me for giving my first one to Ullia," Len rolled his eyes. "And before you ask me who Ullia is, I implore you *don't*. I don't want to talk about it."

"Fine," Shawn said, although Len's request made him even more curious.

Len went back to plucking at the strings of his harp, while Shawn finished his dinner. When he tossed his plate into the fire, Len put aside the harp and arose with difficulty. Motioning to Shawn, he limped away from the glowing campfire. They made their way through the black trees, following the path of starlit sky above them. Drawing up to a wall of pines, Len pulled back a heavy branch and motioned for Shawn to go through. He stepped through and froze as the forest and the cliff ended all at once, and before his eyes spread an immense canyon. It was a veritable fortress of stone: pinnacles, tunnels, arches, and maze-like passages for miles in each direction, like Daedalus's Labyrinth. The moon shone upon it like a massive flashlight, casting shadows from the towers of stone.

Unable to construct the words of his wonder, Shawn didn't say anything. Len put a hand on his shoulder. "We've arrived, Shawn. Behold: Strothar Canyon!"

CHAPTER 14

The Naming of the Two

Tonight was the night. The stranger fidgeted in front of his mirror, pulling his new gold tunic this way and that and combing his fingers through his hair. He could never remember being so nervous and excited. Nifty stood on the floor next to him, grooming his bushy tail. "Gotta look good for the ladies," he pronounced, fluffing his tail. He scrambled up the mirror's side to scrutinize his friend.

"Well, Nifty, how do I look?" The man struck a pose with his hands on his hips and his chest in the air.

"Like a hedgehog fallen in honey!" Nifty tittered.

Scowling, the man shooed him off the mirror. "Impertinent squirrel!" he huffed.

"Hmm, impertinent, eh? Have you been talking with the trees?"

At that moment, a weeping willow's branch curled through the window to snatch hold of the garrulous squirrel, who made a great show of screaming and struggling. The tree spoke in its husky voice, "Now don't you take any mind of this rascal, friend. I'll have him tidy and respectable by the time you're ready."

As the branch receded with the squirrel out the window, their voices faded away, "Ha, respectable! I wasn't finished yet, you hopping, old, hunky-dory horror!"

"Oh, such language I never heard the like of!"

The man took a deep breath and checked himself over once again. *Something's missing. I've got my sword. What else?* He paced back and forth.

"Dear?" a voice murmured from the doorway. Standing at the door, with her slim, green dress bringing out the emerald in her eyes, Melody had never looked so lovely, or so the man thought.

His face lit up as soon as he saw her. "I-I'm ready."

She crossed over to him with a laugh. "Not yet, you're not." Out of the chest in the corner, she pulled the white cloak which Lovely Lake had given him when he first arrived. "You remember what you need to say?" she asked as she put it over his shoulders and buckled the gold clasp on his chest. The man wondered if she could feel the thundering of his heart under her delicate hand. "Thank you so much, Melody. For everything," he spoke in a low voice so it would not tremble.

Her cheeks turned pink as a blossoming rose, and she shook her head. "You are the one who is to be thanked. You've shown me nothing but kindness since the blessed day you came to our fair Island. This is the happiest day of my life. Oh, I could sing right now for gladness!"

"Then why don't you?" he asked, leading her by the hand from his cottage.

"Only if you'll sing with me," she responded.

So together they sang, while the trees hummed along, the creatures bounded ahead of them, and the sunset came down over the sea, casting a dreamy, purple light over the Island of Joy. It was the True Love Song… or TLS as Nifty would say. The song, once it has begun, never ends. Whether the True Loves are together or apart, they are always singing or humming it to themselves. The man felt that he was a completely different person from the man who sang his First Song to Melody above Rainbow Falls. Singing was as simple as breathing now. He didn't think up words but let them come as they wanted. He was quite satisfied with his voice, especially when accompanied by the trees' voices. However, every time Melody opened her mouth to sing, it was like the world hushed, and all hung on her every word.

They were still singing when the rolling, daisy-speckled hills brought them into the Joyful Village. For the first time that the man

Two Sides of the Coin

could remember, there was not a person to be seen. They made their way to the market square only to find tables and trays of food sitting undisturbed around the jumping fountain. The man scratched his head. "Where could they be?"

"I think I know," Melody replied with a mischievous sparkle in her eye. She ran ahead of him, beckoning with one hand. They raced out of the village, through green fields, over Sparkle River, and came out into Flower Meadows. Just as they reached the edge, people popped up like gophers from behind every flower bush. "SURPRISE!" How on earth they all hid so well, the man could not guess. Everybody laughed and shouted to each other whilst, hand in hand, they formed a circle. Melody squeezed his hand before joining her parents. In the midst of all the motion, a dozen animals gathered around the man. In their various squeaking or grunting voices, they all called at once, "Hey, hey! Remember that time when you fell right in that pile of Sweet Friendships over there? Yeah! You remember that? Then Melody—oh, this is the best part—let me tell! I want to tell him."

"I'll tell him," pronounced Nifty.

"Tell me what?" he asked.

The squirrel climbed up his leg to perch on his shoulder. "On the day you arrived," he began in a loud, theatrical voice. All the people went silent and looked at him. He beat his tail. "Go on! Keep talking."

The people complied, breaking out in conversation again. Nifty chuckled. "Sheesh, can't a squirrel say anything without people freaking out? Teehee!" He tweaked the man's ear playfully. "Anyways, when you first arrived, you heard Melody's song coming over the hill and found her. She was sitting right over there, remember? Just singing like any normal day. But then out you came out the forest, sang along with her, and then keeled over just like that!" He slapped his paws together.

The man laughed. "Yes, I remember, though it seems like a dream now. So what is it you wish to tell me?"

The little bunnies wiggled their cotton tails in delight, and the hedgehog chuckled so hard that he had to roll up so as not to poke his friends. Even the reserved lizard had a pleased expression on his face. Nifty leaned forward and whispered, "She didn't know if you would turn good or not. But she wanted to save you, so she gave you her First Kiss!" He bounced straight up in the air. "And tada! You woke up and have been one of us ever since."

The man was speechless. All the commotion around him seemed to fade away. Through blurred eyes, he found Melody in the crowd. She was also crying tears of joy and, distraught at the strange sensation, turned to Millie. "Mother, what's wrong with me? These things falling from my eyes, are they what's called tears? My heart feels like it is being squeezed, and it *hurts!* Yet, at the same time, I am happier than I've ever been."

Millie drew her daughter into her arms. "That's True Love. It's so powerful it hurts, but it's a good hurt. You made the right choice, love."

Meanwhile, Steadfast stepped out, booming, "Please listen everybody. It's time!"

The crowd went quiet, quieter than the man had ever heard. Every face beamed at him as he made his way towards the center. When he stood before Steadfast, the leader put his arm around him. He boomed out, "Welcome, people of joy! Welcome, our wise guardians, the trees. Welcome, all you creatures. And welcome, our dear friend. We have gathered this evening to have our naming ceremony for this new brother of ours. Granted, it is rather belated, for we usually name our children three days after they are born." There was some laughter at that. "We also usually have the child's parents up front to speak for them, but since you are of age, that's not necessary. The rest shall be the same."

Steadfast paused to let the excitement build. The stranger trembled. He was glad when Steadfast declared, "Kneel and present this child before everyone." No one laughed now, but held their collective breaths. Dropping to his knees, the man bent his head under the weight of Steadfast's bear-like hand. "With great joy, you have been anticipated, brother, and with great joy you have arrived," Steadfast proclaimed.

The people, trees, and other creatures shouted, "So be it!"

"Here we have gathered to acknowledge this new brother and grant him a name as well as a place forever among us."

"So be it!"

"What say you, man?" Steadfast asked.

Two Sides of the Coin

The man swallowed hard. *The vow... I have to say it now.* The words were on the tip of his tongue, but he wasn't sure if he could say them. All the breath seemed to have been squeezed out of him. Desperately, he searched for Melody in the crowd. Amidst the sea of blonde-haired men and women, he found her looking at him with such love, he took heart. Drawing a breath, he gave her his word. "I swear to love, support, and defend the Island of Joy and all who dwell here."

"So be it!"

"As the leader of the village," Steadfast announced, "I affirm his chosen name. Henceforth, you shall be known as *Stephen!*"

Stephen arose, crying out with the Island of Joy, "SO BE IT!"

* * *

Clang! Shink—clang, clang! Len was frustrated.

Ping! Shink! Clang—thud. "Rats!" So was Shawn. He bent, gasping, and a bead of sweat dripped from his chin.

"How come you dropped your sword?" Len demanded.

Shawn shook his head. "I don't know. I blocked your strike, but the shock hurt so much, I couldn't hang on."

"First of all," said Len, "you shouldn't have blocked that strike. If you had just moved a little back and to the right, you could've not only saved yourself the pain, but also been in a position to counter. Secondly, *you never let go of your sword*, no matter how much it hurts to hang on. Grip it with both hands if you have to. When you let your sword drop..." Len flicked his blade upwards, letting the point rest an inch away from Shawn's throat. "You're dead."

Sighing, Shawn nodded. He picked up his sword to begin again, but his heart was not in it. The prince had to repeat himself on everything, and even then Shawn did not comprehend. They continued to go through every motion, block, strike, and dodge in slow motion. After a few minutes, the prince disarmed the reporter again, who stared at the ground whilst Len explained what he did, or rather did not do. When Shawn showed no sign of repenting, the prince combined his instructions with injections of idiot, fool, and Sir Sorry Scribbler, intending to rouse him from his apathy. He succeeded only in arresting the reporter's attention for a few seconds, in which Shawn lunged at his head. Then Len moved like lightning, knocking the sword from his hand and explaining for the umpteenth time, "No, stupid, you have made the worst mistake in the book! Never fight out of rage."

Shawn gave a thin smile. "You sound like Yoda," before hastily explaining, "A short, green, er, I mean wise, umm—man, sort of— in this story. He's always saying not to fight with anger."

Len dipped his head. "Well, he's no wiser than any fighter with common sense. When you angrily lash out, you cannot control your motions. Ah! And that is the key to sword-fighting, being in control of your sword. Wielding it like an extension of your arm." Len demonstrated an inch from Shawn's face with three whip-like strikes.

"I wish you wouldn't do that," he complained.

"Then don't let me. Fight, you fool, else I knock you down and tickle your insides with my knife as your enemy would!"

Why does it always seem like Len's my enemy? Shawn thought. He wiped the sweat from his forehead and tried to focus on his lesson. Things had changed in the five days since they had arrived at Strothar Canyon, and Shawn was torn within himself once again. It all began three days ago…

The two travelers walked side-by-side along the top of the cliff. The path was wide enough for them to walk together without bumping, not that a drop would kill them. It was only about ten feet to the ground. Shawn kept his gaze downward. After walking through the valley all yesterday too, Shawn's feet ached. *I still don't see why Len keeps insisting we make our campsite in the middle of the labyrinth. After all, didn't we lose that Fox patrol long ago?* He grumbled to himself. Len had even gone back to the cliff side for the rope, despite Shawn's pleas that there was no way they could tell the rope was Len's even if they found it. But Len was adamant; nothing Shawn said could deter him.

The reporter gave up reasoning with him. Every time he brought up the fact that they had lost the Foxes, Len gave him that pitying smile and murmured in a patronizing tone, "Alright, if you're so confident, why don't we head back to the inn? I never got to finish my dinner."

Len nudged him, interrupting his thoughts. "Hey."

"Hey. Did you see something?"

"No." They walked on for another minute in silence before Len said, "Listen. If I think you need to learn something, I am obligated to teach you. Everything I teach has a reason, though you might not see it, and you'll have to trust my judgment. Do you agree?"

"Of course," replied Shawn. Hardly were the words out of his mouth when the prince shoved him off the cliff side. Shawn yelped, hit the ground feet-first, and collapsed on his bottom. He lay stunned, wallowing in a swamp of confusion. Also, he was half-convinced that he'd broken something. However, when he saw Len smirking overhead, righteous wrath spurred him to his feet. "What was that for?!" he yelled, rubbing his bottom.

Len opened his wings, turned a circle like a giant vulture, and glided down. "You needed to know what it felt like," was his calm response. He grinned and pointed to a cave just across from them. "Would you look at that? A perfect campsite! Excellent work, Rossow!" And he patted Shawn's shoulder. The reporter shoved his fists in his pockets to keep them from leaving a new mark on the prince's face.

The next morning, Shawn's training began in earnest. He exercised the whole day: running through the tunnels, rock-climbing, cliff-jumping, and more. It wasn't all exercise, however. Len introduced him to the longbow, the crossbow, the spear, and swordplay. Yet, although time should have cleared up Shawn's confusion, the days that passed only added to it. Shawn would be concentrating on a push-up only to have his face pushed in the mud and be informed, "Fourteen! You needed to know how it felt, Rossow. Fifteen!" He was also pushed down a hill, into a pond, and into a ditch.

To avoid this, Shawn began walking a little behind Len, but the danger of that soon appeared. As Len turned a corner, a dagger shot out—just missing Shawn's nose—to bury itself in the mossy wall. Enraged, Shawn popped his head around the corner. "Why did you— oh, never mind."

Earlier this morning when he returned after a run, a pebble hit his shoulder. It stung, but Shawn shrugged it off as yet another prank of Len's. The next time, the rock was a bit bigger. Standing in the shallow water, with a spear poised to throw, Shawn jumped as the pebble hit the back of his neck. Of course, all the nearby fish vanished from sight. Shawn whirled around to face the prince. "How does hitting me with rocks teach me anything?"

He threw his spear into the ground and stomped past the prince. Suddenly, it occurred to him that he shouldn't turn his back on Len. Just as he peeked over his shoulder, Len threw another rock. Shawn ducked, to Len's disappointment. The prince acted as if they were playing a game of dodge ball... or dodge-rock, rather.

Though Shawn felt like strangling Len, he stalked away. *I will never, ever understand these people. Is Len going crazy? He was bad enough on the way here, but now he's taking every chance to hurt me! And what am I doing here anyway? All day he makes me exercise and learn stuff, but he never tells me why. Seriously, I should be back in Sanfran Cisco now, making billions, but I'm out in the middle of a blasted valley getting blasted by stones by this loony Fox-prince. Oh, blast! Now what?*

While marching through the narrow passage, livid, Shawn hadn't noticed a strange sound until it was right ahead. An arch formed a grand entrance to his left where the sound issued. Wary of strangers, Shawn pressed his back against the wall and listened. "Be ba dum, do da tum, a fiddle a fum, and a riddle with rum! Heh heh, that's a good 'un, Honest. Is that everything? Well, I should say so. Oh, but I'm just missin' one thing... Heh!"

The creaky voice, dipping up and down, sounded familiar to Shawn, but he couldn't place it. *I may as well go and make the fellow's acquaintance,* he thought. Entering the clearing, he waited for the man to notice his presence. Shawn couldn't have chosen a more interesting person to watch. The man was short and somewhat plump, but he walked with a bounce in his step. He sported a white mustache so curly Shawn wondered for a moment if it was fake. His white hair was slicked with gel, and he wore a black fez. He also wore a jaunty, scarlet tunic with a black vest. A tiny pair of spectacles teetered on his long nose. Wrinkles appeared around the man's sea-blue eyes whenever he smiled or laughed, which he did often and heartily. He bustled about his campsite, talking aloud, and amusing himself with his own wit. As he bent over to search through an enormous pack, he nearly vanished within it. "Where could it be?" he muttered. "Is that it? Heehee, no it ain't. *Definitely* not!"

Shawn stepped forward. "Excuse me, sir?"

The man cried out and promptly fell into the pack. He peeped out from beneath the cover. "Thieves! Vagabonds! Come to steal from a poor merchant, have you? Oh, Honest, your goodness has finally caught up with you. Well, let it be said that Erwinkle didn't go down without a fight! I bet you weren't expecting this—"

So saying, he disappeared, and the bag jiggled as he rummaged about. "Please, good sir," Shawn coughed to keep a laugh at bay, "I am neither thief nor vagabond. I'm not going to—"

"Ha! So say you. Take that!" a black box tumbled from the bag.

Gasping, Shawn jumped back. The box rolled twice, and out popped a hideous creature. "SHRARRHK!" it shrieked.

Dang, he really had me worried for a second. Shawn blinked. "It's a…"

"Goblin jack-in-the-box from the Crow Region," the man crawled out and retrieved his item. "Quite a state of the art little device, donch'ya think? Heehee, this little guy has saved me from many a peril, yessir, yes indeed. And now for the amazing price of twenty shekels you, even you, could own such a treasure. What a deal! So, what'll it be? Give it to you at base price or buy one get one free?"

Shawn held up his hands. "Oh no, you got me all wrong. I don't want your jack-in-the-box."

The merchant tossed the box over his shoulder into the pack. "Am I to presume that you really are a thief?"

"No!"

"Then what are you?"

"I'm a reporter."

"A spy?" The fellow clapped his hands like a child receiving a new toy. "Fantastic! It's my lucky day. Say, young man, how would you like to come work for me in Dreken 'Eils? That's the Sea Dragon capital city,

243

doncha know. I've needed a good spy for awhile. Competition can get pretty tough, and I'm not as young as I used to be. I promise I'll treat ya right, pay ya well, and never, ever cheat! Nope, Erwinkle is *always* honest with his friends!"

"Wait, wait! Rewind." Shawn frowned. "Despite popular opinion, I'm *not* a spy."

"Well, why didn't you say so?" Erwinkle snapped. He crossed his arms and sized up the reporter. "I really had my heart set on hiring some whippersnapper... if only to fight off other thieves and vagabonds." He nodded to himself and asked, "So what do you say about joining in cohorts with ol' Erwinkle?"

"No, I really ca—" Shawn started to say when he realized, *Maybe this is my chance! If I go with the crazy, old merchant to Sea Dragon, I could get a ship, go back to Sanfran Cisco. A real sailing ship, like the kind I used to have back home before...*

The thought hit his heart like a sledgehammer, knocking loose a chest of memories he had strived so long to keep under lock and key. He remembered looking out from his window at the beautiful sunset reflected on the lake, Mom handing him the Lord of the Rings trilogy for his birthday, Dad working with him in the carpenter shop where they built a boat, learning to sail and talk like an old sea dog. Intermixed with these sweet treasures were hidden knives: the long nights waiting in the hospital for news, the "For Sale" sign nailed to the door of their cabin, Dad's cold goodbye when he left for the city, the letter which told him—

Desperately, Shawn slammed the lid on his thoughts, but one more popped out: Mom wouldn't be there to welcome him home with hot chocolate and hugs when he brought the "Millennium Falcon" into the bay. Shawn's face contorted with pain. He turned away from Erwinkle and paced to the cliff. *Get a hold of yourself, Shawn!* he berated himself. Yet the bitter truth of the memory stopped him in his escape-bent tracks. *Even if I did get back to Sanfran Cisco, what then? Who's waiting on me besides Mr. Morri?* Shawn rubbed his face and smoothed his hair. Summoning courage, Shawn faced the little merchant. "Sir... Erwinkle... I can't make this decision in such a short time."

Two Sides of the Coin

"Heh!" grunted Erwinkle. "Well, whether you come with me or not, I'm gonna skedaddle two mornings from now, before the sun has begun to rise. You got that? Not tomorrow morning but the morning after that, before the sun—"

"—has begun to rise," Shawn finished.

"Bright one, aincha? Heehee!" And with that, the merchant picked up his bag (Shawn was mystified how he managed that) and strolled away singing, "Mathildaaaaaa! No girl for me but Mathildaaaaaa! Yes, darlin', only you."

Shawn called after, asking where to meet him if he decided to go. Erwinkle hooked a thumb behind him at the clearing. Long after the strange man had gone, Shawn could hear his song echoing from the canyon walls.

* * *

Shawn came back to himself as his sword clattered to the ground once again. He looked up like a thief caught red-handed. Len sheathed his sword. "That's enough. How am I to teach you when your mind is in the clouds?" He gestured to the sun, which had sunken until it rested on the crown of the tallest mountain. "And besides, it's time for dinner." With his typical energy, the prince trotted away. Shawn trudged after. The wind seemed just as exhausted as the reporter, sighing while it wandered through the valley's mazes.

Alright, Shawn. Time's run out. What do you choose? Shawn laid his head against the cold, unfeeling stone wall. Thoughts spun round his mind until he was dizzy. It seemed like the Island of Despair was on trial, and one witness after another rose to condemn it. The whole court was in agreement except for one annoying, persistent defender. It irked Judge Shawn that the defender didn't seem to care a whit about his safety.

"For my final point," declared an accuser, "It would be pure foolishness to stay at the Island of Despair when we've had three narrow escapes from death in a two month timeframe."

"That may be true, but you might also say that Shawn has also never felt so alive, right? Right?" the defender chimed in. He was booed by the court.

So it continued. Every time the case was almost settled, that defender would speak. At last, Shawn brought the anvil down with the announcement: *I will return to Sanfran Cisco.* At once all the voices were silenced. Shawn raised his head and looked around. The sun had slipped from its mountainous perch, plunging the world into shadow.

The reporter heaved a sigh that seemed to well up from the deepest parts of his heart, and threw his regret to the wind in order to think practically. *Getting away tonight will not be easy, Len being such a light sleeper. After I get up, he will wait for me to return. If I don't, he'll come looking. I could leave before bed. Yes, I could tell him I want to go hunting, and he should not expect me any time soon. Of course, the danger of that is he might ask to go with me or tell me I can't go. And even if he gave permission, he may follow after. I could tell him I'm going to practice with my sword. Man, I can't wait to see the look he gives me when I say that! Hmmm, what else would I want to do in the middle of the night? Fishing, hiking, star-gazing...*

Deep in thought, the reporter drifted to the campsite, about a half mile away. Darth's stomach growled at the aroma of roasting meat. He quickened his pace and soon came around the bend to where the campfire glowed. In the past five days, they had given the campsite a personality. Horse blankets were used as walls for the small cave. It was a tight squeeze getting in, but once settled, the place was remarkably warm and cozy. There was also a small carpet before the entrance which said in flowing letter, "Sweet Nightmares!"

Len had made the campfire from scratch: digging the pit, collecting the stones, and arranging them. Indeed, he had not let Shawn even touch a rock while he worked. Len had also fashioned a spit from pine wood on which their dinner, two rabbits, filled the air with a mouth-watering scent. They had found rocks for chairs and dragged a flat boulder beside the fire pit to serve as a table. Shawn had to step carefully over the weapons, clothes, and other devices strewn about the ground.

Two Sides of the Coin

Len stood up from the fire. "Oh, there you are, Tubby! I was beginning to get worried the fish had eaten you, but I knew you would not tolerate missing dinner even for that."

Shawn smiled. "You got me there. I am hungry." He sat and warmed his hands. "Are the rabbits almost finished?"

Len flipped his dark hair from his eyes. "Ha! Don't deceive me. You wouldn't have shown up yet if they weren't ready, hmm?" Taking a knife, he sliced open a rabbit and steam wafted up to mingle with the smoke. "Just as I thought. They're done."

They dug in eagerly, blowing on their fingers as they devoured the scorching meat. After a few minutes of hungry silence, Shawn commented how nice it would be to listen to music while they ate. Len boasted of the famous orchestra his parents employed that played for them at every meal. Scoffing, Shawn told him about the huge orchestras he had attended, as well as rock, jazz, and country music concerts. After trying to explain what this music sounded like, Shawn waved his hand. "The point is, I have a healthy taste in music."

"That's nothing," Len snorted. "I've been bombarded with the greatest music of the Island since before I was born. Which must be why I turned out to be such a wondrous musician." So saying, he pulled the harp from the packs and strummed a lively tune. It reminded Shawn of a forest with a winding stream. The smooth cords were the wind moving through the trees. The plucked notes were the water's voice. When the music took a comical turn, Shawn imagined a raccoon trying to catch a fish. The notes rose to crescendo before *plunk!* the fish flopped into the stream.

Shawn applauded, and Len bowed. "Thank you, thank you! Improvised, the whole thing." At Shawn's skeptical look, Len muttered, "Well, most of it anyhow. Which reminds me," he pulled a wood object from his tunic, "I carved this for you."

Shawn was speechless as he took the intricately carved wooden instrument, which looked remarkably like a recorder. It was soft and light as a butterfly's wings. For a whole minute, he turned it over in his hands and exclaiming at the pattern of twisting vines. Len shrugged off the praise. Finally, Shawn put it to his mouth and blew a long, clear note. It rang out off the canyon walls, while the shadows listened in silence. He played one note after another, delighted to find he could play a wide range. "I used to play a clarinet in college," he explained. "Who knows? I could've been the best clarinet player in the world if I'd gone into music instead of journalism."

Len ignored the boasting and picked up his harp. "How about you accompany me?" He plucked the strings reminiscently. "Do you know Carpe Noctem?"

"Nope. How does it go?"

Len soon taught him the song, playing the notes one at a time until Shawn could find the correct finger-hole combination. They played through the simple yet lovely tune several times. "Alright my turn," Shawn said. "How about… hmm, Amazing Grace? You do know that, right?"

"Amazing Grace? Never heard of it," replied Len.

This time it was Shawn who played out the melody, and the prince listened. The second time through, he joined in with long flowing chords that added such a depth to the music that Shawn's heart flew. They played until Shawn ran out of breath at the last stanza. Len leaned forward with a rare, genuine smile, "That was a good song."

"The words are beautiful too. The only problem with an instrument that you blow into is you can't sing at the same time," Shawn observed.

"That and your spit drips out," was Len's wry response. "Nevermind, this time I'll play a song with words." Propping the harp against his hip, Len played a song which once again painted images in the reporter's mind. This time it was stately and noble, like a great ship at full sail bursting through the waves. But it was also sad and lonely-sounding.

Shawn listened closely, blowing odd notes a couple times on his flute before putting it down. Len had his eyes closed, and he swayed back and forth to the harp's song. Completing the tune, Len took a deep breath and began to sing with the music. The prince's rich voice, full of emotion, echoed through the tunnels. It was his beloved's song, the one she had sung when he fell in love. Shawn was pulled into the tragic story of two lovers: a sailor and a lady. Len whispered the last line, and ended with a final, rising chord.

Two Sides of the Coin

Waves crashing, calling, crying; my love's eternal heartbeat!

In the quiet that followed, the campfire crackled. It spread a warm, orange glow over the men's faces. Len appeared to be hypnotized by the flames. *Perhaps this is my opportunity! He looks so relaxed,* thought Shawn.

A guilty pang hit him in the middle. *How can you leave now, Shawn? He's your friend, not your captor, for heaven's sake!* That pesky defender was back.

Shawn shooed him away. *No, I've gotta stick to my decision. If I don't, I may never get another chance. Len would do the same if he were in my shoes... wouldn't he?*

"Say, Len..." Shawn commented. "I'm not really tired right now. I want to go, umm, do some sword practice. Yeah, I kinda feel bad about being so scatterbrained this afternoon." Len merely raised an eyebrow. "I'll be back by tomorrow morning," he promised.

Len didn't respond at first. Shawn began to worry he'd fallen asleep when the prince stated, "Fine. You don't have to ask permission to leave camp."

He—he gave me permission to leave! I don't believe it, thought Shawn. Before Len could rethink it, he hopped up, "Well, I guess I'll see you later." He walked to the edge of the campsite, choking on the lie. *Is that all I'll get to say? This could be the last time I ever see him. Just don't look back, Darth, whatever you do. Keep walking! Keep—*

"Say, Tubby?" Len strode towards him.

Shawn froze. *The gig is up!* "Yeah?" he murmured, like a boy caught with his fists full of stolen candy.

"You forgot your sword," the prince chuckled and tossed it to him. Shawn flinched, shielding his face, and barely caught the sheathed sword.

"Thanks, Len," he stammered, "f-for everything. The rescue, the lessons, the dagger, and the flute. I'm truly thankful."

Chirp, chirp, went an oblivious cricket. Len yawned. "Well, that was ridiculously heartfelt. You're welcome." And so they parted ways.

The air was cold away from the fire. Shawn gathered his cloak around him and forced his feet into a run. What he had said lingered in the back of his mind. As fast as he ran, he couldn't escape his guilt. Finally he halted, panting. The sword at his side felt heavier than usual. When he pulled the sword from its sheath, Shawn still got chills from the sound. Yes, the long blade was heavy, yet he had learned to take comfort in its heaviness. He lifted the blade high, admiring the way the moonlight gleamed on the metal. Regretfully, he lowered it. *I can't take this with me. I don't want to be a thief as well as a liar.* Shawn gazed at the grey sky with patches of starlight shining through. *Well, I still have some time before I meet the merchant. Why not a little practice?* The thought was as much to ease his battered conscience as to pass the time. Shawn found his way to the clearing where he and Len had practiced for so many hours.

The moonlight cast a surreal, dream-like quality on the clearing. Shawn took a deep breath and began to practice. Faster and faster, he whirled the blade, not only going through the motions, but feeling them. He pretended there was an opponent ahead of him whom he dubbed Shame. His enemy charged him straight on, mocking the reporter, "Who do you think you are, a knight? You don't deserve to carry that blade! *You're nothing!*"

Shawn struck out at his foe, swinging first at his legs and adding a back-slice to the head. At that moment, Greed attacked from his right. He blocked just in time and kicked him in the stomach. But now enemies appeared from all directions. Shawn whirled and leaped, slashed and blocked: consequently disarming Laziness, killing Fear, and chasing away Depression. When the sound of his foes had faded, he stood alone in the arena, dripping with sweat despite the cold. Shawn looked down at his sword with awe. *It feels like part of my arm!*

However, it was not long before reality came back to him. The moon sank further down with every passing minute. It was time to leave. Drooping with exhaustion, Shawn placed the sword on the dewy grass. He couldn't help running his finger along the groove one last time before he turned away. At once, he froze.

On the cliff top, silhouetted against the moon, towered a hooded figure. His arms were crossed, his hood up, and his cape billowed ghost-like in the wind. In that way, Shawn hardly noticed a pair of wings

Two Sides of the Coin

appear from its back until they were completely unfurled. The wings fluttered as silent and graceful as an owl's as the man descended from the cliff. He landed on all fours. Lightning crackled in livid blue across the sky. When the man stood up to the sound of a crashing thunder, both the cape and wings had vanished. Paralyzed with fear, Shawn's heart hammered in his ribcage like a terrified bird.

The man raised his finger and cried, "Pick up your sword!" It was Len.

So he did follow me! Emboldened by his anger, Shawn yelled back, "What if I decide not to? What if I told you that I'm done with this stupid training? Would you really kill me?"

"Give me one reason why I shouldn't." Len reached down and unsheathed his sword.

Though he tried to hide it, a tremble crept into Shawn's voice. "I'm your friend!"

The prince gave a deep-throated, evil laugh. "Oh, that's a heart-jerker. Friends, are we?" He took a step closer. "Friends must stand on equal ground, and you, poor Tubby, have never done so with me. You lie and cheat me, too cowardly even to face me. Come now, is that your best excuse?"

"You've used all this time and energy to train me—"

"—and you were about to leave it all in the dust. It's true, I poured myself into you. I gave you shelter and protection, putting my reputation on the line for you," he clenched his teeth. "Yet now you spit on it with contempt."

"Len, I know you wouldn't do such a thing."

"I've dealt with traitors before," Len bellowed. "Maybe you shouldn't be so quick to say you know me!" Bolts of lightning struck behind him as if they too were crackling with fury. Shawn backed up, sensing an attack any moment. At the roll of thunder, Len stepped into attack position and screamed his challenge. "Pick. Up. Your. *Sword!*"

The night held its breath as the echo of *"Sword, sword, sword!"* rang down every passageway. They stood in the eye of the storm, and all was deadly still. Then a raindrop fell, followed by two others. The downpour hit mere seconds later. Shawn bowed his head against the onslaught, and the droplets fell from his dark hair onto the resting sword. He could clearly hear the mocking voices of his enemies flung at him from all sides.

"You pathetic coward."
"Liar! Liar!"
"What an idiot."
"Just give up now."
"You're nothing."
You're a rising star.

What? Shawn lifted his head. The voice had sounded so clear in his mind that he wondered if Len had spoken. The prince stood like a statue opposite him, ready to attack. But he waited... waited for him to act. Could Len still believe that Shawn could be—no, that he *was*—a rising star?

Shawn locked gazes with the prince, gave a grim smile, and picked up his sword.

At a crackle of thunder, Len charged. Darth moved into a defensive position with his feet firmly planted and the sword held out in front of him. Len came in swinging and knocked Darth's blade aside. The stroke that would have sent his sword flying this afternoon now failed to defeat him. Clutching his hilt with both hands, Shawn parried Len's second blow with equal force. He pushed back, and their swords moved together in a flashing arc over their heads until Len's was pushed away. For the first time in all their training together, Shawn forced Len to step back.

It was a small victory, but it was enough. Shawn moved at once from defender to attacker. He attacked from high to low, feinting to the left while striking to the right. At Len's every parry, the jarring impact of the clashing blades rattled his bones. Soon his hands went numb from the shocks. Still, too, there was the storm to reckon with. As their fight grew fiercer, so too did the wind and rain, thunder and lightning. Hardly able to see, Shawn's attack faltered, and the prince followed up with a vicious counterattack. His whole self was absorbed in avoiding the slashing blade in the dark. He backed away, not trusting himself to see every strike. Len followed him every step.

Two Sides of the Coin

The cliff side neared. *He's driving me into it,* Shawn realized with a jolt. As his back hit the wall, Len stabbed forward. Shawn, prepared for the attack, dodged to the side at the last moment. Len's sword struck the rock, and sparks danced from the blade's edge. Shawn surged forward with a left elbow strike, which the prince barely blocked. Grabbing Shawn's shoulder, he knee-kicked him in the ribs. As Shawn reeled back, Len landed a punch that knocked him to the ground. Len's sword flashed above him, and he desperately held out his hands to ward off the blow. *Is this the end?*

But when he looked up, the prince stood over him with his sword upraised. "Get up, Rossow!" he barked. "Why are you always on the ground?"

Shawn scrambled to his feet, burning with frustration. "I wouldn't always be on the ground if you didn't push me down all the time!"

Len lowered his sword, his expression unreadable. When he spoke, his voice had changed to a murmur which Shawn strained to hear over the storm. "Yes, it's true, I did push you. I could have been kinder to you. I could have never thrown rocks, pushed you off cliffs, or knocked you down. Yet I knew that someday, someone would do the same to you... except without mercy. I could not let that happen." The prince clenched his fists. "A father who loves his son will beat the tar out of him when he plays with a cobra's hole."

"Your whole island is a cobra's hole!" snapped Shawn.

Len nodded. "So you do understand." He threw himself to the ground, rolled, and came up beside Shawn. He swung at Shawn's feet, and the reporter barely jumped high enough to miss it. Shawn slashed at his head, and Len leaned back, the blade whizzing an inch from his nose. They fought on for neither knew how long. Time and time again, Len knocked Shawn's sword out of his hands. Time and time again, he yelled, "Pick up your sword!" Time and time again, Shawn bent over to retrieve the heavy weapon. Every move Shawn made was a struggle. Even his fingers couldn't grip the blade without difficulty.

Finally, Shawn lifted his hands in surrender. "I get it, Len! I get it. Your intentions were good, but you were wrong to keep me here. I'm not your servant."

"Oh? I saved your life repeatedly. In some regions, you would be my servant, forced to serve me for life unless I released you. I do believe Fox is one of them."

"Really?" Shawn's face drained of color.

Len sighed. "No, not really, O Gullible One. Still, wouldn't you say you owe me something?"

"Why do you think I felt so bad for leaving? I don't have anything to offer." Shawn spread his hands.

The prince regarded him with narrowed eyes. "How about your loyalty?"

"How can I be loyal when I'm a prisoner?"

"You're not a prisoner."

"Then I can go home whenever I please?"

"Where is your home?" Len demanded. His question felt like another blow to the face. Before he could respond, Len continued, "You were always thinking about returning, weren't you? I know it. All the while you were learning and traveling you had it in mind to leave. Yet still I stayed. You tried to leave me once and would've starved in the gallows if I hadn't helped you. Now you regard *me* as your captor. Yet still I stayed. Everyone who knows me thinks I have gone mad at last, trying to teach a stranger our ways. You have proved me a fool. Yet still I stayed."

Overwhelmed, Shawn covered his face with his hands. Len wasn't finished. "Why did I stay? Listen up, fool." The prince poked him in the chest. "Shawn, I believe that you could be one of the greatest knights the Island of Despair has ever seen. Why do I believe this? You ask. It's because you're different than us. There's something great inside you that was never realized by the people who scorned you. You have strength unseen by all, especially yourself. You never reach for greater things because you are afraid to fail. I see it in your eyes. How blind you are! You'll never hit your target if you tell yourself you won't."

As Len spoke, Shawn listened just as he did whenever the prince told stories. Only this was *his* story. Could it be? Was he, Shawn Rossow, the low-salary reporter from Sanfran Cisco, really someone special?

"I don't know…" he murmured, looking away from Len's burning gaze.

"It's time you stopped dancing between two worlds and made a decision. You can stay. Yes, stay and take on all the island's dangers. I would teach you everything you need. But if your desire is to leave… you may." At last, he looked away and said in a low voice, "And I hope you will always remember as you sit in comfort and safety how you rejected your chance to truly *live*."

The prince turned his back on Shawn. Again, he was left alone to wrestle with a choice that would forever shape the course of his life. But he did not call the court into session. This decision was his alone. He sat on a boulder, laid his blade across his knees, and pondered it. *Sanfran Cisco or the Island of Despair: which is my home? What do I want: Television, electricity, and cars; or, castles, weapons, and horses? Are t-shirts better than tunics? Am I a reporter or a knight? Would I rather run to meetings or run for my life? Is it better to die old having lived a boring life or die young after giving everything? Oh, I don't know!* Shawn glanced over his shoulder at Len. The man's head was bowed, and his hands clenched tightly behind his back. *In order to leave this cobra-hole of an island… I have to leave my best friend.*

Moon-fall arrived. The clouds rolled on above them like a great, grey sea. Away in the east, the sky lightened. In time, every storm ceases, the longest nights are broken, and even the hardest choices are made. Shawn rose at last.

Len faced him. His eyes were bloodshot, his mouth grim. However, when Shawn sheathed the sword at his side, his grim expression faded away. Shawn smiled. "Len?" He nodded once. "I'll stay."

Len pumped his fists in the air and cheered at the top of his lungs, which scared the living daylights out of every creature in hearing distance. He hugged Shawn and scrubbed his knuckles over his head. "Yes, you're staying! Not like I was worried, of course."

Shawn laughed, batting him away. "Course not! Len, I want to be your apprentice. Will you teach me?" he asked, hope rising in his chest at the thought of becoming a knight.

"I don't know…" Len crossed his arms and gave a crooked smile. "Can I be sure Shawn the Reporter won't run away again?"

Shawn shook his head. "I'm not the same Shawn."

"Or," observed Len, "perhaps you're not Shawn at all. Ah, I know! It's perfect! You need a new name."

The reporter gaped. "A new name? Well, umm… let me think."

"Heh, what do you think I've been doing all night? That's fine, I am very good at that now," the prince plopped down beside him and stroked his chin. "How do you like the name Elden?" he suggested. "It means 'the *Old* Servant.'"

"I find that in bad taste. Plus, I have other ideas." Shawn's ideas, namely, were to review the names of his favorite characters, seeing if any would fit him. *Not Luke or Han, they're too normal. Aragorn and Legolas wouldn't work either. Too unusual! Well, how about villain names? There's Scar, Sauron, Khan, Darth Vader—hmm, Darth Vader? Too elaborate. I couldn't be called Vader or Maul anyway. Perhaps Darth?* He tested it out loud, "Darth."

"What's that?" asked Len.

"Darth?" he repeated.

Len pronounced the word slowly, narrowing his eyes. "It's an odd name, but I think it just might fit you. Darth. Yes, it does. Are you satisfied with it?"

"I think. I mean, I can always change it later, if it doesn't stick."

"It's settled then!" Len exclaimed.

"So do I have to sign some legal papers to officially change it or—"

"Legal papers, pah! *This* is how we legalize names," Len reached out and pulled his sword from its sheath. "Kneel."

When he had done so, Len touched both his shoulders with the tip of the blade. "I dub you Darth, apprentice to the Prince of Fox. Rise up."

Chills ran down Darth's spine as he rose to his feet. Len held his sword out to him. "For the first order of your master," he looked down at Darth and smiled. "Pick up your sword and *never* leave it behind."

Darth took the sword. "Don't worry, Len. I'm here to stay."

EPILOGUE

The late-afternoon sun beamed down on the little shop, where Honest Erwin finished his story to the children seated before him on the rug. "—and so the man who went to, well, that other place, became known as Stephen. The man who came to our island, after these adventures, took for himself the name Darth. No such thing has ever been recorded in the history of the Islands. Rumors tell of others..." Erwin trailed off. "But those are only rumors, y'understand,"

"Rumors, rumors, only rumors!" chimed the children.

The storyteller chuckled. "Why, that's right! Good for you, kids. Now I do believe there are some peppermint candies hiding around here. Have you seen them by chance?"

They squealed with delight, pointing at the top of his head where a candy jar teetered. "There, Honest! Teehee! The peppermints are on your head!"

Erwin's bushy eyebrows wiggled as he looked up. By then he had moved the jar under the stool. He made a face at the children. "You playing a joke on me?" He peeked down and gasped. "Well, there it is! How on earth did it get there?"

Erwin held it out to them and was informed by a little girl, "You are the one playing jokes, Honest. I forgive you, though."

"Aww, thank ya, dear."

"Did Darth really become one of the greatest knights of the Island of Despair?" asked an older girl. The other children echoed her question.

Erwin tapped his nose. "Let's not get ahead of ourselves, sweetie. We have to take the story one day at a time."

As always, one boy (today called Paulus Romanus) stood aloof until all the others had drifted away. Only then did he creep over and tug on Erwin's tunic. "Honest? You didn't say 'the end' again."

"That's 'cause it wasn't the end," Honest Erwin replied. "In fact, I do believe this adventure's just begun."

And that is that.

ABOUT THE AUTHOR

Malia Davidson is an author, missionary, black belt, and self-acclaimed nerd. She debuted with her first book at age six and has tenaciously clung to writing despite the onset of that condition known as "Growing Up." Her heroes come in all shapes and sizes: from mice to dragons to reporters. She has completed two books and is currently writing two others. Malia grew up in Woodbury, Minnesota. At night, when she and her sister Kalai were supposed to be sleeping, they created their own world with talking animals, pirates, and magical islands. After graduating from high school, Malia joined a church-planting organization called Mission UpReach, located in Santa Rosa, Honduras. She helps teach Honduran kids Bible stories, morals, and wacky VBS songs. Malia prays that God will not take her home until she has finished all seven books of her series. But if He does, she's okay with that too.

Printed in the United States
By Bookmasters